KRISTINE SMITH

RULES
OF
CONFLICT

EOS

An Imprint of HarperCollinsPublishers

This is a work of fiction. Names, characters, places, and incidents are the products of the author's imagination or are used fictitiously and are not to be construed as real. Any resemblance to actual events, locales, organizations, or persons, living or dead, is entirely coincidental.

EOS
An Imprint of HarperCollins*Publishers*
10 East 53rd Street
New York, New York 10022-5299

Copyright © 2000 by Kristine Smith
Cover art by Jean Pierre Targete
ISBN: 0-380-80784-X
www.eosbooks.com

First Eos paperback printing: September 2000

Eos Trademark Reg. U.S. Pat. Off. and in Other Countries, Marca Registrada, Hecho en U.S.A.
HarperCollins® is a trademark of HarperCollins Publishers Inc.

Printed in the U.S.A.

WCD   10   9   8   7   6   5   4   3   2   1

Also by
Kristine Smith
from Eos

CODE OF CONDUCT

In loving memory of Prince,
the best puppy in town

CHAPTER 1

"Name?"

Jani Kilian shifted her attention from her aching stomach to the admissions clerk who held her MedRec card by the corner like a dirty dispo. The woman tapped her stylus against the data-entry grid that rested on the desk in front of her, the staccato impact of plastic on polycoat sounding its *get on with it* song.

"Shane Averill," Jani replied, "just like it says in the card." She snatched a peek at her reflection in the highly polished counter. Chilly, too-dark eyes. Jaw tensed with discomfort. She forced a smile.

The clerk ignored the attempt at sociability. "Date and place of birth?"

Jani heard her voice quiver as she recited the information she'd memorized in preparation for this encounter. The Earthbound accents that echoed through the cavernous lobby made her nervous.

Coming to Felix had made sense after fleeing Chicago. The closest colony to Earth, it was an easy burrow to hunker down in. So obvious a stopping place was it that the Service agents who had no doubt pursued her would have bypassed it for someplace less likely. The Channel Worlds. Or Pearl Way.

But the burrow had proved to be made of quicksand. Expensive but necessary equipment purchases had devoured her finances, forcing her to remain until she could earn enough money to leave. Then her dodgy health had taken a serious downturn.

The stomachaches, I can handle. But not the nausea, the vomiting, the pounding heart. She knew she risked exposure by coming to Neoclona-Felix, but it was the only place on the planet that could treat her properly, and she had grown sick and tired of feeling sick and tired.

It was a matter of minutes now. One blood study or encephaloscan, and she'd be blown.

They promised I had nothing to fear. Cal Montoya, the doctor who had saved her life in Chicago, and those he spoke for. *Promises were made to be broken.* Her stomach clenched, and she leaned into the counter.

"Parents' names and worlds of origin?"

Jani looked around the Neoclona facility's glass and stone lobby as she gave voice to more of the fictitious Ms. Averill's invented history. Shades of purple—the company's signature hue—shone from every surface, even the tinted glass that softened the battering Felician sun. Bathed in shafts of grape-colored sunlight, she felt as though she stood at the bottom of a filled punch bowl.

"I don't suppose you can give me the first letter of your patient string?"

Jani took a steadying breath as the pain in her gut eased. "P-seven-eight-dot-one-two-dash-four-eight-zee—"

The tapping ceased abruptly. "You *know* your patient string *by heart?*"

Jani restrained the urge to turn on her heel, walk out of the lobby, and disappear into the Felix Majora crowds. "It's just a series of encodes. GateWay nearest my birth planet, followed by world code, followed by sector—"

The clerk ran the card through a scanner, then watched the disgorged data as it scrolled down the grid screen. "Shipping administrator for Felix Cruiseways, huh? Figures you can memorize forty-two-character strings." Her haggard features softened at this discovery of a kindred, data-crunching soul. She even cracked a smile. "Is Cruiseways a good place to work?"

Jani eyed the clerk's bright purple shirt. Silver caducei, every detail of snake, wing and staff visible in the holoetching, sparkled from collar and cuffs. The knowledge of what lay behind the symbols made her shiver. Or maybe it was the subarctic temperature of the lobby. "It's all right. I doubt it's any more exciting than what you do here. Besides, with the way Earth-colony relations are headed, the shipping and travel businesses are bound to take a hit. You're better off sticking with Neoclona."

The woman sighed and tugged at her dark blond bangs. Earthbound, judging by the odd twang of her Felician Spanish, and younger than she initially appeared. Mid-twenties, but her attitude aged her. "It just didn't turn out to be as exciting as I thought it would when I answered this posting. 'See the colonies! Meet new people!' " She fingered an entry into the grid. "Check in with the outpatient nurse on thirty-seven. She'll tell you where to go from there."

Jani reclaimed her record card and offered a commiserating grin of farewell. *Dear child, the last thing in the Commonwealth you want is an exciting life*. She waded deeper into the bowl, toward the lift bank. *Trust me*.

They asked her the same questions four more times as she scaled the floors to her doctor's office. Crude way to suss out potential health-care fraud, but with the field of documents forgery as advanced as it was, the human element usually turned out to be the weakest link. Something about the increasing isolation and the proximity of sharp metal instruments and blinking analyzers tripped up less-determined con artists.

But we're the few, the sneaky, the hard-core liars, Jani thought as she followed the latest in the afternoon's series of white-coated backs down a hallway lined with examining rooms. She had reached the seventy-second floor, aerie of department chiefs and other demigods—her appointment had been made with a divinity named Tellinn. Deputy chief of endocrinology. Narrow, slumped shoulders. Shaggy black hair that needed trimming. Lapdog eyes deep-set in a drawn, pale face. Looked as though he could use a little of what he sold.

"This way, Ms. Averill," he said as he led her around yet another corner. "You're complaining of nausea?"

"Yes."

"And you're feeling jittery?"

"*Yes*," Jani hissed. Two decades of experience compelled her to memorize the locations of the nearest exits, the security desk, the dead-end hallways. "At first, it just happened after I ate, but now it's constant."

"Could be one of the food allergies we've been encountering lately," Tellinn said glumly. "Are you from Elyas? Elyans have an awful time when they come here."

"No, I'm . . . not." Could they tell she was Acadian from her pattern of genetic mutations, or would her unique condition swamp out minor colony-to-colony differences? *What won't they find out about me, if they probe deeply enough?*

Jani sniffed the filtered air and shivered again. She hated hospitals. Not that this richly appointed corner of Neoclona's far-flung empire resembled in any way the jury-rigged basement in which, eighteen years before, the company got its start and she received a second chance at life. But old memories died hard, and every time she caught a biting whiff of antiseptic no filter could ever totally eliminate, three faces formed in her mind.

The three empire-builders. Eamon DeVries, who hated her guts. John Shroud, who . . . didn't. And Valentin Parini, who put out the fires that raged between the two polar opposites like the born fireman he was.

John and Val promised I would be looked after. Their representative had spoken in their names—she had nothing to worry about. She looked up and down the hallway as she trudged after Tellinn. *Exit to stairwell—unalarmed—second hallway to the left of the nurses' station.*

"Jesus Christ!" Tellinn slid to a halt so quickly Jani almost walked up his back.

"Not nearly so grand," said the man who had stepped out of the shadowed doorway. "Hello, Hugh."

"Val." Tellinn's voice shrank to a whisper.

"Sorry to drop in so abruptly." Valentin Parini riffled a hand through his ash brown hair. His hazel eyes were large and almond-shaped, his nose a finely molded arch, his cheekbones precipitous. Time's passage had left only thread-fine grooves near the corners of his mouth.

"What—are you—" Tellinn's complexion, moontan to begin with, had turned downright chalky.

The barest hint of recognition flickered in Val's greenbrown gaze as it moved to Jani, then back to Tellinn. "I just punched through the GateWay two days ago. Forgive me for not messaging ahead, but being so near, I didn't see the point." Full lips curved in a cool smile. "Don't worry, this isn't a surprise inspection. John didn't send me to Felix with an agenda."

Tellinn drew the back of his hand across his mouth. "How did you get here? No one mentioned sending out the VIP shuttle."

Val shrugged lightly. "Felix Central Orbital Station to the city shuttleport. Chartered a heliskim. Landed on that new rooftop pad you installed last year. I must say, I do like the sensation of dropping onto my hospital from the clouds."

"Like God Almighty himself," Jani muttered. Val responded to the jab with a knowing smirk, but the glare Tellinn focused on her held murder. And something else. She looked again at Val, who winked.

"Actually, Hugh," he said, pointing to Jani, "I'd like to perform this physical, if you don't mind. I checked the appointment roster at the nurses' station. *Another* food allergy—my, my, they seem to be everywhere these days. They're a pet interest of mine—did you know that?" He waved off the other doctor's protest. "However, my role in all this is strictly *off-paper*. Keep your encode in her MedRec and draw up any scrips yourself. As far as we're all concerned, you're the physician of record." His all-business expression softened. "I'll explain it to you over dinner tonight." Jani swore his eyelashes fluttered. "But only if you can fit me in, of course."

Twin rounds of color bloomed in Tellinn's cheeks. "I—did have something, but I—can cancel." He blinked as though dazed, then handed Val the data-recorder board he had up to that point been holding in front of his chest like a shield. "I'll be in my office." He shot Val a last, stunned look, then walked slowly down the hall and disappeared around the corner.

Val watched Tellinn leave with the discerning eye a gourmet would direct toward the dessert display. Then he turned to Jani, and the look sharpened. "Oh Captain, my Captain." He pointed to the examining-room door. "In there. No sudden moves. Hands where I can see them."

Jani pushed the panel open; it whined under the force. "You haven't changed a bit, you shameless bastard. You sandbagged him." She held the door open while Val sauntered past. "You're more than he can handle, and you know it."

"But with me as a distraction, he won't give you a second thought, will he?"

"He's in love with you!"

"Yes, well. Believe it or not, after a few days with me, he'll be ready for six months without. I'm the white-chocolate cheesecake in his life—a little piece of me goes a hell of a long way." Val set the recorder on a table beside an analyzer. "But, first things first." To Jani's surprise, he held out his arms. "Just a quick hug, Jan. Because I've missed you. Because knowing I'd be seeing you again scared the hell out of me."

Jani hesitated. Then she walked, a little unsteadily, into Val's embrace. He enclosed her lightly, as though she might break. She squeezed back harder. He wore a crisp linen daysuit in light green; the stiff material crackled in her grasp like leaves.

"If you're trying to wring the years out of me, you're too late." He pulled back so he could look her in the face. His eyes glistened. "You look lovely. My one and only girl." He tugged at one of her short, black curls, then ran a fingertip down the bridge of her nose. "That's held up well, I must say."

Jani batted his hand away. "Social climber. You gave me a Family face. Damned bones you could sharpen blades on."

"Bullshit. I passed on the Parini countenance in the only way I cared to."

They grinned idiotically at one another. Then Jani sensed her instincts firing warning shots, and her smile faded. "How did you know I was here?"

Val sighed. "So much for sweet reminiscence." He frowned as Jani extricated herself from his arms. "Well, what can I say, except that there's nothing loyal employees and money can't accomplish. We have spies in every colonial city with a decent port—our Felician contact spotted you soon after you arrived. When you didn't depart immediately for a more out-of-the-way refuge, John started to worry. We decided I should come. John feared you'd bolt if you saw him."

"Did he?"

"Well, maybe I needed to convince him. Sit on him. Threaten him a little." Val crossed his arms and dropped his chin—his skeptical pose. "So?"

Jani shrugged. "I spent all my cash on gear. I needed to earn a berth." She wavered beneath his stare, weighty with paternal gruff. "And I haven't felt good for months."

"That's what John was afraid of." Val fingered the collar of her white trouser suit. "That's very pretty. *Très Felicienne*. You've got five seconds to peel out of it. We have work to do."

First came bloodwork, followed by a series of intrusive swabbings and scopings Jani could have done without, thank you. Then came an upper GI scan facilitated by her swallowing of a biodegradable, capsule-sized camera, and completed in spite of Val's insistence that she stand beside him at the display receiver and watch the full-color, three-dimensional workings of her digestive tract. Her equally adamant reply that he'd find himself *wearing* the camera if she did as he asked put a stop to his goading.

"Last part." Val rolled a stress screen the size of a full-length mirror into the center of the room. "Let's see how those new limbs of yours are doing. Off with the medgown. Get behind the screen. Stand up straight. Move only when I tell you to."

Jani stripped off the tissuelike gown and stepped behind the dull, milky screen. It brightened to translucent glass and emitted a barely perceptible hum.

She looked down at her left arm, then her left leg. No longer numb limbs driven by half-formed nervenets, but fully functional animandroid, the best Neoclona could produce. Replaced almost six months ago, during her first ever visit to Earth.

"Jani, atten-*hut*!"

She snapped to attention, chin up, shoulders back. The screen mirrored her image; she avoided looking at her face. Her light brown skin held up well under the room's chem-illumination. Her legs didn't look too bad.

But, as always, her eyes drew her in. They looked like two black holes staring back from the screen surface. She didn't like using that filming. It was the same brand holoVee actors used, formulated to show up well in the imaging, and less likely to fissure than commercial brands. But it was too dark for real life. People were starting to comment.

Bet they'd shut up if I let them see what was underneath.

"At ease, Captain. Your whole thorax has gone red. *Relax.*"

Jani took a deep breath and thought about white, puffy clouds. "Can I talk?"

"Yeah. Just don't gesture."

"How do I look?"

"All greens and blues—a veritable study in symmetry and stress distribution. The new limbs are fine, of course, but the old musculature has held up very well. We really did an exceptional job on you. I don't believe we've ever topped it."

"Well, you boys always worked best under pressure." Jani's hands clenched, and she thought about clouds again. "Trying to patch me together while holding off the Admiral-General's office and the Consulate—can't imagine much more pressure than that."

"Turn ninety degrees to your right, please." At first, it seemed Val would ignore further mention of their shared past. Then he cleared his throat. "The difficult part was justifying the supplies we ordered. Most of the Consulate staff had been evac'd out of Rauta Shèràa by then, and the ones that remained weren't sustaining the types of injuries to justify the materials we shipped in. It reached the point where I became a daily visitor to the Service Intelligence annex." He chuckled warmly. "Guess that's where I developed my legendary powers of persuasion. Turn your back to me, please."

Jani turned. "The Vynshà had taken the perimeter settlements by then. All they'd left to do was declare themselves 'rau' and send their Haárin advance troops into Rauta Shèràa to prepare the way. The Family members who'd supported the Laum were scrambling to realign themselves. Some pretty formidable names feared for their lives. You'd think Intelligence would have had their hands full getting them out of Rauta Shèràa alive."

Val sighed. "Yes, the Vynshà were exhibiting remarkably human vindictiveness, weren't they? I think Intelligence was concerned John, Eamon, and I were on the same short list. We were bad boys, remember? Turn ninety degrees, please."

Jani rotated slowly. The rough sensapad on which she stood made the soles of her feet itch. "Did you really think they'd have killed you?" She tried to shift her footing, but stopped when she heard Val grumble. "Nema considered the three of you esteemed enemies. A chief propitiator's regard should have been enough to save you."

Val huffed. "We had traveled pretty far into the land of forbidden knowledge by then. Besides, Nema was on his Temple's fecal roster. His regard and a vend token wouldn't have bought us a cup of coffee." A series of clicks sounded as he downloaded the screen data into the recorder. "All done. You can come out now."

Jani eased from behind the screen and reached to the floor for the crumpled medgown. The chill tile helped ease the burning on the bottoms of her feet, but before she could examine the damage, Val called to her.

"Let's have a look at those sweet baby jades of yours," he said as he wheeled the screen against the wall. "Strip off those eyefilms."

"My eyefilms?" Jani backed against the sinkstand. Her ankles prickled. She stifled a cough.

"What's the matter with you?" Val took a step closer. "What's wrong?"

Jani coughed again as her lungs filled with scancrete. "Can't breathe. My feet—" She slumped against the sinkstand. Black patches grew and faded before her eyes.

Val rushed to her. He knelt down, grasped her ankle, and snatched a glance at the bottom of her foot. Then he looked back at the sensapad. "Damn it! Damn it, damn it, *damn it*!" He hurried to the pad platform, tore the thin polymer film from its metal base, rolled it into a tight tube, and shoved it under his jacket and into the waistband of his trousers. Then he rushed to the door, pushing through the gap before it opened completely. "*I need a shockpack!*"

He returned, dragging an equipment-laden skimcart; white coats streamed in after him like a flood of milk. Two of them lifted Jani onto the scanbed while Tellinn clipped a monitor relay to her ear. "Hurry the hell up, Val," he snapped. "Her oxygen saturation's dropping like a rock."

Prodded with probes, raked over by scanners, Jani watched the frantic bustle with growing disinterest. Her world had become one of deadened emotion, blurring color, choppy sound and motion. Out of the corner of her eye, she saw Val work over her right arm, then felt the pinch of an injector. The heaviness in her chest eased, and she inhaled with a wheezy rattle.

"Blood pressure's up. A hundred over fifty-five." The source of the announcement, a silver-haired woman with CHIEF OF STAFF etched into her ID badge fixed Val with a glare. "What happened, Parini?"

Val's eyes locked with Jani's. *They know, Jan*, they said, as the once-glib mouth worked soundlessly. Sweat trickled down the face he'd copied for her, in a basement lab outside a war-torn alien city, when he and John and Eamon had learned enough about her to realize rebuilding her old one wasn't an option.

They know you're here.

CHAPTER 2

"Here, drink this." Val refilled the cup and pushed it over to Jani's side of the table. "Now, while it's hot."

Jani eyed the black, foamy brew with distaste. John's coffee had always tasted like a gift from the gods. Val's, on the other hand. . . . "Don't you think three cups are enough?" She belched quietly. "My stomach's going to go critical any second." She gazed longingly across the table at his iced lemonade. "I think we can ease up on the caffeine—my breathing's fine."

Val had returned to the bar, set in a sunken alcove in the middle of his spacious hotel room, and continued to rummage through coolers and cupboards. "Just keep drinking—you're not out of the woods yet. Damn it, I injected you with enough adrenosol to punch a resistant male one and a half times your weight through the ceiling, and it *just* brought your blood pressure up into low-normal. I couldn't risk giving you more, not with all those expert witnesses around." He slammed the cabinet door.

"I got enough of the fish-eye as it was. 'Wasn't that dose a tad *high*, Val? What were you *doing* to her, anyway?' They know the story of the patient we patched together on Shèrá, and not all of them approved of our methods. I swear they all think I was experimenting on you, and it backfired. You'd think that damned augmentation of yours could have helped you out."

"You know Service augies only work in threatening situations." Jani fingered the tiny round scar on the back of her neck where skull met spine. The large bore canula of a stereotaxic headset had punched a hole there over twenty years ago, then injected the self-assembling components of her little passenger. "Discharge a shooter across my bow, I can get as frosty and functional as you please." Only then would the tiny glands adjacent to her amygdala release their reservoirs of pseudocatecholamines. Sharpen her wits. Ease her panic. Dull her pain.

But if I'm not pissed off or scared senseless, I'm on my own. She pulled in a deep, wheezing breath, and choked down another sip of coffee. "So what happened?" Her stomach gurgled ominously.

Val returned to the table, the results of his explorations clutched in his hands. He piled all the stomach-settling food he could find, dispos of crackers and peppermint candies, by Jani's cup, then fell into the chair across from her. "I've got the head of Security running scan searches and background checks to see who the hell could have put the mat there. I'm not optimistic. It was either a Service or Cabinet plant, and they're probably off-world by now." He fumbled with a packet of crackers. "As for what was in it, I won't know for sure until I test it, and I can't test it properly until I get it home. Whatever it was, it had your number. You stood on it for no more than ten minutes, and the soles of your feet look like someone went after them with a strap."

Jani winced. Her heavily salved feet, encased in thick, truecotton booties, tingled with a maddening, itchy burn. The booties had been treated with anti-irritants and healing accelerants, but they couldn't work miracles. Walking promised to be a real treat for the next few days.

Wherever I happen to be. She checked her timepiece; six hours had elapsed since her episode. Most of that time had been spent in the office of Dr. Fanshul, the tart-tongued chief of staff, who had argued vehemently that it was in Jani's best interest to stay in the hospital overnight for observation. Val had put an end to the debate, and blown his cover in the process, by signing her out under his care. By the time all the signatures were in place, half the facility knew something strange had happened on the seventy-second floor involving one of the "Big Three" and a mysterious "woman in white."

"So?" Val laid claim to one of the peppermints. "Have I fucked up your situation here sufficiently, or should I try for full-page adverts in tomorrow morning's newssheets?" He smiled broadly, his teeth and lips coated bright blue by the candy.

Jani knew he wanted to coax a smile out of her. Under different circumstances, it might have worked. "I have to get off-planet. Within the hour."

Val slumped back in his chair and drummed his fingers on the table. "My ship's having some refit work done. It'll be ready in two days. Let me take you—"

"I can't wait two days."

"You better find a way. Face reality. You almost died. As things stand now, I can hear you breathe across the room— that situation isn't going to change for days. And if you try to do much walking on those feet of yours, you risk a nasty infection."

"Can't you give me something to see me through?"

Val's expression grew pained. "Jan, I'm not sure how the drugs I have on hand would affect you. As you learned to your detriment in Chicago, your response to some common medications has become idiosyncratic." He stared moodily into his lemonade. "For all I know, there's nothing wrong with that sensapad. You may have simply developed a sensitivity to that particular biopolymer, and damn it, if exposure to something like that is enough to knock you for a loop, what else out there could affect you?"

"That's not your problem."

"*Monkey's ass it's not my problem! You*—" Val fell silent. Jani could almost hear the click of a balance as he weighed his words. "Jan, your body is going through some changes right now. We know why, but the how, what, when, and where have us a little baffled." He looked at the ceiling, into the depths of his glass, everywhere but at her.

"Why can't you say it, Val?" Jani took another sip of coffee, and swallowed hard. "Eighteen years ago, you patched me together with tissue manufactured from human and idomeni genetic material. You thought you'd deactivated most of the idomeni genes, but you hadn't. You thought you'd made it so I'd live for two hundred years, but you didn't stop to think what I might live *as*."

Val blinked rapidly. "Jani," he said, his voice cracking, "you're wrong."

"I'm hybridizing. I'm not human anymore, but I'm not idomeni either. I can eat Haárin spices that would blister the inside of your mouth, but some of their herbs and nuts go through me like poison. I can't drink human tea anymore. I can barely choke down anything sweet, but I can peel a lemon and eat it like you would an orange." Jani heard the tremor in her voice. When she tallied up the small things— that was when it scared her. "Nema was right. He said this would happen, that no matter how you tried to stop it, I would continue to change."

"Jani, Nema is a religious fanatic with an agenda as long as my arm. Let's leave your medical care to experts, shall we?"

"And which experts would those be, Val? The ones who got me into this mess in the first place?"

Val flinched as though she'd slapped him. The room lighting accentuated the lines near his mouth, signs of age Jani couldn't find around her own no matter how hard she looked. "Jani, we did the best we could for you."

"That you did, Val, that you did. Thanks to you, I have eyes that look like two corroded copper discs and eating habits that make people stare. I york my guts a couple times a week, and between the nausea and the shivery shakes, my every day is a joy. And let's not forget that this condition of mine has reinforced Nema's grand theory that I'm his heir apparent, which gives him the right to take charge of the rest of my life if I ever let him get his hands on me, which I don't believe I will, thank you!" She glared at the stricken man. "I've had time to think these past few months. Way too much time. I hate being this way and I didn't have a choice. And now that the Service and the Commonwealth government know I'm alive, all they have to do is follow the trail. I'm a goddamn walking disaster siren!"

"Jani, we—" Val's voice cracked. "Do you hate us that much?"

"Do you really want me to answer that?"

"No." He sniffed. Cleared his throat. "You need more in-depth assessment than I can give you here. Come back with me to Seattle. You and I always got along, and Eamon isn't around much these days." He hesitated. "And whatever you think of John, he would like very much to see you."

Bits of memory flitted through Jani's mind. Some were more vivid than others. "Does he still play the violin?"

"Yes." Val's voice lifted hopefully. "You'd enjoy listening to him now—he's gotten rather good."

"Just the three of us basking in one another's company and listening to John fiddle. That sounds familiar." Jani looked out the tableside window. Fifty floors below, early-evening skimmer traffic crammed Felix Majora's main thoroughfare. Above the nearby mountains, barely visible through an artificial forest of scancrete and glass, the setting sun glowed like a weld spot. "You and John live in a dream world. Eamon would know better. He wouldn't be able to shove me out the door fast enough." A cramp shot through her abdomen. She tore open a packet of crackers and forced them down.

"Jan, we can keep you safe. No one will even suspect you're Earthside."

"Really? Is Neoclona a sovereign state? I read the news-sheets, Val. I watch the 'Vee. Funny the stories that keep cropping up. Rehashes about how human-idomeni relations took a dive after Knevçet Shèràa. Garbled rumor about the death of Rikart Neumann. Portraits of Evan as the emotionally battered son and lover. Can't you see what's happening? His attorneys are scrambling for a defense, and I'm it."

"Jani, he gave the order to have your transport blown out of the sky to cover up his involvement in Knevçet Shèràa. Nobody's that good a scrambler."

"Oh yeah? Has he been formally charged?"

"John knows he's guilty. He told me—"

"Has Evan been formally charged?" Jani nodded as the uncertainty flickered in Val's eyes. "The term is *plea bargain*. He's telling the Service all about me. I won't even need a trial—they'd just shoot me at O'Hare."

"We have influence."

"Val, I killed Neumann. My commanding officer. The first N in NUVA-SCAN. The Families are closing rank." She stood and headed for the door. "Your influence and a vend token." She took one step. Two. Before she could take a third, popping sensations worked across both soles, followed by stinging wetness, then raw agony as though she skated over metal blades.

Jani didn't feel herself fall; she only knew she was on the floor. As pain radiated up her legs and she gasped for breath, she felt a hand close over her shoulder.

"You're not running out on us, Jan," Val said gently. "Not this time. And when you finally do go somewhere, it's going to be with me."

In the end, they compromised.

"I don't like this one damn bit." Val snaked the Neoclona staff skimmer down one of Felix Majora's less-traveled side streets. The sleek, silver two-seater didn't meet Jani's standards as a getaway vehicle. It drew the eye like a stone skipping over water. Pedestrians stopped to stare as it passed.

At least it wasn't purple.

"You have to keep your date with Hugh," she said. "He can tell you what they're saying about us in the staff room."

Val checked a street sign, compared it to the name on his directional screen, and frowned. "He's not like that. No matter his feelings, he's always kept his own counsel."

"Oh, I'm sure you can work around his better judgment. Use your legendary powers of persuasion." Jani watched out her window as large commercial buildings gave way to the smaller residential structures of the city's mountain side. It took her some time to realize Val hadn't spoken; she turned to find him eyeing her with ill-concealed discomfort.

"I don't like playing the tart while you're running loose doing God knows what."

"Staying put in my apartment. Packing."

"Packing. Right." Val pointed to the directional's touch-pad. "I like Hugh. The idea of working him repulses me."

"Considering your performance this afternoon, I find that difficult to believe."

"That was *fun*!" Val sighed. "Would've been fun. This is different. There's too much at stake, and I don't know what the hell I'm doing."

"Just find out what they're saying about us. If Hugh asks about me, bring up the massive clinical study you're planning. Tell him you want to base it in a colonial facility for a change. Mention it will need a director. Throw in that famous smile, and you'll be in like a greased weasel." Val shifted uneasily, and Jani forced a grin. "Look, if it's any consolation, I've done the tart thing once or twice. If *I* can do it, you're a lock."

Val stopped at an intersection and glanced at the directional. "You say left, it says right."

"Take a left."

He shrugged and turned left. "Sometimes, at the end of the day, when we've worked to the point of exhaustion and all our internal safeguards have burnt out, John and I will uncork a bottle of wine and talk. About you. Where you could be living, what you could be doing. John does most of the talking." He glanced at Jani sidelong. "I don't think I'll repeat this conversation to him anytime soon."

They turned another corner. The sudden brightness of the streetlights hit Jani full in the face. She closed her eyes against the battering glare; they watered anyway. "Fuck you," she said. "Stop here. I'm getting out."

"What!" Val jerked the wheel in surprise, sending the skimmer over the curb boundary and up onto the sidewalk. The vehicle's proximity alarms blatted as he tried to regain control from the autonav, which fought to turn the skimmer in the opposite direction. By the time he maneuvered into an idling slot near a small playground, residents from nearby buildings had gathered in windows and doorways to watch. Scattered applause sounded as the vehicle shuddered to a stop.

Jani watched a woman across the street point at the skimmer and laugh. "You have a future in this business, I can tell."

"Oh, bullshit!" Val glared at their surroundings. Much of the playground equipment had been dismantled, lighting was intermittent at best, and several less-polished-looking skimmers had already veered by for a look at the spiff new visitor. "I'll be damned if I'm letting you out here—this place is a dump!" He pointed to the directional touchpad. "I don't know why you told me to bring you here, anyway—the address code on Shane Averill's MedRec says—"

Jani popped open her door, but Val dragged her back inside the skimmer before she could flee. His grip on her animandroid upper arm made her gasp—he knew just where to grab and how hard to squeeze. "Shane Averill was a one-shot, wasn't it? Something you patched together to get through the visit to Neoclona? You don't work at Felix Cruiseways, and you don't live at the address in your file!" He struggled to pull the door closed with his free hand. "We're supposed to meet tomorrow morning at your apartment, Jani. Now how the hell are we supposed to do that when I don't know where you live!"

Jani tried to wedge her right leg through the shrinking gap between door and seal. "I'll meet you at your hotel."

"You said you didn't want to go back there anymore. You said it was too risky." Val swore as Jani wriggled halfway out of the skimmer. He tried to drag her back into the cabin without releasing his grip on the door pull, but before he could set himself, the gullwing flew upward, pulling him headlong across Jani's lap before finally wrenching free.

Hot, dry night spilled into the cabin.

"Hey, *lindo, que pa*?" A wiry Feliciano, bare to the waist and sporting a half-shaved head, stood in the gaping entry. He leaned forward while still holding on to the door pull; the stretched pose accentuated his thin waist and bony chest. "What's wrong, pretty man with the pretty skim, you don't get your money's worth?" He leered at Jani. "Hard girl like this don't earn her pay?" He rapped the door sharply, and shapes moved into the range of the skimmer headlights. Four of them. "Maybe we give you both your money's worth."

Jani eased her other knee from beneath Val's body. "When I bolt, you floor it and go."

"Oh shit, Jan, don't—"

Jani kicked out. Before she'd left Val's hotel room, she'd supplemented her booties with three pairs of his socks and a pair of his hiking boots. Her padded and armored feet connected perfectly with Shaved-head's solar plexus; he dropped to the ground. She scrambled out of the cabin and over his gasping form, pounding off in the direction opposite his cohorts before any of them could react. After a few strides, she heard the gratifying whine of an accelerating skimmer, followed by the much-less-welcome sound of pursuing footsteps. She tried to pick up her pace, but her feet burned as though she ran through flame. Her chest ached. Her legs turned to cement.

Behind her, the pounding grew louder.

Then, like a bracing wave breaking over her, an old friend dropped by to pay Jani his respects. Her feet numbed. Her lungs cleared. Muzzy perception crystallized. The ovenlike night air parted before her, then closed behind, buoying her along. She pelted down a side street and through an alley, aware as a cat of the fading noises behind her. The thought that she'd been sick a few hours before and should slow down flitted through the cold white that had become her mind, but she shook it off. Fatigue was for other people. She could surf this way for hours. And maybe she would, just for the sheer animal joy of it.

Hello augie—about damn time.

Through every cell in her body, Jani's augmentation whispered his regards.

But her Service-implanted bootstraps could only take her so far. As she slowed to a trot, Jani felt the first tendrils of panic push through her calm. The neurochemical rush that had eased her pain and opened her lungs slowed to a sputter. Augie worked best and longest for intact soldiers at the top of their game, not for half-animandroid never-weres just released from the hospital.

Jani eased to a walk, in part to conserve her flagging

strength, but mainly because she'd entered a section of Felix Majora where a running woman would attract attention. Office towers and manufacturing facilities loomed on either side as she headed down a wide, well-kept alley. When she reached an entry next to a small loading dock, she knocked twice, then sagged against the doorframe and pressed her hot, wet face against cool, dry metal.

The door opened.

"I saw you coming on the scan." The woman looked Jani up and down and grimaced. Her name was Ileana, and she was Jani's boss. "What the hell happened?"

Jani ducked past her. Inside, the air felt cool and held a soft floral fragrance. "Almost got mugged."

"Where?"

"The Cuarto Montaña."

"What the hell were you doing there!" Ileana flipped her long black braid over her shoulder. "At night? Alone?"

"Fell asleep on the *hojea*." The Felician Spanish slang for the automated public-transport system slipped off Jani's tongue as though she'd used it all her life. "Didn't hear the end-of-the-line alarm until it was too late. They just spooked me. I'm fine."

"Hmph." Ileana eyed Jani's rumpled white trouser suit. Then she looked down at Val's heavy brown boots and wrinkled her nose. "Tell me you didn't do that on purpose." She had matched her own flame orange wrapshirt and trousers with high-heeled sandals of the same color, and had wound a desert-print scarf around her neck. Her thick braid reached to her waist and gleamed with gold oil. Tall and lithe, with a long, angular face, she appeared the well-to-do Feliciana, a mature lady of business. Perfume dealer, in this case.

Appearances could be deceiving.

"It's a long story." Jani entered the main work area, where a man and woman watched over the array that packed the rolls of perfumed adhesive patchlets into cartons. "Maybe I'll tell you about him sometime."

"Ah, man trouble!" Ileana clapped her hands in glee. "Finally, my paper robot shows humanity!" She followed Jani into the tiny employee locker room. "Bring him to lunch tomorrow, Tasia. I must meet him."

Tasia. Jani sat down on the narrow bench in front of her locker. Oh yes, a "T" name; lately, she found it hard to keep track. "Sure. When and where?"

Ileana debated times and places out loud; Jani stifled a yawn as she willed her voice into the background. Post-augie fatigue had overtaken post-augie jitters more quickly than she remembered. But then, lately, lots of things were happening differently than she remembered.

The entry comport buzzed; Ileana, still nattering about restaurants, left to answer it. As soon as she was alone, Jani keyed into her locker and removed a small duffel. The Service surplus bag was made of stiff, dark blue polycanvas, and contained everything she owned. She had taken a risk leaving it there, but she hadn't dared take it into Neoclona, and she didn't trust the security of her flat.

Jani did a quick inventory of her duffel's contents. *My preflight check.* Two pairs of dark grey coveralls, rolled into tight tubes. A pair of battered black boots. Assorted underwear. Her keepsakes: a toy soldier, a holocard depiction of two sailracers, and a gold ring with a red stone.

She examined her boots wistfully. Val's hikers chafed her ankles despite the padding, but felt tight around her feet. That meant her feet had swelled. *If I take his boots off, I won't be able to get mine on.* She pushed her old faithfuls aside and dug farther into the bag.

The scanproof material that lined the false bottom of her duffel had cost Jani most of her cash reserve, but would have been worth it at twice the price. Within the slippery blue envelope rested her shooter, a bulky Service-issue over twenty years old, and assorted gadgetry hooked together by a braided length of red cloth. The devices allowed her to reset a touchlock or interfere with an eavesdropping device. Nothing to strike fear in the hearts of an antiterrorist squad, but they would draw the notice of Treasury Customs and Transport Ministry Security.

Jani stuffed the gadgets back in the envelope, then removed a cracked plastic case from a well-padded pocket.

"Hello, you," she said as she unzipped the case and removed her scanpack.

The palm-sized oval's scratched black cover shimmered dully in the glare of the overhead lighting. Driven by Jani's farmed brain tissue, the device functioned as the repository of a quarter century's worth of documents knowledge. It would have won her envious stares from the other doc techs Jani had met at Felix Majora's Government Hall, and pointed questions from Ileana. Only Registry-listed documents examiners carried scanpacks, and only four others in the forty-nine-planet Commonwealth carried ones that looked like Jani's. And they all worked on Earth.

Pointed questions, followed by pointed sticks. Jani stuffed the device back in her duffel and sniffed the air again. *Isabellita.* The light floral scent had become popular in some rather far-flung regions of the Commonwealth, a reason sufficient to explain the small perfume house's 'round-the-clock operation. Every morning, boxload after boxload departed the small loading dock, bound for the rich colonies of the J-Loop as well as their not-so-rich brethren in the Channel and the Outer Circle.

Wonder if External Revenue's caught onto the fact there's a lot of sweet-smelling sewage out there lately. Jani grinned. The perfume was a water-soluble concoction that could be flushed out of the patch polymer; the polymer could then be reworked into some of the best scanshielding Jani had ever seen. Not on par with the military-grade material lining the bottom of her duffel, but good enough to allow the occasional cruiser filled with unregistered, untaxed cargo to flit through the GateWay chain under the noses of sundry Cabinet branches.

Jani unrolled one of the pairs of coveralls, then began the tricky task of pulling off her pants without removing Val's hikers. Ripping proved necessary, but that didn't bother her. The suit, fashionable and delicate, belonged to someone named Tasia, and Tasia had only minutes to live.

Laughter trickled in from the packing room. This was, without a doubt, the happiest smuggling ring she ever worked with. *Wonder how long it will last?* No operation

like it ever floated for long without springing a few leaks.
The fact that most of the revenue earned by the small network went to finance colonial secessionist groups didn't bode
well for its life span, either.

That was the main reason for her delay, when every nerve
in her body sang for her to *get out now*. She had to finish
out the night, leave things tight. If it ever went to hell for
these people, it wouldn't be because of anything she had
done. Or failed to do. She might have worked at many jobs,
under many names, on a score of worlds, but Jani Kilian had
done them all very well. The habit had sunk its roots during
her short but eventful Service career. *Whatever job you un-
dertake, perform it to the best of your ability, and see it
through to the end.* And so she had, now as then.

Well, no. There had been one particular *then* when she
had not done her best. Oh, she had survived. No one else
had, though, except in her memory.

Knevçet Shèràa, the one bad job that outweighed all the
good.

"Tasia! What's taking you so long!"

Jani bundled the ruined trouser suit into her locker and
limped out to the packing room to find Ileana waiting for
her, holding a documents pouch.

"Guv Hall. Hurry. You have sixteen minutes to file these
quarterlies or those bastards will come after me!" She thrust
the pouch into Jani's hands, then grabbed her elbow and
steered her toward the door.

"It's only half a block." Jani tried to ease out of the
woman's grip. "I could stop for dinner and get there in time."

"Maybe, the way you eat." Ileana eyed Jani's coverall with
distaste. "You eat like you dress. No thought. No one would
ever mistake you for a true Feliciana." She pushed Jani out
the door. "Now move!"

Jani hurried down the street in a lurching double time, her
eyes focused on the brilliantly lit triple towers of Government Hall. Then she glanced back to see if Ileana watched
her, and slowed down when she saw she didn't. Her chest
ached again. Her thigh muscles trembled. She wondered
what Val was doing. Worming secrets from his sometime

love? Or tearing the city apart looking for her?

Good old Val. Her steps slowed as she recalled his embrace. It worried her that it took only a single kind gesture to knock her off-balance at a time when she couldn't afford the least wobble. Now more than ever, she could not drop her guard.

But I'm tired. Tired of feeling sick, of running, of trying to remember what her damned name was. Fed up with being alone.

Jani flashed her Tasia ID for the last time at the Guv Hall security desk—one of the few benefits of being non-Reg was that she didn't have to worry about hand or eye scanning. After she stuffed the pouch in a lobby drop box, she keyed in a request that the receipt be fiched to Ileana instead of to her.

That final loose end tied off, Jani crossed the wide avenue and headed for the *hojea* platform, dodging skimmers and jostling through groups of the well-dressed leaving their businesses for a night on the town. One, a day-suited man whose night out must have started that morning, bumped her roughly, then staggered on, muttering curses at the world in general. Not a Felician accent, Jani noted. Earthbound. No surprise there. Lots of Earthbounders worked on Felix.

She stepped onto the platform and surveyed the scene around her as she waited for the train. Across the street, she saw the man who had bumped her standing in the Guv Hall entryway, watching her. Then the street weaved and roiled like a banner in the wind. Just as she sagged to her knees, Jani heard footsteps close in from behind. Then it all went black—

CHAPTER 3

"So what do we do now, Quino?" Evan van Reuter flipped his stylus from one hand to another. "We've been waiting for one goddamn piece of paper for two hours."

Joaquin Loiaza shot a look uptable at the SIB chief investigator. But Colonel Veda was engaged in anxious discussion with the Judge Advocate's representative, and didn't appear aware of the mutterings at the far end of the conference table. "In truth, Evan, we've been waiting for two goddamn pieces of paper. The *Hilfington* roster would be nice, but we'll take the *Kensington* master if we have to."

"By my count, this makes the fourth time in a month they've misplaced documents."

"Yes, their track record does fail to impress. I must consider how to turn that to our advantage." Joaquin rubbed his chin thoughtfully. As always, the old-coin aspect of his close-cropped brown hair and regal nose was offset by the pinched look around his turtlelike eyes.

Caesar with a migraine. Evan tapped the stylus on the table and stole another glance at Colonel Veda. Since she sat, he could only see her from the waist up. Closely trimmed black hair. Creamy brown skin. A noble face, handsome rather than pretty. He'd yet to see her smile, but he guessed those dark brown eyes could sparkle given the right encouragement. He knew from other stolen glances that her Service summerweights hugged lovely curves.

Her first name's Chandra. A soft, lovely name. Yes, in another lifetime, he would have asked Durian Ridgeway to don his go-between hat and invite her to an assignation in one of the rented flats the Interior Ministry had scattered throughout Chicago. In that other lifetime, she would have accepted.

But in this lifetime, Durian is dead and Veda thinks I'm a worm. Evan struck the stylus against the table—tiny shards of poly sprayed across the surface as the writing tip shattered. "What difference do the ship records from the evac make?" He swept the plastic bits over the tableside and onto the carpeted floor. "They know I was there—that's why I'm in trouble now."

Joaquin sighed. "Pretend you're still a cabinet minister and use your brain. We want to build sympathy. Highlight the hardships you endured during the idomeni civil war and the evacuation, the hardships that still haunt your memory eighteen years later. The terror as the Haárin stalked Rauta Shèràa, slaughtering the fallen Laum, while their Vynshàrau puppetmasters watched from the surrounding hills."

"You make it sound like a 'Vee melodrama. All that's missing is the closing clinch with the girlfriend to the strains of the Commonwealth anthem." Evan smiled to mask his unease. He had many reasons to dread his memories—he didn't relish the thought of his own attorney dredging them up again.

Especially the memories he'd deny to the grave.

Joaquin's stylus scraped across the surface of his recording board. "Only you would see it that way. A more sober-minded individual would have lived in constant fear."

Evan's smile died. Fear? Of what? The bombs? The panic? The rumors of a massacre by a human of twenty-six Laumrau in a place called Knevçet Shèràa? That the Haárin might ignore their cultural conditioning and avenge the disorderly deaths of their enemies by slaughtering the remaining inhabitants of Rauta Shèràa's human enclave?

That his government would find out the things he'd done? That escaping execution in Rauta Shèràa only increased his chances of meeting that fate back on Earth?

"Fear?" Evan felt the sweat trickle under his shirt. His hands shook. His left knee ached. He needed a drink. "What do you know about fear?"

Joaquin ignored the question. "Most especially, we need to emphasize that there were times during the voyage home that you didn't think you'd make it back to Earth alive."

His stylus broken, Evan dissipated the urge to twitch by tugging on his security cuff. *My electronic leash.* Nice of his jailers to make the black-banded monitor look like a timepiece. He wondered if it fooled anyone. "Living through two months of crappy food and cramped quarters isn't going to win me any sympathy from this crowd. It's their way of life."

"Keep your voice down!" Joaquin glanced anxiously at Veda. "Remember your place. No one has to tolerate your pithy commentary anymore." He clucked his tongue, then returned to his note taking.

Evan felt the lump in his gut grow and twist. Not long ago, people stood in line to tolerate his pithy commentary and whatever else he cared to dish out. It had been six months since the life he'd always known had ended. Six months since the roof had caved in.

And we know who snapped the support beam, don't we? Evan could see her face as clearly as if she sat across the table from him. Hair as short and black as Veda's. Eyes as dark. Skin as smooth. Look, as cold.

Jani, who killed the Laumrau and, before that, his Uncle Rik. Whom he tracked down and pulled from the gutter eighteen years later, because he had needed her a lot and still loved her a little. Who repaid him first by killing his friend Durian, then by destroying his life.

Jani.

"Excuse me."

Evan looked up to find Veda standing before him. Up close, he could see the fine etching of lines that decorated the corners of her eyes. So, there were smiles bottled up in that well-conditioned body. He wondered for whom she saved them. He tried to inject some softness into his expression—imagining what lay hidden under that trimly tailored summerweight shirt made it easy. *Grey isn't her color; he* forced himself to focus on her face. No, it would have to be soft yellow or cream, something that would complement the undertones of her skin. . . .

Joaquin's puckered asshole of a voice shook Evan out of his sexual reverie. "Have the vanished rosters reappeared yet, Colonel?"

A muscle throbbed in Veda's cheek. "No, Mr. Loiaza, they have not. The ranking documents examiner has been contacted, however, and we hope to have them first thing tomorrow morning."

"Do you?" Joaquin managed to inject more cynical skepticism in those two words than less-skilled attorneys could in an entire summation. "I find it very distressing that documents that could play an important role in my client's defense have gone missing as easily as last week's newssheets."

Veda's chest rose and fell. Evan found the movement hypnotic.

"Not a very skillful diversion, Counselor." The Judge Advocate's representative, a geeky youngster whose name Evan kept forgetting, drew up to his full-yet-unprepossessing height. "Let's not lose sight of the essential facts. Your client is responsible for ordering the deaths of sixteen members of this Service. Add to that his collusion in the deaths of the Bandan research team at Knevçet Shèràa and his role in the illegal importation of idomeni augmentation technologies—"

"All alleged, Counselor. My client has not been charged." Joaquin's voice grew dangerously soft. "He's here to assist you in your investigation of Jani Kilian's murder of her commanding officer. Unless you're having difficulty uncovering documents pertinent to that case, as well."

The meeting ended with a terse assurance from Colonel Veda that the documents would be available by morning. Evan watched her stalk out of the conference room, his eyes greedily recording the sway of her walk in the long-deprived recesses of his memory. "Was that necessary?"

Joaquin tossed his recording board into his briefbag. "Evan, just because you have a hard-on for Veda doesn't mean I have to cease doing my job."

"Pithy, Quino."

"Let that be a lesson to you."

The SIB hallways mirrored the stripped-down aesthetic of the conference room. Evan fingered the austere beige sacking that cloaked the walls near the lift bank. *Roshi probably picked out the wall coverings himself.* Hiroshi Mako took pride in his functional, unadorned Service. He had battled to the dizzy heights of the Admiral-Generalcy with one goal in mind, to salvage his beloved Blue and Grey. They were a true military now, he claimed, instead of the Family police force they had been in the Bad Old Days.

Those Bad Old Days were pretty good to me. But then, Evan could admit his bias. Anything that improved a Family's place in the Commonwealth was right and commendable, and anyone in the NUVA-SCAN Family network who claimed to feel differently lied. Now, however, in these days of restless colonies clamoring for autonomy and argumentative idomeni demanding trade agreements that encroached more and more deeply into human territories, wise Family members kept such sentiments to themselves.

Family first. Even though, as far as the van Reuters were concerned, the Family had for years consisted of him and him alone.

"Rather fine qualifying match on the 'Vee this evening," Joaquin said. "Live from Geneva—Gruppo Helvetica vs. some poor colonial appetizer."

A scene flashed in Evan's mind. Tanned, coltish legs pumping—black ponytail flipping. *Daddy, watch me—!* His eyes stung. "Soccer's not my game, Quino."

"It *is* the Commonwealth Cup." Joaquin grew thoughtful. "Although God knows what the upsurge of colonial pride will wash out of the drains if one of those teams actually wins it this time."

"Serena used to play on her school team." Evan blinked until his vision cleared. "I haven't watched a match since she died."

Joaquin shifted his feet. "Evan, I—"

"Just drop it." He braced for a clumsy apology. When

none proved forthcoming, he turned to find his attorney regarding him with impatient admiration.

"If the people of Chicago could see you at this moment, they'd storm Sheridan to free you." The man exhaled with a rumble. "You're my client. My responsibility is to you. Everyone's heard the rumors. Let me place one official story about the children—"

"No."

"Damn it, it's the prime example of how your late father manipulated everyone around him! He subjects Martin to an experimental personality augmentation at the age of three—eleven years later, Martin dies during the boating mishap he'd arranged to kill Serena and Jerrold."

"Thank you for mentioning it. I needed that."

"The deaths of your children destroyed any chance you and Lyssa had to rebuild your marriage."

"Our marriage was a joke from the start." Evan thumped the lift bank keypad with his fist. "We've discussed this before. I haven't changed my mind. Use anything but the children. Let them rest in peace. End of subject." The lift door finally opened. He limped in, left knee clicking with every stride.

"Since you brought up colonial pride, Quino, here's a question. I heard on CapNet that Acadia and the other Channel Worlds have lodged some kind of protest concerning the arrests of political prisoners despite insufficient evidence. One of those prisoners wouldn't happen to be Jani, would it?"

"As soon as Kilian is found, the SIB is required to notify us. If Veda lets us down in *that* regard, not even your esteem will prevent me from tearing her apart." Joaquin boarded the lift and punched the pad for the ground floor. "Apropos of nothing, how is the Crème Caramel doing?" The mention of roses erased the discomfort from his bony face.

"Fine, Quino." Evan bit his lip to keep from grimacing. At his flower-loving attorney's insistence, he had planted a small rose garden in the rear yard of his prison-home and tended the blooms faithfully every day. Joaquin claimed that the image of a disgraced ex–Cabinet Minister tending his garden as he once tended his constituents would excite sympathy from the public, but Evan nursed the conviction that the man just needed a place to stash the overflow from his own extensive cultivations.

"I hope you didn't fertilize it yet. You need to wait at least another two weeks."

"Yes, Quino."

"Then you must use the special mix I gave you for the Jewellers' Loop hybrids, not the standard mix I gave you for the others."

"Yes, Quino."

"And you must wait until late afternoon. Spread no more than two hundred grams around the base of the plant, then follow with a liberal watering."

God help me. "*Yes,* Quino."

By the time the lift reached the ground floor, Evan had mentally dismembered the Crème Caramel with an ax and was about to start on his attorney. The door swept aside; he stepped out of the car and almost collided with a man dressed in summerweights. Short. Stocky. A round, tawny face cut by a perpetual scowl. Black eyes hidden by sloping cheekbones and drooping lids.

"Hello, Roshi." Evan stepped around the supreme commander of the Commonwealth Service, then dodged sideways to avoid his aide. "Inspecting your fences, are you?"

"Evan." Admiral-General Hiroshi Mako pulled up short, then looked in apparent disinterest from him to Joaquin. Only if you looked hard could you detect the mild working of his broad jaw that betrayed his unease. But then, what could he say? *How are you? What brings you here?* "Hellish weather we're having." When in doubt, there was always the weather.

Evan racked his brain for a suitably neutral reply. "Plays hell with the roses."

Mako's eyes clouded as he watched the lift doors close. He stepped aside as his aide grabbed for the closing door and thumped the keypad—unfortunately for him, the man's efforts proved wasted. "You raise roses? Ah yes, I saw something about that on one of the news shows." Mako's guttural bass kicked upward a tone in grudging interest. "Tamiko raises them, too." His voice warmed as he spoke his wife's name. "The J-Loop varieties give her the hardest time, judging from her muttering. She refuses to accept mere climate as an excuse for failure to thrive."

"She should contact Dr. Banquo at the Botanical Gardens—the woman was born on Phillipa and knows everything about Jewellers' Loop hybrids." Joaquin leaned forward in shared conspiracy. "The secret is in the fertilizer."

That's government in a nutshell. Evan caught the aide eyeing him and tugged at his somber, dark blue jacket. *Do I look that bad?* He had lost weight, and he hadn't been sleeping well, but what else would you expect—?

"Damn."

He turned to find Joaquin standing with his hand pressed to his stomach and a look of stricken concentration on his face. "Watch my bag." He dropped his briefbag at Evan's feet and hurried toward a discreetly marked door near the lobby entry.

Evan answered Mako's questioning look. "New cook. She tends toward a heavy hand with some of the more pharmaceutically active colonial herbs."

Mako winced in sympathy, then turned to his aide. "See if you can find out which herbs she used, Colonel. The last thing we need at next month's off-site is an attack of the trots."

"Yes, sir." The man pulled a small handheld from the slipcase on his belt and muttered a notation.

Evan watched the man; whoever he was, he didn't look like the typical Base Command poop boy. Distinctive, in the close-clipped, wire-lean way that typified Roshi's New Service. The nasty scar that grooved his face from the edge of his nose to the corner of his mouth accentuated his sharp-featured homeliness, its dull white color a marked contrast to the sunburnt red-brown of his face.

But it was the way the man looked at Evan that drew his attention. Not the pointed monitoring of the bodyguard, but the more analytical assessment of one who searched through his mental ID file, matched, tagged, shrugged, and moved on.

I know a hatchet man when I see one. Evan had employed enough of his own. He snatched a glance at the man's name tag. "Colonel Pierce." He offered a nod, but didn't try to shake. One too many snubs when he had held out his hand had driven that lesson home.

"Sir." Pierce nodded back, but kept his hands at his sides.

"You're lucky to be lakeside in this weather." When in doubt . . . "At least you get some breeze."

Pierce made a point of not looking Evan in the face, instead concentrating on the floor indicator located above the lift doors. "Yes, sir. That we are, sir." His voice proved nasal and harsh. It could have been the lower-class version of Evan's own Michigan provincial, but odds were the muted remnants of a Victoria colony twang would prove the more accurate choice.

From Pearl Way, are we? Evan felt his long-dormant curiosity stretch out a paw. It was a hell of a long trip from that far-flung network of worlds to the Admiral-General's side. At one time or another, Pierce had proven himself extremely talented. Or extremely useful.

The lift returned to the first floor. "Good-bye, Evan." The relief in Mako's voice was gallingly evident as the door opened and he and Pierce stepped in. "Enjoy your roses."

Evan watched the door close. Mako took care to avoid his eye. But Pierce glanced at him just as the panels meshed, his scar twisting his disgusted curl of lip into a caricature of a sneer.

"I'm back. What's left of me." Joaquin drew alongside, then bent slowly to pick up his bag. His complexion was waxen, his eyes, narrowed to slits. "Let's go."

Evan followed him out the door. After the coolness of the SIB, the late-afternoon heat made him gasp. "How are you feeling?"

"Like I've been punched in the stomach." Joaquin gestured to his driver, parked in the nearby visitor's oval. "I can't decide if it was the cherryvale leaves in the salad or the folsom in the gravy."

"Probably a combination of both." Evan watched his lawyer's sedate black double-length slide to the curbside and felt the envy twinge. He'd had an entire fleet of black double-lengths at his beck and call, in that other lifetime. Triple-lengths. Sedans. One cherry red Sportster he missed particularly. He had planned to take Jani for a ride in it, as soon as the weather and her stiff-necked mien had permitted.

The best-laid plans, all blown to hell.

He eased into the passenger seat beside his rose-loving attorney and looked out at the bowl of poured concrete that some architect had inverted and dubbed the Service Investigative Bureau. Odd area of Sheridan for the supreme commander to be wandering, despite his reputation for digging into the daily workings of the base.

Whatever's going on, he needed his hatchet along to check it out. Evan remembered the feeling—he had dragged Durian Ridgeway along on so many cleanup projects, the man had earned the nickname *the janitor.*

Made one wonder what service Scarface had performed to merit the confidence.

"Did an officer named Pierce serve on either the *Hilfington* or the *Kensington*, Quino?" Evan must have done a good job keeping the curiosity out of his voice—Joaquin barely glanced up from his handheld.

"Crew rosters are included in the documents we've requested from Veda, Evan. I can't answer that question until I have them in hand."

Evan nodded. "It's just that he looks familiar." He tapped his thumb on his knee and watched Joaquin's face in the angled reflection of the driver's rearview mirror. "I could have seen him at the Consulate, I suppose."

"Those rosters we have, thanks to your father's meticulous recordkeeping. I'll have one of the clerks check when I get back to the office." He looked at Evan with an air of quiet interest. "Do you recall the circumstances under which you think you saw him?"

Evan shook his head. "No. Sorry. If anything comes to me, I'll let you know." With that, he dropped it. He had known Joaquin for over thirty years and had worked with him professionally for fifteen. The man sensed a possible lead; therefore, he would *check.* Whichever Service records he could access. Whatever other official sources he could tap. Then, just to make sure he hadn't missed anything, he would assign an agent or two to work the unofficial side of the street, to research Pierce's past from the cradle to what he had for breakfast that morning, and see where the reports overlapped.

Or didn't.

And then I'll know. It didn't have to be big—it just had to hurt. A failed marriage. An embarrassing relative. A rumor of cheating in school. Something to fling in Pierce's battered face the next time they met. *Pierce, Pierce, I'd heard of a Pierce who—oh, I'm sorry. Are you related?*

The skimmer passed beneath the base entryway. The shadow of the Shenandoah Gate darkened the vehicle interior; the illuminated names of the Greatest War dead inscribed on the stone's surface shone like stars. The sudden nightfall shook Evan out of his bitter daydream. *Why the hell am I bothering?* Did he crave a respite from his legal travails? Or did being rebuffed at by a colonial counter-jumper aggravate him that much?

Which colonial counter-jumper am I thinking about? He rubbed his aching knee and pushed thoughts of Jani from his mind.

CHAPTER 4

"I can't find it, Mr. Duong."

Sam looked up from the stack of files that he had balanced precariously on his lap. "Which is *it*, Tory? The *Hilfington* passenger roster or the *Kensington* master?"

The Clerk Four shifted from foot to foot. "Both. Neither." Her eyes filled. "Mr. Odergaard said that Mr. Loiaza threatened to notify the Prime Minister."

Sam closed the file he had been rooting through and hoisted the pile from his lap to the tabletop. "He can try," he said as he smoothed his rumpled civilian greys. "Prime Minister Cao does not jump to the beat of lawyers who make a show of stamping their well-shod feet."

"But Mr. Loiaza is *Mr. van Reuter's* lawyer."

"That's no great honor." Sam stood, shivering as conditioned air brushed across his sweat-damp back. He could visualize the light grey shirting darkened to charcoal, and wondered if he dared escape to the locker room for a shower and change of clothes. It wouldn't make the hell that the day had become go any more smoothly, but at least he would feel better. Comparatively speaking. He felt a battered wreck now.

"Mr. Odergaard says that if we can't track down the docs in the next half hour, you have to contact Lieutenant Yance." Tory's eyes widened. She was seventeen years old—the Clerk Four position was her first job since graduating prep school. Judging from the mounting panic on her round, fresh face, she would be starting her second position sometime next week. "Mr. Odergaard says—"

"As second shift Tech One, Mr. Odergaard is responsible for the live documents on his watch." Sam folded his arms. "I am the archivist. The dead belong to me."

Tory's agitation ceased, replaced by the so-still attitude Sam had encountered more and more frequently as the weeks passed. The weeks since ex–Interior Minister van Reuter and his lawyer had begun visiting Fort Sheridan. The weeks since they had begun asking for documents from the Service Investigative Bureau Archives. Documents describing murder. Mutiny. Conspiracy. Documents that could not be found.

And everyone blames me. Little Sam—you know him. Small, wiry chap. Hair like tar. Face like a daze.

He stepped from behind the table and beckoned for Tory to follow him back to the aisle after aisle of paper-crammed shelving that constituted the SIB stacks. *Because they think I'm . . . unwell.*

"Unwell or not, *K* still comes after *H.*" He waited at the stack entry for Tory, who lagged behind. He'd gotten used to that, too. The aversion people evinced at having to work with him, talk to him. The vague feeling that people just wished he'd go away.

We have that in common, van Reuter. The ex-minister's hawklike visage surfaced in Sam's memory. From the stairwell scuttlebutt he had heard, the man who had once been the *V* in the NUVA-SCAN technology conglomerate had become a pariah amongst his own. Isolated. Maligned. Blamed for every misstep taken by the Families in the last twenty years.

Sam felt a chill sense of kinship with van Reuter, in spite of the crimes the man was alleged to have committed. *It's all your fault, and no one wants to hear you explain.* He held the door open for Tory, and maintained his air of polite reserve as she dodged past him into the stacks. A great thing, to have so much in common with such a great man.

*   *   *

"I apologize for taking you away from your work, Sam. I understand you've been very busy."

"That's all right, Doctor."

"Look into the light."

"Yes, Doctor." Sam lifted his head and stared into the red glow, positioned a scant meter in front of his face. At first, it shone with a single, steady beat. Then it fluttered, skipped, skittered across its source surface like a bug in a bottle.

Another light joined it. Another. Finally, an entire series of red pulses stuttered and popped, filling his range of vision like a silent, monochrome-fireworks display.

After a few minutes, the reversal began. Fewer lights. Fewer. Mad perturbations slowed and steadied. A handful of lights. Five. Three. Two. One.

Stopped.

Sam blinked, worked his neck, yawned. Sitting in the dark had reminded him how tired he was. The *Hilfington* rosters had finally turned up. Tory had found them shoved in between two accounts-receivable folders, under the letter *P*. *One crisis averted.* But the *Kensington* rosters remained missing, as were so many other things. The day's single success did little to lessen the pressure Sam felt from Odergaard, who felt it from Yance, who felt it from the Head of Archives, who in turn had to deal with Veda's foot on her neck.

Normally, he despised his visits to Sheridan's Main Hospital. But today, the relief he felt at being able to leave the SIB basement made him want to cry.

The room lights blazed to life. Sam shut his eyes against the assault.

"Did that bother you at all?"

He opened one watering eye to see Dr. Pimentel standing near the examining-room entry, his hand still resting on the lighting pad. He shrugged. "I found it interesting, at first. Then it became irritating."

Pimentel hung his head. He seemed to grow older with each passing visit. The blond hair, more dull and lank. The eyes, more fatigued. He had to be at least twenty years younger than Sam, no more than thirty-five. What did he do that drained him so? "Irritating? How?"

Sam struggled to construct an explanation. It seemed such a trivial thing, hardly worth the effort. "It appeared so . . . tentative. I kept waiting for it to make up its mind."

Pimentel continued to watch him from his post by the door. Then he walked back to his seat next to Sam's examining table with the round-shouldered trudge of someone who bore the weight of the world. "Sam." He always took care to pronounce Sam's name in proper Bandan fashion— *Sahm* rhymes with *Mom*, not *Sam* rhymes with *damn*. "I subjected you to that test for a reason. If you were indeed augmented, as you claimed during your last visit, you would not have been able to look into that light for more than a few seconds without it affecting you."

Sam thought back to his previous visit. Tried to think back. It had been sunny . . . no, rainy . . . wait, they hadn't had any rain for over a month. Or had it been two? "Affecting me?"

The ergoworks in Pimentel's seat creaked as he leaned forward. "Blink patterns are designed to affect Service augments in very specific ways. You've been here often enough in the past few months to have heard the term *takedown*. That's when we use blink patterns to halt the progression of an unwanted overdrive state, a situation where the panic-dampening function of the augment asserts itself in a non-conflict situation. We do it both as a semiannual precautionary treatment, and, when necessary, to short-circuit an acute event."

"I told you I was augmented?" Sam reached into his shirt pocket and pulled out his Service-issued handheld. He kept all his appointments in it. And his little notations. Where the men's room was, for example. Well, the SIB was a large building—it was an easy thing to forget. *What did I tell Pimentel, and when?* He'd kept no record of that, unfortunately.

"Yes, Sam. You did." Pimentel glanced at the handheld, his tired eyes flaring with curiosity. "The aftereffects of a takedown aren't pleasant. The patient can feel fatigued and disoriented for as long as a week after treatment. Unfortunately, much milder versions of blink patterns can have a similar, though lesser, effect. For that reason, many augments develop an aversion to the color red, and become highly agitated when exposed to arrays of blinking lights. We take that into account here at Sheridan, where the augmented population stands at twenty-seven percent. Certain types of lighted displays and exhibits are expressly forbidden. Enforcement becomes difficult during the various holiday celebrations, of course." He grinned weakly. "But it's different in the world outside the Shenandoah Gate. No holds barred in Chicago, a city you visit three to four times a week." He grew serious. "Am I right?"

Sam nodded, resisting the urge to check his handheld again. "I visit the city, yes."

"You visit the various Service Archives to research the names for inclusion in the Gate. You travel at night, from what you told me. You find it easier to work when no one else is around. You take the Sheridan Local Line, which passes the Pier exhibits, the Bluffs Zoo, the Commonwealth Gardens. They each have thrill rides. All-night exhibits." Pimentel's weary gaze never left Sam's face. He seemed to be prompting him, reminding him of his life. As though—

As though he doesn't think I can remember on my own.

"I guarantee you, Sam," the doctor continued, "if you were augmented, you couldn't look at those exhibits, because *every* augment I examine mentions having a problem with at least one of them when they visit the city. Some wear special eyefilms to filter out the light. Some wear hearing protection because they've developed related sensitivity to any sound resembling emergency sirens or explosions. But every one of them does *something*, because otherwise, they become very sick very quickly.

Sam's chest tightened as his anger grew. "You knew from my encephaloscan that I didn't have a Service-type augmentation?"

"Yes, Sam. You're the one who seemed to require convincing."

"My augmentation is different." Yes, that was it. Pimentel must have only asked him whether he was augmented, not what type of augmentation he had. He hammered Sam with vagueness, then called foul when Sam responded in kind. *Don't ask me what I remember, Doctor, ask me what I know.* "It's not a Service augmentation. It's something else."

"Define *something else,* Sam."

"It was supposed to make me hear things. See things. Feel things, deep in my body."

"That's an odd function for an augmentation. Why was it made that way?"

"Because they wanted to study my reactions. Because they wanted to see what I'd do."

"They?" Pimentel glanced down at his recording board, then back at Sam. "Who's they?"

"The ones—" Sam blinked away images that flashed in his eyes like the patterns. Faces. Gold. White. The gold ones spoke. He couldn't understand the words. "The ones who put it there."

Pimentel continued to write, the scratch of his stylus filling the small room. "Were you implanted against your will?"

"Yes."

"You felt paralyzed? Not in control?"

"Ye—" Sam could feel it again. The clench of anger that told him he was being maneuvered "Have I told you this before?"

Pimentel shook his head. "No, this is new. For the past few months, you've been insisting you're a xenogeologist. You showed me papers you'd written, books you'd had published." He pocketed his stylus and rocked back in his seat. "You had taken those papers and books from the SIB Archives, Sam. They weren't yours."

"No, I—"

"Sam, the e-scan didn't reveal a Service augmentation. It only confirmed what we've known for months. You have a tumor, in your thalamus, that's affecting your memory. It causes you to forget events that really happened, and to substitute fabrications to fill in the gaps."

"A tumor?" Sam poked the back of his head, then let his hand fall back into his lap. Silly. It wasn't as though he could feel the thing if he probed long enough.

Pimentel nodded. "It hasn't increased in size over time, but we need to remove it."

"I'll die."

"If we take the tumor *out*, why would you die?"

"They—they told me I'd die, if anyone took it out."

"No, you won't, Sam."

"Yes, I will!" *I know.* "This . . . tumor—it's not hurting me, it's not affecting my life, my work."

"Sam, it *is* starting to interfere with your ability to do your job." Pimentel stood and walked to his desk. "You've built a reputation over the years as a first-class archivist. But now you're losing papers, forgetting where you filed them, making up stories that they were stolen." He leaned against the desk as though he needed the support. "You need treatment."

Sam stared down at the floor. Dull grey lyno, flecked with white. He recalled seeing a stone that resembled it. Holding it in his hand. The where escaped him, however. The when.

"Sam, you don't state the names of any family or friends in the Emergency Notification block in your chart."

"There is no one."

"No one you can talk to? No one you feel you can trust?"

"No."

Pimentel returned to his seat. "Do you know what a ward of the Commonwealth is?"

The clench returned, stronger this time. "It means I'm supposed to trust a member of the government to take care of me."

"No, to help *you* take care of yourself. And it isn't just one person. It's a committee. In your case, it would consist of an impartial civilian official, a Service adjudicator, and a medical representative." Pimentel smiled. "Most likely me, as your attending physician."

"No." Sam slid off the examining table. His feet struck the lyno that reminded him of stone. "I've trusted members of the government to take care of me before. That proved a mistake."

"When, Sam?"

"I don't remember." *Don't ask me what I remember. Ask me what I know.*

* * *

He waited until after midnight to return to the SIB. Odergaard had left a note requesting Sam stop by to see him before start of shift later that day. That didn't bode well. If previous events repeated, that meant another document had turned up missing.

Sam sat at his desk, head in hands. Pimentel had made him promise to consider the wardship, and he had said he would. Anything to get out of that place.

No one cuts into my head. Ever. He left the cubicle maze of the doc tech bullpen and walked down the hall to the vend alcove. He bought a cup of tea, striking the beverage dispenser with a timed series of thumps the techs had discovered made it disgorge an extra mouthful into the cup. Since he was the alcove's only visitor, he had his pick of tables. He chose one in the corner, farthest from the entry.

He activated his handheld and pulled up the file he had unfortunately found many reasons to update over the past weeks. In one column, he had listed all the documents that had gone missing, in the other, the ones that had eventually turned up. He sorted, ran a discard, and examined the few items that still remained outstanding.

The roster. Shipping records. Death certificates. The roster and records belonged to the CSS *Kensington*, the flagship of the group that executed the evacuation of Rauta Shèràa Base.

And the death certificates? *Ebben. Unser. Fitzhugh. Caldor.* Three officers and a Spacer First Class, who died during the evacuation.

Sam stared at the small display and tried to divine a pattern from the list of documents. Like flecks in stone, they seemed anarchic, unconnected. But he sensed history, just as he would if he studied the stone. If he subjected the stone to elemental analysis and investigated the site at which he'd found it, he would know how it formed, and why. So, too, with these documents—they could be broken down, as well. Every entry had another piece of paper to back it up, and when he had uncovered those pieces, well, then he'd know, wouldn't he? He never liked to conclude ahead of his data.

At the beginning, it was enough to know that sufficient reason existed for the data to be collected.

He sipped his tea, heavily creamed and sugared to obscure the bitterness. Not like at his old stomping grounds on Banda. *The university*. There, they knew how to make tea.

"And I knew how to drink it." He recalled overhearing a shopkeeper brag to another customer one day as he made his purchases. *No one in Halmahera knows tea like Simyam Baru—*

Sam paused, then checked the nameplate on his handheld. *Duong*. First name Sam, rhymes with Mom.

"My name is Sam Duong." But pictures formed in his imagination again. He saw himself encased in ice, then heard the hissing crackles as fissures formed in the block. Water dripped as the melting progressed, revealing who he truly was. Another man, who hated hospitals, too.

Again, not something he remembered. Something he knew.

CHAPTER 5

Evan stood before his shallow bank of roses and inventoried the status of each bush in turn. "The Crème Caramel's looking good." He dictated the observation into his handheld as he hefted a branch laden with butterscotch blooms. "Tell your Dr. Banquo she knows her fertilizer."

Banquo . . . Banquo. Evan paused, his finger pressed against the handheld touchpad, as the names cascaded in his head. *Banquo . . . Mako. Mako . . . Pierce.* "It's been over two weeks, Quino. I just wondered if you'd scrounged anything about Colonel Pierce. The more I think about that name, the more familiar it sounds." That was a lie, but he'd had lots of time to ponder the colonel's snub, and the more he thought about it, the more it bothered him. Information flitted throughout military bases at speed—he wondered if Pierce knew something, something that made him feel he didn't need to hide his dislike for his fallen minister. Perhaps the Service had reopened its investigation of Jani's transport explosion. Perhaps it had found a witness, someone who had stumbled past the comroom just as Evan had contacted the fuel depot where the transport was hangared. Saw him enter the comcode. Heard him say the words.

Do it.

He grunted in pain, and looked down to find he had gripped the Crème's branch too hard, driving the thorns into his hand. He hunted through his pockets for a clean dispo, dabbed at the welling beads of blood, and moved on to the next shrub. "I'm not sure about this Wolfshead Westminster. It's still washed-out rust instead of bright orange, but I don't know what you expect. It's a cold-weather hybrid that thrives by waterside, and we're only in the middle of the hottest, driest summer in thirty years." He flicked off the device and shoved it in his pocket. "Report's over for the day, Quino. You want to see how your goddamn roses are doing, drive up here and check them yourself."

His knee ached less than it had for weeks—a walk seemed in order. He strode to the end of the garden, then turned and paced alongside the two-meter-tall hedge that defined his boundary with the neighbor who he'd been told worked for Commerce Purchasing. Then he made a balance beam of the edge of his patio and finished the traverse by walking along the latticed polywood fence that formed the barrier between him and the neighbor who he'd been told slaved for the Commonwealth Mint. He knew better, of course. Prime Minister's Intelligence, both of them. He'd have bet his last bottle.

When he cut by the garden and stood again at the spot at which he had started, he checked his timepiece. "Elapsed time for inspection of the van Reuter fences—seventy-two seconds." And he had even walked slowly this time.

How do people live like this? Cheek by jowl. Sounds of their lives commingled into one vast blare. Everyone knowing their business and them knowing everyone else's, without one minute's privacy or peace. They all must have developed a zoo-animal mentality, he decided, living their lives as their instincts compelled them without caring who saw what.

"Sir!"

Evan turned. Halvor, his aide, stood on the patio, looking befuddled as usual. *"Yes?"*

The young man hesitated. "You have . . . a visitor, sir."

Evan trudged up the shallow incline toward the house he thought of as his Elba. "Quino isn't supposed to stop by until tomorrow."

Halvor's face, smooth and rounded as an overgrown baby's, flushed pink. "It's not Mr. Loiaza, sir."

"Well, who is it?"

Halvor told him.

Evan took care to follow his aide at a carefully calculated distance. Too close, and he'd seem anxious. Too far, and he'd seem apprehensive. *Stay calm . . . stay calm.*

After the glaring brightness of the outdoors, it took a few seconds for his eyes to adjust to the dimmer light of the sitting room. He didn't register the figure standing in front of the curtained window until it spoke.

"Hello, Evan." John Shroud stood with his back to him, his attention focused on the view of the rear yard. "You're due for a medical checkup. Compassionate visitation, the Jo'burg Convention calls it. Guess who drew the short straw?"

Evan motioned for the flustered Halvor to leave the room. He sank into his favorite lounge chair and waited for the hushed click that indicated the door had closed. "You expect me to believe you flew in from Seattle just to check my vitals?"

"You're an ex–Cabinet Minister, Evan. You rate Big Three attention."

"Bullshit."

Shroud turned slowly. "As you wish." He had employed his albinism like a fashion accessory, as usual. Today, he resembled a polished marble of a medieval monk. He'd brushed his stark white hair forward and had dressed in ivory from head to toe, the collar of his jacket draping like a cowl. His height, thinness, and long face reinforced the image, as did his blanched skin, drawn tight across cheekbone and brow. Disturbing, no matter how often you'd seen him. The ambassador from the Other Side.

I should have expected this. Evan wished he'd had the sense to prepare, but except for a quick swig prior to tending his roses, he'd had nothing to drink that morning. As ever, abstinence proved a mistake. He always felt more in control with a half liter of bourbon warming his insides. "What really brings you to Chicago, John?" As if he couldn't guess.

"It's been raining for two solid weeks back home."

Shroud's bass voice rumbled like a knell. "I need sunshine, even if all I can do is look." He strolled to the sofa and sat down. "Besides, I don't often get the chance to visit the capital." He stretched out his long, thin legs and crossed them at the ankles, then looked around the room, sharp eyes taking in the cramped dimensions, the shabby furniture, before coming to rest on Evan. "Cozy," he said, with a ghost of a smile.

Evan responded in kind. "I think so."

"Quite a change from the old Family estate."

"Quite."

"Smaller."

"Yes."

"A woman's presence, of course, is what makes a home." Shroud's smile withered. "I never had the opportunity to offer my condolences. Lyssa's death came as a shock to us all."

Evan tensed at the sound of his dead wife's name. "Thank you."

"I spoke with Anais last evening, at one of Vandy's interminable dinner parties. Milla's staying with her for the summer. Lyssa's aunt and mother together again, after so many years. Sad how it takes such tragedy to reunite sisters." Shroud shook his head. "Anais had a great deal to say about Lyssa's death. I think she used it as a shield to avoid discussing that idiotic food-transport screwup she helped engineer that upset the idomeni so, but then Family gossip has always been more riveting than idomeni food philosophies."

"Transporting foodstuffs in sight of their embassy was incredibly stupid." Evan leapt at the chance to dismantle Anais's diplomatic blunder. He was starved for news from the capital. Besides, he didn't want to discuss Lyssa's death. "I understand the idomeni almost packed up and returned home?"

"Not as long as Nema draws breath." Shroud's air of mild interest never altered. "Tell me, was Lyssa's skimmer crash really an accident or did you arrange matters, as Anais claims?"

"I didn't—" Evan's fingers curved around a nonexistent glass. "Despite assurances to the contrary, I'm fairly certain the walls have ears." He pulled up his sleeve to expose his security cuff. "And I'm not altogether confident about the jewelry, either."

Shroud pressed a hand over his heart as though taking a pledge. "Jo'burg also allows us our privacy. And in case anyone's forgotten that, I'm well fitted out in the counter-monitoring department. Now, back to Anais—"

"I didn't realize you and she were so close."

"We're not." Shroud draped an arm along the sofa back. "But she does bend every ear she can these days." The smile again. "And you do have a history of engaging in that sort of thing."

Silence stretched. Just before it snapped, a muted tapping sounded. Evan offered up a silent thank-you. "Come in."

Markhart, his housekeeper, entered pushing a beverage trolley. She was elderly, short and compact—a white raisin of a woman in a shapeless tunic and trousers—but she possessed enough wit to compensate for Halvor's lack of same. Despite the smiling greetings, she detected the tension between the two men. She maneuvered the low-slung trolley between them like a barrier and, after waiting for a small nod from Evan, left them to serve themselves.

"As I was saying." Shroud leaned forward and poured himself coffee from the carafe. "An old habit is an easy fall-back, and you've one that's hard to break. Killing people when they become dangerous, or inconvenient—"

"I've never killed anyone." Evan cracked the seal on a bottle of bourbon. "My attorney would be very interested to hear you've been telling people otherwise." He filled his tumbler, then added a splash of soda. His hands shook. His voice didn't.

Shroud's shoulder twitched. "You've never done the dirty yourself, no. Someone else interfered with Lyssa's augmentation so that she hallucinated herself into a fatal crash. Durian Ridgeway strangled that poor dexxie last winter." He stared into his cup, grimacing as though some ugly scene played itself out on the coffee's reflective surface. "Someone else placed the bomb on Jani's transport."

Evan took a large gulp of his drink. Liquid heat warmed

him like an internal sun. "*Someone else*. Those are the two words that will have me sleeping in my ancestral bed by Christmas."

"You think so?" Shroud set his cup down on the sofaside table. He stood, reached inside his jacket, and removed a folded documents slipcase from his inner pocket. "I received this by special messenger two months ago, about the time the first of those pro-Evan stories appeared in the news." He unfolded the slipcase and removed a single sheet of parchment. "That is, I received the original, which is safely locked away. This is a copy."

Evan's heart skipped as his stomach went into free fall. It took all the willpower he could muster to keep from pulling away as Shroud held out the blue-trimmed white page for his perusal.

"It's an old Consulate comlog, a list of all the outgoing communications made by executive staff on the day Jani's transport exploded in midair." When Evan made no move to take the document, Shroud placed it across his knees. "You gave the order to have the bomb placed on board. The time, location, and comport code all identify you as the person who called the Service fuel depot outside Rauta Shèràa just before the transport that was assigned to pick up Jani and the other members of the Twelfth Rover Corps departed for Knevçet Shèràa."

Evan took a sip of his drink, more to moisten his dry mouth than for the alcohol. "That isn't enough evidence to convict."

"It's a start." Shroud returned to his seat. "It may even be enough to persuade Li Cao to turn you over to Commonwealth Intelligence for a dose of Sera."

"Truth drug?" Evan managed a harsh laugh. "Even if her Prime Ministry was at stake, Li would never set that precedent. Not if she thought there was the slightest chance it could come back to haunt the Families."

"If the colonies keep threatening to cancel Service base leases and limit port privileges for Commonwealth shipping, she'll set it." Shroud tasted his coffee and sighed contentedly. "If Nema keeps dangling access rights to idomeni GateWays in front of her nose like the weighty carrot it is, she'll inject you herself."

"Nema's a figurehead. The Oligarch will never allow him the authority to make deals like those."

"On the contrary, his influence grows every day. Cèel may despise him, but he knows the old bastard understands us better than any other Vynshàrau in his government. He needs him."

Evan took another swallow of bourbon. The colonies could be slapped down with a few good embargoes, but the unpredictable Nema added a new dimension to the term *wild card.* "I can't speak for the idomeni," he said in an effort to rally, "but I know for a fact the colonies have no authority to cancel those leases."

"Well, they're using the argument that if their signatures were necessary to validate the agreements, there must be some power behind them. Would you want to be the Prime Minister who tells them, no, we just let you sign off so you'd think you mattered?" Shroud plucked a cookie from the sweets tray. "You're in a nasty position, Evan. Li needs a head to stick on a pike to show the colonies she's acting in good faith, and yours is the most expendable. You're the last van Reuter. No desperate relatives to scurry about assembling a defense, no wide-eyed offspring to parade before the holocams—" He stalled in mid-chew, his face reddening.

Evan watched the man's growing embarrassment with grim satisfaction. "You were saying, John?"

"My apologies. Some things are off-limits, even during the final rounds."

"Go to hell, you bleached bastard."

Shroud dropped the remains of the cookie on his saucer. "You're alone. I'm offering you a chance to keep your head."

"At the risk of losing yours? Withholding evidence in a murder investigation is a capital crime."

"You're the murderer being investigated. I doubt you'll be filing a complaint." Shroud shook his snowy head. "No, what *is* in your best interest is to develop amnesia when Service Investigative asks you questions about Jani."

"I couldn't do that. They've already received preliminary

reports from my attorney as to what I'll be saying. If I back down, they'll know something's wrong. And if they don't, Joaquin sure as hell will."

"You're a maintenance alcoholic who's gone without proper medical care for months." Shroud's look turned professional—it was obvious from his stern expression that he didn't like what he saw. "You've lost weight. You look like hell. I'm sure your nutritional indices would indicate several key deficiencies, some of which can lead to memory disturbance." He spread his long-fingered hands in an offering gesture, as though what he promised was worth a damn. "It's the cleanest way, and with me signing off on any diagnosis, there will be no questions."

"Selective amnesia?" Evan picked up the comlog with his thumb and index finger and tossed it atop the beverage trolley.

Shroud folded the document back in its slipcase and tucked it away. As was his habit, he'd filmed his eyes to complement his clothing—the pale gold-brown irises formed the only spots of warmth in his cold face. "I'll schedule you for a complete work-up at the downtown facility. We can discuss matters further then." He set his cup aside, then reached alongside the sofa and hefted a large carryall onto his lap. "Now, in case one of us ever has to testify as to what occurred here, if you wouldn't mind undressing . . ."

Shroud's preliminary examination proved mercifully quick. He drew blood deftly and completed swab samplings well before muscles tightened and gag reflexes kicked in.

"Do you just dislike eating," he asked as he watched Evan dress, "or are you consciously trying to starve yourself?"

Evan yanked on his shirt. So what if his ribs showed? They had for as long as he remembered. "I like good food."

"As a modest complement to plenty of good wine, I'm sure." Shroud rummaged through the carryall, removing a variety of bottles and cartons. "Get started on these. The bottles contain supplements. The cartons contain food additives and mixes. Drinks. Soups." He concentrated on arranging the containers atop the trolley. "I only ask because I'm required by law, not because I personally give a damn, but are you sure you want to continue with things as they are? A brain insert and a gene retrofit, and it could all be a distant memory."

Evan tucked in his shirt. "I'm a content drunk, John. Leave me be." He tightened his belt, using the last of the holes he'd punched only last month.

"As you wish. Your left knee requires a rebuild. The stabilizers you had inserted last winter were only temporary." Shroud hestitated. "I heard Jani had something to do with that."

"Ah, don't mince words, John. She cornered me in my office and cracked my knee to keep me from running off." Evan flexed the joint, which emitted its inevitable click. "Just before she crippled me, she killed Durian Ridgeway. The sheets called it suicide, but she broke his neck." He remembered it well, since he had been ordered to identify the body. In the interest of efficiency, he'd been told, but he had known better. He had stood in Durian's office, supported by Justice officials on either side, injured leg numbed to the hip. The crime-scene tech lifted the corner of the tarp and someone bit out, *Take a good, hard look.*

The images sneaked up on Evan now, sceneshots etched into his brain. Durian's goggled eyes. The unnatural twist of his neck.

He walked over to a wall-mounted mirror and concentrated on hand-combing his hair. "Durian. Rik Neumann. The Laum encampment at Knevçet Shèràa. Our Jani has a pretty lengthy history herself, and those are only the deaths we know about." He watched Shroud shift containers back and forth. "She's lived on the thin edge for almost twenty years—God only knows what else she's guilty of."

Shroud's head shot up. "I don't care." His eyes glittered, their fervor promising stakes and bonfires to anyone who crossed him. The monk gone mad. "I'll do whatever it takes to save her. If that means jumping down the hellhole and dragging the entire Commonwealth in after me, I'll do it."

Evan watched the color rise in Shroud's cheeks like fever. *You lovesick fool.* What did he expect in return for his risk-taking, gratitude? *You've picked the wrong girl, Johnny boy—trust me, I speak from experience.* He walked to the trolley, picked the largest cakelet he could find, and popped it into his mouth. "Jani had managed to get her hands on that log just prior to my arrest. After that, it disappeared. Any idea who sent it to you?"

Shroud eyed him warily, then shook his head. "None. All my efforts to retrace the delivery route petered out." His manner grew more distant as he calmed. "Whoever it was, they knew how to cover their trail. And they knew I had the background to understand what the information in that log implied. And the willingness to use it." He closed the carryall and hoisted it to his shoulder. "Good-bye, Evan. See you in a few days."

Evan charged Markhart with seeing Shroud to the door. He refilled his glass, this time without soda, and wandered out into the backyard.

He tried to consider his options, but thoughts skittered away like beads from a broken string. He studied his fingers, which had stiffened, the nail beds tinged with blue. He shivered. *I'm in shock.* He remembered the sensations from that day on the lakeshore, just as he remembered the other things. Lyssa's screams. The chill smoothness of Serena's small hand as he touched it for the last time.

"He doesn't like you."

Evan wheeled to find Markhart standing behind him. She stood only a stride away, so near that she had to tilt her head back to look at him. *She's so short.* He'd known it, of course. He just hadn't realized it. "I don't like him, either. You don't have to like the people you work with."

The woman pondered, her worn face grave. "My sister scolds me for working for you. She says you're a killer. But she works at Sheridan, and her husband's retired Service, so her viewpoint is skewed." Her voice, made ragged by nic-sticks, was shaded by a muted accent Evan couldn't place. "Others don't think that way."

Down the street, a dog barked. Evan stiffened. "And what way do those others think?"

"They think that whatever you did, or didn't do, you paid."

Markhart's normally aloof demeanor softened. "Because of the children."

The barking increased. Another dog joined in, followed by the whining hum of older-model skimmers. Evan's heart thudded. "Is that what you think?"

Markhart sighed. "I think you're a very sad man." She frowned at the glass in his hand. "I think you drink too much." She smiled sadly, lined face crinkling. "Maybe you don't want me to think anymore." She squared her hunched shoulders. "Now I have a dinner to prepare. Another one that you won't eat."

"What are we having?"

"Tomato-dill soup from one of the boxes Dr. Shroud gave you. And kettle beef." She raised her chin in response to Evan's scowl. "They only allow me so much to run this house, sir, and I can't afford real animal on what they give." She nodded. "But there's fresh peas I need to shell, so if you'll excuse me."

"Wait a minute," Evan said, "I'll help." He started out walking alongside her, but as shouts and laughter sounded from the surrounding homes, he quickened his pace until his knee crunched with every stride. Shroud's visit had rattled him—he normally sequestered himself indoors long before this. He always avoided the outside in the afternoon, when school had let out for the day, and the children returned home.

CHAPTER 6

The skimchair stalled as it floated down the gangway leading from the shuttle gate into the O'Hare Service Terminal concourse. Jani gripped the sides of her floating seat as two members of her escort tried to wrestle it through the narrow arch. After one particularly hard push, the chair shuddered, bucked, then bounced to the floor and back up into the air. Her stomach turned. The acid rose in her throat.

"How many mainliners does it take to push a skimchair?" Jani *thought* she muttered under her breath. Every other person and device in the concourse chose that moment to fall silent, however—her commentary cut the air like inappropriate sounds usually did.

The mainline lieutenant who steered glanced over her head at the mainline lieutenant who ruddered, then at her. "Do you have any suggestions, Captain?"

"The signals from the doorscan and the skimchair lift array are confounding one another. Ask someone from Port Security to shut down the doorscan until you can push me through."

The looie grimaced. He was a man of action, who preferred pulling and grappling and nauseating his passenger to asking for help. He released the chair grudgingly and strode off in search of a Security guard, the red stripe on the side of his trousers flicking like an ambulatory exclamation point.

Jani crossed her arms over her queasy stomach. Then she

looked through the arch at the third member of her escort, who had entered the concourse ahead of them and now sat perched on the arm of a nearby bench, regarding her with mock solemnity. He had worn the same sideline summer-weights since they'd departed MarsPort; days of wear had left the light grey short-sleeve and steel blue trousers rumpled, the sideline white trouser stripe puckered. His pale skin, black, curly hair, and stocky build would have marked him as Josephani Dutch even without his accent, which sounded like Hortensian German with the edges ground down.

Piers Friesian. Major. Defense command, out of Fort Constanza. Appointed by the staff Judge Advocate to see to her defense. A nice enough man. She wondered what he had done to deserve her.

He rocked back on his tenuous seat and locked his hands around his knee. "I heard the news walking by one of the kiosks. Acadia Central United won its final qualifying match. They defeated Jersey Conglomerate four to one."

Jani managed a smile. "That means they've drawn a first-round bye."

"The merry dance starts in two weeks. Guess who I'm rooting for?"

"Josephan Arsenal."

"You got it."

"Won't make it out of the quals." Behind her, the rear-guard looie swallowed a chuckle.

"Says you." The light in Friesian's eyes dimmed. He glanced over the top of Jani's head at Rearguard, who stepped around the skimchair into the concourse and took a seat beyond hearing range. "How are you feeling?"

"Fine, sir."

Friesian ran a hand over his face. "Fine, sir. You said that at Fort Constanza, just before that stomachache dropped you like a rock. You also said it just as we broke through Felix GateWay. Right after that, you passed out, then awoke two days later speaking street Acadian and insisting you were fifteen years old. I don't think the medical officers will ever be the same. Neuro was *not* his specialty."

"I was fine by the time we reached MarsPort."

"Yes, you were. You did tell me that. I thought we might actually get some work done. Then you ate lunch and became royally sick." His impatience broke through his even speech like flecks of foam on smooth water. "Your 'fine, sirs' aren't worth much, are they?"

Jani tugged at her own baggy short-sleeve. From what little she could remember of the last three weeks, it had once fit her perfectly—otherwise, she wouldn't have been issued it. How much of a weight loss did that imply? Five kilos? Ten? "What do you want me to say, sir?"

"I want you to call me Piers, and I want you to level with me."

Jani examined her right arm, halfway between elbow and wrist, where a tiny, round wound had healed to form a darkened scar. Her new Service ID chip lay implanted beneath. They had her now. If Security activated the proper codes, they could pinpoint her exact location in a room and tell whether she sat, stood, or did push-ups.

She looked through the arch into the heart of the concourse. Functional furnishings, well maintained and spotless. Lots of steel blue and silver on the walls and floor, accented by splashes of mainline red in the chair cushions and fixtures. Through the wide windows opposite her, trim shuttles and sleek aircraft glinted in the summer sun.

Every object she looked at, every surface, every blue-and-grey uniform, told her where she was, and what waited for her. *My name is Jani Moragh Kilian, Captain, United Services. Eighteen years ago, at a place called Knevçet Shèràa, I killed Colonel Rikart Neumann, my commanding officer. Now I've been brought here to pay.* He had deserved to die, but that wasn't the point. The Service frowned on the individual Spacer making that judgment, and they had a time-honored method for showing their displeasure. The firing squad. "I'm scared, Piers."

Friesian eyed her in puzzlement. "I'm not saying you have nothing to worry about. But considering the state of your health, you're doing yourself no favors holding back from me." He stood as Lieutenant Forceful came into view, a Security guard in tow. "We'll talk after we get checked in at

Sheridan. After you check in at the hospital."

Shutting down the doorscan worked as Jani said it would, much to Forceful's disappointment. Their journey to the lower-level parking garage was punctuated by his comments as to how he could have jazzed the mech if only he'd had the time.

He made up for the loss, however, by brute-forcing the side conversion panels of their skimmer so the passenger opening could accommodate the skimchair. His joy multiplied manyfold when Friesian asked him to expand the interior space by pulling out one of the seats. Rearguard and the driver, a corporal with a squint, struggled to keep from laughing as they fielded the components that came flying out the door.

Jani eyed the pearl grey, triple-length that had been provided for their transport. The enamel coating shone wetly, even in the dull light of the garage. "What's with the chariot?" she asked Friesian.

He pointed to her seat. "It was the only vehicle available that could hold a skimchair."

"What about a brig van?"

Another look of puzzled appraisal. "Jani, why would you expect a brig van?"

Jani fell silent. *They stuck me with an idiot,* she thought as Forceful and Rearguard loaded her into the skimmer. The Judge Advocate was required by charter to provide for her defense, but the charter said nothing about the quality of defense they had to provide her with. Friesian obviously had no idea what crime she'd committed or what the Service planned to do to her after they convicted her. He'd sit at the Officers' Club bar after her execution and wonder where the hell it all went wrong.

As they departed the garage, the sudden change from half-light to full glare of summer caught them all by surprise. Jani shut her eyes to stop them tearing, while Rearguard exploded with a sharp burst of sneezing. The Boul artery on which they rode seemed to glimmer in the heat. Chicago had been buried beneath mountains of snow the last time Jani had visited. Now, she could see the verdant patches of parkland

and clusters of low houses, backed by the distant skyline.

Their driver took them on a route that skirted the city—within minutes, they left the crowding traffic behind. The four-lane skimway they rode cut along a line of homes obscured from view by large stands of trees.

"The South Bluffs." Forceful gazed out the window and sighed. "This is the low-rent section, and still all I can afford to do is look."

"Why would you want to live here, Don?" Rearguard sniffed as he took in the view.

"Because it's the *Bluffs*, Lou. Once a man can call this place home, he knows he's arrived."

Jani caught the look that passed between Friesian and Rearguard Lou, the chins-up camaraderie of those who had scaled the barriers of opinion since they decided to make the Service their career. That opinion originated in the homes they passed now. *All you with the wrong parents, wrong names, wrong accents, raise your hands.* Friesian looked down at his lap, while Lou concentrated on the view out his window.

The skimmer exited down a corkscrew ramp, then turned onto a two-lane road that ran along a massive fence built of arched whitestone and metal bridging. The five-meter-high barrier stretched ahead as far as Jani could see.

"Have you ever seen the Shenandoah Gate, Captain?" Rearguard Lou asked her. "It was erected to honor the tens of thousands who died at the Appalachian Front during the Greatest War." That those thus honored had died for the Earthbound side could be discerned from the gleam of resentment that lit his eyes.

"This year's the seventy-fifth anniversary of its completion." Don seemed oblivious to the other man's displeasure. "The archivists are working night and day researching names for addition to the Placement Rolls." He shook his head in wonder. "It took the artisans eleven years to encode the gridwork and apply the coatings. Isn't it gorgeous?"

Jani caught the iridescent flickers of the names of the fallen as the sunlight played over the holoetching in the stone. "Lieutenant, in case you haven't noticed, you're talking to three colonials."

"It's a *Service* monument, ma'am." Don smoothed the front of his short-sleeve. "Besides, well, I hate to state the obvious, but the reason you're touchy is because your ancestors were asked to leave after the dust settled. Because they lost."

" 'Asked to leave'?" Jani smiled. "I like your choice of words, Lieutenant. Just for clarification, what words does your side use to refer to the internment camps and prison ships?"

Friesian tugged at his collar. "I read an editorial in *Blue and Grey* requesting a reevaluation of the Gate," he said hurriedly. "Over two-thirds of Service recruits come from the colonies. It does seem counterproductive to risk alienating them before they set foot on the base."

Don's eyes widened in surprise. "But sir—!"

"It's a matter of perspective, Lieutenant," Jani interrupted. "You're honoring yourselves because you won. You had the biggest governments and the richest companies behind you. You won control of the technologies and the freedoms and the privilege to dole them out. You won the right to send my ancestors to the colonies to work in your friends' factories and fields. You were quite happy with the outcome— you didn't need to examine it further. It was left to us as the losers to figure out the hows and whys, and after we did, we felt a little irked." She ignored Piers's warning look. "What do you know about the Battle of Waynesboro?"

Don frowned, as though she'd insulted his intelligence. "It was the turning point in the battle for eastern North America, ma'am. Major Alvin Cao came to his senses and brought his fifty thousand over to hook up with van Reuter's Fourteenth Armored out of Philly."

Jani nodded. "And if he hadn't come to his senses, as you say—we prefer the phrase *turned traitor*, the *C* in NUVA-SCAN was his price—Everhard would not have lost DC and the rest of the Eastern Seaboard wouldn't have dominoed in response. And there would have been no March to Albany."

"Yes, ma'am, but—"

"Seven thousand four-hundred eighteen losers died during that march. Their bodies were sprayed with dissolvant and tossed in ditches because your side judged *them* the traitors, undeserving of proper burial. A many-times-great-grandfather of mine was one of those losers. The only place his name is inscribed is in a Bible my father keeps in his workroom. Like I said, it's a matter of perspective."

Don nodded. He actually seemed to be listening, which was more than many Earthbounders did. "Can you say your side wouldn't have done the same thing if they'd won?"

Jani hesitated. She was colony, yes, and proud to be so. But life had left her few illusions about people, especially after the blood started flowing. "No, I can't. But that's not the point. The point is, all the dead merit remembrance. Even the ones who lost. Because first you forget who, and then you forget why. And then it happens all over again."

The skimmer turned onto the Fort Sheridan entry and passed beneath the Gate's main archway. The cabin darkened; the names inscribed inside the arch winked and faded. Then the view lightened; the sight of the numerous shade trees and multicolored shrubbery decorating Sheridan's rolling lawns dissipated the tension.

Borgie would have been in heaven, Jani thought as they passed teeming walkways that joined row after row of low-slung white-and-tan buildings. Her late sergeant hadn't been the most conventional of Spacers, but if you'd scratched him, he'd have bled blue and grey. He'd often told her that the only reason he'd ever visit Earth would be to walk the paths at Fort Sheridan. *I wish you were here.* She would have enjoyed listening to his blunt-edged take on her current predicament. She could have used the laugh.

"We'll be checking you into the Main Hospital first." Friesian leaned close to Jani so he could speak softly. "If you're through with the history lecture, that is." He sat back, eyes slitting as though a headache had placed a call.

In contrast to the glass-walled grandeur of every Neoclona facility Jani had ever seen, Fort Sheridan's Main Hospital showed squat and homely. Its white-cement surfaces were smooth and squared off, its windows short and narrow. Only ten floors, but what it lacked in height, it made up for in sprawl. Patients undergoing fitness therapy could get their day's exercise simply by trotting around its circumference.

Lou took it upon himself to maneuver Jani's chair to the hospital entry as Friesian supervised Don's refit of the skimmer. "*Bienvenu à Chicago, Capitaine,*" he whispered as he leaned forward to adjust the lift settings, touching his fingers to his forehead in a surreptitious salute.

"*Vous êtes un Manxman, Lieutenant?*" Jani didn't need to ask—the harsh tones of Man French branded him easily.

"*Oui, Capitaine.*" He backed away as Friesian approached. "*Vive la Manche,*" he mouthed, using the Channel Worlder's nickname for their network of planets.

A subversive Manxman. Jani touched her own forehead in return. *Quite a happy family the Service has here.* She sat back with a jolt as Friesian propelled her a shade faster than necessary into the cool depths of the hospital.

"Turn slowly, and walk back toward me."

As Jani tried to reverse her course, her right knee buckled. She grabbed the rails of her treadway just in time to keep from falling. "This thing is hard to walk on."

"There has been motor-nerve axon damage," a voice piped from behind the large analyzer that received signals from both the treadway and the numerous sensor buttons that studded Jani's arms, legs, trunk, and back. "I'm downloading the specific sites into her chart now."

The doctor who stood at the far end of the track offered Jani a quiet smile. Tall, thin, tired-looking—Hugh Tellinn's blond brother. "We'll be starting rebuild immediately. Along with digestive-enzyme adjustment and heme infusion." He held out his hand and helped her down the two short steps to the floor so the waiting nurse could pluck the buttons. "Are you feeling all right, Jani? You look dazed."

"I didn't expect to get herded into myotherapy so quickly." She glanced at the man's name tag. *R. Pimentel.* No rank designator visible on his medwhite shirt. Jani had yet to hear a title other than *Nurse* or *Doctor* over the past few hours, but she figured Pimentel for at least a major, judging from the way the other white coats deferred to him. Possibly even a colonel.

"We've been receiving your MedRecs via message central transmit for the past ten days, so we had a good idea what to expect. The *Reina*'s medical officer had a lot to send—let's just say this department's Misty account has topped out for the quarter." He continued to support her as they walked out of the therapy room and into an adjoining office. "Now, we need to ascertain your current status, judge whether it has improved or worsened, and commence the appropriate treatments as soon as possible." He helped Jani lower into a visitor's chair, then took a seat on the other side of the cluttered desk.

Jani looked around. Two filled bookcases, double-stacked with bound volumes and wafer folders. Holos of Admiral-General Hiroshi Mako and Prime Minister Li Cao. A watercolor of a pleasant-looking woman holding a little girl. "So what happened to me, Colonel?"

"Colonel?" Pimentel's brows arched. "How did you arrive at that conclusion?"

Jani pointed behind him, to the narrow window. "You have a view."

"Well, I hate to break it to you, Captain, but this is Fort Sheridan, and we have windows to spare." Pimentel sat back. "But yes, I am a colonel."

"Full?"

"*Yes*. But I'm also a psychotherapeutic neurologist. Owing to the types of conditions I treat, I find it easier for both me and my patients if we leave the ranks in the lobby." Pimentel picked up a stylus from his desk and regarded the unlit tip. "We think the drug used to subdue you on Felix triggered this idiosyncratic reaction of yours. We may be dealing with a disease called porphyria, but thus far, we've been unable to identify the specific genetic mutation."

"A human genetic mutation?"

Pimentel hesitated. "For now. Until we have more data."

"Neoclona has a lot of data—why don't you request my file?"

Pimentel tapped the stylus on his knee. "Heme is manufactured in the bone marrow and the liver. Heme in the bone marrow is incorporated into hemoglobin; heme in the liver is incorporated into electron transport proteins, some of which metabolize drugs. The synthesis of the molecule is complicated; several intermediates and enzymes are involved. When a person possesses lower than normal activity of one of the enzymes, the precursors build up in either the bone marrow or the liver, depending on the enzyme involved."

When he's angry, he spouts techno. Jani decided to play good girl. He seemed to mean well—if she was nice to him, maybe he'd tell her why she was talking to him in his office with his family's picture on the wall instead of in a locked room in the brig infirmary. "I'm deficient in one of these enzymes?"

"Yes. Porphobilinogen deaminase, to be precise."

"Your wife married you because of your way with words, didn't she?"

Pimentel looked startled for a moment. Then he grinned bashfully. "PBG deaminase, for short. That makes your flavor acute intermittent porphyria. Its cardinal symptoms are the abdominal pain you developed at Fort Constanza, the psychotic episodes you experienced on the *Reina Adelaida*, and the neuropathy, or muscle weakness, you're showing now. It's extremely rare these days. Not life-threatening, usually—most people who have it don't even realize it. We normally only find it in the far-flung colonial outposts, where things tend to slip through the cracks."

"So people are usually born with it?"

"*Always* born with it. It's a genetic disorder, not something you acquire."

"That depends, doesn't it?"

Pimentel tossed the stylus back on his desk. "You know, whenever two or more doctors get together in the same room, the talk eventually turns to Neoclona's first patient. 'S-1.' Shèrá-1. The woman John Shroud wanted to make live forever." He seemed to stare past the painting of his wife and daughter, to someplace far away. "I've never met a legend." He looked at Jani. "Do I think something he did to you in

Rauta Shèràa has come back to haunt you? I'm by no means Dr. Shroud's greatest fan, but I'd like to keep an open mind, for now. First, we need to stabilize your diet and repair the nerve and liver damage you've sustained." He reached for his comport pad. "You look exhausted. I'm going to have you taken to your room."

"My room?"

"I'm admitting you, Captain." The tired eyes grew steely. "I'll make it an order, if that's the only thing you'll accept."

They gave her a private room, owing to her rank. Dinner consisted of a fruit milk shake and dry toast; when she complained about the sweetness of the shake, they scrounged hot sauce to kill the flavor. She waited for Pimentel to burst in and order her out of his hospital for the murderer she was, but all he did was poke his head in and say good night. She waited for the guards to be posted outside her door, but they never came. She waited for Friesian to come and inform her of the charges against her, but the second-shift head nurse, a no-nonsense blonde named Morley, told her Pimentel had asked him to hold off until tomorrow.

They're not going to shoot me for Neumann's murder; they're going to shock me to death. Jani lay back against her soft Service-issue pillows, in her dove grey Service-issue pajamas, and worried herself to sleep.

CHAPTER 7

"Good morning, Jani."

Jani looked up from her magazine to find the morning nurse standing in the sunroom doorway.

"You have a visitor." He stepped aside. "You can go in now."

"It's about time." Lucien Pascal brushed past the man and strode into the room. When his eyes locked with Jani's he smiled broadly, at first glance the walking equivalent of a bright summer day.

"Hello." He dragged a chair over to the sunny corner Jani occupied, white-blond hair flashing in the diffuse sunlight. He'd acquired a tan since she'd last seen him—his grey short-sleeve looked silver against his skin, now almost as brown as hers.

"How did you get in to see me ahead of my lawyer?" Jani watched his shoulder muscles flex beneath the fitted shirt as he positioned his chair. The southerly view wasn't bad, either. "They're not going to let him in until this afternoon."

Lucien held up his arm to show her the thin silver band encircling his wrist. "Outpatient monitoring."

"They let you come here for your takedowns? An Intelligence officer?" Augmentation was one thing she and Lucien had in common, although his prototypical version had boosted the nonempathetic aspect of his personality in addition to adjusting his panic response. "I thought they'd put you in secure lockdown in case you started talking."

"No, I only come here for psych evals." Lucien's eyes, rich brown and normally as lifeless as spent embers, flared with disdain. "I had my last takedown at the Intelligence infirmary. Before that, they were supervised by Eamon DeVries—he's Anais's personal physician."

"Now that's a match made in hell." Jani shivered at the memory of DeVries' rough examinations. *Did that hurt, Kilian? Well, too damned bad.*

"But enough about me." Lucien fixed her with an angry stare, every trace of good humor extinguished. "You never even said good-bye."

"I'm sorry."

"I had your escape route all planned. I also had interested parties to answer to for your disappearance. What happened, didn't you trust me?"

Not completely. "You know I don't trust easily."

"I thought you understood me well enough to make an exception." He tugged at his outpatient band. "Hell of a lot of good your secrecy did you. They still caught you."

"If you came here to cheer me up, you're doing a good job."

"I came here to deliver a message." To Jani's surprise, Lucien slipped into Middle Vynshàrau, complete with posture and gestures. *"The chief propitiator of the Vynshàrau bids the glories of the day to his most excellent Eyes and Ears."*

"You—" She stopped. Counted to ten. Twice. "You're working with Nema?"

"Attached to the idomeni embassy—security liaison," Lucien said in English. "I'm under arms at all times"—he lifted the flap of his belt holster, revealing an empty compartment—"except when I enter the loony bin and need to check my shooter at the front desk. Can't let the crazies get their hands on the weaponry, can we? They might take over, and then where would we be?"

"About where we are now. Who do you report to?"

"All embassy staff report to the Xeno branch of Justice. So, not only am I in constant contact with your most powerful ally, I also have an in at the ministry that's building the case against your old boyfriend." He grinned wolfishly. "Kind of makes you want to treat me nicer, doesn't it?"

"What else did Nema ask you to tell me?"

"Is that an apology?" Lucien held a hand to his ear. "I can't tell with all this interference."

"*Lucien.*" Jani tried to stare him into submission, but he glared back in sullen stubbornness. He could get testy when he felt unappreciated, but in this case he had justification. He had earned Exterior Minister Anais Ulanova's enmity when he forsook her patronage to throw in with Jani, and the animosity of a Cabinet Minister could destroy more than just a career. *Right, Evan?* "I'm sorry I bolted."

"Apology accepted." Lucien's smile bloomed anew.

"So what else did Nema say?"

"That you must watch and listen, as is your way. He also wanted me to ask you if the ring fits yet?" He ended with a teeth-baring grimace, an imitation of Nema's version of a smile.

The red-stone ring. Her Academy graduation gift from her esteemed teacher. Each of the six special students who had received their degrees in documents examination from the vaunted idomeni university had received one. Everyone else's had fit, but when Jani had tried hers on, she couldn't push it past her second knuckle. *Not anymore.* Several nervous sizing tests in Felix Majora confirmed the now-comfortable fit. "Tell him no."

"He told me that ring's a monitor. When it fits, you'll be hybridized enough to begin training to become his successor. Is that true?"

"Lucien, I'm human." *Officially. For now.* "That mitigates against me becoming the religious leader of a whole other race, don't you think?" *That and the fact the Service will have come to their senses and shot me by then.*

"But he said—"

"The hell with what he said. Just because he says things doesn't make them fact!"

"Keep your voice down!" Lucien looked toward the sun-room door, on the alert for eavesdroppers. "You know, he wanted me to rig myself so I could record you. He said he wanted to hear your voice. I don't think I'd want to be in the room with him after he heard *that*."

"Oh, it wouldn't be bad. He'd disregard it as unimportant." She was only the Eyes and Ears, after all. A tool. Her thoughts and fears didn't matter. *And I have thoughts and fears, you bet I do.*

Lucien rose and walked across the room to the holoVee display. "Keep your mouth shut until I set up some interference." He activated the unit and flipped through the programs, stopped at an opera broadcast, and jacked up the audio until the swell of voices filled the room. "What's the matter with you?"

"Ask my doctor—he keeps the running tally." Jani watched Lucien stroll back to his chair. Part of her could have watched him forever. The part with the brain wished he'd go away. "What's happening with Evan? What sort of plea bargain has Justice offered him? What's he given them concerning me?"

"Slow down." Lucien sprawled unServicelike and picked at his nails in irritation. "His attorneys are worried—they don't like the publicity this case is drawing."

"They need publicity. They need to show what a great guy Evan was and what an evil influence I was."

"Well, that's not what they're getting. The Earth news services aren't carrying anything about you. The colony services are another story. On FelNet, Felix is complaining about the arrest of colonials with insufficient evidence. In the smoke-filled rooms, the Felician governor called your capture kidnapping and filed a formal complaint against the Service. She's threatening to cancel the landlease for Fort Constanza. She can't do that, legally, but that doesn't seem to concern her. Acadia and *toute La Manche* back her up. They're threatening to boycott the Commonwealth Cup—"

"*What!*"

"—but they've been sweeping the prelims, so they may decide defeating the Earthbound teams serves their cause better." Lucien chuckled. "Nema takes a different tack. He asks about you in meetings with the PM, usually after she inquires after rights to use the idomeni GateWays near the Outer Circle."

"That doesn't answer my question about Evan."

"If he attacks you, he has to admit the part he played in your transport explosion."

"That's the point of the plea bargain. He tells them how much I hated Neumann, and they let him off the hook for ordering the bomb to be planted on my transport."

"His pride won't allow him to admit what he did. That being the case, he'll sit in his little house forever."

It can't be that easy. "They haven't charged me with Neumann's murder yet." Jani rolled up the magazine and whacked herself on the thigh. "I shouldn't be here. I should be in a brig infirmary waiting to get scanned and strip-searched."

But instead, colonial governors were lodging protests on her behalf.

What the hell is going on?

Lucien looked at his timepiece. "Test time—I have to go. Then it's off to the city. I'm in charge of an advance team checking out Chicago Combined. Nema will be meeting with their botany professors. They're going to discuss the possibilities of idomeni-humanish hybridizations. For plants." He stared down at his shoes.

"Lucky you," Jani said, ignoring his allusion. "Has he been behaving himself?"

"No." Lucien looked up with a smile. "He left the embassy without his guard the day before yesterday. They corralled him in a park. Some kids were teaching him how to use the seesaw." He stood, then pulled her to her feet as well. Before she could react, he leaned down and kissed her on the cheek. His lips felt warm and soft; he smelled of soap and clean clothes.

Jani backed away. When he tried to pull her to him again, she placed her hands against his chest and pushed.

"That's OK, I thrive on rejection." He hunched his shoulders and kicked at the floor. "The least you can do is walk me to my appointment."

The halls were filled with people, including two colonels

and a major, all mainline. The sight of all that red-striped brass compelled Lucien to behave. Somewhat.

"If you still feel strongly about that strip search after you get out of here, let me know." He walked down the hall toward the testing labs. "I'm an expert in that sort of thing." He paused to wink at her before disappearing around the corner.

Jani leaned against the wall for a few minutes and recovered her blond-addled wits. Then she wandered back to the sunroom. *The colonial guvs are making a stink.* And if the tension over the Shenandoah Gate was any indication, Service solidarity in a colonial crisis was not guaranteed. *And Nema's raising his own brand of hell.*

But in the end, what good would their interferences do? She traced the Pathen Haárin word for garbage on a wall with her finger. *Their protests and a vend token, Lucien.* Or a Vynshàrau ring.

Pimentel placed a drop of her blood on a cartridge tester. "The only reason John Shroud is still walking the streets rather than occupying a prison cell is because he's convinced certain people he's closing in on the secret to eternal life."

Jani sat on the edge of her bed. *I hope he won't be drawing any more blood.* The crook of her right arm already looked like a dartboard and stung to the touch. "What happened to your open mind? He saved my life." She waited for Pimental to reply, but he continued to manipulate testing materials and capillary tubes. "Cal Montoya from Neoclona Chicago treated me about five months ago," she said as she settled back against her pillow. "He prescribed enzyme supplements to help my digestion. He didn't say anything about porphyria."

Pimentel returned the testing equipment to his crammed carryall. "What else would you expect? Can you imagine the damage to Shroud's reputation if it got out that he had inflicted a genetic disorder on his legendary patient? That 'word from the mountaintop' aura is the main thing Neoclona has going for it. Service Medical has never bought into their mystique. Our physicians all receive their training in unaffiliated schools. And even Shroud will admit, if squeezed hard enough, that our people can hold their own against his by any measure you can think of."

Jani squirmed beneath her covers. She would be the first to admit her feelings for John had never made sense. In the months they'd been sequestered together, he'd treated her as either goddess or entitlement, depending on his mood. *Galatea to his Pygmalion one minute, oyster to his pearl knife the next.* For her part, she'd exploited his affection even as she ached for his touch; as the years passed, she'd come to resent him mightily for the things he had done to her. Every time her gut cramped or her muscles spasmed as though torn, she cursed him, yet when someone attacked him, she felt compelled to jump to his defense. "He thought he was helping me," she said, knowing how weak it sounded, to her ears as well as Pimentel's.

"He helped you, all right. I've spent the morning studying your tissue scans." He straightened her blanket with a sharp tug. "It amazes me you can speak kindly of him, considering what he did to you. He treated you like an experimental culture. Genius he may possess—unfortunately for you, he lacks the judgment and ethics to go with it. Every half-baked hypothesis that stewed in his brain concerning the benefits of human-idomeni tissue hybridization, he tried out on you. And now here you are, forced to cope with the consequences of his criminal negligence." Pimentel picked up the carryall and regarded her levelly. "You need sound medical care. You don't need John Shroud or one of his acolytes trying to fix you with the same useless tools with which he broke you in the first place."

Friesian breached the Morley-run defenses at midafternoon break. The enforced downtime had done him good. His fresh summerweights fit crisply, with not a pucker to be seen. He had gotten a haircut as well, and had shaved so closely his cheeks shone like a baby's.

"It felt good to sleep in a grounded rack." He led her into a vacant office located around the corner from her room. "All my friends live for ship duty, but I'll take a nice, solid planet any day." He closed the door, sat down at the desk, and pulled file folders and loose papers from a black-leather documents case.

Jani sat across from him and watched the desktop disappear beneath a layer of Service paper. "You've been working?"

"Oh, yes." He glanced at her in surprise, as though hitting the stacks directly after coming off a three-week-long haul was the most normal thing in the world. "Spent the better part of yesterday afternoon filing motions. Extensions, mostly, since you and I weren't able to work together to prepare your case. I also visited the Service Investigative Bureau Archives." The eager look in his eyes altered, becoming harder, more cold-blooded.

Jani caught a glimpse of Friesian-in-court and grudgingly admitted she liked what she saw. "What did you find there?"

"Better to ask what I didn't find." Finally, he removed a small watercooler and a couple of dispo cups from the case's side pocket, then dropped the case to the floor beside his chair. "Anything relating to your history after your transfer from First Documents and Documentation to the Twelfth Rovers. It's as though you disappeared."

Jani picked through a stack of papers. Most were formal requests to examine documents, formatted in the current style—lightest blue parchment with a stylized eagle watermark. Friesian had noted the places where she needed to sign. "That makes no sense. That's their case."

Friesian grinned. "Exactly."

"They're up to something." Jani crossed her arms, tucking her hands in her sleeves in an effort to warm them. *Why do they keep these rooms so damned cold?* She'd supplemented the long-sleeved winter-issue pajamas with a winterweight robe and two pairs of socks, yet she still felt cold. "They can't let me get away with this."

"Get away with what?" Friesian's voice grew measured. Another courtroom tic surfacing. "Jani, why do you believe you're here?"

Is this a trick question? She tried to cross her right leg over her left. The weak limb wouldn't budge, forcing her to grab a handful of pajama leg and hoist up and over. "Check the posting board in any colonial Government Hall."

"We aren't in a Government Hall now, and I want to hear it from you."

But I don't want to say it. Once she said the words, that would be it. No going back. No pretending the past eighteen years had never happened, that her Service career had continued uninterrupted, that she was simply in hospital for her annual physical. She stared over Friesian's head at a point on the blank wall and listened to her words as if they emerged from another mouth. "I'm wanted for murder. The murder of Colonel Rikart Neumann, my commanding officer."

"The correct wording is, *Wanted for questioning in connection with* . . . Hardly the same."

"Words."

"In my game, words count." Friesian freed a recording board from beneath one of the piles. "Jani, what you're actually charged with is Article Ninety-two of the Service Code. 'Missing movement.' " He unsnapped a stylus from its board niche, activated it, and began writing.

"Miss—" Jani tried to speak, but the words stalled in her throat. *They're saying I missed a ship.* Neumann dead. The patients dead. Twenty-six Laumrau and fifteen Rovers. *And they track me for eighteen years and arrest me for missing a ship.* "That—that's a joke."

"You think so?" Friesian continued writing. "As the highest-ranked documents examiner in the Twelfth Rover Corps, it was your sworn duty to ensure that the paper under your control made transfer during the evac of Rauta Shèràa Base. According to the charge, you failed to appear at your post the night the evacuation took place." Friesian picked a document off the top of one of the piles and studied it. Older Service paper—pale grey parchment. Paper from Jani's time. "The Night of the Blade. The night the Vynshàrau took over."

"The Twelfth Rovers—" Jani shivered. She felt even colder now. "The Twelfth Rovers never made it back to Rauta Shèràa Base."

"No, but you did, according to Colonel Veda. One of the documents that went missing recorded your transfer, via people-mover, from Knevçet Shèràa to Rauta Shèràa Base."

"That never happened!"

Friesian tapped his thumbs on the edges of his board. "What did happen?"

"From the beginning?" Jani pulled her robe more closely around her. "We were sent to Knevçet Shèràa to hook up with the group of Bandan xenogeologists who had been trapped by the fighting and escort them back to Rauta Shèràa."

"You were a documents examiner. Why bring you on a pickup?"

"Neumann said he needed me to confirm their papers. What he really needed me for was to validate and code their patient files for transport back to Earth, but I didn't realize that until too late." Jani blew on her hands—so cold. "The first patient died soon after. Her name was Eva Yatni. Then Simyam Baru mutilated himself, and I tracked down Neumann to find out what the hell was going on. We fought. That was when I killed him." She stared at her hands, skin paled from inner chill. "The Laumrau staff fled to the hills, warned their compatriots that word of their collusion with humans would get out if they didn't act. So they started bombing. Yolan Cray died during the first wave. She was my corporal. A wall collapsed on her. Then the bombing stopped."

She could hear the silence again, the silence that fell after the last shatterbox found its target. Silence too afraid to open its eyes. Silence with its heart torn out.

"A Night of Convergence." Friesian cleared his throat, then poured himself water from the cooler. "The idomeni government conducted an investigation that confirmed the action you took against the twenty-six Laumrau encamped outside Knevçet Shèràa."

"It wasn't an action—I killed them one by one as they took a sacramental meal in their tents."

"They also advised us that they have no interest in pursuing any type of case against you at this time." He paused to drink, then pressed the cup against his forehead. "That part of your story, at least, can be confirmed."

Jani recrossed her legs. She still needed to hoist her right. "What do you mean, confirmed?"

Friesian sighed. "Ever since I started working this case, all I've encountered is one rumor after the other." He pressed fingertips to forehead. "Rumor that the doctors who founded Neoclona salvaged you from the transport van Reuter allegedly arranged to have bombed. Rumor that they kidnapped you off the street and smuggled you offworld to experiment on you. I hear different stories every day concerning how Rikart Neumann died." He picked up the documents bag and rummaged through the flaps and pockets until he freed a small packet. He tore it open, shook a bright pink tablet into his hand, and tossed it into his mouth, washing it down with water.

Jani reached for one of the dispos—Friesian took that as a cue to pour her some water. She let him. Her hands had started to shake—if she tried to serve herself, who knew where the water would end up? "What other stories do you need? I'm admitting I killed Neumann."

Friesian handed her the cup. "On the *Reina*, when you were still holed up in the infirmary and giving the medical officer fits, you insisted you had sneaked out during a shift change and disabled the fire extinguishers. Your accounting of your movements was so accurate, the chief engineer ordered a ship-wide inspection. You hadn't touched a thing, of course. You'd never left the infirmary."

"You don't believe me."

"What *I* believe doesn't matter. What anyone else believes doesn't matter. Solid proof, *paper* proof, proof that can be researched and confirmed, is what the prosecution needs to support this or any charge and the only thing against which we need to mount a defense. And so far, they've shown me nothing to connect you with Neumann's death."

"You're—" Jani loosened the neck of her robe. She felt much warmer now. Her heart pounded. "You're saying they won't charge me, that I spent all these years running for nothing. You're saying they have no case."

"That's exactly what I'm saying."

"Because the paper's gone missing."

"If it ever existed at all."

"I don't understand any of this."

Friesian leaned forward and selected papers from the various piles. "I had a long talk with Roger before coming to see you." He grinned at Jani's puzzled look. "Dr. Pimentel. He feels you're under a great deal of stress. Much of it, he adds, is self-imposed." He handed her one of the documents requests, along with a stylus. "I want to do what's best for you, Jani. I wish I felt you trusted me more."

Jani braced her hand on the arm of her chair. In spite of the support, her hand still shook so badly that her normally crisp signature showed blurred and crooked. "Do I have a choice?"

"That is not what I want to hear." Friesian took the document and handed her another. "Roger did tell me he feels you're improving. The muscle weakness may last for a few more weeks, but you're responding well to the diet they've put you on and the other therapies they're trying out. You could be released in the next few days."

"To do what?" Jani stared at the paper she held. *Extended Residence Agreement*. A Transient Officers' Quarters contract. "Work with you?"

"Such a luxury, the Service cannot afford. They have an Academy-trained documents examiner in their grasp, and they can't afford to let her go unutilized." Friesian pointed to the TOQ contract. "You're being returned to duty, Captain Kilian. With restricted movement, I should add. You'll be confined to base until we close the book on this." He reached into another pile and removed an official-sized steel blue envelope, its flap crosshatched with white security seals. He smiled cautiously and handed it to Jani.

She traded the TOQ contract for the envelope. The crisp parchment snapped like plastic between her fingers. "Do you know what's in here?"

"Um-hmm."

"Are you going to tell me?"

"No. You have to open it."

She held her breath as she broke the threadlike seals, removed the sheets of pale blue parchment, and unfolded them.

"What do you think?" Friesian's smile strengthened. "You've been assigned to your old outfit. First Documents and Documentation."

Reporting to Lt. Colonel Frances Hals. Foreign Transactions, third floor, Documents Control. Simple wording for simple actions. Three days from today, at 0830, she would present herself to Lieutenant Colonel Hals, dressed out, scanpack in hand. The Service's Oldest Living Sideline Captain reporting for duty.

Friesian gathered the documents and returned them to his case. "Roger feels it's in your best interest to work again. Use your skills. 'Chip off the rust,' he calls it. In the meantime, I'll work my end, and we'll meet regularly to discuss any developments."

Friesian insisted on playing the gallant, so Jani let him escort her back to her room. On the way, they passed a patient leaning against the wall, arms crossed in front of his chest, staring at nothing. He looked like he'd been through a war himself—bronze-haired and lean, with a long, weathered face cut from edge of nose to end of mouth by a deep, age-whitened scar. He looked at them as they passed—his eyes held confusion and bewilderment and mute question. *Takedown malaise.* Jani knew how he felt. The next time she looked in a mirror, she'd see the same eyes staring back.

CHAPTER 8

They discharged her two days later.

"You've shown marked improvement." Pimentel said. "But you're to check in every other day until further notice. The noise from the firing range occasionally entertains us—if it bothers your augie, come in and we'll fit you with hearing protection." He handed her a rectangular blue bag that looked like a Service toiletry kit. "Your scrips and instructions are in here. If you have any questions, anytime, call or stop in." He reached into the front pocket of his medcoat and pulled out a small, cartridge-tester-like device.

"This is your diet monitor. It's like a scanpack for food. Run it over every item you want to eat—it determines kcals as well as fat grams, protein, etc, and it keeps a running tally. If it squeals, you can't have what you just scanned." He held the small box out to her. "We'll be able to tell if you cheat and trust me, so will you."

Jani accepted the device with a grudging nod. "I know what it's going to tell me. More fruit milk shakes." The sweet sludge had remained a staple of every meal. She had run through the kitchen's entire supply of hot sauce in a day and a half, and had been forced to resort to plain black pepper to kill the taste.

Pimentel led Jani out to the lobby and was about to show her out the door when a woman standing near the entry desk raised her hand. He ran a hand over his rumpled medwhite

V-neck. "Jani, I'd like to introduce you to someone."

The woman made no move to meet them, but remained by the desk. She was perhaps twenty years older than Jani, with steel grey hair trimmed in a blunt, chin-length style. Her eyes were dark, her skin, olive. She wore summer-weights and a crisp white medcoat, and cradled a recording board.

"Ma'am, it's good to see you." Pimentel executed the straight-backed sharp nod that took place of a salute indoors. "Captain Kilian, I'd like to introduce Dr. Carvalla, our chief of staff."

Dr. Major General Carvalla, Jani amended, taking note of the twin silver stars adorning the sides of the woman's short-sleeve. "Ma'am."

"Captain." Carvalla's broad face broke into a genuine smile. "You have been giving my people a workout." She glanced at Pimentel, who looked starstruck. "It's not often I meet someone who served on Shèrá. We're contemporaries of a sort. I served as medical officer on a ship stationed in that area. The *Kensington.* You may not have heard of it, considering the circumstances at the time."

Jani's grin froze. "The flagship of the group that evac'd Rauta Shèràa Base—yes, ma'am, I had heard of it." After she escaped John's stifling care, she had spent several nerve-wracking days evading the crews that took over the human sector of the Rauta Shèràa shuttleport as she tried to wangle a billet on a civilian ship. Everywhere she had turned, she had seen someone sporting the names *Kensington, Hilfington,* or *Warburg* on a jacket or lid. "I'm sure the evacuees recall you fondly."

"*Perhaps,*" Carvalla replied dryly. "Quarters were close, and supplies were scarce. I think the fondest memory the evacuees have of us was saying good-bye." She glanced at her timepiece. "Well, it's time for rounds. Take care of yourself, Captain. I'm sure I'll see you again." She nodded to Jani and Pimentel in turn, then walked to the rear of the lobby to join a doctor cluster waiting near the lift bank.

"She's wonderful. The best thing that ever happened to Service Medical. Fair. Forward-thinking." Pimentel's boun-

ciness lasted until he walked out of the hospital and into the
full blaze of summer. "God, it's hot! Are you sure you don't
want someone to drive you to the TOQ?"

"No. I looked it up on the base map Morley gave me—
it's not that far." Jani took a deep breath of hot, dry air, felt
the chill leave her for the first time since her arrival, and
waved good-bye to Pimentel.

She walked down the long drive leading from the Main
Hospital, then turned down a series of shorter, tree-lined
streets named after famous generals. Hillman Avenue. Dra-
gan Row. Starcross Way. Earthbound generals. She could
imagine Borgie's peeved Man French mutterings as to the
inequity of the situation. She could sense him walk beside
her, as he had a hundred times at Rauta Shèràa Base.

They'd both acquired reputations by then, Jani as the stiff-
necked anti-Family doc jock who reacted to threats by making her own, Borgie as a quick mind ruined by a quicker
temper and the penchant for the freelance deal. Jani had uncovered evidence of one such operation, an attempt to divert
scanpack supplies to a Pearl Way broker. She had quietly
shut it down, then had taken Borgie aside and explained why
it was in his best interest to keep his damned hands out of
her patch. Struck by the fact that she had figured out his plan
so easily, *and* that she declined to turn him in to Base Security, he had decided to adopt her. Hers was a worthy mind,
he had told her, for an officer. From then on, he took her on
rounds of his own, and explained to her the things he felt a
deskbound paper-pusher needed to know to survive in the
Old Service. Much of the information had come in handy
during her years underground. To say she owed Borgie her
life didn't say enough. To say she'd let him down . . . well,
that didn't say enough, either.

Jani took her time examining the Sheridan grounds. The
rolling lawns. The locations of intersections and main drives.
She walked easily, her discharge summerweights and relaxed
manner marking her as a new release on her way home.

She and Borgie had talked about many things over the
months. The fine art of breaking and entering. How to plan
an escape. Primary routes. Back-up plans. Acquiring and se-

creting provisions and weapons. And other preparations.

They get us with that damned chip, Captain. They can track us anywhere with that thing. All they have to do is enter your code into systems and activate. How you deal with that depends on how desperate you are.

Jani checked her trouser pocket, the one that contained the scalpel she had swiped from a supply cart. In another, she'd stashed the half-used tube of incision sealant she'd found sitting atop the nurses' station counter, along with the topical anesthetic and a bandage pad. She'd operated on her scanpack often enough. She wasn't squeamish, and thanks to augie she had a high tolerance for pain.

The most important thing, Captain, is to choose your moment well. They won't give you a second chance.

"Frankly, Sergeant, I'm surprised they're giving me a first one." Jani slowed to a stop in the middle of the road and considered the strangeness of it all. *Piers thinks I'm lying about Neumann.* Because Veda needed paper to back up charges, and Jani's records were missing. *Where are they?* Who was responsible for their disappearance? Why were they involved? What did they expect to gain? Did they think to lull her into a false sense of ease, only to spring charges on her later? The unexpected attack was the hardest to fend off—she didn't want to be caught unawares. *I need to know who's been fiddling with my records.* And her records were stored at the SIB.

She started walking again, reaching a nameless cul-de-sac and trudging up a path leading to a five-story whitestone box set well back from the road, surrounded by low hedges. South Central Transient Officers' Quarters. Her home for the duration, however long that turned out to be.

The TOQ lobby proved just as plain as the exterior. The cheers and excited commentary that sounded from a side room indicated a well-attended Cup broadcast in progress.

Jani found her room on the mezzanine floor, a quick ten-step flight up from the lobby. Three small partitioned spaces: a sitting room cum office equipped with a desk and comport, a bedroom, and a bath. Spare furnishings of honey-colored polywood. Cream walls. A single narrow window in the sitting room, looking out over the cul-de-sac.

Her enthusiasm ramped when she laid eyes on her old duffel, resting small and lonely on the frame couch. "They really worked you over," she said as she dug through the depleted contents, removed her scanpack from its half-fastened pouch, then fingered the ragged edge of what had once been the scanproof compartment. They'd confiscated her shooter and gadgets. Someone, however, had taken the time to wrap her keepsakes in a tissue envelope.

She stashed her stolen medical supplies, the scalpel in the catch-all tray on her desk, the anesthetic, glue, and bandage, in her bathroom cabinet. *Hide in plain sight.* A nosy visitor would think she had a strange taste in letter openers and the tendency to cut herself with same, not that she planned to make a run for it as soon as circumstance allowed.

She opened her small closet to find the Clothing Elf had seen to her gear. She perused the six different styles of uniforms hanging within, then removed her unmarked hospital summerweights and donned a fresh set of her very own.

Jani found her ribbons and badges in a small box atop her dresser. She attached her bronze sideline captain's tabs to her collar, the silver scroll and quill of Documents Services to her shoulder tabs. They'd awarded one-year colonial service ribbons back in her day; she pinned the two green-and-gold-striped rectangles over her left pocket, where they glistened like pieces of spun-sugar candy.

They'd even allowed her the gold marksman badge she'd worked so hard to win when her mainline cohorts had told her she had no chance. Expert. Short shooter. *You'd think they'd have held that one back.* Might as well shout it to the worlds. *Hi, I'm Jani. Shot twenty-seven—killed them all. And you are . . . ?*

She applied makeup. Spritzed her hair with water and trimmed her more straggly curls with the nail cutters that came in her toiletry kit. *Captain Paragon girding for the File Wars.* She smiled despite her disquiet.

Her feelings toward the Service made about as much sense as her feelings for John Shroud. Pride in her Commonwealth had nothing to do with it—she'd been too much a colonial to feel patriotic and too much of a skeptic to see Acadia's rebel factions as any more than self-serving delusionaries. *I joined up for the same reasons that receptionist joined Neoclona.* To get away from a deadend homeworld. To meet different people. To learn. She'd never resented the routine, since working with the idomeni guaranteed things never remained routine for long. She'd even liked the uniforms; she'd never been an avid follower of fashion, and had been quite happy to turn the clothes part of her life over to someone else.

Give me a scanpack and a stack of paper, and I'm happy. If they'd assigned her anyplace but Rauta Shèràa Base, she might have even made the Service a career. *I like to fade into the background, and there's no place you can fade better than the Service.*

The one time she had broached that opinion to Borgie, however, he had laughed till he cried. *You're an action person, Captain,* he told her after he recovered sufficiently to speak. *You like digging into things you shouldn't. Turning over rocks. You don't toe the line—hell, you're a peacetime nightmare. You're one of those poor souls who needs a war.*

As it turned out, she was a nightmare even then.

She was in the middle of brushing her teeth when the doorscanner buzzed.

"Hello!" Lucien pushed past her into the sitting area, laden with packages. "I unpacked your gear this morning," he said as he tossed his brimmed lid on the couch and set a basket of cut flowers atop the end table. "I hope you appreciate it."

"So you're the Clothing Elf." Jani stood by the door, toothbrush in hand, and watched him unpack and store disposable cups and wipes, sundries and supplies for the desk. Instead of summerweights, he wore dress blue-greys. A black-leather crossover belt cut a diagonal swath across his steel blue tunic. His grey trousers were cut down the sides with the requisite mainline red slash, and the holster on his belt was fully packed. "Was today 'take your idomeni ambassador to university' day?"

"Yeah. His security picked the time at the last minute. Most propitious, they said, but I think they just wanted to shake the reporters. Nema was as excited as hell. He got into everything." Lucien reached into one of the bags and removed a small glass-and-gold clock. "This has a *good* alarm," he said as he set in on the desk. "The one on the comport isn't loud enough, and you can't set it to repeat."

Jani ducked into the bathroom to finish her teeth. "I found soap, hairwash, and toothpaste in here. I'm surprised they couldn't stick a clock somewhere."

"They used to. Stopped last year. They said it was the officers' responsibility to keep their own time."

"Are you sure it wasn't because the clocks were getting swiped by the occupants?"

Lucien poked his head around the bathroom entry. "We are talking about officers and gentlepeople, not *occupants*. And the word is *reappropriated*, not *swiped*."

"They must have been good clocks. How many got reappropriated in a year, on average?"

"One hundred fifty-three. They could even survive direct shooter fire. When magnebolting them to the tables didn't work, Housekeeping called it a wash. You really do have a suspicious mind, you know that?"

"Only because people keep living down to my expectations." Jani rinsed her mouth, then fixed the damage the toothpaste and water had inflicted upon her makeup. "I doubt human nature gets checked at the Shenandoah Gate."

"Don't let a superior hear you say that, or you'll get an earful. The New Service is a proud organization. It does not embrace the malcontent."

"Then why does it have its hand down my trousers?"

Lucien laughed. "You've got me there." Shoulders still shaking, he tossed a wrapper in the trashzap and disappeared around the divider.

Jani edged out of the bathroom, leaned against the divider, and watched Lucien set out an assortment of newssheets. When he still worked as a security officer on Anais Ulanova's staff, he had been deftly inserted into the crew list of the CSS *Arapaho*, the ship Jani had traveled on during her first trip to Earth. His duty had been ostensibly to serve as her steward; his true function had been to uncover her real identity. Even after the ruse had fallen through, he had still insisted on performing his cabin-attending duties. She'd had fresh flowers every ship day, liqueur waiting after dinner, laundry done daily.

He even massaged my neck once. She had just spent hours combing over some of Evan van Reuter's files, and the conclusion that her ex-lover was guilty of bribery and conspiracy, among other nasty things, had resulted in a tension headache that left her photophobic and unable to move her neck.

But Lucien fixed. Did he ever. In the five weeks they spent together, that was the closest he came to getting her into bed. Letting him get those hands on her was one mistake she had no intention of repeating. But, if he wanted to spend part of his day replenishing her flowers and reading materials, she wouldn't turn him down. "Is that everything?" she asked as she watched him stuff more wrappings into the trashzap.

"No." He stepped into her bedroom, then turned to her and crooked his finger for her to follow. "One final surprise." He held up the last package, removed the silver-and-black wrappings with a flourish, and held it out for her inspection.

She found herself staring into two shining brown eyes framed by a fringe of fur. "A teddy bear?"

It was an old-style toy, designed to do nothing but sit. Light brown fur, the closest match Lucien could find to his own hair. A black-plastic nose capped a snubby muzzle and a winsome, sewn-on smile. The uniform of the day consisted of a dark blue field sweater and fatigue pants, complete with a little blue garrison cap clutched in one fuzzy paw.

"What do you think?" Lucien propped it against the pillow, then reached out to adjust its sweater.

"It's too cute for words." Jani eyed the creature in bemusement. "I haven't had a teddy bear since I was three."

"That explains a lot." Lucien ran a finger along the edge of the bed. "You know, I've been told I have teddy-bear-like qualities."

"Yeah, you're both glassy-eyed and stuffed." Jani tapped her timepiece. "I have things to do."

"The first thing you're doing is dinner with me, but you're not going anywhere looking like *that*." Lucien pulled a comb from his trouser pocket. "This is Fort Sheridan. There are Appearance and Standards officers behind every bush." He recombed Jani's hair and made her retuck her shirt. Then he reached into his inside tunic pocket, removed a thin black rod, and tapped the side—a blue-green light flickered from one end.

"You carry a *micrometer*?" Jani watched him run the lighted end over her badges, check the readout, then pop the rod in his mouth like a nicstick as he adjusted the placement of one of her colonial service ribbons. "You can't tell me the A&S-holes are that picky."

"The wha—!" The micrometer wobbled as Lucien tried to suppress a laugh. "Depends whether they've met their quotas. They go on a binge about once a quarter; those demerit fines can really chew up your pay. You learn not to take chances." He touched Jani's short-shooter badge. "Expert. Really?"

"No, some officers steal clocks, I steal badges." She pointed to the micrometer. "That's bullshit."

"And you're all roses, my DI used to say, so suck it up." Lucien knelt carefully on the carpeted floor and measured Jani's trouser hems.

"You had a DI? I thought you emerged fully formed from a recruiting holo." She watched him run a dispo over one tietop. "And don't tell me that shoe's dirty because I just polished it."

Lucien looked up at her and shook his head in dismay. "You'll thank me for this later."

"This entire exercise is just an excuse to touch me."

"If I wanted an excuse, I could think of much more interesting ones than this." He yanked at her other fastener and retied it more neatly. "What are you going to name him?"

"Who?"

"The bear. He needs a name."

"Oh, it's a 'he,' is it?"

"Of course." Lucien straightened up and stood before her in all his mainline glory. His hair shone more brightly than his badges, which in turn gleamed enough to flash the roomlight like stars. He'd pass any measurement test devised by man—oh yes, if you struck him, he'd ring. "What are you going to name him?"

Jani took a step backward. "Val," she replied quietly. "After my old friend, Val Parini."

Lucien looked heavenward and sighed. "I set out your gear, do your shopping, save you from A&S wrath, and what thanks do I get?" He pointed to the two badges decorating his own tunic pocket. "I have you beat. Expert, short *and* long shooter."

"You had a head start. You were born with half the equipment." Jani grabbed her scanpack from the desk, stuffed it into her belt pouch, dashed out the door, then waited for Lucien to catch her up. After some bickering while he adjusted her garrison cap, they proceeded to dinner.

They ate at the South Central Officers' Club, and watched a freshly transmitted Cup qual match on the bar-mounted 'Vee. The German provincial team versus Elyas Amalgam in an Earthbound-colony tussle. Elyas was up five–zip at halftime—most of the faces at the bar appeared rather glum.

The temperature outside had reached record levels, according to the ServNet weather broadcast. Forty Celsius, with no cool-down expected for at least a week. The 'Vee viewers nursed their drinks and looked out the floor-to-ceiling windows to the bright, shimmering lawnscape beyond, delaying as long as possible the inevitable walk outside.

Jani stepped out onto the patio, sighing with pleasure as a Rauta Shèràa–quality blast of hell-spawned wind sucked the moisture from her eyefilms.

Lucien drew alongside. "Want to check out the beach?"

"We're not dressed for the beach."

"We can change." He handed her a dispo of water. "You don't even have to buy a swimsuit. You were issued one."

"Was I?"

"Yep. They're dark silver this year." His look grew pointed. "That color would look great against your skin."

"Would it?" Jani brushed off Lucien's subdued leer. "I want to go to the SIB." She chewed a mint leaf she'd plucked from her fruit cup—the fruit had been torture to choke down, even with pepper and hot mustard, but she found the gnawed mint leaves followed by a cold water chaser refreshing. "I need to talk to an archivist."

"You start working tomorrow, not tonight. Tonight, you're supposed to relax and have fun." Lucien flashed a smile, white teeth brilliant against tanned skin. "That's what I'm for."

Jani let his rich brown stare draw her in. A less-experienced soul could drown in those cool, dark pools. Luckily, she knew how to swim. "Can I ask you a question?"

Lucien leaned closer. "You know you can ask me anything."

"Are you using me to get close to Nema, or Nema to get close to me?"

His head snapped back. His smile vanished. He strode out onto the lawn. "A little of both. Does that matter?"

Jani remained silent. She knew he didn't like it when she tossed his affections, such as they were, back in his face, but she didn't relish him treating her like one of his suckers either.

He paced in front of her, with the occasional glance to see if she watched. "At least I tell you."

"Only because I already know."

He slowed to a stroll, then to a halt, and looked at her, his face a study in line and shadow devoid of emotion. Then the smile returned, grimmer and more knowing. "It's too hot for the beach. How about a walk along the South Marina docks? At least the walkways are covered."

"SIB."

"There's the indoor games room."

"SIB."

"We could see what's playing at the Veedrome."

"SIB."

"SIB." Lucien tugged at his tunic collar, then fanned his

face. "Can I at least change into summerweights first?"

Jani studied him with what she liked to call her criminal eye. *If I were stealing documents, would I worry if I saw you show up in the middle of my shift?* She contemplated his trim, rangy frame, displayed to perfection in the formal uniform. His hard stare. Most particularly, she studied his packed shooter holster. "No. I like you just the way you are."

SIB Archives, like most repositories Jani had known, had been originally designed to be much smaller, then expanded over time to its divinely ordained size. The area, which took up half the basement, was comprised of an interwoven network of secured storage rooms and jury-rigged tech bullpens. She and Lucien walked through the hallways twice, drawing questioning looks from the techs who filed and performed preliminary doc checks in cubicles or at open tables.

Lucien eyed his surroundings with a complete lack of interest. "Forgive me for questioning your absolute authority, but what are you going to do?"

Jani stopped before a bulletin board and read some of the postings. The usual announcements of parties. Lost jewelry in the washroom. A memo from SIB Safety complained about the lousy clear time during the last evacuation drill, and promised repeat exercises until people "got it right." "I thought I'd play the registrar. Poke around. Ask a few questions."

"Oh. You mean overstep your jurisdiction and meddle in things that are none of your business."

"It's my ServRec that's missing—I have a right to look for it."

"Hmm. What do you want me to do?"

"Look like your day won't be complete until you arrest somebody."

"You know, I like being a lieutenant. Someday, I'd like to like being a captain."

"It's overrated." Jani entered the archives room with the most traffic and walked around the perimeter. She opened a file drawer, leafed through a report that lay open atop a desk, and smiled at everyone who looked her way.

"May I help you?"

Jani turned and found herself being subjected to the critical appraisal of a rotund man in civilian summerweights. "I'm Odergaard. Tech One on this shift." His face was flushed, his skin shiny, as though he'd just been taken from the oven and basted.

"Captain Jani Kilian, First D-Doc." She cocked her head toward Lucien. "This is Lieutenant Lucien Pascal, Intelligence."

Around them, the skritch of styli stopped. Whispers fell silent.

Odergaard's gaze widened as it flicked from Jani's name tag, to her scanpack, then to Lucien's sidearm. "Is there a problem?"

"I'm trying to obtain access to my Service record, but I've been informed by my attorney that portions of it have been mislaid."

What ruddiness remained in Odergaard's face after *Kilian* and *Intelligence* vanished upon mention of the word *attorney*. "We have been transferring files from the Judge Advocate's to new bins in this building for the past few months, and the inevitable cross-ups have, of course, occurred—"

"I'd like to speak to the shift archivist." Jani made a show of looking around the room.

Anger flared in Odergaard's eyes. "That would be Mr. Duong." He took a step, then hesitated, but another look at Lucien's sidearm decided him. "This way, please."

They walked to a more sheltered work space in the far corner of the room. A small, dark-haired man sat at a workstation, entering document tag numbers into a grid. Most of the numbers were blue, but the occasional red string could be seen. Red had meant "missing in action" when Jani interned in Consulate Archives. She doubted that had changed in the years since.

"You're running inventory." Her voice lowered in commiseration. "I always hated inventory."

The man turned with a start. Older, fifties probably. Earthbound Asian or Bandan—Jani wouldn't know until he opened his mouth. And suspicious. The look he shot at Odergaard held that special brand of distrust reserved for meddling managers.

Odergaard spoke first. "Sam—"

Sahm—he's Bandan. Jani smiled. This could wind up working quite well.

"—this is Captain Kilian from First Doc—"

"*Apa kabar, señorìo.*" *Greetings, sir.* Jani's Bandan wasn't perfect, but it was formal, which came in handy when working with the pedantic precisionists that usually populated the archivist ranks. She held out her hand to the man. "*I'm looking for my life—can you help me find it?*"

He looked up at her. His eyes were old brown—dull, with yellowed sclera. His face held confusion, as though he remembered her face but couldn't recall her name. "*You speak Bandan?*" His handshake consisted of the barest touch. His voice emerged very small.

"*I lived there for a time. Near the university.*"

"*You know the university! I worked there for years—*"

As Duong rattled on, Jani heard Odergaard grumble under his breath. Yes, they were being rude, but she needed Duong's help more than his boss's, and she couldn't help thinking that Odergaard deserved to get his tail twisted.

Duong rose from his chair. "*I'll show you my dead,*" he said as he gestured for Jani to follow him. "*Maybe in my dead, is your life.*"

"*Maybe.*" Jani wondered if Duong's Bandan expressions ever colored his English. Bandan was an interesting language, but it tended toward the poetic, and some of the literal translations struck the uninformed as odd.

Just as they were about to cut across the hallway into Duong's file bin of choice, a younger man in sideline summerweights blocked their path. His yellow collar tabs marked him as a lieutenant. His holstered scanpack marked him as the ranking examiner on the shift.

"Lieutenant Yance." Odergaard transformed into a round-shouldered hand-rubber. "This is Captain Jani Kilian. Her attorney, Major Friesian—"

"Captain." Yance nodded sharply. "I think the documents you're looking for may prove much more accessible than you've been led to believe." He brushed past her into the bullpen, all shined shoes and elbows.

Jani glanced at Lucien. "I don't want to talk to the ranking."

"They sure as hell don't want you talking to Duong." The first glimmers of attention showed on his face. "Odergaard almost jumped out of his skin when you started speaking Bandan."

"*I did not put those there!*"

Jani hurried back into the bullpen, Lucien at her heels. She recognized Duong's voice, and the mounting panic she heard in it.

The bullpen residents had swarmed around Duong's work space. Jani shouldered through them in time to see Yance pull a thick file from a desk drawer. Light grey parchment in a light grey folder. Old Service paper.

"What else has he got in there?" Yance craned to look around the bulky Odergaard, who was down on his knees, pulling more files out of drawers.

"I did not put those there!" Duong rocked from one foot to the other as though the floor scalded his soles.

One of the techs made a "slow down" motion with her hands. "Mr. Duong, please—"

"*I did not put those there!*"

Jani thumped Yance on the shoulder. "Lieutenant, what's going on?"

"Captain, please." He leaned close. "He's done this before, ma'am. He has a problem."

Odergaard twisted around. "I found some of the van Reuter stuff, too."

Jani glanced at the faces surrounding them. Some held surprise, others, disappointment. One or two sneered. "I don't like this," she said to Lucien.

He held up an open hand in an "oh well" gesture. "But it looks like you've got your records back, so what difference does it make?"

"You would think that, wouldn't you?" Jani stepped around Yance, who was busy talking into a handcom, and planted herself between him and the shaking Duong. "Mr. Duong?"

Duong looked up at her, eyes wide and glistening. "I did not put those there."

"You didn't lock my life away in your drawer?"

"*No!*"

Jani looked into Duong's stricken face. She had no reason to believe him—she had known him for all of five minutes. *He's an archivist.* Archivists had earned a well-deserved reputation for strangeness. Sometimes they grew jealous of the documents in their charge, resented others touching them, using them. Sam Duong could just be one of those disturbed few who had decided that if he couldn't have them, nobody could.

Do I believe that? She considered the trembling figure before her, and tried to get the sense of him. She had lived by her instincts for eighteen years—they'd served her well. It was only when she disregarded them that she found herself in trouble.

She touched Duong's arm. "I believe you."

It took a moment for her words to sink in. When they did, the tension drained from Duong as though someone had flipped a release, and he slumped forward.

Jani snaked her arm around him to keep him from falling. "Get this man to the infirmary!" She eased him into the arms of two techs, who helped him out of the room.

"You really shouldn't have said that, Captain. It only encourages him." Yance ran his scanpack over one of the papers, waited for the display to show green, then repeated the action with the next. Judging from the thickness of the piles, he had a long night of ID confirmation ahead of him.

Jani fingered a page from her Service record. *My transfer orders to the Twelfth Rovers.* She could almost feel Rikart Neumann's presence in the paper, like a layer of grime. "So he's done this before?"

"Nothing this blatant. Misfiles that he claimed someone else must have done."

"What made you suspect?"

"A tip."

"Anonymous?"

"*No*, ma'am. A very reliable source." Yance hesitated in mid-scan. "I don't like this either, ma'am. But if he's a threat to the paper, we have to shut him down."

Jani looked at Lucien, who responded with a shrug. "I'd like two copies of these docs. Send one set to Major Piers Friesian, Defense Command, this base. Send the other to me at the South Central TOQ."

"Yes, ma'am." Yance entered a notation in his handheld, then returned to his scanning.

Lucien left the bullpen with the light step of a newly released prisoner. "I didn't know you spoke Bandan." He slipped a finger between his tunic collar and his neck and cursed the uniform designer responsible.

"Enough to get by." Jani felt a twinge of self-reproach as she recalled the excitement on Duong's face as he conversed in his native tongue. It was pathetic how little it took to win a person over.

She strode ahead of Lucien up the stairs and through the lobby. As she burst through the lobby door, she barely missed colliding with a man trying to enter. The red trouser stripe combined with the hardware blared "mainline colonel." She was treated to a surprised glare as he brushed past her.

Jani stood in the entry and watched him snap across the lobby and down the stairs. Typical hard-ass brass, but he had a couple of distinctive features. Hair the color of bronze, and a long, weathered face cut from edge of nose to end of mouth by a deep, age-whitened scar.

CHAPTER 9

The incident with Sam Duong nibbled at Jani's tenuous calm as she readied for her first day as a reactivated Spacer. After a scanner-approved breakfast in her rooms, she strode the walkways to Documents Control, adjusting the tilt of her garrison cap until it mimicked everyone else's. She slung her black-leather briefbag over her left shoulder, again in imitation, and rested her arm across the top. *Everything the same as everybody else.* Just another way to disappear into the crowd.

The morning air held a metal tang, as though it had been on the fire too long. The hot wind desiccated everything it touched. She savored the heat as she followed the signs and markers, finally pulling up in front of a building that, but for the rimming of hedges, could have twinned the TOQ.

Jani trotted up the Doc Control steps as quickly as her weakened right leg would allow. She paused in front of the doorscanner, waited for it to read her retinas, then held her breath as the lock whirred and the door clicked open and she entered a close-controlled building as Jani Kilian for the first time in eighteen years. She listened to the echo of her tietops as she strode across the tiled lobby, and wondered at the firm tone of her oh-so-Service voice as she asked a passing lieutenant the location of the Foreign Transactions Department.

Before she entered the anteroom leading to Lieutenant Colonel Hals's office, Jani dug her orders out of her briefbag and checked the date and time against a wall clock. *Right day?* Check. *Right time?* Check. *So where is everybody?* All of the office areas she had passed on the way had been empty. She scanned the doorways and desktops for clues to explain the lack of human occupation, but no scrawled note informing all that the department meeting had been moved or that someone down the hall had brought in doughnuts surfaced to clarify the situation.

At the sound of the half hour, she stepped up to the adjutant's desk, positioned just outside the colonel's door. Lieutenant Ischi, who according to the nameplate should have been manning same, was nowhere to be seen.

Then Jani heard sounds emerge from the inner office. Sharp rises. Sudden falls. The cadences of argument. Either the voices were very loud, or the office soundshielding very poor. She'd have bet her 'pack the quality of the shielding was just fine.

She knocked on the door, and the voices cut off abruptly. One beat later, a woman called out, "Come in."

Jani touched the entry pad. The door swept aside to reveal two men and one woman standing around a large goldwood desk. The woman stood on the business side, hands braced on the edge. The men, one older, one younger, stood opposite her. The older man looked angry. The younger looked like he wished he were somewhere else.

"Colonel Hals?" Jani remained in the open doorway, looking from one worn face to another. "Captain Kilian reporting, ma'am." *What the hell have they been doing?* Their summerweights were sweat-stained and rumpled, their hair, matted, the older man's face alarmingly flushed.

"Do we look that bad, Captain?" Hals asked. Her voice held tired humor, along with the barest trace of New Indiesian singsong. She was shorter, heavier, and lighter-skinned than Jani, her curly, dark brown hair twisted in a tight bun. Pleasant-looking, if you ignored her heavy-lidded eyes and fatigue-drained complexion. "Please. Come in."

The younger man gestured toward the older. "This is Major Vespucci, ma'am," he said to Jani. "Our Procedural specialist."

Vespucci nodded. He was dark-haired and fleshy, his small eyes set in a permanent squint. It was Procedural's job to make sure a department had access to the latest form revisions—Vespucci had the humorless look of a man who liked controlling the codes.

"And I'm Lieutenant Ischi," the young man added with a smile. "Tech wrangler and department dogsbody." He was Eurasian, tall and trim, with big, bright eyes and good bones.

Jani removed her orders from her briefbag and walked across the office to hand them to Hals. "Ma'am."

Hals accepted the documents with a small smile. "We'll start you off by having Lieutenant Ischi show you to your office, Captain. I'd like to see you back here at oh-ten." She acknowledged Jani's "good morning, ma'am," with an absent nod, and resumed her conversation with Vespucci, this time at a lower volume.

Ischi bounded out of Hals's office, his relief at escaping evident in his wider grin and expansive gestures. "This way, ma'am." He led Jani down one short hall, then another, finally pulling up in front of an unmarked door. "I'm expecting your doorplate in this afternoon's delivery from Office Supply. They drop off three times a week—let me know what you need, and I'll add it to the next list."

Jani stepped past him into her office, close enough to catch a whiff of deodorant on the cusp of failure. *If an A&S-hole catches sight or scent of you, Lieutenant, you're a goner.* What had he and Hals and Vespucci been up to?

The office was long and narrow. No furniture except for a desk and couple of chairs. Inset bookcases, so at least she had shelves. A single-pane window centered the far wall. Through the portion not blocked by tree branches, she could see the edge of a charge lot. Pimentel was right—Sheridan did have windows to spare.

"Sorry about the view, ma'am."

"At least I'm not looking through bars."

"Ma'am?"

"Nothing." Jani wandered over to her desk. The workstation, comport, and parchment imprinter all looked like they'd just been removed from their cartons—the workstation touchboard still bore its protective plastic wrapping. "Has Systems initiated this yet?"

"This afternoon, ma'am." Ischi's grin tightened. "My apologies."

"Hmm." Having an uninitiated system meant she'd be spending the morning straightening her desk. She walked to the window, looked out at her tree, then turned back to Ischi. "Do you mind if I ask . . . ?" She gestured toward his unkempt uniform.

The light left Ischi's eyes. "We spent last night at the idomeni embassy, ma'am. They keep it pretty warm in there."

"The *whole* night?"

"Yes, ma'am."

"What time did you arrive?"

"Nineteen-up, ma'am."

Jani counted. "You spent over twelve hours there? Doing what?"

"Verifying and cataloging instruments of negotiation, ma'am. Concerning the Lake Michigan Strip."

"I've never heard of that."

"You will," Ischi replied flatly. He nodded sharply and turned to leave. "By your leave, ma'am. I'll nudge Systems about getting you up and running."

Jani watched the door close. Her door. In her old department. In a close-controlled building. On a Service base. *And everyone's fighting, they look hot and confused, and the idomeni have them back on their heels.* Almost two decades and six GateWays removed . . . and nothing had changed a bit.

"Come in, Captain. Have a seat."

Jani walked slowly across Hals's office to disguise her residual limp, and lowered into the visitor's chair.

Across the desk, Hals continued to page through her ServRec. She had showered and changed her uniform. The ends of her bound hair were tightly curled from damp, the creases of her short-sleeve sharp enough to cut parchment.

Jani tensed each time the woman's gaze was arrested, then raked her memory to recall which item could have claimed her attention. The SIB-decimated file held little useful information. Jani's Rauta Shèràa job history. Her specs. Her education and training. She knew it didn't contain what Hals no doubt most wanted to know.

So, Captain Colonel-Killer, what did I do to deserve you?

Hals closed the ServRec, then traced along its sides with her fingertips. "So—"

Jani squeezed the arms of her chair.

"—you're Two of Six. The Eyes and Ears." The woman offered a quick half smile.

"Yes, ma'am," Jani replied carefully.

"I'd just begun my sophomore year at Montserrat when the news arrived that six humans had been chosen to study documents sciences at the Rauta Shèràa Academy. That made my decision to major in paper rather than law easier for my parents to swallow." Hals tipped back her chair and tapped her fingertips together. Index to index, middle to middle. "How did that bit of doggerel go? One of Six for Tongue of Gold, Two for Eyes and Ears, Three and Four for . . . for—"

"Hands of Light." Jani felt the heat crawl up her neck. "Five and Six for Earthly Might."

Another fleeting smile. "The late Hansen Wyle was your mouthpiece. He was One of Six."

"Yes. Ma'am." Jani glanced around the lieutenant colonel's spare office. Of all the things she expected to be questioned about, this hadn't even made the top twenty. "Gina Senna was Three. Carson Tsai was Four. They were musicians—musicians impressed the idomeni. That's what *Hands of Light* means." She waited for Hals to respond, but the woman only watched her silently. "Dolly Aryton was Five. Her mother was a Neumann. Ennegret Nawar was Six. He's the *N* in SCAN. Hence the Earthly Might." She wished she had the nerve to sit quietly, wait out Hals's silences. Memories of past calls-on-the-carpet returned *en force*. The dry mouth. The ragged thoughts. The gabbling to fill the relentless quiet. "We were eighteen when we wrote it. We thought it sounded very enigmatic."

"I'm not asking you to defend it, Captain." Hals paused

and held a hand to her mouth. Her jaw flexed as she suppressed a yawn. "As you no doubt recall," she continued, eyes watering, "Foreign Transactions covers a rather broad range of dealings. These usually involve records and equipment transfers to the colonies. We do, however, occasionally monitor transactions with the idomeni. Unfortunately, as you also no doubt recall, that five percent of our duties can take up eighty percent of our time."

Jani nodded. "Food shipments into Rauta Shèràa Base used to result in some marathons. I remember the one time we tried to ship in beets. The idomeni have beetlike vegetables, but they're grown in the Sìah valleys in the central plains. They don't grow in the northern regions, so the Laumrau didn't want to let them in."

Hals leaned forward. "So what happened?" She spoke quickly. More than polite interest—she *wanted* to know.

"We gave up after three straight days with no breaks. Nobody liked beets that much." Jani could still remember the hot, stagnant air, the simultaneous collapse of everyone's deodorant, her CO at the time nodding off in a corner. "Sometimes, you have to give them what they want. It usually pays off. They gave in to us later when we wanted to bring in peanut butter. Of course, we were willing to fight for peanut butter. I think they knew that." She chuckled, until a glance at Hals's blank expression silenced her.

"You make it sound so homey, Captain." She fingered a corner of Jani's file. "Why are they so picky about their food?"

Ask me something easy, like the meaning of life. "They place great value in order—that significance cuts across sect lines. Order that nourishes the body also nourishes the soul. Eating certain types of food at certain times maintains that sense of order. Exposure to certain foods only during certain seasons of the year. A balanced diet taken to the extreme."

"Don't they ever eat anything just because it tastes good?"

"They're not a very sensual people when it comes to appetites, ma'am. One theory has it that their brains work similarly to those of humans who've been stressed to the point of burnout. They only feel extremes. Nuance escapes them."

"Do you believe that?"

"I'm not a xenoneurologist." Jani wavered under Hals's probing gaze. "No, ma'am, I don't believe that. They're alien. We just don't understand their nuance."

Hals's eyebrows arched. "Do you include yourself in that *we*, Captain?"

Jani hesitated, then shook her head. "No, ma'am. However, I also don't underestimate their capacity to surprise."

Hals nodded wearily, as though she'd had the idomeni capacity to surprise up to *there*. "Ask Lieutenant Ischi to provide you the background information concerning our involvement with the Lake Michigan Strip. I'll be interested to hear your take." She tapped absently at her comport pad. "By the way, during your time in Rauta Shèràa, did you ever know a female named Onì nìaRauta Hantìa?"

"Hantìa?" It had been years since Jani had heard that name. She recalled a smooth, arrogant voice, like barbed satin. "She was member of a scholarly skein, training to be a Council Historian. The equivalent of an archivist."

"She may have been an archivist then. She's the Vynshàrau's chief documents examiner now." Hals opened, then closed Jani's folder. "Did you know her?"

Yes. Jani watched Hals fidget. *But I think you knew that.* It looked as though her new CO possessed a capacity to surprise, as well. "We were at the Academy together."

Hals nodded. "I thought it might be likely, judging from your ages." She looked at Jani. Through the fatigue in her eyes, a hard light shone. "It will be nice to have someone with your experience in this department."

"Ma'am." Jani knew a dismissal when she heard it. She stood, rubbed her damp palms against her trousers, then came to attention. "Good morning, ma'am." She backed up one step, executed about-face, and headed for the door.

"Captain."

Here it comes. Jani stopped. Turned slowly. What would it be? A question about Neumann? Evan?

Hals sat back, her brow furrowed. She wanted to ask Jani *something*—that was obvious. Maybe she was having trouble deciding where to start. How do you question mutiny, when you're on the business side of the table? "Never mind," she said. "Make sure you see Ischi about the background report."

"Yes, ma'am." Jani walked out of the office, left a note for the absent dogsbody requesting the report, then cut through the anteroom into the desk pool. Most of the chairs were filled; a few of the uniformed occupants paused in their work to cast her curious glances.

She entered her office to find someone from Systems bent over her workstation. She fled to the quiet of the women officers' lounge, locked herself in a toilet stall, and slumped against the cold metal partition. *Crazy.* Her heart pounded. Her stomach ached. *They want the wait to drive me crazy.*

By the time Jani felt settled enough to return to her office, the Systems tech had departed. The presence of a steel blue folder in the middle of her desktop told her that Ischi had delivered the background report.

She closed the door and sat at her desk. Paged through the file. Inserted the attached data wafers into the workstation slot. The mechanics of work calmed her. She slipped the report on like a favorite shirt, and read. Eventually, she sat back and propped her feet up on the desk. Laughed out loud a few times.

It was the funniest story she'd read in years.

"Ma'am?"

Jani glanced up to find a freshly fitted-out Ischi standing in the doorway, holding a steaming mug in one hand and a covered plate in the other.

"I thought you might want something to eat." He held up the plate with the hopeful air of a father trying to persuade his child to come out from under the bed. "You've been in here for over five hours."

"I have?" Jani checked her timepiece, and whistled. "I have." She lowered her feet to the floor. "Time flies when you're having fun."

"A couple of us did hear you laugh once or twice." Ischi walked in and let the door close behind him. "Three times, maybe." He set down the cup—the heavenly aroma of true-bean drifted across the desk. "We tried to figure out what was so funny." He removed the protective cover from the plate to reveal a sandwich and a piece of cake, and placed it before her.

Jani wrapped her hand around the mug, then motioned for Ischi to sit. "What the hell was Anais Ulanova thinking?" She sipped the coffee. Black. No sugar. Strong enough to warp enamel. She almost moaned in rapture. "She orders a lakeskimmer to transport mixed foodstuffs to the Commerce Ministry, even though the idomeni embassy sits smack between them and the verandas where all the idomeni take meditation facing the water."

"*Exposure to unknown food.*" Ischi perched on the edge of his chair, elbows on knees. "*Breaking the sacred plane.* Those phrases have been ringing in our ears since this began. Tsecha and the other priests spent three months decontaminating the embassy, and they're still not happy."

"And to keep it from happening again, all they want are land, sea, and air rights to a two-kilometer strip stretching from their embassy proper, across the lake, to the eastern side of the Michigan province."

"And scanning rights. And boarding rights. It's the scanning rights that we're worried about. They could monitor flyovers of experimental craft." Ischi's clear young brow furrowed in consternation. "I think they're overreacting, personally."

"You're lucky they're still in Chicago." Jani took a bite of the sandwich. Cold roast beef on buttered bread, with slices of pickled hot pepper on the side. "If the Oligarch had had his way, he'd have recalled the whole crew back to Shèrá. Morden nìRau Cèel has been looking for an excuse to cut diplomatic ties with us ever since they reopened." She bit a slice of pepper—Ischi cringed as he watched her chew. "It was a miracle that Nema talked him into only decamping to the Death Valley enclave. I wonder how he twisted his arm?"

"Nema?" Ischi chewed his lip in puzzlement. "Oh, the ambassador's other name." He eyed Jani intently. "Would you call him that to his face, ma'am?"

"No. To his face, I'd call him *nìRau*. Or *nìRau ti nìRau*, if I wanted to be really formal. Or *inshah*—that's informal High Vynshàrau for *teacher*. Not that he'd mind if I called him Nema, but I wouldn't feel right." Jani pondered her half-empty cup. "So, Lieutenant, what's the word. Did the Exterior Minister insult the idomeni on purpose?"

Ischi's guileless manner altered. His eyes narrowed. His voice deadened. "That's Diplomatic's call, ma'am. They don't discuss those matters with us."

"Why not? You're part of this enterprise. You can watch as well as they can."

"We're not qualified, ma'am. So we've been told. We've been told a lot of things, lately."

He wants to say more. That was obvious as hell. *He just needs a push.* And unlike with Hals, she could provide the helping hand. "Out with it, Lieutenant," she said coldly.

Ischi's words tumbled, laced with frustration and anger. "We've been getting questions from Diplo for weeks, ma'am. 'When's she coming? When's she going to be here?' "

"Their point?"

"Burkett, ma'am. Brigidier General Callum Burkett. Head of Diplo. He said you're halfway to being idomeni and you have no business being in a uniform, much less as a member of FT." Ischi swallowed. "I'm quoting, ma'am."

"I understand."

"FT doesn't hold with that opinion, ma'am."

"Glad to hear it."

"Inasmuch as we're allowed to express opinions. Ma'am."

Jani stood, stretched her stiff back, and walked to her window. "The first students the idomeni allowed into the Academy weren't diplomats, but documents examiners. To the idomeni, the order is in the paper, and order is all. They expect you to participate. They expect you to be able to make decisions and negotiate binding agreements because, I guarantee, their examiners sure as hell can."

"Hantìa," Ischi grumped. "She keeps trying to push Colonel Hals into saying things—"

"And Hals has been told to keep her mouth shut and scan

the paper." Jani tugged at the window shade so hard she crooked it. "I went to school with Hantìa. If she senses weakness, she is merciless unless you hit her and hit her hard. She expects you to—that's the born-sect tradition of challenge and counterchallenge. She's making overtures, inviting Hals to begin the negotiation process. If Hals keeps ignoring her, first she'll become confused, then she'll feel insulted, and at that point, no amount of diplomacy is going to lessen the perceived offense."

"We're more important than Diplo thinks we are?" Ischi's voice bit, like he'd just had a long-nursed belief confirmed.

"Oh, yes."

"What can we do?"

"I don't know." Jani returned to her desk and picked up her cup. "Hals seems to realize she needs to do something. I kept getting the feeling that she wanted to ask me questions, but she couldn't work up the nerve."

"That's Vespucci. By the book—" Ischi swallowed his comment and stood up. "By your leave, ma'am—I have a tech meeting to prep."

"They were arguing about me, weren't they? About how involved I should get in this?"

"I think you'd better speak with Colonel Hals about that, ma'am." Ischi kept his eyes fixed on the floor. "I can set up an appointment for you first thing tomorrow morning."

"Please do, Lieutenant." Jani took another sip of coffee, then leaned against her desk and absently examined her cup—

"By your leave, ma'am." Ischi about-faced and made for the door.

—bright blue with a black griffin rampant on a gold shield. "Stop right where you are, Lieutenant!"

"Ma'am." Ischi snapped to attention a mere step from freedom.

"What is this?" Jani held the cup within centimeters of his nose.

"It's—a coffee cup, ma'am."

"And?"

"It's blue, ma'am."

"*And?*"

"It has a bird on it."

"No, Sergeant, this is not a bird. This, Corporal, is a griffin. Do you know what a griffin is, Spacer?"

"Ma'am."

"It's the emblem of something called a Gruppo Helvetica, a worthless assemblage of overpaid has-beens who are going to get their asses flayed as soon as they play a *real* team."

Ischi remained at attention as he looked at her sidelong. "Bet?"

"Name it."

"The officers have a pool."

"Put me down for Acadia Central United, all the way."

"You're on, ma'am." Ischi removed a handheld from his trouser pocket and coded an entry. "It's a fifty-Comdollar stake, payable before the first round begins. Ten percent off the top goes to the charity of your choice so we don't get gigged for gambling. Where do you want yours to go?"

"Colonial Outreach."

"Colonial Outreach, it is." Ischi tucked the device back in his pocket. "It'll be a pleasure to take your money, ma'am," he said as he departed, with a clipped coolness that would have given Lucien pause.

Jani stuck her tongue out at him as the door closed. Then she returned to her desk, and her report, and the balance of her meal.

It was dark by the time Jani departed Doc Control. Had been dark for hours—the only people out and about were third-shifters on their way to work. *Pimentel is going to have my ass.* She stopped by the South Central out of guilt and assembled dinner from the leavings of the salads and soups. Everything scanned edible. Good thing. She'd forgotten to scan the sandwich and the cake, and one of them had made her wheeze. Considering the only other things that made her wheeze were shellfish and biopolymers, unscanned foods were now officially expunged from her menu.

Her walk had slowed to a trudge by the time she entered

the hostel lobby. But she detoured to the holoVee room anyway, just to decompress.

"In other news," the disembodied voice of the announcer continued, "reaction to the idomeni ambassador's visit to the Botany Department of Chicago Combined University, undertaken in an effort to promote scientific exchange between the Commonwealth and the Shèrá worldskein, remains mixed. Negotiations are currently under way to allow teams of human and idomeni botanists to conduct joint research in selected sites throughout both our domains. This would be the first time such exchanges would be allowed since the idomeni civil war, and agriculture officials fear these programs could draw attention and funding from the more traditional research that has been conducted in the colonies for decades."

As the announcer continued his narration, Arrèl nì Rau Nema came into view, flanked by white-coated human scientists. His golden skin seemed to shimmer in the bright sun. Gold coils flashed from his ears. His straight, pale brown hair had been braided into a series of thin loops that trimmed his head like fringe. He wore the usual clothing of a male of his skein and station: light brown trousers tucked into knee-high brown boots, open-necked shirt in the same dusky color, an off-white overrobe trimmed with crimson. A human wearing so many clothes in the extreme heat would have looked sweaty and wilted, but Nema looked sharp and energetic.

Jani stepped closer to the display. Several Service officers stood behind Nema, eyes fixed on the crowds. Lucien, she noted, wasn't among them.

"I have most enjoyed my visit to this place," Nema said. His light voice sounded clipped, flat, English falling easily from his thin lips. "So much have I learned, and truly."

One of the reporters shouted a question. The scientists frowned and tried to herd Nema away, but he planted his feet and rounded his shoulders. His stubborn posture made Jani smile.

"I am curious of all things in this city," he said. "*All* things." He paused, then looked straight at the holocam. "My eyes and ears are always open to that which I must know."

Amber eyes tunneled. Through the hours. The distance. Straight at her. "Knowledge is power, isn't that what all humanish believe? Then so must we labor together, to build our power."

He bared his teeth in a skeleton-like grimace. The expression was the idomeni equivalent of a smile, though it looked in no way benign. Jani had always referred to the expression as *Grim Death with a Deal for You*. The term seemed more appropriate now than it ever had.

Another reporter shouted another question, but before Nema could respond, the white coats maneuvered him into a nearby building.

Jani turned and walked slowly from the room. Up the stairs. Down the hall.

Nema's turning the screws to keep me out of jail because he wants me to look for something. She changed into pajamas, set out her late dinner, ate. *Something powerful.* She washed, burrowed into bed, nestled Val the Bear on the adjoining pillow. *But what?*

Did it matter? She esteemed Nema, and always would. And who could help liking him? *But he could teach John a thing or two about treating people like objects.* She had taken care to leave his ring in her bag. It was a keepsake, from a time long past. She didn't have the ability, or the will, to jump when he called anymore.

She punched her pillow, thought of the scalpel on her desk, and knew she should start planning her escape. *Not now.* Later, when she could think more clearly. When thoughts of victimized archivists and troubles with the idomeni didn't prey on her mind. When she'd seen everything through to the end. Left things tight.

She fell asleep slowly, fitfully. Her stomach had started to ache again.

CHAPTER 10

Sam sat on the scanbed and watched the morning sun stream though the examination-room windows. The light fractured into rainbows as it struck analyzer displays, flashed like flares as it reflected off metal stands. He found the brightness cheering. So different here than in the SIB basement.

In some respects.

"You understand my problem, don't you, Sam?" Pimentel activated one of the analyzers. "Why I'm reluctant to discharge you?"

Sam twisted the end of his bathrobe sash around his fingers. "I understand why you believe you have a problem, Doctor. I do not, however, understand why you feel it must become mine."

Pimentel dragged a lab stool next to the scanbed and sat down. He closed his eyes and pinched the bridge of his nose. "Sam, it's gone beyond simply taking on other people's pasts and calling them your own. You've been caught in a direct lie about your work. You'd never lied about your work before. Your condition is deteriorating."

"Your opinion."

"My *medical* opinion, Sam. It's worth a lot." He leaned forward, his hands splayed across his knees. Narrow hands, for a man. Thin fingers. "I've spoken with your immediate supervisor, as well as his supervisor. They told me what happened the other night. They told me about finding two drawers' full of missing documents in your desk."

"I did not put them there."

"You checked out those documents. Your name is on the sign-out."

"Be that as it may. I did not hide them."

"Sam, according to Lieutenant Yance, no one else has access to those particular papers." Pimentel stood. He wore summerweights, although as usual he had left his rank designators in his desk drawer. "You were put in charge of everything connected with Rauta Shèràa Base because you possessed a reputation beyond reproach and organizational abilities Yance called second to none." He paced in front of the bed, his hands inscribing strokes and circles in the air, a conductor without his baton. "You were able to surmise a series of events from just a few documents. You knew where the holes were, where people needed to look to fill them. You figured out paper protocols the idomeni hadn't used since the Laumrau fell from power. 'Almost as if he'd worked there himself,' was how Yance put it."

Sam nodded. "I understand research."

Pimentel stopped in front of him. "Yes, you spent years building your reputation. Refining your expertise." He braced one narrow-fingered hand on the edge of the bed. "Every day you delay the removal of the tumor increases the chances that you could suffer permanent brain damage, and with that, permanent damage to your expertise. Even with the knowledge base we have, some things can't be fixed." He leaned close. "Sam, please let me schedule you for surgery."

Sam edged away from Pimentel. His view of the door was blocked by the way the doctor had positioned himself. If he tried to slide off the bed, Pimentel only had to move a little to his right to stop him. He didn't like that. He hated the sensation of feeling trapped. He hated the sight of Pimentel's spindly hands. "No."

"Sam—!"

"No, Doctor! That's my decision, and unless you hold me prisoner here, there's nothing you can do about it!" He slid off the bed and darted around Pimentel until he stood in a direct line with the door. "I will be leaving this place as soon as I change my clothes."

"*Sam.*" Pimentel struck the scanbed with his fist. Once. Twice. "I assume you've given no thought to what we spoke of the other day."

"No."

"I can't stand by and watch a man destroy himself. If you persist on this course, I will initiate the paperwork necessary to have you declared a ward of the Commonwealth."

"You can try, Doctor." Sam bolted from the room, almost colliding with an orderly pushing a skimcart laden with equipment. He mumbled an apology and scurried down the hall, the ends of his sash bouncing off his knees like clappers in a silent bell.

No doctors inside my head, ever again. He'd die if he let them in. He knew it.

He weaved up and down halls, ignoring the signs, using doors and nurses' stations and inset lights as his guides. Things that couldn't be moved, couldn't be changed. *There's nothing wrong with my memory.* Not for the things that mattered. Escape. Freedom. Keeping the doctors out of his head.

Sam turned the corner onto the hallway that led to his room and collided with a uniformed man walking in the opposite direction. Dress blue-greys, unusual for that area of the base. Sam looked up into the man's face and stifled a cry. *Scar.* From his nose to his mouth. It drew the eye like any accident. Sam barely kept from blurting out that he was in the right place to get it fixed.

The man brought his hands up to chest level, palms toward Sam, as though to grab him. But in the same motion, he backed off a step. The hands dropped. "My apologies." He smiled—not the most pleasant sight. "I came by to pick up some test results, but I can't find the lab drop."

"Scan or wet analysis?"

"Scan."

"Two halls to the right. Middle door. Blue." Sam's gaze flicked over the man's badges and designators. Any more, and he'd have looked ridiculous; any fewer, and he'd have looked like everybody else. Then Sam looked at the name tag. "Colonel Pierce."

"Yes." The man looked over the top of Sam's head, toward the distant goal of the ScanLab.

"I've seen you before." Sam nodded in recognition. "On ServNet broadcasts. You accompany the Admiral-General to meetings." He rattled off the particulars as though the man's ServRec lay open on a desk in front of him. "Pierce. Niall. One I, two Ls. C-number M-five-six-dash-three-three-dash-one-one-one-S. You were a sergeant, assigned to the CSS *Kensington.* You led A Squad, Platoon Four-oh-nine-eight, during the evacuation of Rauta Shèràa Base, during the Night of the Blade."

Pierce lowered his gaze slowly, his scar smoothing as his smile died. As each detail found voice, he grew more and more still, until Sam thought he had turned to stone. "You have the advantage of me, sir," he said, so quietly not even his scar moved.

"Yes," Sam said, "I do." He sidestepped Pierce and broke into a trot, darting into his room and pushing the door closed. He pressed his ear to the panel, straining for any sound. He didn't trust doctors, no, but he trusted colonels even less. He couldn't remember why, although he knew there had to be a reason. Sufficient for now that he simply knew, that the instinct that helped him hack his trails through paper would see him clear to the door with regard to doctors who wanted to take away his freedom and colonels who wanted to know his name.

He tossed the robe in a corner, followed by the pajamas. Pulled his clothes from the tiny armoire and dressed as though the room were on fire.

Ward of the Commonwealth. Sam cracked the door open, eased his head out, checked the hallway for colonels and doctors. Then he dashed out of the room and down the hall in the direction opposite the way he had come, not stopping until he found a doc tech office.

"Excuse me." He stepped just inside the doorway and waited for one of the techs to attend him. "I can make changes to the personal data in my file here, can't I?"

"Yes, sir." A young woman approached him, smiling. Younger even than Tory, and no one was younger than Tory. "What changes do you need to make?"

"Next of kin."

The tech scanned his patient bracelet with her handheld, then waited for his file to open. "Name, please?" she asked, her stylus tip poised above the device input.

"Jani. Kilian. She is a captain, on this base."

"Could you define the relationship, please, sir?"

"Friend." His only friend—this he believed with all his heart. *She believed me.* She had looked him in the eye and told him so, when everyone else preferred to trust in the lies. *She'll take care of me.* He couldn't pinpoint why he felt so sure, but he did. He knew he could trust her. He just knew.

CHAPTER 11

Evan burrowed into the plush rear seat of the Neoclona double-length and watched with a mixture of excitement and dread as the Chicago skyline filled the windscreen. Months had passed since he'd last seen the city.

My arraignment. He had stood before the Ministers' Bench of Cabinet Court and watched men and women he'd grown up with look upon him as a stranger as they exiled him to his rose-infested Elba. *All except Anais.* Her scrawny face had been aglow with gloat. Evan treasured that memory, sick though it seemed. At least she'd considered him an enemy vanquished, rather than an embarrassment to hide away.

Since then, but for his sojourns to Sheridan, he'd remained rooted to his suburban patch. His jailers met his medical needs with biweekly visits from the local Neoclona annex, and had shunted aside his other needs as unworthy of their attention.

But what John wants, John gets. Joaquin suspected nothing. He'd even waxed enthusiastic about Shroud's sudden interest in Evan's health and dismissed his client's protests that the good doctor's real interest revolved around Jani Kilian. *John's a good Family man,* he'd said. *He didn't get where he is today by acting like an obsessed fool.*

"Quino, I'm afraid that's exactly how he got where he is today." Evan ignored the driver's questioning stare in the rearview, and soaked in the city views with the rapt attention of a condemned man watching from his tumbrel.

The driver maneuvered down traffic-jammed State Street. "We're early, sir," he said as he weaved around a triple-parked people-mover. "I can drive around the block, if you wish."

Evan held out his hands, palms facing down. No trembling. The half liter he'd downed for breakfast had seen to that. "Go on in. I'm ready."

Finding Val Parini waiting for him by the VIP-lift bank didn't surprise him. Shroud was the master, Parini the dog. *And I'm the stick of the day.*

"Hello, Ev." Parini looked ill—ashen skin, bleary eyes. His trousers and short-sleeved pullover were rumpled, as though he'd slept in them.

"Val." Evan congratulated himself that his own black trousers and black-and-blue-striped pullover looked much sharper. *The last thing I need is that bleached bastard thinking I don't give a damn.* He followed Parini into the lift, and swallowed hard as the car shot upward and he felt his feet press against the floor.

"How've you been?" Parini stuffed his hands in his pockets and leaned against the wall. "Considering."

"All right. Considering." Evan forced a smile. "Tired."

Parini stared up at the ceiling. "Yeah, I know the feeling. I just got in from Felix. Six-week round-trip, not counting the couple of days in between to catch my breath." He yawned. "I'm getting too old for that stuff."

Evan nodded politely. "Business?"

"Special patient. Someone you know."

"Our social circles overlapped, Val. Care to narrow it down?"

"Jani Kilian," Parini said, contemplating the light fixture. "You remember her. Tawny damsel. Had a little accident a few years back."

Evan flinched as the car decelerated. At least the lift mechanism's hissing whine drowned out the roaring in his head. "You saw her?"

"Yes. She slipped out from under, though, as she is wont to do. Unfortunately, she walked right into a Service trap.

She's at Sheridan now." A corner of Parini's mouth curved. He knew surprise when he smelled it, the son of a bitch. "Didn't Quino tell you?" He tsked. "Bad Quino. She's been there almost a week." The lift slowed to a stop and the door opened.

Evan lagged behind Parini, eyes locked on the back of his neck. *Just one good shot*—Ridgeway's crumpled body flashed in his mind, and the urge evaporated. "There was nothing on the 'Vee or in the sheets."

"Yeah, I don't know how the hell they managed to keep it quiet." Parini led him down a wide corridor. One side was glass-walled—glimpses of the Commerce Ministry compound and the lake beyond could be seen between the highrises. They stopped in front of an unmarked door enameled with a purple so dark Evan at first mistook it for black. Parini palmed it open.

Evan expected to enter an examining room—matte white surfaces, analyzers and viewscreens, a scanbed in the corner. Instead, he walked into an opulent sitting room—eggplant-colored walls, bloodwood bookcases and tables, Persian carpets.

A panel slid aside and Shroud stepped into the room. The feverish glisten in his eyes spoke of freshly applied filming. Violet, this time, a perfect match to his daysuit jacket. "You're early."

"Sorry, John," replied Parini, not sounding sorry at all. "Guess what? Loiaza didn't tell Evan that Jani's at Sheridan."

Evan glanced around nervously. A large holoVee display dominated one corner, a pillow-strewn daybed, another. *No way in hell I'm letting these two creeps examine me in here.* "I'm sure Quino had his reasons."

Shroud gestured for Evan to sit. "He must be realizing that taking you on as a client wasn't the wisest career move he ever made. I sense damage control in progress. You need allies." His rumbling voice grew measured. *"Quid pro quo,* as we discussed before."

Evan looked at Shroud, who regarded him with relaxed contempt, then at Parini, whose distaste held an edge. *Master told dog I'll help them.* He sank into a cushioned lounge chair and immediately reached for the bourbon decanter that rested on the nearby low table. "I've known Quino for over thirty years. He doesn't leave clients to twist in the wind." He poured a shot, tossed it back. Of course Joaquin had a reasonable explanation for not telling him about Jani. Which Evan would be damned interested in hearing as soon as he returned to Elba.

Parini flopped into a chair opposite Evan. "Jani's not in the news, either. ServNet's no surprise—they do what Roshi Mako tells them to do, and he doesn't think Service issues are the public's business. But I talked with Dory in Commonwealth Affairs, and she said CapNet must have agreed to self-censor. She said that they only do that when they get pressure from the PM."

Shroud joined them. The chair he chose was less padded and straight-backed. You could have used his spine to draw a plumb line. "Jani's news on ChanNet because she's from La Manche. She's news on FelNet because she was captured there under circumstances embarrassing to the Service and Felix is looking for an excuse to renegotiate the lease for Fort Constanza. No one's made a fuss over her in Chicago because she's not news in Chicago."

"You're wrong, John. There's a sizable Acadian population here in the French Quarter who would love to know what's going on." Parini ignored the beverage service and instead plucked at a bunch of grapes, popping them into his mouth with ballistic force. "I bet Nema has something to do with it. He's been twisting arms all over town. He'd start a shooting war on the Boul Mich if he thought it would free his Eyes and Ears."

"Nema doesn't exert any control over Earth-based broadcasting."

"Just because you hate him doesn't mean he has no influence, John!"

Evan listened to the two men bicker with the uneasiness of someone who found himself the captive audience to a marital spat. He looked from the animated Parini to the over-controlled Shroud, and the question that had been the subject of dinner-party debate for twenty years parked itself inside his head and refused to leave.

Do those two . . . fuck? Both sides offered cogent arguments, Parini's many boyfriends and Shroud's revolving-door women notwithstanding.

Evan refilled his glass as his well-calibrated people-filter chugged in the background. *No, not lovers.* He still felt his master and dog theory explained the relationship. *And sometimes dog refuses to stop barking and master has to go to the window to see what the fuss is about.*

Shroud picked up a nicstick dispenser from the table and turned the rectangular case end over end. His spindly fingers invited the image of spiders tumbling a victim in a web. "Why would Li and Roshi want to keep Jani's story quiet?"

"I can tell you the reason they gave," Evan offered. But first, he sipped. Shroud had him by the short hairs, true, but he also stocked the finest bourbon. "Commonwealth security. CapNet will sit on news if they're told releasing it could threaten internal stability." He'd exercised that option many times when Lyssa still lived, as her behavior grew more uncontrollable and her public displays more embarrassing.

Shroud snorted. "What could Jani do to threaten Commonwealth stability!"

The three of them looked at one another. For one brief moment, their thoughts coalesced. Only Parini felt it appropriate to smile.

Shroud coughed. "Let me rephrase that. What happened to her on Felix that could threaten Commonwealth stability?"

"John, she almost died!" Parini looked at Evan. "Those Service morons injected her with Tacit, an experimental sedative. It knocked her liver for a loop."

Shroud struck the nicstick case against his thigh. "Tacit is safe." The rattle of the plastic sticks against metal punctuated every word. "Instances of hepatotoxicity have never been recorded."

"For *humans*, John. It hasn't been tested on idomeni—"

Evan shut out the men's argument and considered his own uncomfortable thoughts. *I asked Joaquin about illegal arrests of colonials and he brushed me off.* The man had offices on Felix—the staff would have Misty'd him immediately if rumors of Jani had surfaced.

My own attorney's holding out on me? Why?

"Evan?"

He looked up to find Shroud glaring at him.

"Let me repeat the question. In your opinion, is Jani's case important enough to cause a furor?"

Evan nodded. "You said it yourself, John. The colonies are flexing their muscles, and the idomeni, especially Nema, are jumping feetfirst into the fray." He should have worked it out himself, but living in exile, he couldn't access the catalyzing snippets of information that had once fueled his life. "Li faces reelection next year. I'm betting that right now she wishes Jani had never been found."

Shroud scowled. He had the moody, tightly wrapped look of a blanched El Greco. "What about Roshi?"

"He's in a more difficult position. His proud New Service is over two-thirds colonial. If he prosecutes Jani, he risks a breach that may never heal at a time when a mixed-bag force may be called upon to quell colonial unrest. But on the other hand, it's not in his best interest to seem soft on mutiny and murder." Evan tried to put himself in Mako's shoes—problem was, he didn't know the man well enough. How far would he go to preserve what he had worked so hard to build? "He could be planning a quiet trial and execution." That would explain Roshi's presence at the SIB. The born field officer, checking personally on the progress of his investigative branch's most sensitive case in decades.

Shroud's voice droned funereal. "There's no such thing as a quiet execution." He reached for the beverage tray—to Evan's surprise, he chose bourbon, too. "Well, Val, what do your sources tell you about the mood on Sheridan? Is Jani's presence rallying the colonials?" He poured three fingers, added a single ice cube, and threw back a healthy swallow.

Evan checked his timepiece. Only midmorning. *Not a good sign, Johnny—don't tell me I've found a drinking buddy.*

"I'll admit, it's pretty quiet." Val slung his leg over the chair arm and flicked grapes into the empty vase in the center of the table. In between tosses, he shot anxious glances at the door. "Considering that Service Diplomatic has been pulled in to help settle that idomeni food fiasco, I wouldn't be surprised if they dragged Jani in as well." He shrugged at the surprised looks that greeted the statement. "That's what she used to do on Shèrá. She has more head-to-head experience with the idomeni than anyone else at Sheridan."

Shroud's jaw dropped. "They wouldn't."

"They would if they're desperate." Evan could hear the disbelief in his voice when he, of all people, should have known better. "I've sat across the negotiating table from idomeni. After a couple of hours, you've forgotten your name, much less what you're there for. If you meet them on their turf, you have to contend with the heat and the paralyzing sensation that every move you make is the wrong one. If they meet you on yours, you have to sanitize rooms, knock out walls, and relocate all the vend alcoves." And if the Service needed Jani now, they sure as hell didn't need him to give evidence against her. God, he must have been braindead—why didn't he think of it before?

The door opened, and a man entered. Mid-thirties. Tall, thin, and mopey. The type Lyssa would have dubbed *homeless puppy.*

"Sorry I'm late." He wore medwhites; his dark hair covered his ears and fell to his collar. He displayed the all-knees-and-elbows gangliness of a twelve-year-old as he lowered into the chair next to Evan.

Parini, Evan noticed, watched the man's every move with a look of eager expectancy. *This is his new toy?* Quite a change of pace from old Val's usual pretty boys.

Shroud looked aggravated. "So happy you could finally join us, Doctor." He refilled his glass, this time adding ice. "Evan, this is Hugh Tellinn. He's an old friend of Val's, from our Felix Majora facility."

To Evan's surprise, Tellinn held out his hand. If he knew his ex–Interior Minister's recent history, it didn't show in his face or his attitude. "Endocrinology," he said, as though that explained everything.

"That's Hugh's way of saying, 'hello'," Parini said with an uncertain smile.

Tellinn looked at the floor rather than his boyfriend. "I've been studying the results of the tests Val performed on Jani Kilian." He braced his feet on the edge of the table. "Has anyone bothered to bring you up to speed on the state of her health, Mr. van Reuter?"

Parini held up a hand. "Hugh—"

Tellinn ignored him. "I thought that's why we were here. I thought that's why you're suborning perjury, because of your fears for Jani's health."

Shroud tilted his glass back and forth; the clink of ice echoed. "My fears for Jani's health consume my every waking moment, Doctor."

"She's very ill."

"Is she?"

"I believe she suffers from multiple metabolic and endocrine disorders, the most serious of which is a type of acute intermittent porphyria."

"Really, Doctor?"

"Really." Tellinn either didn't see Parini's increasingly frantic gesturing, or once more chose to disregard it. He looked at Evan. "Porphyrias are genetic diseases. Miscues at various points along the heme biosynthetic pathway. Jani wasn't born with the condition, according to the Service scans in her patient file. Therefore, she must have had it thrust upon her during a period when she was undergoing tissue rebuilding, rebuilding performed by someone who didn't know as much as he thought he did about the idomeni genome." He looked down the table at Shroud. "First, do no harm."

Parini's hand stopped in mid-slash.

Evan watched Tellinn. What had first seemed like clumsiness now revealed itself as an overwhelming effort to retain self-control. The man clenched his armrests. His whole body seemed to vibrate with deep-seated rage. *He wants to pound Shroud into the carpet.* Suddenly, he looked capable. The pup had wolf blood. "Well, well, John. Hugh's saying that when you reassembled Jani, you gave her a life-threatening disease."

Shroud ignored him. His stare never left Tellinn. "In your opinion, Doctor."

Tellinn's glower remained just as steady. "I believe the facts speak for themselves. Dickerson and Yevgeny have published a series of papers in *JCMA* describing an illness affecting members of a Haárin enclave on Philippa that is analogous to acute intermittent porphyria. The genetic mutations involved do not match those for the human AIP variant, and the idomeni ban on exchange of medical information has made it impossible for us to pinpoint them." His voice leveled as his eyes deadened. "Therefore, while Service Medical may have an idea what's wrong with Jani, they're unable to nail the diagnosis and therefore the definitive genetic retrofit. Which means they're falling back on heme infusions and dietary controls until they design methods to identify and fix her particular mutation."

Parini jumped in. "I'm also very concerned with the quality of the medical care Jani's receiving—"

Tellinn's blank look silenced him. "On the contrary, I have always found the Service Medical staff I dealt with at Fort Constanza to be very sound. What *I* fear is that Jani's ongoing hybridization has led to the development of so many anomalous metabolic disorders that the diet and drug therapies Service Medical has put her on could lead to serious adverse reactions."

Shroud started to speak, then stopped. His gaze flicked from one face to another, gauging mood without daring to look too deeply. Then he dug down and excavated a fragment of the old John. "In your opinion, Doctor," he said, his voice like a tomb.

Evan understood Shroud's reluctance. He'd felt it himself these past months. *Will you please tell the court what you knew and when you knew it?* And Shroud knew, damned right he did. He knew that Jani's hybridization had led to problems, and that Service Medical wouldn't know how to treat her. *And you've alienated them to the point that they won't ask for your help or let you anywhere near her.* Enter Evan, stage right.

Tellinn graced his agitated lover with a bare glance. "That's why Val persuaded me to accompany him to Chicago, because my opinion counted."

"I wouldn't overestimate your value to this enterprise," Shroud replied. "It wouldn't be the first time Val thought with his prick."

Parini's face flared red. "You should bloody talk!"

Tellinn showed no reaction to either Shroud's insult or the breaking storm. He stood up and turned to Evan. "When is your next visit to Sheridan scheduled, Mr. van Reuter?"

Evan could feel Shroud's glare brand the side of his face. "Early next week."

"Well, perjure yourself as you never did before. Jani won't live out the month if you don't." Tellinn nodded to him, then shambled out of the room.

Parini struggled to his feet. "Damn it, John!" He tripped over the edge of a rug but bulled onward, rubbing his knee and cursing as he stumbled out the door. "*Hugh! Wait!*"

Shroud watched the hot pursuit with a disgusted grimace. "Poor Val. He certainly can pick them."

Evan listened as Val's shout rang down the hall. "Jani's survival instinct is knife-edged—she knew the Service was looking for her. She knew her medical problems were so distinctive, she'd attract immediate attention. Yet she still braved a visit to Neoclona-Felix." He remembered the last time he saw her, just before Justice arrived to arrest him— her lips tinged blue from lack of oxygen, her breathing a rattle he could hear through his haze of pain. "She must have felt like hell."

"I'd worry about myself, if I were you." Shroud stared into the dregs of his glass. "Now repeat after me, I do not remember . . . I do not recall . . ."

After a final warning from Shroud on the benefits of acquiring alcoholism-induced amnesia, an actual condition with the name of Korsakoff's syndrome, Evan was passed off to a series of staff physicians. They lectured him on diet, scanned his brain, and scoped his knee. No one gave any indication that they cared who he was or who he had been. Oh, how the mighty had fallen.

His rage mounted as he descended to the parking garage, entered Shroud's loaned skimmer, fast-floated through the Chicago streets. By the time the driver deposited him in the front yard of Elba and reset his security bracelet, his hands shook and his head pounded. Markhart showed her good sense by remaining silent when she met him at the door. Halvor showed even greater sense by staying out of sight entirely.

Joaquin's secretary put him on standby. By the time the attorney's sere image formed on the comport display, Evan had to grip the edge of his desk to keep from punching his fists through it. *"Why the hell didn't you tell me Jani was at Sheridan!"*

Joaquin blinked slowly. "You heard that from Parini, I'm sure. The man's a shameless gossip. Why Shroud tolerates him, I'll never know." He pressed a hand to his forehead. "Evan, I only learned myself the day before yesterday."

"So why didn't you *tell* me the day before—"

"Because I knew you'd do just what you're doing now— work yourself into needless panic." He paused to sip from a cup. Tea, most likely. Earl Grey, flavored with plenty of personality-enhancing lemon. "She was seen being pushed through the O'Hare Service concourse in a skimchair. Immediately upon arrival at Sheridan, she was admitted to the Psychotherapeutics Ward. I understand she has since been released, but is under constant medical monitoring."

Evan's fingers cramped. He eased his grip on the desk and sat down. "They've got her working with the idomeni, don't they?"

"She is on restricted duty, yes." Joaquin riffled through a folder. "In the Foreign Transactions department."

"Her old department at Rauta Shèràa Base." Evan opened the bottom desk drawer and pulled out a half-empty bottle. "Shit."

"Evan, calm down. She hasn't been deposed yet, but she

will be. We can't control what she'll say, but we will be able to counter. Is that clear?"

That's what you think. "Yes, Quino." He cracked the bottle seal and took a healthy swig.

"Good." Joaquin closed the folder and pushed it aside. "So, how did your examination go?"

Shroud grabbed me by the balls and squeezed. "Fine."

"Good, good." Joaquin stilled, then reached for another file. "By the way, why did you ask me to check into Niall Pierce's background?"

Pierce? The visit to Neoclona had rattled Evan so much, everything else had slipped his mind. *Oh, Scarface.* He shrugged. "I don't know." Finding the man's Achilles' heel didn't seem important anymore.

"Well, you always did have a nose for the nasty." Joaquin sniffed. "He's a Victorian. Orphaned at age four. Ward of the Commonwealth. Entered the Service twenty-three years ago under the Social Reclamation Act, a nice way of saying join up or go to prison. Numerous disciplinary actions against him—a wonder he wasn't booted out." His eyebrows arched. "As a last resort, he was transferred to the Fourth Expeditionary Battalion. After that, he seems to have grown up, and the nasty ends."

"Fourth Expeditionary?" Evan perked up. "They're the ones who got us out of Rauta Shèràa."

"Yes, the Fourth was Roshi's old crew, wasn't it?" Joaquin continued reading. "Roshi's good with the hard cases. Pierce thrived. Promotion through the enlisted ranks followed. To top it off, his actions during the Rauta Shèràa evac earned him a battlefield commission." He glanced up over the top of the file. "Was it that bad?"

Evan took another swallow before answering. "Yes."

"We should make more use of it." Joaquin read on, his brow wrinkling. "Pierce has actually become something of a scholar in his spare time. Master of Literature from Chicago Combined. Published a well-regarded essay on *Macbeth*— who would have thought? For the past few months, he's been a regular visitor to the PT Ward. He's augmented, of course—most combat Spacers were back then. Some of them go on to develop augment depression—he's apparently one of the unlucky."

Past few months—define few! Evan had always hated it when aides became vague about time—it always meant they hadn't done their homework. "Can you be more specific as to the date?"

Joaquin looked up with a start. "Early this year. Right after your arrest, as a matter of fact." He pulled a disc out of the file. "Here, why don't I just transfer this to you. I'll code it as legal communication so no one can monitor it. If you think you recall meeting him during the evac, let me know." He inserted the disc into his comport. "Now, if you're sufficiently becalmed, perhaps you'll let me get back to work." It wasn't like Joaquin to request permission, and this time proved no exception. His image sharded, leaving Evan to stare at the blue standby screen.

He waited for the data transfer to complete, then called up Pierce's file on his comport display. Joaquin had covered the high points, but the details revealed the more complex picture of a self-destructive young man undergoing a complete transformation under the firm guidance of the only father figure he had ever known. "Boy, Niall, you'd fall on a sword for Roshi, wouldn't you?" If every great man had his dog, Mako had bred an attack animal in Pierce.

Evan rested his head against the chairback and let his mind wander. *I get arrested.* Directly afterward, the son the A-G never had starts cracking up. "But Roshi doesn't let him down. He keeps him by his side to play escort and take notes on diarrhea-inducing herbs." However much Pierce esteemed Mako, the feeling seemed mutual.

"What else happened after my arrest?" Well, relations with the idomeni became more interesting. Nema started talking GateWay rights and trade routes as soon as the fact that Jani Kilian lived became widely known.

"Jani's alive—Pierce goes downhill." Evan pondered, then shook his head. "Coincidence." He stared into space for a time. Then he scrabbled through his desk for a recording board and stylus and reread Pierce's file, making notes along the way.

CHAPTER 12

It might have been a dream. Could have been a dream.

Jani rode a waveglider. But she had no arms to steer the board, and skimmed out farther and farther on the lake. The shoreline disappeared from view. Skies darkened. Wind howled. The waves grew higher and higher, breaking over her again and again before finally flipping the glider like a vend token. She tumbled through the air. Into the water. The cold wet closed over her, pulled her down. She could see nothing in the frigid blackness, but she could hear.

Voices.

No.

One voice.

Neumann's.

Welcome to my home base, Kilian.

Deeper. Darker. Colder.

I've been waiting for you.

Pain. In her stomach. She pressed the side of her body against the floor, and tried to drive it out with cold.

"Jani!"

She curled in a ball.

"Somebody call an ambulance!"

Tighter. Tighter. If she made herself small enough, she could sink between the tiles, disappear into the floor, and leave the pain behind. It wouldn't fit. It was too big.

"Hurry up! She's in here!"

Pimentel glowered at the cartridge tester. "You're the gate-keeper, Jani. You're the one who controls what you eat. Your scanner doesn't come equipped with little hands to clamp over your mouth." He looked at her over the top of his mag-nispecs. He wore summerweights rather than his usual med-whites; his shirt was rumpled, and his hair needed a trim. Some A&S-hole would make his or her quota and then some the next time he stepped outside.

Jani sniffed the air, then continued to breathe through her mouth. According to Pimentel, Lucien had stopped by her room to take her to breakfast. When she didn't answer the buzzer, he had broken in and found her semiconscious on her bathroom floor. She had come to in Triage. Taken a deep breath. Passed out again when the smell from the next alcove hit her. There, a burn team attended to a firing-range acci-dent. The young woman's shooter had backflashed; the half-formed pulse packet had burnt through her summerweights and seared her right side from shoulder to knee.

"Please don't admit me," Jani whispered. Even though she now sat in an examining room on the opposite end of the building, she swore she could detect the odor of burnt flesh in the air. Burnt, like Borgie and the others. Burnt as she had been, too, but she had survived. "I don't want to stay here."

Pimentel removed the magnispecs. "Jani, you are in no condition to leave. Acute intermittent porphyria can affect the autonomic nervous system. Part of that system controls the adrenal glands, which, along with your thyroid, are the sites of your secondary augmentation. While you were in Triage, you started talking to someone who wasn't there. I'm concerned that stimulation of your adrenals is aggravating your primary insert, and you don't need the threat of augie psychosis on top of everything else." He held out the re-cording board and stared at it. "I'm going to schedule you for an augmentation imaging. Today. And you're staying here until that's done."

*   *   *

Jani sat on a skimchair in the imaging lounge and spooned another mouthful of fruit sludge from the overlarge container. Strawberry, supposedly. Judging from the texture, "straw" was a given, but she'd fight to the death the "berry" part.

The clip of footsteps in the hallway gave her an excuse to drop the spoon in the remains of the semifrozen glop. The door swept aside and Friesian bustled in; he slid to a stop when he spotted her.

"Pimentel called," he said as he took in the skimchair, her hospital-issue robe and pajamas. "Said—they found you—in your room." His voice was choppy, his face flushed. It was a healthy run from Defense Command. "What happened?"

"Didn't eat right. Got sick."

"*Jani.*" Sweat beaded his forehead and soaked his short-sleeve. He pulled a dispo from his trouser pocket and mopped his brow. "How do you feel now?"

"Fine."

" 'Fine,' she says." He sat down on the sofa next to her chair. "And we know what that's worth, don't we?"

Jani remained quiet and stirred the remains of the sludge.

Friesian shook his head. "Pimentel thinks one of the reasons you suffered this episode is because you're under a great deal of stress. I told him I had a piece of news I thought might reduce that stress substantially. When he heard what it was, he suggested I share it with you." He sat back, arms at his sides. He looked as exhausted as Jani felt. "I received a call early this morning from a Colonel Bryant, a member of the prosecution. We had a very interesting talk. I'm expecting an offer to work out a deal anytime now."

Jani kept poking at the sludge. "No trial?"

"Just a hearing."

"How do you know they're not just pulling your leg?" She set the container on her chairside table and wiped her condensation-wetted fingers on her robe.

Friesian tugged at his damp short-sleeve. "I've been at this game a while. I know when someone's playing with me and I know when they're scrambling. This is a scramble like nothing I've ever seen. They want you settled and out of here."

Jani sat back. As she shifted, the skimchair rocked. The motion sickened her—she had to swallow hard before speaking. "Makes you wonder what's the rush, doesn't it?"

Friesian flexed his neck forward, back, then side to side. His cervical vertebrae cracked like knuckles. "*No*, it doesn't. My job is not to run after the prosecution and ask them why they're not going after you harder. My job is to get you out from under with as little penalty as possible. *And* to keep you from shooting yourself in the foot, which from the notations in your record appears to have bordered on a second calling!"

After a flare of anger that set her stomach to clenching, Jani decided not to argue. She felt too sick. Besides, truth was truth. "So what would I be looking at?" She leaned forward. Her lower back balked, and she braced her elbows on her knees for support. "A plea bargain?"

Friesian glanced at her, then looked away. "Not quite. More an arrangement that would see justice served, while taking your condition into account."

"My condition?"

"Your emotional and physical health, both now and at the time of the infraction."

Infraction? That made it sound so . . . A&S. Jani sat up carefully. "Go on."

Friesian hesitated at the tone in her voice. "This arrangement would be worked out by a panel of experts. In your case, the panel would consist of an adjudicating committee, your attending and consulting physicians, a prosecutor from the JA, and me."

"Who sits on the adjudicating committee?"

"A judge and two members of Service Medical unaffiliated with your case."

"No trial?"

"What would be the point? We would admit you did what you were charged with. Your physicians would explain why you did what you did. The prosecution would delineate the consequences of your actions. Then, it's up to the committee to decide a fair punishment, while at the same time protecting you."

Why do I have a feeling what I need protecting from is the committee? "And you expect what?"

"A general medical discharge. A verdict that while you may have been somewhat aware of what you were doing when you missed being evac'd from Rauta Shèràa, your physical and emotional states contributed to your disregard of the consequences."

"How can you define my physical and emotional states when no one will believe me when I tell them what happened?"

"Jani, we need to make a determination according to what we *know* happened. What we have paper on. The effects of the experimental treatments you received from John Shroud. Your guilt over the deaths of your comrades in the transport crash. Your inability to prevent the deaths of the patients at Knevçet Shèràa."

Jani rested her hands on her stomach. The nausea had eased, but the fruit sludge settled like a weight, heavy enough to push her through the chair. "What does a general medical entail these days?"

Friesian's shoulders slumped. It was as if he'd braced for a fight, then realized there wouldn't be one. "It entitles you to a partial pension. You'd give up the right to sign yourself as *Captain, Retired.* No access to ship-stores discounts or emergency travel on Service vessels. But you'd still retain rights to medical care, which in your case, I believe, is the most important consideration."

"Jail?"

"Sentence would be limited to time served."

"Which was?"

"Your incarceration at Fort Constanza."

"One week in the brig infirmary?" She searched Friesian's face for some sign of wonderment or confusion, any indication that he felt mystified. She certainly did. "You really believe they will offer me this deal?"

"Bryant indicated it could be finalized within a week."

"And that I should take it?"

"I would recommend you do, without hesitation."

"Just walk away?" She watched Friesian nod.

The realization settled over her gradually, like the slow-motion buckling and flattening of a sailchute after a landing. *They're letting me off the hook.* She licked her dry lips, swallowed. *I killed Rikart Neumann, and they don't care.*

I wonder why?

Jani felt a slight tingle, the mild frisson of the shock not completely unexpected. She used to feel it back at Rauta Shèràa Base, when she'd show up for an audit. The catch in a voice. The sidelong glance. The sense that things were going on that other people didn't want her to know about.

I'm being diddled. She sat back and clasped her hands over her still-sore stomach. It didn't do to get excited—a person could miss things if she let herself get carried away.

Eyes and Ears open—that was always the key.

Friesian rose, walked to the wall opposite, and thumbed through the tacked-up notices on a message board. "By the way, I received a packet in the interdepartmental mails from a Lieutenant Yance in SIB Archives. It contained missing portions of your ServRec. He noted in his cover memo that he had sent copies to you, as well. At your request." He walked back and stood in front of her. "What were you doing at the SIB?"

Jani grew conscious of a disquieting sensation. A flashback to her teen years, and her papa standing before her. Same stance as Friesian. Same probing glare. "Just looking around," she replied softly. A voice caught out past curfew.

"Just looking around?" Friesian rubbed his face. He suffered the curse of the dark-haired and pale—only midmorning, and he already looked like he needed a shave. "The next time you feel an overwhelming urge to stick your nose where it doesn't belong, call me."

"I have the right to find out what happened to my ServRec."

"No. You have the right to come to me, and say, 'I wonder what happened to my ServRec.' To which I would reply, 'Why do you believe it's applicable to your case?' And if I liked your answer, I would contract with a registered legal investigator and have them look into it, so that if something did turn up, it would have been uncovered properly and we will have had a chance to deal with it. Your case is still open, Jani, and that means the rules of discovery are in force. Everything we find, the prosecution gets to see and vice versa. That being the situation, it really isn't advisable to turn over every rock you find just to see what crawls out!" He covered his face with his hands. "Damn it! You're a documents examiner. You of all people should know better."

Jani folded her arms. The chair rocked some more, but it didn't upset her stomach as much. She felt stronger. "If it's the truth, why bury it?"

"So that we don't wind up uncovering a mess we can't deal with!"

"You mean you don't want to know what you don't know." Jani cocked her head to look him in the eye. "All those things you've heard about me. It's starting to occur to you that they might be true, isn't it?"

"Not related to this case. Therefore, not my concern." Friesian flexed his neck again and returned to his seat. "I don't think Pimentel would be very happy with me right now. That's the end of legal talk until you get out of here."

Jani picked up her fruit sludge and stirred the melted remains, just to have something to do with her hands. The repetitive motion helped her think. "Sometimes you walk around a big place like Sheridan, you keep seeing the same faces. Makes the place seem smaller somehow."

Friesian rocked his head back and forth in a "so-so" nod. "They probably live or work in this area of the base. Makes sense they'd crop up regularly."

"Hmm." Jani gave the spoon another turn. "There's this one guy who's popped up a few times. Full colonel. Nasty facial scar."

"Oh, him." Friesian frowned. "Niall Pierce. Special Services."

"What, is he famous or something?"

"No. He's just the A-G's right hand." The frown turned to a grimace of concern. "You haven't made yourself known to him in any way that I should know about, have you?"

"I don't know what you mean."

"No, of course you don't." Friesian clasped his hands and slowly twiddled his thumbs. "You remember what Spec Service is?"

"They're the hatchet team."

"No, they provide special assistance and advice to the commander on technical matters and other O-three situations."

"Out of the ordinary?"

"You remember that? That is reassuring."

"I remember lots of things." Jani grabbed a handful of pajama trouser and hoisted, right leg over left. "That's a pretty wide gulf between the A-G and a colonel in Spec Service. What's the deal with Mako and Pierce, they marry sisters or something?"

"Better than that." Friesian eyed her thoughtfully. "They served together on the CSS *Kensington*."

"Really? The *Kensington* flagshipped the evac of Rauta Shèràa's human enclave."

"Yes, it did. Mako was her captain. Sergeant Pierce played an integral role in the ground assault."

"*Sergeant* Pierce?"

Friesian nodded. "Yeah, that man earned himself a field commission. For that matter, all the members of the *Kensington* crew have done well over the years. Dr. General Carvalla was Medical Officer. General Gleick, the Sheridan base commander, was Mako's exec. Aliens, anarchy, hostile fire, a threat to the Commonwealth—that evac had it all. Even the hot water they got into after they returned to Earth added to the aura."

Jani uncrossed and recrossed her legs, worked her neck, did her best to seem only mildly interested. "Did they botch the evac?"

"No, nothing that serious. They mishandled some remains. Problem was that the remains belonged to Family members. Mako had to testify at a Board of Inquiry about what happened. He knew a witch-hunt when he saw one, and went on the offensive. Named names with regard to some of the garbage that went on at Rauta Shèràa. Rumor has it that those records will remain sealed for two hundred years." He looked at Jani, and stood.

"That's it. You look beat, and I don't want Pimentel coming after me with a bone cutter." He looked at her with kinder eyes, and smiled. "This is going to work out for you. You just need to get your strength back, listen to your doctor, and stay away from the SIB." The courtroom light flared. "Promise?"

Jani nodded. "Whose remains?"

Friesian sighed. "Oh, no one important. Just the members of Rauta Shèràa Base Command who died during the evac. You probably knew them—Ebben, Unser, and Fitzhugh."

What do you know—those three bastards didn't make it offworld alive. "Think they died accidentally or on purpose?"

"Not your problem. Do you promise?"

Jani nodded in the here and now as, meanwhile, a part of her returned home to Ville Acadie. Her father had meted out her punishment, and explained to her that it was for her own good. And that part of her sat on the couch, head hung low, and murmured agreement as she planned her next escapade. *Mais oui, Papa.* "Promise."

Pimentel fingered his workstation touchpad once. Twice. "The augmentation scan does show some low-level stimulation in the regions around your primary insert." He spun the desk display so Jani could see it. "See." He pointed at a multicolored blob that pulsed in the lower middle area of the translucent overlay of her brain. "We're seeing moderate hyperactivity in your thalamus and in the area of the insert nearest to your amygdala. Now, your tendency toward vivid dreaming is indicated by your elevated Dobriej values"—he tapped a row of numbers that scrolled along the top of the display—"and combining that with the excitation in your limbic system and diencephalon—"

"*Roger!*"

"Fight or flight and sensory areas," he said, switching to lay-speak without missing a beat. "Memory." He snatched a dispo out of a box on his desk and wiped a smudge from the surface of the display. "I don't think I'm telling you

things you don't already know. You're one of those augments who tends to hallucinate under stress. The porphyria
may be aggravating this tendency. The usual monitoring we
perform may need to be stepped up in your case." He shredded a corner of the dispo.

Jani thought back to Pierce's post-takedown expression.
The bewilderment. The desolation. *Is that what you're offering me, Roger?* "What do you recommend?"

Pimentel shrugged. "Well, my first suggestion is always
to remove the augmentation. Your records show you were a
borderline case. We have ample justification." He rested his
elbow on his desk and tapped a finger along his jaw. "Of
course, even the most challenged augment is reluctant to give
up the benefits. I don't believe I need to explain those to
you."

"No." Augie had saved Jani's life too many times for her
to give him up now. *Like most men, you're trouble, but I
still think I'll keep you.* "Next option."

"Hmm." Pimentel's jaw-tapping slowed. "We'd be entering to experimental areas."

"Roger, my entire adult medical history has been an experimental area."

Pimentel gave a snort of laughter. "Quite." The tapping
stopped. "I'd like to try to take you back."

"Take me back where?"

"To what you were before Shroud got his hands on you.
I've been consulting with some researchers in our Gene
Therapeutics lab. To say they're itching to get their hands
on you doesn't do their enthusiasm justice." He smiled like
he had a present for her hidden in his pocket. "I'd like to try
to make you human again. One hundred percent."

Jani pulled her robe closer around her and looked past
Pimentel to the sunlit scene outside his window. She longed
to sit in the dry heat and let it bake her to the bone. *Always
cold . . . always sick.* And what if she developed a bacterial
infection and the bug did things to her that it wouldn't do to
someone normal? Someone human?

I'm one of a kind. And a damned lonely one, at that.

Nema will be devastated. But then, he wasn't the one passing out on the bathroom floor, was he?

She wouldn't have even considered the option if Friesian hadn't told her about the deal. Odd feeling, having a future to worry about again.

What do you want to be when you grow up, Jani Moragh? To be left alone. And the best way to guarantee that was to be like everyone else. "I think I'd like to give it a try." She shoved her hands into her sleeves to try to warm them.

"It won't be pleasant."

"I'm used to that."

"I know." Pimentel tapped an entry into his workstation. "Like I said, I'd be turning you over to the Gene Therapeutics group. I wouldn't even think of treating you myself. I know my limitations, unlike some." He eyed her sharply. "I'd like to wait until you get this legal mess behind you. Piers feels it may be wrapped up in a week or two. I'll set up the first appointment for you for month's end."

"Fine." Jani tried to scoot out of the visitor's chair, a task made more difficult since she didn't want to remove her chilled hands from her sleeves. "Can I leave?"

"Hang around for another hour and make an appointment to come in tomorrow for a follow-up. Then you can go." Pimentel raised his hand. "There is one more very small thing. Sam Duong."

Jani sat back. "That man from the SIB. The archivist."

"Yes." Pimentel's shoulders sagged as his bright mood evaporated. "How well do you know him?"

"I don't, really. I'd never met him before two days ago."

"Never met him before." Pimentel picked up his recording board and entered a notation. "The reason I ask is, he has no relatives. Up until this morning, he had no friends, either. None he'd admit to, anyway." He massaged the back of his neck. Talking about Sam Duong seemed to tighten him up. "He authorized a change to his MedRec a few short hours ago. He named you as his next of kin."

"*What?*" Jani slumped in her chair—the ergoworks whined in their effort to keep up. "Did he say why?"

"I was hoping you could tell me."

"I was there when he fainted. His supervisors were pulling missing documents out of his desk and he was yelling that he hadn't put them there. . . ." *Oh.* "And I told him I believed him."

Pimentel knocked the back of his head against the headrest of his chair. "Jani, why did you tell him that?"

"Because I didn't like what was happening. His supervisors were taking him apart in front of his coworkers, which you do *not* do, I'm sorry, and he was in a state. I tried to calm him down." Pierce's face appeared in her mind again. Mako's right hand. "Thinking back, I don't consider it outside the realm of possibility that Sam Duong was framed."

"Framed?" Pimentel's massaging action moved to his forehead. "Jani, if you knew his medical condition, I think you'd change your mind."

"So tell me." Jani crossed her left leg over her right—the left felt stronger and she didn't need to hoist. "If I'm his official next of kin, I have the right to know."

Pimentel rapped his work station touchboard; the image of her brain splintered into oblivion. "Sam Duong first visited me about six months ago. It was at about that time that papers in his charge began disappearing, and his supervisor was concerned that perhaps Sam was having some problem he didn't want to talk to an on-site counselor about. Encephaloscan revealed the presence of a tumor in the paramedian posterior region of Sam's thalamus—"

"*Roger.*"

"—and you need to know where it is, because the location defines the clinical symptoms. He suffers memory defects, amnesia. Immediate memory is especially affected."

Oh. "So if he did something this morning, he'd forget it by this afternoon." *Like putting papers in his desk.*

"Yes." Pimentel reached into the front pocket of his short-sleeve and removed a small packet. "He will also work to fill in those missing memories. In addition to distortions of fact and outright lies he has shown the tendency to adopt the lives of those in his archives as his own." He stood up and walked to his bookcase, atop which a watercooler rested. "Two months ago, he brought me a book. I don't recall the title, but the subject was geology. Not popular geology, either. This was a university-level textbook." He tore open the packet, dumped the contents into a glass, and added water. "He said he wrote it." Pimentel stirred the resulting pale yellow liquid with his finger, then tossed it back.

"Maybe he did."

Pimentel set down the empty glass. "The book had been written by a man named Simyam Baru."

Jani's mind blanked. She had to consciously make the effort to not cry out. To breathe. "Did—" She stopped, and tried again. "Did he say he was Simyam Baru?"

Pimentel shook his head. "Not outright. But he insisted he'd written the Baru book, as well as another written with a woman, a fellow professor—"

"Eva Yatni."

"Yes." Pimentel walked back to his desk and sat on the edge near Jani's chair. "To complicate matters even further, he consistently refuses treatment because he claims removal of the tumor will kill him. Then along you come, telling him you believe him when he says he didn't take your files. He probably figured you'd believe the rest of his story, too." He touched her shoulder. "You don't know how much it pains me to tell you this."

Jani stared past him out the window. "I visited Banda about fifteen years ago." She'd arrived during the summer. Just as hot as Chicago, but more humid. She'd spent the first three months of her visit indoors—she didn't possess the heat tolerance that she did now. "I wanted to know them. What they had done, how they had lived. I studied their work, what I could understand of it. Talked to their friends." The view blurred—she blinked it clear. "The tumor's in his thalamus?"

"Yes."

"I had been able to get hold of the Knevçet Shèràa patient files, but I didn't understand most of what I read. I knew the Laum researchers were experimenting with altering perceptions. Sensation. And I remember Service Medical tested my thalamus repeatedly before they augmented me. So the thalamus is involved in those functions."

Pimentel nodded. "Very much so."

"Then the Laum would have implanted there."

"Oh, Jani . . . There is no reason for you to have to go through this. I can have someone from MedRec bring up a waiver of rights. You sign it, and your name will be removed—"

"No." She stood up slowly. Her left leg felt strong, but her right was still wobbly. "Not until I talk to him."

Pimentel held out his hands in exasperated plea. "He has an explanation for everything. He will tie you in knots."

"Then I'll bring an all-purpose knife." She shuffled to the door. "I'll explain to him why I can't act as his next of kin, then I'll come back and sign your waiver." She waved goodbye without turning around. "Promise."

Jani returned to her room to find Morley bustling in an unusually bubbly fashion. Lucien had stopped by to see his favorite captain, she said, and he had brought her some clothes, wasn't that nice of him?

"He's a peach." Jani waited for the nurse to leave, then picked through the small duffel Lucien had packed for her. *Wonder how he got in my room in the first place?* Had he broken through a panel? Jazzed the lock? Charmed the building manager into giving him the code?

She pulled her panties out of the bag. As she shook them out, a small piece of paper fluttered to the floor. Handwriting of calligraphic neatness, written by someone who placed a grid sheet beneath his notepaper to keep the lines straight.

Call me at I-Com Four West-7. L

"Signing our name with an initial now, are we?" Jani tucked Lucien's note into the pocket of her summerweight trousers. "Intelligence, Communications branch." Hell, if he'd wanted her room code, he probably just brute-forced it out of systems.

She finished dressing. Styled her hair. Put on makeup. Tried to avoid consciously thinking the thought that skirted the edges of her mind.

What if someone else got out? What if I'm not the only one anymore?

"No." She checked her badges, packed her gear. "I'll talk to him. That's all. I'll explain to him why I can't do what he wants me to do." And if she slipped in a few questions about life on Banda, or the university, or the best place to buy kimchee, or the Great Boiled Shrimp Debate, well, that was fair. Her questions deserved answers, same as anyone else's. And she'd get them. Not wanting to know what she didn't know was a philosophy she wasn't familiar with.

CHAPTER 13

Jani walked into her TOQ suite, tossed her cap and duffel on the chair, and walked from room to room looking for signs of Lucien. He had replaced her old newssheets. Not with the *Tribune-Times* or the *Commonwealth Herald*, however, but with colonial sheets. Weeks-old issues of the *Ville Acadie Partisan* and the *Felix Majora Vox Nacional*, transmitted to Service Intelligence via Misty and printed out on fiche.

The *Vox* was littered with editorials demanding the shuttering of Fort Constanza, interspersed with the usual calls to secede. The *Partisan* reported the presence of the Acadian governor in Chicago to discuss matters related to "colonial rights." The article mentioned "an incident involving an Acadian colonial in Felix Majora that remains shrouded in mystery."

"Nothing mysterious about it. I was shanghaied." For the express purpose of being coddled and petted while the Judge Advocate tore apart the Service Code looking for an excuse to let her go. "After that, they're going to make me human again." Then what? A civilian consultancy? An extravagant flat in the city? The social whirl, capped off by her favorite lieutenant sunny-side up whenever his schedule allowed?

"Pull the other one—it sings 'Oh, Acadia.'" Jani tossed the newssheets aside and continued her inspection. She found fresh flowers in both the sitting room and bedroom. Val the

Bear sat perched against the bedroom vase, a banner pinned to his chest.

"You're out of uniform," she told him as she detached the note. *I found the scalpel on your desk—don't even think about it.* This time, Lucien hadn't even bothered with an initial. Jani crumpled it and tossed it in the trashzap, following with the missive she'd found tucked in her underwear.

She had made another circuit of the bedroom before she spotted the thick, pale blue envelope lying on her bed. Another slip of white paper had been attached to the closure flap.

My, aren't we the colorful personality?

Jani shredded that note before consigning it to the flash-flame. Messages in underwear were cute, and knowing Lucien had been rummaging through her bedroom had its seductive aspects. "But there's a line, Mister, and you just crossed it."

She hefted her ServRec and adjourned to her sitting room, plucking Val the Bear from his floral roost on the way. "Simyam Baru escaped from his room," she told him. "I thought I'd locked him down well enough, but he wasn't as far gone as the other patients, and he figured out how to crack the Laumrau code locks." She sat on the couch and propped Val against a pillow in the opposite corner. "Only two other patients still lived at this point—he released them from their rooms. Orton was blind—they'd severed her optic nerves so they could input directly into her visual cortex. Fessig could still see. On him, they'd performed a tactile-aural synesthetic reroute." Jani looked into the bear's shiny eyes. "He felt everything he heard. Whispering and instrument hum felt like ants crawling over him. Normal speaking voices felt like slaps and punches, depending on their pitch."

The three of them jumped Felicio and Stanleigh, who had run down to the garage to secure the exits as soon as they realized patients had escaped. "They had to secure the exits manually because we couldn't control ingress and egress from central systems. You see, the bombing started right after the Laumrau hospital staff cleared the building and fled to their sect-sharers in the hills."

Shatterboxes first, to disable systems and blow infrastructure. "That was when Yolan died, when one of the operating theater walls collapsed on her."

Then came pink, the brilliantly hued microbial mist that took up where the explosives left off. "We tried to wash it out of the air with water—within the first half minute after release, it's still concentrated enough that you can do that— but the shatterboxes had damaged the pumping system, and we couldn't maintain pressure in the hoses. The pink diffused and got into everything."

Instrument cards liquefied. Boards turned to jelly.

"So we couldn't control the doors—we had to shut them manually. That was the first mistake I made—I should have guessed the Laumrau would try to pink us. I should have locked down the doors and vents as soon as they'd fled."

Val regarded her patiently.

"I know. I'm digressing." Jani prodded him with her toe. "So Fel and Stan ran to the garage to check the doors, and Baru, Orton, and Fessig jumped them and stole the control card for the people-mover." But the vehicle had been damaged by the shatterboxes. "I think the pink got to it, too. I watched it from the roof—it barely made it over the first rise."

Then she saw the Laumrau pursuit craft, a sleek, bullet-shaped demiskimmer with bank-and-dive capability. "It flitted over the rise after the 'mover." She picked up one of the throw pillows and hugged it to her chest. "I heard the explosion. Saw it. A blown battery array emits a very distinctive green-white flash. John confirmed it later." Granted, over two months passed before he could examine the site, but he'd had a lot of experience in crash investigation by then, and he knew what to look for. "He said from the condition of the wreckage and the human remains he found, no one could have survived."

Val the Bear cocked an eyebrow. Well, not really, but it was easy to imagine.

Jani nodded. "Yes, I know. You could have said the same

thing about what happened to me." She cracked open the envelope and removed her file, shaking and riffling both in case any more *communiqués petits* awaited discovery. Then she lay back, rested her head against the bolster, and paged through her Service record. Most of the material that covered her time under Neumann was still missing, but what remained still told quite a story.

The excerpts she read could be considered hilarious or depressing, depending on the judgment of the reader. She could understand Lucien's dismay. The role she played in the midnight requisition from Central Supply of several sorely needed parchment imprinters and systems cards had earned her the undying enmity of the Rauta Shèràa Base Supply officer, the threat of a court-martial, and a personal invitation from Colonel Matilda Fitzhugh to eat a shooter.

"No mention is made, of course, that the reason they kept Documents and Documentation undersupplied was because they'd been shunting equipment into the J-Loop black market for a year and a half." Jani glanced over the top of the report at Val the Bear. "Instead they dropped the charge against me because of 'insufficient evidence' and spread the rumor that Evan used the Family *du piston* to get me off the hook. Forget the fact we hadn't spoken in six months." She straightened the pages and moved on to the next episode.

"Oh yes. My first run-in with good old Rikart." Jani could visualize Neumann in his dress blue-greys, the narrower black belt of the older-style uniform squeezing his thick middle like a tourniquet. Broad-beamed. Wide, jovial face cut with a narrow mustache. Father Christmas in middle age. "A personal buddy of Phil Unser, which told one everything one needed to know right there. He started out second-in-command of Base Operations. When he tried to kneecap Documents and Documentation by incorporating us into Ops, I wrote a report." She leafed through the fiched copy, forty-eight pages of carefully delineated argument as to why a nonindependent documents section would be detrimental to the Service as a whole and Rauta Shèràa Base in particular. Her "fictional examples" had contained everything but the names and dates.

"There were twenty-three transfers after I submitted it for General Review." Her commanding officer had reamed her for not clearing the report with him before submission, and yet another notation of "insubordination" was added to her record. "I couldn't figure out why they didn't just boot me out."

The answer came in a message, which she had found tucked in the outer pocket of her scanpack pouch during an idomeni-Service conclave a few weeks later. The pouch hadn't left her belt—she'd never been able to figure out who passed the message to her and when.

Think if this had been a knife, the first line had read. It got better after that, but not much.

> *Nice report, Kilian. You think like a crook, but you need seasoning. When you get sick of protecting the litter-runts of the Commonwealth, I'll be waiting. Rikart.*

"And do you believe he signed that note?" A few weeks later, he had her seconded to the Twelfth Rovers to help her make up her mind.

Jani reassembled her file and tucked it back into the envelope. Val the Bear had toppled over and lay flat on his face. *I know the feeling.* She sat back, cradled her head in the crook of her arm, and let her gaze drift. "Piers didn't answer my question about how Ebben, Unser, and Fitzhugh died. I'd bet 'on purpose' myself." Her eyelids felt heavy. Her stomach growled.

She stared at her comport message light for a full minute before she realized it blinked. "Lucien, go away." She struggled to her feet and shuffled to her desk. "I'm mad at you." She hit the playpad so she wouldn't have to look at the flickering light anymore—she meant to delete the message immediately, but the face flashed before her fatigue-blunted reflexes could kick in.

Lieutenant Ischi's pensive aspect filled the display. "Captain? Ma'am, I know you're not feeling well. But if there's any way at all you can manage to stop by the office today, it would be greatly appreciated."

Jani checked the time-date stamp on the message. *Only an hour ago.* Odds were good the bodies hadn't cooled yet, although Ischi's expression aside, she had no reason to assume Hals and Vespucci had gotten into another fight about her. *And if you pull this one again, it sings "The Hymn of the Commonwealth."*

"All eight bloody verses." She recovered her garrison cap from its resting place and tottered out the door.

Jani entered the Foreign Transactions desk pool to find Ischi and several techs clustered by the coffee brewer. Ischi stood fists on hips and head thrust forward—the traditional lecture posture of a frustrated tech wrangler trying to cut the stampede off at the pass.

"Colonel Hals is a helluva lot more aware than you are of the problems we're facing, Mister!" he barked, his nose a finger's breadth away from that of a pasty-faced SFC. "And the sooner you stop bleating your unique blend of garbled fact and outright fiction, the better off we will *all* be!" He was about to launch into round two when another tech's eyes rounded, and he turned to follow her stare.

"Captain Kilian, ma'am!" His turnabout-and-present was so quick, the object of his ire barely ducked an elbow in the nose. "The colonel will see you shortly. Please follow me."

Jani fell in behind Ischi in the best Officer's Guide manner, waiting to draw alongside until they had passed into the anteroom. "Having a bad day, Corporal Coffee Cup?" That got a smile out of him. "Ah, the joys of personnel."

"Doylen's an idiot. He listens at doors, catches half the words, and rearranges them in the worst order possible." Ischi stopped at his desk and paged through the assorted stacks. "The problem is, it's hit the fan, everyone knows it, and they're diving for cover."

"So what's the latest?"

"Hals is being relieved and FT split up. Some of us will be shipped to colonial postings and the rest shoved back in the main pool."

"*What?* What brought that on?"

"A complaint by Hantìa. She claimed Colonel Hals is incompetent and that her mistakes have hampered negotiations." Ischi kept his eyes fixed on his paper rearranging. "All the errors are Hantìa's fault. She held back vital data, waiting for the colonel to ask for it. But she wasn't allowed."

Sounds like the Hantìa I knew and hated. Jani jerked her head toward Hals's door. "Who's in there now?"

"The colonel, Major Vespucci, and Colonel Derringer from Diplo." Ischi exhaled with a rumble. "Come over to *explain* the situation."

"Right." Jani circled around the distracted lieutenant and punched Hals's doorpad. She ducked into the office and forced the panel closed on Ischi's wailing "Ma'am, not yet—"

Hals sat at her desk, face drawn. Vespucci sat across from her, the look he directed at Jani suffused with outrage.

Derringer sat on the short side of the desk between the two, his mainline stripe drawing the eye like a warning flare. He stiffened when he saw Jani—the leg that had been crossed ankle over knee slowly lowered until foot hit floor. His was the rangy build and sun-battered face that came from a bin labeled "middle-aged officer-standard issue." He looked like he knew the answers. Jani would have bet her 'pack he didn't understand half the questions.

"Ma'am." She snapped to attention as well as her weakened right leg would allow. "Captain Kilian reporting as ordered."

Vespucci's voice emerged level and hard. "You don't have an appointment scheduled, Cap—" He had twisted so his back faced Hals, but they must have worked together for so long, they'd developed psychic communication. Hals's stare bored through the back of his head—he turned to face her slowly, as though in a trance, and fell silent.

"Captain, it's obvious some mistake has been made," Derringer said sharply. "Please leave us."

Jani clasped her hands behind her back. Lifted her chin. Dug her heels into the carpet. Just like old times—ready, steady, into the deep end. "I know what this meeting is about,

sir. I find it alarming that Diplo has taken it upon themselves
to decide a course of action without consulting the one officer in Foreign Transactions who is a known authority on
idomeni affairs."

Derringer stared past Jani at the door, as though waiting
for Ischi to make an appearance. "And who would that be,
Captain?"

"That would be me, sir."

His gaze shifted to her. Even Vespucci's had held more
warmth. "Captain, I realize sideline conducts itself more
loosely than mainline, and I also realize documents examiners as a whole pride themselves on their unmilitary behavior. But you are out of line here, and I am ordering you to
leave this room."

"Captain Kilian is *my* direct report, Colonel, and we are
in my physical jurisdiction." Hals's soft Indiesian accent contrasted sharply with Derringer's twangy Michigan provincial.
"If we are indeed so concerned about proper military behavior, I believe those two points give me the deciding vote as
to whether she stays or leaves." The look she directed at Jani
said, OK expert, this better work. "Carry on, Captain."

Jani heard voices outside. She reached behind her and
pressed down on the doorpad—the doormech scraped as Ischi tried to open it from the other side.

"Sir." The scuffling outside the door grew louder, and she
leaned harder on the pad. "It is my informed opinion, as a
Service officer experienced in dealing with the idomeni, that
removing Colonel Hals from any further contact with this
matter is not a sound decision. It will prove detrimental not
only to immediate Service dealings with the idomeni, but to
future Service and Commonwealth dealings with them as
well."

Derringer looked from Hals to Vespucci, then back at Jani.
He hadn't expected this. He had no fallback position, no
support, and no idea what to do next. "It has not been officially determined that you outstrip everyone in the Diplomatic Corps with respect to idomeni experience, Captain."

"Fair enough, sir—in that case, I have two questions for
you. One, how many years did the senior Service negotiator

attached to this matter live on Shèrá and two, how many idomeni languages do they speak and is High Vynshàrau one of them?"

"That's three questions." Hals's expression was bland, but tiny embers of rebellion glowed in her eyes.

"My mistake, ma'am," Jani replied with equal flatness. "I do apologize." She looked at Derringer. "Sir?"

Derringer shifted in his chair. He wanted to refuse to answer, but three pairs of sideline eyes let him know that wasn't an option. "General Burkett spent one year at Language School and a six-month stint at our embassy in Rauta Shèràa."

"Is he a colonial? Some colonials have had a great deal of day-to-day experience dealing with the Haárin."

"No, he is Earthbound by birth. However, he did do a ten-year stint in the J-Loop, where large populations of Haárin do reside. He tells stories." The corner of Derringer's mouth twitched as the gauntlet hit the floor.

Jani nodded. "I began my course of study in documents examination at the Rauta Shèràa Academy at the age of seventeen. Four and a half years to degree, with my final year spent under direct tutelage of the being who currently serves as idomeni ambassador. After that, two and a half years at Rauta Shèràa Base, the majority of that time spent as a Food Services Liaison and an Import-Export Registrar. After that, eighteen years—"

Derringer held up his hands. "Captain, no one is denying your expertise—"

"Only my loyalty?" She stared at him until he looked away. "I am fully aware of the low opinion any member of the traditional Service would hold of me. But your opinion of me is not the primary consideration here. The primary consideration here is the continued lack of regard being shown the documents examiners assigned to this matter and the confusion this engenders in the idomeni, who consider examiners as qualified to negotiate and determine policy as any diplomat."

Derringer sucked his teeth. "Captain, we have discussed this with the ambassador at length, and while he questions our reasoning at times, he has shown himself willing to see the human side of things."

"Sir, FT isn't dealing directly with the ambassador, who is an exception to almost every rule regarding traditional Vynshàrau behavior. FT is dealing with the documents examiners, who have been reared from birth to operate in the diplomatic sphere." *Except for Hantìa, but I'll worry about that inconsistency later.*

Derringer glanced at his timepiece. "Captain Kilian, negotiations for the Lake Michigan Strip have grown more and more heated over the past several days. The Prime Minister and members of her Cabinet are currently attending at the embassy, and we have been called in as well. There is no time to waste." He stood. "The decision on how to proceed has been made."

Jani leaned against the doorpad. The voices and scrabblings had stopped long ago. All she could hear was the voice in her head that whispered *gotcha*. "NìaRauta Hantìa issued the complaint against Colonel Hals and the Vynshàrau demanded FT presence *all* this afternoon?"

Derringer hesitated. He'd grown sick of answering her questions—that was obvious—but he knew alarm when he heard it. "Yes."

Hantìa, you witch, you set me up. "Sir, they know I'm here. They want me to attend. They've issued the sort of challenge they know will flush me out." *They know me.*

Vespucci screwed up the nerve to open his mouth again. "Aren't you taking a lot on yourself, Captain? You'd think the outcome of these negotiations hinged on you."

Jani worked her neck. Her back hurt. Pimentel would strangle her if he knew where she was and what she did. *I wish I had never checked that comport light.* "Sir, I'm sure I sound arrogant, but I know them. They've always acknowledged the actions I took at Knevçet Shèràa. This is their way of formally recognizing me. Everyone here wishes I'd dry up and blow away, but ignoring the unpleasant in the hope it will disappear is not their way. I'm anathema to them, but I'm the devil they've always known. In a culture that values open disputation and the concept of the esteemed enemy, the thought that you could be hiding me is as repugnant to them as a food hoarder during time of famine is to us. They want to see me. Let's get it over with."

CHAPTER 14

Brigadier General Callum Burkett proved the taller, greyer edition of Colonel Derringer. And more frazzled. Seeing Derringer arrive at the embarkation zone with Hals and Jani in tow did nothing to calm him down.

"*Goddamn it!*" He slid into his seat in the rear of the Diplomatic steel blue triple-length and glared across the compartment at the three of them before settling on Derringer. "Intelligence is stepping on our necks for even talking to the idomeni about the Strip, the PM is mixing up Family politics and defense policy *again*, and now you take it upon yourself to jettison the only firm decision we've been able to make in three months!"

"Who drove the decision?" Jani looked from Derringer to Burkett. "It was a bad decision. Who drove it? Ulanova?" She flinched as the skimmer passed beneath the Shenandoah Gate. It wasn't political opinion, but a shocklike tingle that radiated up her right arm. "It's in her interest to destabilize colony-idomeni relations. One way to do that is to blow systems here, and let the backflash take out a few of the Haárin-colony arrangements that have formed over the years." She flexed her arm, then rested it in her lap instead of on the armrest.

"The origin of the decision isn't your concern, Captain." Burkett didn't bother to look at her, or even turn her way.

"Captain Kilian raised some valid points, sir." Derringer

sat with the tense nerviness of a man who wanted with all his heart to punch out the canopy and go out over the shooters but had been ordered to go down with the demi instead. "Major Hanratty's been pushing for months to allow dexxies into the negotiations."

"Hanratty's a *xenolinguist*, Colonel." Burkett's sarcastic tone bit almost as much as the pain in Jani's arm. "Are you suggesting we let someone who watches sceneshots of conversations for a living decide Commonwealth defense policy?"

"Can't do any worse than you're doing now." Jani's right arm throbbed now—she tried massaging it and barely suppressed a cry. "Hantìa and her skein-sharers are attempting to treat Colonel Hals and her skein-sharers as equals. She assumes Colonel Hals is playing coy, and she wants to shake her up by challenging us all. She doesn't expect you to drop the colonel like a hot rock; she expects you to stand behind her. If you show her that isn't the case, you've only reinforced the Vynshàrau opinion that humanish are disordered and unseemly, and you've done it by insulting a documents examiner, which just triples the injury. Is battling for a strip of airspace so important that you're willing to risk an irreparable fracture between the Commonwealth and the Shèrá worldskein?"

"You're suggesting we allow an alien race with whom relations are tenuous at best the unfettered ability to scan any flyover that cuts through that slice of sky?" Burkett's voice twinned Evan's—level, deep, and sharp. Reason enough to dislike him. "It's—"

"A primary corridor into and out of O'Hare, yes, I know." Jani struggled to keep from yelling, to keep from responding to Burkett's voice. "Are you naïve enough to believe they aren't already doing just that?"

Derringer shot her a "please shut up" glare. "Publicly admitting the fact could set a nasty precedent."

"With whom? The colonies? Are we so independent that you need to worry about negotiating treaties with us?" She tried to work her fingers, and her thumb cramped. *Augie, cut me some slack.* "You want some advice from someone who's negotiated with the idomeni for years? Give them the Strip. Show them that you acknowledge that Exterior Minister Ulanova's actions were insulting and that you want to repair the damage." Their skimmer floated down a wooded lane—the trees met over the top to form a leafed canopy. *I'm sure this is lovely.* She wished she could appreciate it.

Burkett glowered across the compartment at Derringer, who tried to sink into his seat. They'd reached the first low-rise complexes that marked the northern outskirts of Chicago. The driver exited the thoroughfare and ramped onto the Boul artery. It wouldn't be long now.

Hals tapped her window softly with one knuckle. "Maybe we can talk to the ambassador about Hantìa, and he can order her to back down. The consensus, as I understand it, is that if we can convince him of something, he'll drive the point home to the Oligarch."

"No, ma'am—we definitely do not want to do that." Jani tried to filter the impatience out of her voice. Trying to find the words to explain the obvious aggravated her anyway, and her aching arm didn't help. "You have been challenged, and you must meet that challenge openly."

"But the ambassador understands us."

"Nema *is* different than the rest of his sect-sharers, ma'am, yes. He likes us. He finds us fascinating." *He has plans for us, too, but if Gene Therapeutics has its way, that won't be my problem anymore.* "He understands our concerns to some extent, but only on an abstract level. Just because he looks you in the face when he talks to you doesn't make him an honorary humanish. He's not your addled Uncle Arthur, he's the chief priest of his sect. I've watched him accept and offer *à lérine.* I've watched him fight and I've seen him bleed."

"I've seen the scars on his forearms. They look like he's wearing lace sleeves under his robe." Derringer winced. "But *à lérine* are only ceremonial fights. Acknowledgments of your enemies. They're not real battles—no one dies."

"Not usually." Jani rested her head against the seat back. The pain had stabilized to a steady pulsation. "Nema fought many of those battles for the right to come here as ambassador. His religious skein-sharers followed him here because he's their dominant and his way is their way. Same for the diplomatic seculars who owe primary allegiance to Morden nìRau Cèel, the Oligarch. They came here because it was their leader's wish. But we're the disordered humanish who do not know our food, and they believe that in living with us, they've sacrificed their souls. Your refusal to concede them the strip tells them you do not consider that sacrifice important. Give them the Strip. They will give it back. That's not what they want—what they want is an acknowledgment of what they've lost." Even though she answered Derringer, she looked at Burkett. "You're thinking like a humanish soldier, and in doing so, you're making a mistake."

Their skimmer ramped off the Boul and down a two-lane access road lined by thick hybrid shrubbery that served the dual purpose of absorbing sound and obscuring idomeni property from prying humanish eyes. As they wended down the road, they passed the first of the manned checkpoints. A tall, ropy Vynshàrau stood in the guardhouse, a long-range shooter hanging by a cross-strap across her back.

"Is that the sort of being you want to allow access to our nav paths, Captain?" Burkett snorted softly. "It's obvious you aren't much of a soldier."

Jani looked him in the eye. He lifted one brow in surprise—he must have thought he'd insulted her. "No, sir, I am not. I will be the first to admit it and the last to deny it."

"You have no business participating in this matter."

"They just need to see me, sir." *After that, I can go back to being your private shame.*

After the gate guards checked the skimmer through, it pulled inside the embassy courtyard, an austere, sunstone-tiled space lined with shoulder-high silverleaf shrubs. The small triangles of sunstone, colored in shades of creamy gold, had been laid in whorled patterns. The courtyard surface looked as though huge fingers had pressed down from above, leaving their prints behind.

As junior officer in the happy convoy, Jani disembarked first. Her arm still ached, and her stomach had joined the chorus, yet she took the opportunity to stroll around. The

late-afternoon sun warmed her; the glare of its reflection off
the light-colored stone hurt her eyes.

This brings back memories. The bare façade of the embassy was featureless but for a set of banded bronze doors.
The poured scancrete fence that barred their view of the
sweeping grounds and the city beyond was three meters high
and topped with crosshatches of ornamental blades.

At least, they're supposed to be ornamental. Jani wouldn't
have wanted to be the one to determine whether the edges
had actually been dulled. Idomeni steel cut deep, and the
hair-thin wireweave that ran down both sides of the edge
ripped flesh and left nasty scars.

A few minutes later, the people-movers bearing the rest of
Foreign Transactions and Diplo lumbered into the courtyard.
Disembarkation began immediately, but it still took time.
Jani had plenty of opportunity to bask in Major Vespucci's
scowling regard as he watched her through the FT mover's
rear window.

As soon as the vehicles had emptied, the embassy doors
swung open and a brown-robed Vynshàrau diplomatic suborn beckoned to them. The Service personnel lined up single
file, lowest-ranking first, with the civilian techs inserting
themselves at predetermined points according to their number of years in the department. Jani looked at Hals, who
stood off to one side. The woman walked over to her, her
face grooved with tension.

"Burkett told me I'm to remain out here." Her eyes glistened with barely contained tears. "Sit in the FT mover and
wait for you." She blinked rapidly, then turned away.

"And your response is what, ma'am?" Jani edged away
from the gathering of closed mouths and open ears. "I will
back you to the wall, for what it's worth."

Hals looked across the courtyard, where Burkett stood in
huddled conversation with Derringer and another mainline
officer. They'd changed their trousers in the interim, switching out their crimson stripes for slashes of dark green. Nema
would be the only being in the embassy allowed to wear red
in his clothing. The idomeni considered it a holy color.

"He'll change his pants for them, but not his mind." Hals

shook her head. "If I buck him on this, he'll level me."

Jani dragged her toe along a whorl of stone. "One Service dictum I remember—and I don't remember many—states that if you value your career more than you value your job, you're the wrong person for both. Now if you stay out here like a good little sideliner, you'll still have a career. You may pass some of it in a shelter waiting for the idomeni shatterboxes to stop falling, but you'll still have your scanpack if the pink doesn't eat it and you'll have a pension if we've reestablished a viable monetary system by the time you retire. Assuming you're still alive."

A flare of temper erased some of the strain from Hals's face. "Kilian, has anybody ever told you you're a judgmental pain in the ass?"

"Good, ma'am, I hope that made you feel better." Jani reclaimed her place in line, one step ahead of the stone-faced Vespucci. "Doesn't do a damned thing to answer the essential question, but one should take every opportunity to vent one's frustrations, I've always believed."

Hals adjusted the set of her garrison cap. "You honestly feel my not participating in these negotiations could alter the tone of idomeni-human relations for the worse?"

"Yes, I do."

"I will have to deal with the consequences of this much longer than you will."

"It will affect your *career*, yes. It may even end it. But I can give you the names of four people who would be more than happy to take on a dexxie who knows how to do her job."

Hals hesitated. "Senna, Tsai—"

"Aryton and Nawar. Yes, ma'am."

A small grin brightened Hals's features. "Not you?"

Jani shook her head. "You don't want to work for me— I'm a judgmental pain in the ass."

The grin flashed. Then Hals reset her cap once again and slipped into line behind a stricken Vespucci.

"She could be court-martialed for this," he rasped in Jani's ear.

"Thanks for the support, Major," Jani tossed over her shoulder as the line started to move.

The first thing that struck her was the heat, followed by the stark, ascetic look of the unadorned hallways and rugless, tiled floors. The Vynshàrau favored the colors of the desert in their interior decoration—cream, white, and tan predominated. But in deference to their allied sects, they allowed some splashes of variety, such as the leaf green and sky-blue curlicues inset in all the lake-facing windows. *Pathen,* Jani recalled. The silver-and-copper wireweave chandeliers, however, that resembled the blades lining the top of the fence, were of Sìah design, since the Sìah were renowned for their metalwork.

So stark, yet so beautiful. Jani struggled to remain in formation as exhilaration washed over her. She felt drunk. Ecstatic. She wanted to skip down the hallway and pound on all the doors. *That would go over big.*

"Colonel!"

Jani heard Hals groan. She turned in time to see Burkett storm up the hall.

"You will return to Sheridan immediately." He drew alongside Hals and beckoned for her to accompany him.

Jani sidestepped out of line to stand beside Burkett. "You're making a mistake, sir."

He turned on her, his voice deadening. "You are expected to defer to the trained diplomats on this team, Captain. After you make your token appearance, you're out of here right behind her."

Jani nodded. "Yes, sir. I'll go," she said in a voice loud enough to echo down the cavernous hall. She pointed to Hals. "She. Stays."

The faint buzz of humanish and Vynshàrau voices reached them as Cabinet and Council officials filled the open doorways. Burkett's sweat-slicked face showed his extreme displeasure at putting on a show. "This discussion is finished, Captain. You have your orders." He gestured to one of his staffers, who had drifted uneasily into the hallway. The woman immediately beckoned to a larger, less timorous-looking Service Security officer, who started toward them.

"Glories of the day to you, my dear-rest friends!"

The familiar singsong stopped the Security officer in his tracks. Hals gasped. Burkett closed his eyes. The other members of FT and Diplo buzzed and whispered.

Jani smiled.

Nema stalked toward them, his off-white overrobe billowing behind him like a churning wake. "Such argument. I left Cabinet Ministers in order to hear more." In person, his skin appeared darker than Jani remembered from the winter, gold-brown rather than ocher, the result of frequent trips to the Death Valley enclave.

Burkett stood at attention. "NìRau, permit me to apologize—"

"For what, General? Open disputation is most seemly. Most as idomeni. Otherwise, humanish are so as walls, we do not think you alive." Nema looked each of them in the face, a born-sect taboo he seemed determined to topple single-handed. His eyes widened as he bared his teeth, resulting in a startling, and to some, unpleasant expression.

They don't see what I see. To Jani, Nema's rictus sardonicus was the welcoming grin of an old friend. An *aggravating* old friend. Presumptuous. But nevertheless . . .

Nema stepped between Jani and the rattled general and gripped her chin between his thumb and forefinger. "You have brought me my Eyes and Ears." He tilted her face back and forth. "*a lète onae vèste, Kièrshiarauta,*" he said to her, voice pitched higher than normal as a show of regard. *Glories of the day to you, toxin.*

"*a lète ona vèste, Nemarau.*" Jani pitched her voice high as well, and added a greeting gesture, crossing her left arm over her chest, palm twisted outward. She tried to tilt her head to the left and offer the traditional single nod, but Nema's firm grip prevented her. "NìRau, I can't move my head."

"Apologies, nìa." His hand dropped away, and he stepped back. "So, you have come to assist me with this stupid food business. Such ignorance. You are most well?" His voice held a touch of skepticism, but he restrained the gestures that would have clarified his feeling. Whatever Lucien had been telling him, he either didn't believe, or didn't like it.

"NìRau Tsecha." Burkett's eyes held that wild look most humans acquired after they'd been around Nema for more than five seconds. "We didn't expect to see you this afternoon."

"I know that, General." The glint in Nema's amber-on-amber eyes indicating that dashing the expectations of humanish Burketts was all part of the fun. "But when I heard my Eyes and Ears was to be here—" His gaze fell on Hals, and he bared his teeth again. "Ah, Colonel Hals, you have met challenge! Onì nìaRauta Hantìa will be most pleased—she thought you dead." He took her by the arm and towed her down the hall and into the documents examiners' meeting room.

Burkett bent close enough to make Jani flinch. "This does not end here, Captain." He turned and whispered something to the Security officer before disappearing into the Diplomatic meeting room.

Jani followed the still-stunned stragglers down the hall to the examiners' room, realizing after a few steps that the Security officer shadowed her. She probed her arm again. The ache had intensified in the last few minutes—the muscles in her lower arm had started to twitch. *What the hell is this?* Delayed reaction to Pimentel's prodding and poking?

"My, my, my."

Jani turned. Exterior Minister Anais Ulanova stood in the nearest doorway, regarding her with the cool arrogance Jani recalled from her first visit to Chicago. In deference to idomeni religious sensibility, she wore a wrapshirt and trousers in dark brown rather than the usual Exterior burgundy. A younger woman stood next to her. Ivory skin and hair. Pale blue eyes glittery with nerves. She wore black and grey, the official Interior colors. McEnnis, Jani recalled from news reports. Evan's interim replacement.

"Captain Kilian." Ulanova nodded. "Although I recall you went by the name 'Risa Tyi' when you visited us last." She leaned toward McEnnis and whispered something in her ear. The woman's eyes widened.

Jani smiled at McEnnis, who took a step backward. "I

can imagine what she's told you about me. Some of it might even be true. I hope for your sake you can figure out which is which—you need that skill dealing with her." She waved farewell and started down the hall. "I'll give Lucien your regards, ma'am, the next time we come up for air." The look of outrage that Jani saw on Ulanova's face just before she slipped into the examiners' room was worth the little fib.

The windowless meeting room proved hotter than the hallway by several crucial degrees. Judging from the mutterings Jani heard, summerweights felt itchy and clingy; dress blue-greys would have been downright dangerous.

She only felt mildly warm herself, but if another twelve-hour marathon stretched before them, who knew how she'd hold up? *But that's a big if.* She glanced behind her and saw the Security officer standing in the doorway, watching her. A lieutenant, his mainline red bars switched out for religiously insignificant dark green. Unarmed, since he technically stood on idomeni soil, but far from helpless, judging from his muscular arms and chest.

If I tried to bolt, he'd just pick me up and toss me over his shoulder. Or break her in half, depending on how much of a fuss she made. She approached him slowly, arms at her sides, hands open and visible. "Lieutenant."

He nodded. "Ma'am."

"May I ask why you're following me?"

"After you meet with nìaRauta Hantìa, I'm to escort you back to Sheridan, ma'am."

"Odds are I'll be needed here."

"General Burkett's orders, ma'am."

Right. Jani walked to the central U-shaped table, where Nema stood surrounded by the members of Foreign Transactions. Most faces held shock or surprise. Ischi's shoulders shook. Hals had covered her mouth with her hand. Even Vespucci grinned.

"And only the player standing in the net can use hands?" Nema toed weakly at the floor. "All the others have to *kick*?"

"Like this, nìRau." Ischi mimed a short, hard pass to Vespucci, who in turn pretended to block the nonexistent soccer ball into the floor with his formidable stomach.

"Really? Such I do not understand." Nema looked at Jani, his posture crooked with dismay. "Why did you never tell me of this, nìa!" He clasped Ischi by the arm and pulled him to one side, gesturing for Vespucci to follow. The sounds of crumpling parchment soon emerged from the huddle. The two men then broke away and kicked a paper ball back and forth as Nema stood on the side and scrutinized every move.

Jani watched the exhibition until she grew conscious of a stare boring through the side of her face. "Colonel."

Hals sauntered to her side. "Captain." She peeked around Jani and nodded toward the strapping lieutenant. "Is he here for you, me, or us?"

"Me. As soon as Hantìa and I meet, Burkett wants me out."

"Then we must meet now," entoned a voice from behind. Feminine, but grating, like nails down a slate. "So that I can laugh as you leave."

Jani turned slowly. She kept her eyes straight ahead, so she would look the idomeni in the upper chest, not the face. Tan robes. The lower curves of shoulder-grazing gold oval earrings. Light brown hair twisted into short helices and wrapped with silver cord. Same regal posture she remembered from Academy. Same damned voice. "Hantìa."

"Kièrshia." The Vynshàrau stepped back and studied her. Side-to-side examination, followed by top to toe, looking everywhere but in her eyes. "You are not what you were." She tilted her head slightly to Jani's right, a posture of moderate respect acknowledging their shared past.

Jani tilted her head to the left, mimicking Hantìa's regard, as she allowed herself oblique glances at the jutting cheekbones and squarish jaw. "Only physically." She lapsed readily into High Vynshàrau; it seemed more appropriate, somehow. "In my soul, I am as ever."

"You left your soul at Knevçet Shèràa. So you are as nothing. That, I always knew."

Jani twitched the fingers of her left hand, a gesture of disregard. She heard no other voices, and knew all eyes were on the two of them. "You are not an archivist, as was planned."

"No." A bow of head as right hand reached up and gripped left shoulder. A posture of sadness. "NìRau ti nìRau Cèel had need of me here." The hand dropped. Hantìa straightened. "A great need, and truly." She turned to Hals, and switched back to English. "Colonel."

Hals nodded stiffly. "Hantìa."

"We must work now. Soon, there will be too many damned papers to count." Hantìa stalked toward the other Vynshàrau examiners, who had gathered on the opposite side of the room.

Hals cocked her head. "Did she just say what I thought she said?"

"She's been taking English lessons from Nema." Jani smiled, but her good humor faded as she watched the lieutenant cross the room toward her.

"Ma'am." He stopped in front of her and gestured in the direction of the door. "This way, please."

Jani looked at Hals, who watched her warily. *I could stand my ground, and fight to stay.* Nema would rush to her aid— he'd probably even offer her asylum. *Wouldn't that do wonders for diplomatic relations?* Ulanova might even persuade Cao to send in armed troops to take her back. Not that they'd succeed, but the invasion itself would constitute a declaration of war.

What do I care—I'd be free.

But at what cost? She looked at Ischi, who bounced the paper ball from knee to knee. At the other members of FT, who grinned and watched. She didn't even know their names.

Better I don't—the list is long enough. No more, if she could help it. No more.

"All right, Lieutenant." She took one last look at the unadorned, sand-colored space, then fell in behind.

"*Nìa?*" Nema broke away from Ischi and Vespucci and beelined toward them. "Where are you going?"

"Back to the base, nìRau. General Burkett's orders."

"*Orders?*" The pitch of his voice lowered so he sounded hoarse. His shoulders rounded. "Is it not true that to stand here is to stand in Rauta Shèràa? Is it not true that in this room, my word is as orders?"

The lieutenant's eyes widened as the tall, *angry* ambassador closed in. "Sir."

"So do I order you to leave this room, Lieutenant."

"Sir—nìRau—General Burkett—"

Jani stepped between the lieutenant and the oncoming Nema. "NìRau! Please!"

"Go to your paper, nìa! Obey me!" Nema's guttural voice sounded a distinctly idomeni warning. He waited for Jani to back away before closing in on the hapless Security guard. "I will speak of this to General Burkett, who gives orders within my walls!" He grabbed the young man by the arm. The lieutenant tried to pull away—his eyes widened when he realized he couldn't break the Vynshàrau's grip.

"*So.*" Nema pushed him out the door and directly in the path of a young diplomatic suborn, who sidestepped neatly.

"NìRau ti nìRau? You are needed." She spoke English with a heavy Vynshàrau accent, swallowed *t*'s and back-of-the-throat *r*'s.

"Not now, nìaRauta Vìa."

"*Now*, nìRau ti nìRau." Vìa rounded her shoulders in a posture of aggravation. Not as hunched as Nema, but the twist and twirl of her right hand indicated that it was only a matter of time. "Exterior Minister Ulanova and Suborn Oligarch nìRau Lish are discussing taxation of Elyan Haárin settlements."

"*Discussing*, nìa?"

Vìa hesitated, then raised her right hand, palm facing up, in silent plea.

Nema's voice dropped to a John Shroud-like resonance. "My Anais makes trouble, as always. I would challenge her myself, but she is too short to fight." He looked at Jani, and his posture saddened. "I see my nìa Kièrshia for so short a time, and now I must leave!" He walked back to Ischi and took the wad of paper from his hand. "I must play goalie." He tossed the parchment ball from hand to hand as he strode out of the room.

Jani turned back to the table, which held surveys and maps

and other documents applicable to the Strip negotiations. She couldn't recall the last time she'd seen Nema that angry. *And all because of me.* "How much longer do you think I have to live, ma'am?"

Hals sighed. "At least until you get back to Sheridan." She unholstered her scanpack. "Burkett wouldn't want civilians to find the body."

The verification session lasted six hours, not including the forty-five-minute interruption for the Vynshàrau's late-evening sacramental meal. By the time they adjourned, Jani's stomach ached from hunger and her right arm had numbed and stiffened from pain. The meeting room smelled like old socks. She hadn't broken a sweat to speak of, but everyone else in FT looked like they'd been caught in a shower. The only consolation was that she felt so exhausted, Burkett's welcoming scowl as he met her in the hallway didn't make her feel worse.

"If you think the ambassador's influence is going to get you off the hook, Kilian, you're sadly mistaken." He hustled her and Hals past the rest of FT and Diplo, through the entry and out into the courtyard, where the lieutenant from Security waited by the triple-length.

"General Burkett!"

Everyone stopped, turned, stilled.

Nema stood in the embassy entry, surrounded by a half dozen of his brown-clothed guards. The shortest equaled him in height. The tallest outstripped him by a head, which made her at least two-one. All were armed. Twin shooters. Knives.

"You are taking my Eyes and Ears away from me!" His sibilant wail echoed off the blade-topped walls. He tucked his hands into his sleeves while six gold faces watched every humanish move. "But you will not take her for long?"

One word from him. Jani watched six pairs of gold hands hover near weapons while around her, grim-faced mainline Security patted their empty holsters. *All they're waiting for is one word from him.*

Burkett gaped. Swallowed. Found his voice. "Bloody hell." Service decorum went out the window as he pushed

Jani into the skimmer, then bulleted in behind her as Hals and Derringer piled in through the other side. The driver shot out of the courtyard and sped past the checkpoints without slowing. No one spoke until they cleared idomeni property.

CHAPTER 15

Jani barely managed to undress and set her alarm before tumbling into bed, visions of the glowering Burkett dancing in her pounding head. She had overheard him in heated discussion with Derringer as they had departed the embarkation zone—the phrases *Office Hours* and *nail down our options* had cropped up with depressing frequency.

Well, if Hals had a shot at nonjudicial punishment, she might not wind up too badly off. Besides, wasn't there an old Service saying that a Spacer without at least one Article 13 on his or her record was unworthy of the name?

Makes me a Spacer for the ages. Jani had stopped counting after number five. She buried her face in her pillow and fell into troubled sleep.

"—anytime now."

Jani jerked awake at the sound of the intruding voice. Reached out. Grabbed a handful of—

What the—? She opened her eyes and saw herself reflected in a glassy brown stare. She released her grip on Val the Bear's throat and lifted her muzzy head.

"I said, feel free to wake up anytime now." Lucien had dragged her desk chair into the bedroom. He appeared much too comfortable, feet propped on the mattress's edge, chair tipped back precariously.

"How 'n hell d'you get in here?" Jani worked her jaw, yawned, stretched her stiff legs.

"Facilities should invest in better locks," he said by way of explanation. "If you get up now, you'll have forty minutes to shower and dress before you have to hightail it to FT."

"I need to eat—"

"So you shall. I have breakfast set out in the sitting room."

"It has to be scanned—"

"I came and got the scanner before I got the food. It's all clear."

"Aren't you the efficient one?"

Lucien tugged at his short-sleeve. "Why's it so warm in here?"

"Because I like it." Jani's voice rang clearer that time. "How long have you been sitting there?"

"Half hour." He offered her the knowing sort of smile that made her teeth clench. "Did you know you talk in your sleep?"

"Do tell." Jani twisted around and sat up, catching her bedcover just in time. She still wore panties, but her bandbra rested amid the muddle of clothing heaped on the bedroom floor. *Make that, "had been heaped."* Le steward extraordinaire had taken care of her dirty laundry along with everything else.

"You're going to have to tell me about Piers sometime." Lucien's gaze drifted from her face to points south, lingering on her bare shoulders. "I see you don't believe in pajamas."

Jani yanked the sheet up to her neck. "Out."

"I don't either."

"Get *out*!" She tried the melodramatic "pointed finger thrust toward the door" move and almost dropped her coverage.

"I love it when a woman loses her . . . temper." Lucien did a side roll out of the chair and darted to the door. He ducked through the opening just as Val the Bear impacted the panel at a height even with the back of his head.

"So, tell me about your trip to the embassy." Lucien poured coffee for both of them, then settled back, mug in hand.

Jani crunched toast as she checked out her scanpack. "How much have you heard?"

"Only the disobeying a direct order part."

"How did you hear about that so soon?"

"Diplo contacted I-Com to ask if they could borrow some recording equipment. Night Desk contacted me because I'm in charge of the storage bins." Lucien reached across the desk to Jani's plate and snatched an apple slice from her overladen fruit cup. "Woke me out of a sound sleep at oh-three up. Burkett must have started amassing his weapons as soon as you returned to Sheridan."

Jani dropped her half-eaten toast on her plate. "And those weapons would be?"

"You'd better contact your lawyer first thing you get to your office." Lucien brushed a nonexistent spot from his immaculate shirtfront. "His name wouldn't happen to be Piers, would it?"

"I'm surprised you have to ask." Jani stabbed halfheartedly at her fruit. "Did you hear any fallout concerning Sam Duong?"

"Why would I?" Lucien finished his coffee and started piling dirty dishes onto the take-out tray. "That sorry situation is none of my business."

"Since when did that ever stop you?"

"It's none of yours, either."

"He made it my business." Jani set down her fork. The memory of the man's desperation ruined what remained of her appetite. "He put me down as next of kin in his MedRec."

"Because you said you believed him?" Lucien made a point of setting Jani's fruit cup on the desk before picking up the tray. "I knew you'd regret saying that."

"I don't regret a thing. I think he may have been set up."

"And why would anyone bother to do that?" Lucien walked about the room gathering newssheets and plucking wilted flowers from the bouquet. "He's a clerk."

"He's a clerk who's been overseeing the compilation of Rauta Shèràa Base and Knevçet Shèràa documents for years." Jani felt a twinge of satisfaction as Lucien hesitated in mid-pluck. "I think he uncovered something, and that something's buried in the missing documents. I think somebody stole the paper, then hung Duong with a *crazy* tag so that he'd get blamed for the docs being missing."

"That's a lot of thinking."

"Admit it—did you ever observe a scene better calculated to destroy a man's reputation?"

"So he works for an asshole." Lucien took his time folding an old newssheet into a loose cylinder. "Make that two assholes." He shoved the paper tube into the 'zap. "What do you think he knows? Or doesn't know he knows?"

Jani didn't answer. Instead, she picked another mental spare fitting out of the bin and checked it for size. "Did you ever hear of Niall Pierce? He's a colonel in Special Services."

Lucien frowned. "The guy who almost ran into you in the SIB lobby."

"Does everybody know him?"

"Just by reputation." Lucien glanced at the clock. "We better get going."

They spent valuable minutes arguing about the breakfast she hadn't eaten. By the time they departed TOQ, the walkways had cleared of first-shifters, which meant that if Jani didn't get a move on, she'd be late. *Not at a time like this.* Her back issued a string of complaints as she broke into a double-time trot.

"I saw Pierce at the hospital, too. He was standing outside the office where I met with Friesian." She pressed a hand to her right side as a stitch took up residence.

Lucien loped beside her with disgusting ease. "Think he was listening?"

"He wasn't that functional. Takedown malaise had him by the throat."

"So he had a good reason to be there. Your running into him was a coincidence."

"We've got quite a few coincidences jostling for space here, don't we?" Jani eased to a slow jog as the Documents Control white box came into view. "You said he had a reputation."

Lucien hesitated. "I've heard things about him."

Jani detected an edge in his voice. That meant he didn't want to discuss Pierce. *That* meant it was time to push. "I know he was at Rauta Shèràa. I know he nailed a field commission after the evac, and that he's Mako's man."

Lucien shot her a "how did you know that?" look. "He and Mako are an odd couple. Mako comes from a cultured background—he doesn't like to admit it, but he's descended from a long line of Family affiliates. Pierce joined the Service to stay out of prison."

Jani gasped in relief as they eased to a walk—her sidestitch had evolved into an entire wardrobe. "What was he up for?"

"Weapons-running." Lucien tapped her on the arm to get her attention—together they saluted a pair of sideline majors walking toward them. "Even after he joined up, he still got into trouble. Fights. Smuggling. Disobeying orders. All that changed after he was transferred to the Fourth Expeditionary. Mako straightened him out. When they returned to Earth, Pierce even went back to school, got a degree at Chicago Combined. Literature, of all things. He doesn't look the type."

Jani pulled in a deep breath. Another. "So? What are you—not telling me?"

Lucien blinked. "What makes you think—?"

"Save the coy-boy routine for someone who buys it and—spit it out!"

Coy Boy eyed her in disapproval. "If you got out of bed at a reasonable hour, you wouldn't have to push yourself."

"*Lucien.*"

"I found the anesthetic, glue, and bandage in your bathroom. I trashed them and hid the scalpel."

"I'll get more."

"You don't want to escape now. You're having too much fun sticking your nose where it doesn't belong."

"Answer the damned question!"

"Mako saved the Service."

"That's old news." Jani kept an eye out for Hals as they pulled up in front of the Documents Center. "Tell me something I don't know." She walked a figure eight. Her pounding heart slowed.

Lucien strolled to the walkway's edge and kicked at the stone border. "At first, it didn't want to be saved. The Old Guard needed to retire. Some of them didn't want to go."

"But Mako, with the help of loyal underlings like Pierce, helped them make up their minds."

"He was promoted to J-Loop Regional Command after Rauta Shèràa. The promotion was designed to reward him officially and at the same time get him out of the way. It didn't work." Lucien stepped over to Jani and leaned close to her ear. "That's where he started cleaning house. Not everything he did was by the book. That's not common knowledge."

"It was well before your time, too. How did you find out?"

"I *am* in Intelligence."

"And you've sneaked peeks at files. And Anais probably told you things." Jani sniffed. Lucien had used scented soap that morning. A light, musky odor, barely detectable. "And you have this way about you that makes people spill their guts."

"You think so?" He moved closer and brushed against her arm. "Care to tell me what way that is?"

"Oh, I think you know." She stepped away and started up the Doc Control steps, then turned back. "I wonder if Pierce had anything to do with what happened to Sam Duong?"

Lucien shook his head. "Why would he want to bury Rauta Shèràa documents? If anything, he'd want to get those out in the open."

"You'd think that, except Mako was called before a Board of Inquiry after the evac team returned to Earth. He bulled his way through it, and emerged victorious."

"So?"

"So maybe something in the Rauta Shèràa documents would sully that victory."

Lucien sighed in annoyance. "I suppose anything's possible."

"Think you could find out more about ex–weapons runner Pierce?"

"That's what I like about you—you never ask for much."

"You owe me." Jani stared at Lucien—he dropped his gaze eventually. "You had no right to pick through my stuff, no right to take that scalpel, and no right to read my ServRec."

"It made for an enlightening afternoon." He looked up at her, cheeks flushed from exercise, stony eyes alight with cool appraisal. "You really could have gone places if you'd behaved, you know that?"

"If I'd shut up and played along, you mean?"

The light dimmed. "There are plenty of ways to make your point without impaling yourself in the process." Lucien snapped a salute and clipped down the walkway to wherever he went, sweat-darkened hair gleaming in the sun like a tarnished halo.

"Your mail, ma'am."

Jani looked up from her equipment transfer report. Ischi stood in her doorway, holding a thin packet of paper mail. If past behavior held, he was using mail delivery as an excuse to talk to her. That was fine—she had a few questions for him, too. "Come on in, Lieutenant. Have a seat."

He slipped inside and settled into the visitor's chair. "I hope you're well after last night, ma'am." Residual excitement animated his haggard features. "I taught the idomeni ambassador how to play soccer!"

Jani smiled. "Yes, you did."

"He sure got upset when Burkett tried to get you bounced." Ischi placed her mail on the desk, one piece at a time. "Think he could put in a word for the colonel?"

"Where is she?" Jani had gone directly to Hals's office as soon as she'd arrived, only to find it dark. She had reconnoitered intermittently ever since, but it was after lunch and there was still no sign.

"Emergency meeting scheduled with Major General Eiswein, head of First D-Doc."

"In this building?"

"No, ma'am. Eiswein sits up at Base Command. North Lakeside sector."

"I should go." Jani closed her report folder and stood up, but the look of alarm that flared across Ischi's face compelled her to sink back down in her chair.

"We've been told to stafo, ma'am."

Sit tight and await further orders. "By whom?"

"Eiswein, ma'am. Her exec transmitted the order when he came to escort Hals to North Lakeside."

Shit. Jani sat back down and thumped her fist on the arm of her chair. "She did the right thing. The Vynshàrau would not have understood her absence, and that would have crippled negotiations."

"Yes, ma'am." Ischi poked moodily at her mail, then slipped an ivory envelope out from the pile. "Your raffle number came."

"My what?"

"Your raffle number." He slid it across the desk to her. "Every month, the A-G hosts a garden party at his house at Far North Lakeside. Invitation's by raffle—everybody gets a number issued them once they get entered into Base systems." He offered a perfunctory grin. "Hottest ticket in town."

"Is it that great?"

"My number came up last spring." He wrinkled his nose. "It was still cold, and it rained. The tent was heated, though, and the food was great." His smile brightened. "Mrs. Mako's beautiful. She took folks on a tour of her greenhouse. Lot of the guys went just to check her out."

Jani opened her desk drawer and swept the envelope inside. "Well, neither flowers nor beautiful women interest me, Lieutenant, but thanks for the heads-up."

Ischi's face darkened. "Sorry, ma'am." He stood. "Do you think the ambassador could do anything to help, ma'am?"

"I'll see what I can do." Jani punched out the one base code she knew. "What's Major Vespucci's take on this?"

"Um." Ischi rose and backed his way to the door. "No one's talked to him, ma'am. At least I haven't." He departed, leaving Jani alone with the blooming face on her comport display.

"Hello." Even a transmission of Lucien's smile lit up the

room. "Called to ask me out to dinner? The answer's yes."

"Actually, I called to ask you for Nema's private code."

The happy expression snapped off. "I can't give you that."

"Can you tell me if FT's comports are being monitored for outgoing."

"No."

"No as in 'no, they're not,' or no as in 'go to hell'?"

"*Will you*—" Lucien's face blanked as his eyes followed something over top his display. A walk-through, most likely, which meant he resided in a desk pool.

"Don't you have an office?" Jani asked, just to rub it in.

"In a sane world, the lieutenants would have the offices and the captains would be out on the street, but that day is not yet come."

"You've become a philosopher."

"And you're still a pain in the ass."

"Hals has been at North Lakeside all day."

"And they told you to stafo?"

"Yes."

"Then do it!" The display sharded as Lucien signed off.

Jani rested her head on her desk, every once in a while pressing her fingertips to her tightening scalp. By the time she lifted her head, her incoming call alarm rang.

"Jani." Friesian's expression would have darkened the bottom of a mineshaft. "Why didn't you call me immediately?"

"I—"

"Things like this aren't just supposed to drop down on me from the sky. Things like this are supposed to be told me by my cooperative client."

"But—"

"Are you busy at fifteen up? Good. See you here. Defense Command Three South, Room Three-oh-four."

"I don't need legal counsel for Office Hours."

"You need legal counsel to get up in the morning." The display fractured once more.

Jani stared at the message light, which still blinked. Someone had called her while she talked, or rather, listened to Friesian. All of a sudden, she had become very popular.

"Good afternoon, Captain Kilian, this is Captain Brighton

from Diplomatic," said the professionally dour woman. "I am calling to inform you of your Office Hours appointment with Brigadier General Callum Burkett for the day after tomorrow. The exact time and date have been applied to your calendar. Details have also been provided to your attorney, Major Piers Friesian, Defense Command. Good day."

Jani fled her office just as the incoming message alarm rang yet again. She hurried into the desk pool and over to one of the techs, who was busy stuffing paper mail into mailboxes. "Do you have anything that needs to be walked anywhere?"

"Ma'am?" The young woman dug into one of the OUT bins. "This needs to go to the SIB, but I can—"

"Perfect." Jani grabbed the envelope and darted out the door. *Always have a reason to go where you're going.* Especially if it gave you a reason to get the hell out of where you were.

The afternoon proved a copy of every one previous—deliciously hot and dry. On her way to the SIB, Jani stopped off at a ship's stores kiosk and shopped. She bought a creamy white coffee mug decorated with a brushlike crimson flower. *La fleur feu*—the fireflower, the emblem of Acadian Central United. Just enough of the old red to make a statement, but not enough to drive her augie up the wall. *Take that, Corporal Coffee Cup.* She'd savor the look on Ischi's face the next time she visited the brewer.

If we're all still working together, that is.

She also bought a canister of Bandan loose tea. Halmahera Black, an expensive blend of hothouse hybrids. She asked the items be packed in separate carriers, and headed to the SIB.

She dropped the envelope in the appropriate mail slot, then descended the stairs to the basement. *He may not be in yet.* Second shift didn't start until fifteen up. But Jani knew Sam Duong would be at his desk. She doubted he had anywhere else to go.

CHAPTER 16

Sam leafed through one of the few files that remained on his desk. Names to check for inclusion in the Gate—at least they still allowed him that much. It meant more trips into Chicago, since Yance had revoked his SIB archive access. But, truth be told, he needed the time away from the basement. Not that people said anything to his face, but he knew they talked. He could tell by the way that they looked at him. Pity could come in many flavors—angry, disgusted, disappointed. But it was still *pity*. He'd have preferred it if they'd hated him. At least hatred stood on its own two feet.

He heard the voices in the cubicles around him waver, and assumed yet another visit from Odergaard. He braced for the sight of that red face rising over his cubicle partition like a florid sunrise.

"Mr. Duong?"

Sam stilled at the sound of the voice. He looked up slowly.

"Hello." Jani Kilian smiled down at him. "I wanted to talk to you about . . . well, I think you know what I want to talk to you about." She held out one of the two silvery plastic bags she carried. "I've even brought a facilitator."

Sam smiled weakly. "In Chicago, we just call them bribes."

"How indelicate." She beckoned for him to follow with the hurried backward hand wave of a child. "Let's go."

Sam stood, paused, then stepped out of his cubicle. All

eyes fixed on him, from the split-shifters readying to leave for the day to the second-shifters straggling in like the first wet splotches of a rainstorm. He followed Kilian into the hall—the pressure of stares lifted like the removal of a weight.

"Is there a breakroom around here?" She looked one way, then the other. "I have a meeting at fifteen up. That doesn't leave us much time."

"This way." Sam led her down the hall to the vend alcove. Three split-shifters sat at one of the tables by the entry, reading newssheets and smoking nicsticks. He led Kilian to his favored table in the back of the room. She fell into one of the chairs and handed him the bag.

He opened it. "Shrimp tea! I used to drink it all the time." He removed the dark green canister and turned it over and over in his hands. "I can't afford it anymore since the tariff increase." He hurried across the alcove to the beverage dispenser and drew a dispo of hot water. "I should have properly boiled water in a pot," he said as he slid back into his seat, "but I will make do." He cracked the canister seal, removed the slotted scoop from the inside of the top lid, filled it with the loose leaves, and snapped the lid closed. "I need orange rind for proper brewing, but oh well." He dipped the scoop into the hot water and watched the ebon essence leach from the black leaves. It dawned on him that Kilian hadn't spoken for a while. He glanced over at her to find her staring at him.

"You know it's called shrimp tea?" Her voice sounded weak. "It says Halmahera Black on the label."

Sam shrugged. "It's shrimp tea. Some people think if you filter it through boiled shrimp shells, it's supposed to unlock hidden flavors."

"Does it?"

"No. Makes it taste like crap." He removed the scoop, tapped it gently against the rim of the dispo to remove the excess liquid, then set it aside. "Some people can convince themselves to like anything, I suppose, if it's outrageous enough. Big fight about it at the university, sometime back."

"The Great Boiled Shrimp Debate." Kilian sat back and

folded her arms across her chest. She looked as though she shivered, but how could anyone feel cold in this heat? "Mr. Duong, when did you work at the university?"

Sam thought. Thought some more. He knew the wheres, most times. As always, the whens gave him problems. "Twenty years ago, I think. Could be more. Could be less." He tapped his temple. "It's my head. I have a problem with my memory that bothers Dr. Pimentel."

"He told me about your condition. I had the right to know, since you'd knocked me."

"Knocked . . . ?"

Kilian cocked her head to one side, then the other. "N.O.K. Nok. It's dexxie slang for naming someone your next of kin." She exhaled sharply, like a breathy laugh. "Like I said, Pimentel told me about your condition. I'm going to test your allegedly poor memory by asking you some questions, OK?"

Sam set his cup down. Oh well, it was fun while it lasted. "I didn't hide your papers in my desk."

Kilian waved her hand dismissively, her face grave. "I'm not asking you about that. I want to know about the other papers."

Grave is the right word for her. Like the grave light that shone in her too-dark eyes, black as the tea in his cup. "*Kensington* records." He took a sip of the grave. "The death certificates showed up this morning."

"In your desk?"

"In my locker."

"Really?"

"I did not put them there."

"I believe you." Her voice held a quiet strength. "What kinds of *Kensington* records?"

"*Kensington* records from the *Kensington*." Sam grinned at his bad joke. That made one of them. "Rosters. Shipping records."

"And the death certificates?"

"Four certificates. Ebben, Unser, Fitzhugh, and Caldor."

"Major General Talitha Ebben. Base commander, Rauta Shèràa Base." Kilian grimaced, as though it hurt to say the name. "Colonel Phil Unser was her exec. Colonel Matilda

Fitzhugh ran the Special Services branch, and reported directly to Ebben."

"Wasn't that unusual?"

"No. Spec Service always reports to the base commander." Kilian struggled to her feet and walked unsteadily to the beverage dispenser. "When did those particular documents go missing?" She chose black coffee, and held the dispo with both hands as she trod back to her chair.

"I don't—" Sam paused to drink, and wished he could enjoy the tea without the questions. "I don't remember."

"Do you recall the causes of death?"

He shrugged. "There were rumors the Haárin killed them."

Kilian's eyes clouded. Cold tea. She looked down at the steaming dispo, which she still held in both hands. She didn't seem interested in drinking the coffee, only in absorbing its heat. "That would mean they died from stab wounds, since they died during the Night of the Blade."

Sam nodded. "The Haárin only used swords and knives that night, to kill the Laum. To cleanse the city."

Kilian set down the cup then pressed her palms to her cheeks. "You mentioned a Caldor, too. I don't remember a Caldor in the command staff."

"Spacer First Class. Died during the final round of bombing. A barracks wall collapsed on her." Kilian's look grew pained—Sam wondered why.

"I heard Mako mishandled the remains." She drew her hands away from her face; their coffee-warmth left redness behind. "He had to answer questions when he returned to Earth, but those records are sealed."

Sam shrugged. "So we'll never know. They all died during panic, so there was no follow-up investigation. No images of the scenes of death appended to their certs."

"No proof," Kilian said.

"Proof." Sam drank down the balance of his tea, before it looked like Kilian's eyes. "I think of so many deaths. They left behind no images, either. No proof." He crumpled the dispo between his hands. "All I have are flashes of thought, things I know."

Kilian leaned forward, eyes downcast. She looked like

someone trying to see over the edge of a cliff without drawing too close. "Like what?"

"Like . . ." Sam ground the crumpled cup against the tabletop, and blurted out all the things he knew. "Like I never walk on the beaches here because of the sand. I hate sand. And heat. And hospitals and doctors and the way Pimentel looks at me when he tells me he wants to cut into my head for my own good." He worked his hand back and forth, grinding the cup into the marble-patterned poly. "There is no good in that, not for me. And he promises I'll be fine and he says they'll take care of me but even though he speaks I hear the words come from somewhere else and I don't remember where. I just know it isn't here." He picked up the flattened cup. "And I can't remember why I hate any of it. I just know I do."

Kilian sat back slowly. She looked older now, years of age added in minutes. "You don't want the surgery?"

"No. No cutting in my head. I know I'll die if they cut into my head." He reached across the table and touched her hand. Still so cold, as though no amount of heat could warm her. "And I knew, I *knew* when you said you believed me that . . ." He pulled back. "That if Pimentel tried to force me, you'd stop him."

Kilian tucked her hands beneath her arms. "How do you know?"

"Because I just know. Like I've been telling you." Sam stood, picked up his smashed cup, and tossed it in the sink so it could dissolve. Water-soluble cellulosic. No trashzaps in the SIB archives. Too great a risk of fire, and fire here would destroy so much. "Do you know what it's like, to know something in your bones?"

Kilian hesitated. Her eyes looked strange, glistening, as though she suffered from fever. "Yes."

Sam bent close. "Well, that is how I know I can trust you." He stood back, and pointed to the wall clock. "Five minutes to fifteen up. You'd better go."

Kilian followed him down the hall, into the stairwell, up the stairs, not drawing even with him until they had crossed the lobby. "You can trust me this time. I won't let you down." She left without smiling, or nodding, or offering him her hand to shake.

Sam stepped up to the lobby window. He watched Kilian leave the building, set her garrison cap on her head, and walk out into the brutal sun, and wondered why she said, "this time." He watched her cross the lawn to a stone bench set beneath a stand of oaks, and wondered why she took the time to stop and sit if she needed to make her fifteen up meeting. He watched her set her bag on the ground, then lean forward and cover her face with her hands. He thought back to her tired eyes and drawn face, and wondered if she suffered a headache and whether he should run out to her and offer her some painkiller.

Then he watched her shoulders shake, and wondered why she wept.

CHAPTER 17

"Sir!"

Evan cringed as Halvor's voice cut through the humid afternoon air. His hand jerked. The motion activated the trimmer he held; the edge brushed across a branch of the rose he'd been pruning. He swore as a fist-sized Crème Caramel lolled on the end of its damaged stem like a broken-necked doll's head. Reactivating the trimmer, he made one more slash and put the fragrant bloom out of its misery.

"Sir!"

"What is it!" Evan wheeled to face his bleating aide.

Halvor stopped short. He looked from Evan's face to the flower in his hands. "S-sorry, sir, but Mr. Loiaza's here."

Evan entered the sitting room to find Joaquin sitting on the sofa leafing through the contents of his documents case.

"Sorry for the surprise visit, Evan." He removed a recording board and several folders, placed them at his side, then dropped the case to the floor. "I received some rather alarming news this morning, however, that necessitates a reevaluation of our strategy."

"Let me guess." Evan lowered into a lounge chair opposite the sofa. It wasn't until he tried to grip the armrests that he realized he still held the trimmer and the rose. He tossed them one after the other atop a chairside table as though he had meant to carry them inside, as though this unexpected visit from his attorney hadn't rattled him in the least. "Something to do with Jani."

Joaquin nodded. "I received a call from your dusky Colonel Veda this morning. She informed me that the SIB can find no evidence linking Jani Kilian to the mutinous murder of Rikart Neumann."

Evan picked up the slaughtered rose and examined it. The petals looked edible—warm butterscotch tipped with peach, like blush on smooth skin. He gripped one velvet edge and yanked. "Did she tell you what they *did* plan to do with her?"

"You aren't going to like it."

Evan laid the petal on his knee, then tugged at another. "I don't like it already." He'd expected news like this since his visit to Neoclona, but he'd hoped he was wrong. He should have known better. Politics, not to mention life, had taught him that what you dreaded most usually came to pass.

Joaquin tapped the writing plane of his recording board with his stylus. "She's to be tried by an adjudicating committee. All indications at this time point to a medical discharge."

"Prison time, at least?"

"No."

"You're kidding!"

"Her health, by all accounts, is not good. Add that to the lack of evidence against her."

Evan tore the petal he held in half. "Oh for chrissake, everyone at the Consulate knew how much she hated Neumann!"

Joaquin smiled grimly. "A funny thing happens to people after they swear an oath. Suddenly, their words become gold and they become misers."

"I'm a free-spender. Why doesn't Veda ask me?"

"Again, it's a question of corroboration." Joaquin unclasped the fasteners of his jacket and sat back more easily. "Everyone knows what you have to say. But without anyone to back up your story, and without the paper to back them up, it's your word against Jani's, and, like it or not, she does have her sympathizers. Some of them are very vocal, and one in particular is riveting."

Evan added the bisected petal to the row forming on his knee. "Nema?"

"He does cut an intimidating figure when he isn't invading playgrounds and wowing them at Chicago Combined." Joaquin frowned in disapproval—in his dignified universe, responsible diplomats did *not* engage in invasions and wowings. "And as much as Cèel despises him, he'll support him when it comes to harassing us."

"Imposing trade sanctions." Another petal. "Looking the other way when colonial smugglers take refuge in their ports."

"Exactly."

As Evan annihilated his flower, Markhart entered bearing a tray. She glanced at him out of the corner of her eye—whatever she saw made her quicken her pace. She set the tray down on a side table and, since Joaquin preferred to be waited on, did the honors as server. She poured his tea and Evan's bourbon in efficient silence.

"She's a prize, Evan," Joaquin said after she had departed, sipping his tea appreciatively as he paged through a file. "Now, where were we?"

"Discussing our contingency plan." Evan swept up the petals and tossed them, along with the rose remains, back on the table. Then he dug into his trouser pocket and removed the recording-board wafer that contained his work-up of Niall Pierce. He carried it on his person as a precaution. He hadn't wanted to risk Halvor or Markhart accidentally erasing it or throwing it away. Or reading it. "Here. Have a look at this."

Joaquin accepted the wafer hesitantly. "What is it?"

"You said we should use more of my Rauta Shèràa experience. Now's our opportunity."

Joaquin pursed his lips. Aggravated turtle. Then he slipped the wafer into his board's reader slot, sat back with cup in hand, and did as Evan asked.

His brow furrowed every so often. He laughed once. That angered Evan, since he hadn't written anything funny.

When he finished, he set the board beside him on the sofa and contemplated his tea.

Evan ignored his bourbon, picking up the mangled rose instead. "Well?" He stripped another petal.

Joaquin didn't look at him. "Have you ever considered writing thrillers?"

"What the hell's that supposed to mean?"

"I mean that this tale of yours is the most convoluted, seat-of-the-pants thing I've read since Vladislav's *The Hijack of the Sainte Marie*."

Evan sent rose parts scattering as he bounded to his feet. "Oh come on, Quino!" He paced the room. "Name the Family that doesn't have something like that in their history!"

"Evan, there's a difference between the information bandied at parties and that used to defend oneself in court. What you have here"—Joaquin pointed to his recording board—"is speculation, and defamatory speculation at that."

Evan parked himself in the window seat behind Joaquin. "I thought if you wrote it down, it's libel."

"It needs to be published in a public venue to qualify as libel, and no one will publish this if I have to smash the wafer to bits myself." Joaquin twisted around so he could look him in the face. "You honestly believe it?"

"Yes."

"That Niall Pierce was involved in felonious activities at Rauta Shèràa Base and that Roshi Mako has squelched the Kilian investigation to prevent those goings-on from being discovered?"

"*Goings-on?* Christ, Quino, you make it sound so polite." Evan swung the rose by the stem, whacking the remains of the bloom against his thigh like a riding crop. "*Yes.*"

"You give me nothing to work with. You say ships from the Fourth Expeditionary often docked at the Rauta Shèràa transfer point, but you offer no proof that Pierce crewed on any of them. You don't even give me the names of the ships so I can check."

"He must have been on one of them. It's the right time frame." Evan pointed the vanquished rose at Joaquin. "All you have to do is get hold of the Fourth Expeditionary vessel records and comb the docking data and the crew lists."

"Track every move made by a half dozen GateWay-class

vessels over a period of at least three years. Is that all?"
Joaquin pinched the bridge of his nose. "And if we found
Pierce had indeed visited Rauta Shèràa, even that he had
visited the city multiple times, what good would that do?
The same people who can't remember Jani Kilian's actions
aren't going to recall the occasional pass-throughs of a non-
resident enlisted man."

"You left out the clincher." Evan stood and paced some
more. It made sense, damn it—why couldn't Joaquin open
his mind! "Pierce's emotional health went into a tailspin after
it became known that Jani was alive. Jani knew everything
about what went on there—she'd know what Pierce did and
when he did it. He sees his career diving into the 'zap—he's
scared to death she'll rat him out."

"Evan." Joaquin pressed his fingertips to his forehead.
"That's too much coincidence, even for Vladislav."

"You said yourself that Pierce had a criminal past, and
that he didn't change his ways after he joined the Service."

"He did change his ways in the Fourth."

"Are you sure! How do you know he just hadn't learned
to hide his crimes better?"

Joaquin blinked. He had the dazed look of a man who'd
taken one too many punches. "Evan, my sources are very
sound, and they tell me—"

*"Just get off your bony ass and check, you son of a bitch—
that's what I'm paying you for!"*

Silence fingered through the room like ice crystals spread-
ing through freezing liquid. Joaquin blinked with reptile
slowness, as though unable to believe that he'd heard what
he'd heard.

Then the comprehension dawned, and his face reddened.
"We'll blame that outburst on the tension you're under and
move on." He fingered the lapel of his staid dark blue jacket.
"So, you claim Pierce was involved with the criminal net-
works working out of Rauta Shèràa Base, that an investigation of Jani's relationship with Rik Neumann would have
revealed his guilt, and that Roshi arranged to scuttle said
investigation, not to mention jeopardize a thirty-plus-year career, in order to protect him." He picked up his recording

board and readied his stylus. "Explain the field commission."

"I touched on that at the end." Evan stalked the room, picking up petals as he went. "I think Roshi threw the lieutenancy at Pierce as a bribe, to make him behave." He shrugged. "The other possibility is that Pierce really earned the promotion. Being a criminal wouldn't necessarily prevent him from acting bravely."

"You're leveling serious charges against a man who is widely acknowledged as the savior of the Service."

"His decision to save the Service could have started with Pierce. He salvaged one lost boy, decided he'd found his calling, and went on to rescue the whole damned system."

"You honestly believe this?"

"*Yes*. How many times are you going to ask me that?"

Joaquin deactivated his stylus and powered down his recording board. "John Shroud called me yesterday. He needed to speak to me about your medical condition."

Oh shit. "I can imagine what he said."

"No, I don't think you can." Joaquin stashed the equipment in his documents case, then gathered the files. "I was going to delay telling you. I thought the news about Kilian enough of a blow for one day." He motioned for Evan to sit.

Evan returned to his chair. The glass of bourbon at his elbow whispered *remember me*. "Shroud would say anything to save Jani's skin, Quino. Keep that in mind." He took a golden swallow and waited for the next volley.

Joaquin leafed through a folder, then closed it and stuffed it in his bag. "You've been classified as a maintenance alcoholic since your mid-teens. During most of that time, you received the quality of medical care necessary to guarantee your good health while allowing you to indulge your dependency." He shot Evan an irritated look. "But there were times, John said, when you didn't care for yourself as you should have. Your tour of duty on Shèrá was one of those times."

"He's a liar! I—"

"According to medical-annex records, you failed to follow your mandated treatment regimen. You worked too hard.

Played too hard as well. With that Kilian woman, and other wild companions."

Evan drained his glass and reached for the bottle. "You make it sound like the second rise of Sodom and Gomorrah. We threw a few parties."

"Quite." Another moue of distaste. "The point is that John's opinion of your past health casts doubt on whatever testimony you have to offer, while his diagnosis of your present condition has effectively scuttled your ability to act in your own defense."

Shroud, you bastard. "I'll have a talk with him."

"I would advise against your contacting him personally, Evan. Going through proper channels at a time like this can only work in your favor."

Evan knew how to decode that remark. "You've already discussed his findings with Veda."

"I was compelled to by law. To allow things to continue with your competency in doubt would have constituted the worst sort of malpractice."

"My. *Competency?*" Evan sagged into the seat. "Any test that old Snowy wants to throw at me, I'll take. Just set the date."

Joaquin avoided his eye. "I don't want it to come to that, Evan. Really I don't."

"He's got you believing it, hasn't he? That my mind is gone."

Joaquin clasped the fasteners of his documents bag. "I need to reopen some doors I felt we could close, start exploring the Haárin connection to the goings-on at Rauta Shè-ràa Base."

Evan felt his reflexes slow, his mind numb, as though he'd already downed the second liter of the day. "I don't recall that ever being more than rumor."

"It is now. Do admit, it's not completely outside the realm of probability. Hansen Wyle did die in one of their bombing raids, and the images of the slaughter of the Laum during the Night of the Blade are very potent. You feared for your life, Evan. You were ill. You became involved in things you shouldn't have, something we will admit. You thought it possible the Haárin could come after you the same way they went after Kilian after Knevçet Shèràa."

"You're going to blame the transport bombing on the Haárin?"

"Based on the tone of the time, it's possible." Joaquin stood and refastened his jacket. "Reasonable doubt, Evan. Let that be your mantra for the next few months." He picked up a rose petal that had drifted onto the sofa cushion and flicked it absently onto the serving tray.

Evan watched him. Funny, the Joaquin Loiaza he had known for years had never ignored an injury to a rose—odd that he hadn't yet commented on Evan's prolonged torture of the Crème Caramel. Very odd. "Quino, give me the wafer back."

Joaquin gave him a blank look. The turtle befuddled.

"The *wafer*. You accidentally left it in your recording board. I'd like it back, please."

"All right." Joaquin unfastened his bag, removed the board, and popped out the wafer, all with the thin-lipped haste that implied he had more important things to do. "Here."

Evan took the disc and slipped it in his pocket. "What are you up to?"

Quino released a rattling sigh. "I'm up to getting you out of this house. What else would I be up to?"

Following his solitary dinner, Evan sat at his workstation and perused the public data banks open to someone with his restricted access. He looked up Korsakoff's syndrome, and studied the descriptions of the associated memory defects. They were rare thanks to the advances in addiction maintenance, but they did occasionally occur in alcoholics who received inadequate medical care.

"Bullshit." Evan activated his recording board and spent some time writing descriptions and events from his past, beginning with his mid-teens. Then he checked the facts against the holos and sceneshots archived in desk drawers and cabinets.

The neckpiece his father wore to his graduation from Sarstedt. Black-and-gold diagonal striping. *Check.*

The color of the bunk blankets on the *Excelsior*, the cruiser that transported him to Shèrá and his first diplomatic posting. Maroon. *Check.*

The flowers Lyssa wore in her hair on their wedding day. White Mauna Kea orchids. *Check.*

The weather on the day he was sworn in as Interior Minister of the Commonwealth of Planets. Blue sky sunny and cold as a witch's tit. *Check!*

He left the room only once, to confirm with a befuddled Markhart what he'd had for lunch the previous day. Vegetable soup. Cheddar bread. Pear tart. *Got it.* Combed the newssheets to assure himself he had indeed watched the holoVee drama he remembered from the night before.

He slumped in his chair, the desktop and the surrounding floor scattered with confirmatory remnants. *There's nothing wrong with my memory.*

And if he didn't act quickly, that fact could keep him marooned on Elba for the rest of his life.

He adjourned to bed, exhausted. Slept. Dreamed. Of Jani.

She looked as she had before the crash. Rounder, cuter face. More compact, curvier body.

She wore the nightgown he'd bought her for their first anniversary. A gift both for her and his twenty-four-year-old hormones, a murderously expensive confection imported from Phillipa. Transparent film from neckline to floor, cut with an opaque swirl that covered just enough and no more.

She straddled him, the gown's skirt hiked up to reveal her satiny thighs. She said something that made them both laugh. Then she leaned forward, shoulder-length black hair veiling her face, and kissed him.

The scene shifted. No more nightgown. Just her flawless skin, lit by unseen illumination to the shade of the Crème Caramel. Perfect breasts. Narrow waist. Swell of hip. Head thrown back as she moved above him, called his name, cried out—

He snapped awake, mouth dry, heart pounding. *Damn it— anybody but her—!* He groaned as the ache of an erection overtook him; he dispatched it in the usual manner.

He got out of bed, showered, switched into fresh pajamas. Then he collected a bottle and padded downstairs and outside to his sheltered patio.

The night air was weighty with heat and the unfulfilled longing for storm. Evan sat, propped his bare feet on a table, and drank. Then he laid back his head and counted the stars.

I visited some of you. Committed crimes. Then returned home to the life that had been made for him, a glossy thing with a hollow center built on a foundation of sand.

"Didn't turn out the way you planned, did it, Dad?" He kept his eyes focused on the night sky as he spoke to his dead father. Then he decided that was being optimistic, and looked down at the flagstone instead. "I started out so full of promise." But the posting to the Rauta Shèràa Consulate, meant to be the first step in a great career, devolved into disaster, followed by full-blown, tail-between-the-legs retreat.

The journey from hell. A detour to Phillipa to take on supplies added two weeks to an already-interminable journey. By the time Evan touched down at O'Hare, he had lost fifteen kilos and, despite the efforts of the *Hilfington* medical officer, much of his hair. Stress, he'd told his mother, who had broken down at the sight of him. To Dad, he'd said nothing. *You did the right thing,* his father told him as they walked down the VIP Concourse. *You did it for Rik.*

He'd come home to the hard looks the bereaved sometimes bestowed on the survivors. *And to the funerals.* Rikart Neumann's memorial service, sans body, followed by Ebben's, Unser's, and Fitzhugh's, that might as well have been. Closed caskets all, because of the condition of the bodies. Severe decomposition caused by improper storage, his father had said. Criminal negligence, the mourning Families maintained.

Sloppy of Mako. The forceful performance he'd given before the Board of Inquiry assured that the furor didn't damage his career, but still. . . . *All he had to do was put the bodies in the damned freezer.* What the hell had he done, stuffed them in body bags and shoved them in the hold?

Evan sat and watched the moon, his mind emptying with the bottle. No more thoughts of death. Jani. Lyssa. His children. By the time he returned to bed, he felt numbed. *Nothing wrong with my memory.* But then, that was the problem, wasn't it?

CHAPTER 18

Jani sat at her desk, her hands moving over her workstation touchboard at their own pace, in their own world. She was sufficiently adept at report assembly that she didn't need to concentrate on what she did in order to do it. Lucky for her.

With the help of some cold water and borrowed makeup, she had pulled herself together by the time she met with Friesian, at least on the outside. Their discussion began contentious, with a gradual shift to tense treaty by the end. Yes, he would sit at her side during her Office Hours with Burkett and yes, this did complicate any possible deal with the Judge Advocate. Her special knowledge of idomeni customs would weigh in her favor. Any pressure applied on her behalf by the idomeni ambassador would not. Nema had been told exactly that after he called Burkett in person to protest her treatment, and seemed to understand when told that his interference would only complicate an already-messy situation. At least, he had nodded his head in a positive manner. When Jani had commented on the many ways such a head-nodding could be interpreted, Friesian had once again broken out the bright pink headache tablets.

That meeting finished, she had returned to FT to find no one had heard from Hals. The desk-pool techs watched her with coiled-spring wariness when she emerged from her office to get coffee, which she drank from a dispo. Her Acadia Central United mug joined the Gruppo Helvetica in the bottom drawer of her desk. Ischi hadn't been in the mood to take a joke, and she certainly hadn't been in the mood to make one.

Jani entered the last of the data-transfer parameters into the report grid, applied the macro, and sat back to watch the report assemble itself, section by section. Part of her monitored the formatting and data retrieval with an eye that could detect a problem without consciously thinking about it. The rest of her decamped to the dark corner of her soul and pondered whether Sam Duong could actually be Simyam Baru.

He looks so different. She caught a glimpse of her skewed reflection in the display surface. *Join the crowd.*

She wondered if she could dare broach the subject. She wondered where she would start. *Hello, Mr. Baru. Do you remember me? I'm the one who let it happen, the one who didn't act quickly enough, the one who let you die.*

Do you remember me?

I've never forgotten you.

"So this is how the other half lives."

Jani looked up to find Lucien leaning against the doorjamb, arms folded, examining her office with a doubtful eye.

"I thought there'd at least be furniture." He sauntered in and paced a circle in the large empty space between her desk and her window. "Great view," he sniffed as he walked past the pane. He flopped into her visitor's chair and put his feet up on her desk. "Do you know what time it is?"

Jani checked her timepiece. "Twenty-one seventeen."

"Have you had dinner?"

"No."

"When's your next appointment with Pimentel?"

"Tomorrow."

"He's going to be perturbed."

"Probably."

"Well, that makes three one-word answers in a row." Lucien tugged at his trouser crease. He looked extremely crisp, as though he'd changed into a fresh uniform just prior to dropping by. "Are you angry with me for not giving you Nema's code?"

"No." *Not much.*

"Good, because I spent the whole day busting tail for you."

"Really?"

"That's *five* one-word answers in a row. What's wrong?"

Jani watched page after page of her export-license agreement pull itself together from portions of other people's reports. *That's how Roger thinks Sam's mind works.* Every day, every hour. *And I have no good reason to think otherwise.* "I talked with Sam Duong today."

"And?"

"He's sick."

"I could have told you that."

"I think he might—" No, she couldn't give the possibility voice. Not yet. "I think he might have a very good reason for being the way he is."

"That's not what you were going to say." Lucien plucked her stylus holder from her desktop and toyed with the charger. "Doing anything tomorrow afternoon?"

"Burning a candle for my Office Hours appointment. Otherwise, no." Her workstation signaled the report complete, and she forwarded it to Hals's system for sign-off. "Why?"

"Interdepartmental soccer match. I'm captain of the Fourth Floor Wonderboys. Star halfback, and a joy to watch."

"Modesty becomes you."

"We're playing a team from North Lakeside." Lucien rattled off a tinny drumroll with two styli. "The Specials."

Jani smiled for the first time since her SIB visit. "Spec Service?"

He grinned. "I thought that would get your attention."

"Pierce play?"

"No, but he attends all the games." One stylus became an orchestra-leading baton. "I juggled our schedule and brought the match forward six weeks. The Sports and Activities department is not my friend anymore, if you know what I mean. That's what I spent all day doing, when I should have been reading security investigation reports about the next place Nema's visiting." Lucien pointed the other stylus at Jani like an overlong accusing finger. "If anything happens to him at the Commodities Exchange next month, it's all your fault."

"I'd worry about the Exchange, if I were you." Jani brushed off his aggravated stare. "I need to think of how to approach Pierce."

"You need to think why you're putting your ass on the line for a sick old man you don't even know." Lucien hunched his shoulders and sank down in his seat. "I bet you wouldn't do it for me."

Jani considered the not-so-veiled cry for sympathy. "You know what I think about sometimes?" She deactivated her workstation and dimmed the desk lamp. "What you told me in the sunroom, the first time you visited me."

Lucien shifted uncertainly. He had expected her to protest or reassure him—he wasn't sure how to respond. "I told you I was working with Nema."

"You also said you reported to Justice. Now that makes me wonder—after Nema gets his and they get theirs, what's left for me?"

Lucien pouted. "What do you want?"

"Your mind." Jani finger-locked her desk drawers. "According to Sam, all the missing documents have shown up except for some records for the CSS *Kensington*. Death certs bubbled to the surface today. One, an SFC named Caldor, was directly attributable to the Haárin bombing. But the other three, Ebben, Unser, and Fitzhugh—mishandling their remains was the main reason Mako was called before the Board."

"Ebben—Anais used to talk about her." Lucien kept his gaze locked on his shoes. "They were best friends."

"They deserved each other. Talitha Ebben CO'd Rauta Shèràa Base. Phil Unser was her exec, and Matilda Fitzhugh headed Spec Service."

"Anais always felt the Haárin killed Ebben in revenge for Knevçet Shèràa." Lucien glanced at Jani and shrugged apology. "That's a big reason why she likes to stick it to the idomeni whenever possible. She knows it's bad policy, but she can't help herself. She hates them. She thinks they used the Night of the Blade as a cover to settle scores."

Jani shook her head. "The idomeni don't operate undercover like that—that was why the Laumrau's conspiracy with Neumann upset them so."

"Maybe if they felt angry enough, they'd make the exception."

"No." Jani twisted in her chair to stretch her stiff back. "They'd feel no compunction about admitting to killings they felt were justified.

Lucien removed his feet from her desk and leaned forward. "So how did they die?"

"The obvious answer is that they were murdered by humans. Problem is, the list of suspects is endless. They were involved with every smuggler, fence, and racketeer in the J-Loop and Pearl Way. It could have been that as the war entered the final stages, they defaulted on agreements with people who wouldn't take 'sorry, there's a war on,' for an answer."

"But you'd know if someone like that had killed them, wouldn't you?" Lucien asked. "What's the point of making an example if it's just going to get swamped out by background noise?"

"Maybe the signs were there, but Mako's botching erased them." Jani contemplated her comport, then glanced across the desk to find Lucien eyeing her in a much-less-attractive manner.

"And where were you during the night in question?"

"Very funny."

"You were in the city that night, weren't you?"

"I had just fled the hospital. I was trying to get to the shuttleport, wangle a berth out of there."

"Any witnesses?"

"*Thanks.*" Jani tapped out a search on her comport, then rang through the code that appeared on the display. "Good evening, Mr. Duong," she said to the sad face that appeared.

"Captain!" Sam Duong's expression lightened. Then his brow furrowed in concern. "Are you feeling better? You didn't look well when you left."

"I'm fine," Jani replied, avoiding Lucien's questioning look. "Mr. Duong, who signed the death certs for Ebben and the rest?"

"Oh. They're locked away now, and I can't—" His eyes widened. "Car—*Carnival!*"

Jani shot a dirty look at Lucien, who had clapped his hand over his mouth to muffle his laughter. "Don't you mean Carvalla?"

Duong blinked uncertainly. "Maybe." He jumped as an alarm bleat sounded at his end. "Disaster drill—I must go!" His face froze, then fractured, leaving Jani to stare at the darkened display.

Lucien stood up with a growl. "Work day over—let's go. We can go to the South Central Club and watch soccer and argue."

The darkness felt comforting, like a warm blanket. Jani felt her mood lift at the sight of people dressed in base casuals—light grey T-shirts with steel blue shorts or pull-on pants—and at the squeak of trainers on scancrete that cut the still air.

But she needed to talk to someone, and Lucien wouldn't do. Not for this. He had no use for sympathy. She doubted he had much use for hope either.

She tapped his arm. "Is there a Misty Center nearby?"

"Why?" He pointed down the walkway, toward the brightly lit entrance of the South Central Officers' Club. "At twenty-two up, drinks are two for one."

"I don't think Pimentel wants me to drink."

"So I'll drink yours, too."

"*Lucien.*"

"Why now?"

"Because I need to talk to someone." Two someones, really, whom she should have tried to talk to long before this.

"Code?"

"Acadia one-two. Ville Acadie TG-one-seven-X-one."

"Name of contact?"

"Declan and or Jamira Kilian. Ninth Arrondissment, Seven Rue D'Aubergine."

The civilian clerk continued to read items off a checklist attached to a recording board. "You realize sending family messages via Misty is considered nonessential use of an essential service?" She sniffed quietly.

Jani leaned against the wall of the transmission booth and folded her arms. "I seem to recall that the real reason message central transmit was invented was to relay Cup match results more quickly between bases." She sniffed louder. "Apocrypha, I'm sure."

"If you brought a Form Eight-twelve from your CO defining this as an emergency communication, I could waive the fee." The clerk's high-pitched voice kicked up an additional third. "This is going to chew up half your monthly. Are you sure you don't want to go ServNet?"

Jani nodded. "I'm sure." In a way, she was punishing herself for taking so long to get around to this. She should have done it sooner, but when she thought they were going to kill her, she didn't see the point.

She handed her ID card to the clerk for scanning, then pressed her thumb against the input pad to authorize the deduction from her salary account.

"The instructions are—"

"I've Misty'd before." Jani slid into the chair behind the console. "Thank you."

The clerk executed a jerky about-face and closed the door after her. The last thing Jani saw was Lucien's face disappearing behind the sliding barrier, lips thinned in exasperation.

She straightened her shirt, fluffed her hair, then fiddled with the adjust angle on the relay screen until the slider base squealed in protest. She sat quietly, took a couple of steadying breaths, then punched the timer countdown on the side of the screen.

The changing colors marked the seconds. Red. Orange. Yellow. Green.

Green.

"*Âllo, Maman. Papa. C'est Jani.*" She fought the compulsion to stare down at her hands, forcing herself to hold her head up so the relay could light her properly. "I know I look different. I was assured my voice hasn't changed, though. I hope you can recognize it." She spoke slowly, pronouncing words in her head before saying them, but they still sounded strange when she said them aloud. That's what she got for working so hard to lose her Acadian accent.

"You probably know what's going on here." Memories of ChanNet's scandalmongering reputation dampened her enthusiasm. "It's not all true, what they're saying. I hope I can explain it all to you soon." She struggled to think of a neutral topic, something as far removed from Knevçet Shèràa and Evan van Reuter as possible.

"*Vive Le Rouge!*" Well, the supposed nonpolitical status of the Commonwealth Cup was a joke, but she had to say something. "They drew a first-round bye. I wish they didn't have to depend so much on Desjarlais, though. One-man teams don't win the Cup. I wish Gilles would get off the disabled list. If they knew his leg wouldn't heal in time for the prelims, they should have signed Stewart. He was worth the money. Good halfbacks are always worth the money." OK, that did it for sports. What was next . . . ?

"It's very hot here." She saw half her paychit disappearing under a sea of banality, and berated herself for not planning the call better. "I don't mind it, though." She watched the timer blink, studied the controls rimming the display. She had trouble looking at the display directly. Too much like looking someone in the eye.

"There's a tag line that runs along the bottom of the message—you need to use same systems to reply. So you can't go to Vickard's—he used out-of-date equipment when I still lived home, and I doubt he's changed. Go to Samselle, or Fredericka." It struck her that it had been over twenty years since she'd walked down a Ville Acadie street. "If they're still in business, that is.

"I couldn't—" Her throat ached, thinning her voice until it sounded like the clerk's. "I couldn't contact you before now. I wanted to. I even tried a few times, but—" She looked into the grey depth of the display. "I'll explain, someday soon." She dropped her gaze. "If you want to listen.

"Say hello to Mirelle. And Yves. And tell Labat that if he's making book on my sentence, whatever he guessed, he guessed high." She doubted that line would get past the censors, but no harm in trying, especially if the thought of a light sentence might give her parents some peace of mind.

The timer light pulsed faster. An alarm chirped. "I have to go." She forced a smile. "I'm going to watch a friend's match tomorrow. Everyone plays soccer when the Cup rounds are on. But I understand he's quite good. He told me so himself, so it must be true." She watched the timer count down, concentrating on the colors as she struggled to keep her voice steady.

Yellow. *There's this man, Maman.*

Orange. *I thought he died because of my mistakes, but now I think he's alive, and I don't know what to do.*

"I love you." She waved weakly. "*Au revoir.*" She watched the timer flutter red and wink out.

She sat in the dark and tried to collect her thoughts. Her heart skipped as a pounding knock fractured the silence.

Lucien dogged her elbow as soon as she stepped into the hall. "He told me so himself, so it must be true. I agree with your remark about halfbacks, though—small thanks for little favors. Who the hell is Yves?"

"What did you do, flash your Intelligence ID at the control room door and muscle in?"

"Better me than standard censors." He leaned close. "I let through the line about the short sentence. Feel free to thank me again." He eyed her expectantly. "Yves?"

Jani brushed past the Communication annex's single lift and pushed open the door to the stairwell. "I went to school with him. Just a friend."

"He must have been some friend if you're saying hello after twenty years." Lucien's voice bounced off the painted walls, drowning out the clatter of their hard soles on the stairs.

"Mirelle's an old school friend, too."

"Hmm." Mirelle didn't interest him.

"Labat runs the local off-track." Jani led the way through the building's clunky double doors. "When I joined the Service, he laid four to one I wouldn't make it through OCS."

"Did he ever give you a reason why?"

"He said I never met an argument I didn't like." Jani ignored Lucien's not-so-muffled guffaw.

Noise and officers packed the South Central from wall to wall. Casuals and summerweights stood three deep at the bar—Lucien executed cuts and weaves that offered an enlightening preview of the next day's match. Jani, meanwhile, staked out the sole empty table, a wobbly two-seater with a commanding view of the men's room door.

"Place is a madhouse." Lucien set down the drinks, followed by a basket of popcorn. "You should have told your parents hello from me. Let them *think* you're having fun."

Jani stared glumly at her fruit soda, interspersed with a few envious peeks at Lucien's beer. *I wish I could get drunk.* Hoot and holler and roll up the rugs. Find a warm, hard body who'd be as happy to vanish with the dawn as she would be to let him.

"Heard anything about Hals?" Lucien shifted his chair so he could watch the door, the 'Vee match, and the room panorama all at the same time.

"No." Jani picked at the popcorn. "I wish Eiswein would tell us something—the pressure's building, and people are starting to snap."

"Who's next in line?"

"Guy named Vespucci. Major. Doesn't like me a bit."

"What did he have to say?"

"Nothing. I don't think he left his office all day." Jani had been relieved that she didn't have to put up with Vespucci's accusing glares, but it did bother her that he didn't try to rally the troops behind their absent leader.

"Think he's a pouter?" Lucien clucked in disgust. "It's always fun to have a pouter in the department. They want people to come to them, and when no one does, they crawl in a hole and seal the entrance." He took a swallow of beer. "Funny he didn't send Hals's adjutant around with the 'I'm in charge' announcement. That kind usually does."

Jani squinted in the direction of the 'Vee screen to try to see who played. But the haze from multiple flavors of nicsticks hung in the air and seeped into her films, stinging her eyes and blurring her vision. "Ischi came to see me, but he said he hadn't checked with Vespucci about anything."

"He came to *you*?" Lucien's arm stopped in mid-swig. "Really?" He set the bottle down slowly. "Hals talk to you a lot?"

"Not too much."

"She took your advice about bucking Burkett, though, didn't she?" He nodded knowingly. "And your advice ran opposite Vespucci's, I bet."

"Yeah, but—"

"He thinks you've end-arounded him. He's jealous."

"Oh, come on!"

"I've seen it before." Lucien waved a sage finger. "You have to nip this in the bud. If Hals doesn't show up tomorrow morning, you need to go to Vespucci and ask his advice."

"He won't give me the time of day."

"Nah, he sounds like the gloating type. You'll want to punch him in the mouth by the time you're through, but at least people will know order's been restored." He shrugged at the look of profound dismay on Jani's face. "Sorry, that's the way it is."

Oh goody—something to look forward to. Jani sipped her fruit juice. Carbonated, which did nasty things to her still-achy stomach, and much too sweet. She stood up and surveyed the surrounding tables in search of a spice dispenser, her eye scanning for shape without transmitting details to her brain. When she finally realized who sat across the room at the far end of the bar, she barely ducked in her seat in time to avoid being seen.

Niall Pierce was alone. People crowded him from every side, but that didn't make a difference. You could always tell. The eyes focused straight ahead. The hunched shoulders. The only communication between him and what filled his glass.

You look the way I feel. It crossed Jani's mind that he might have waited outside Documents Control for her to emerge and then followed her to the Misty Center, then here. The thought didn't bother her as much as it should have. She watched him sit still and silent, then tipped her soda imperceptibly in his direction, a toast to their shared misery.

CHAPTER 19

Jani left Lucien on her doorstep, pleading fatigue and the need to prepare herself to play supplicant to Vespucci. He looked dubious but departed quietly, leaving her with the promise to stop by at 0730 to take her to breakfast.

She talked to Val the Bear about Sam Duong. Wondered what Borgie's take on Lucien would have been. Slept fitfully. Dreamed of drowning again, Neumann's jolly chuckle providing background music.

Oh-five up found her suffering the wide-awake lassitude of the truly exhausted—too numb to sleep, too enervated to rise. She got up anyway, showered and dressed in a plodding daze, and departed the TOQ just as the sun began its creep above the lake horizon.

She bought breakfast at a kiosk, then dumped it in the trash untouched. Watched a frazzled lieutenant endure an impromptu inspection by two A&S-holes with recording boards. Kept a weary eye open for Pierce as she trudged to Documents Control, arriving just in time to meet Vespucci coming from the opposite direction. She saluted. "Good morning, Major."

"Captain." Vespucci returned the salute grudgingly, then hurriedly mounted the steps.

Oh no, you don't! Energized by a jolt of anger, Jani chased him up the steps and through the entry, finally catching up to him by the lift bank. "I wondered if you'd heard anything from Colonel Hals, sir."

Vespucci's face brightened in surprise. "You mean she hasn't been in touch with you?" He drew up straighter, the first glimmerings of smugness imbuing his fleshy features. "She called me first thing yesterday morning. Meetings with General Eiswein all day yesterday. Hammering out proposals for a revamping of Foreign Transactions."

Jani stepped aboard the lift, her benumbed brain struggling to wedge that tidbit amid all the others. *You were in contact with her yesterday and you didn't tell anyone!* Lucien had overestimated her tolerance. They hadn't even entered the office, and she already felt like punching Vespucci.

Instead, she stepped to the front of the car and concentrated on the control-panel lights. Red, of course. Not the smartest decision to stare at them, considering her current state. *Screw it,* she thought, as the indicators flickered. The fatigue faded from her limbs as she rode the glow. "What else did she have to say, sir?"

"That's confidential, Captain."

"Can you at least say if she's—" *—under arrest?* "—if she's well, sir?"

"As well as can be expected, considering the trouble you stage-managed her into." The lift stopped—Vespucci crowded out the door as soon as it opened wide enough and bustled down the hall. "You may think that Academy mystique of yours fools people, but some of us know a destructive malcontent when we see one."

Jani's tietops slid on the slick flooring as she wheeled around the corner. "Whatever you think of me, sir, the rest of FT deserves to hear something. Is the department breakup on hold? Are folks going to be shipped out to colonial postings tomorrow?"

"We were ordered to sit tight and continue at our jobs, Captain. That's all anyone needs to know right now." Vespucci strode through the desk pool, ignoring the hopeful "good morning, sirs" that greeted his appearance.

Jani glanced around the desk-pool area. Already, the paper mail had piled up in the collection boxes, and dirty dispo cups and plates littered desktops and tables. The coffee odor permeating the air had that sharp, stale tang. The high gloss had dulled already, and Hals had only been gone a little over a day. *Ah, shit.* Vespucci showed his worth by allowing it to happen, but he was all they had to work with right now, and it was apparently up to her to nudge him into his designated mooring. *I've become a diplomat.* And she had about two seconds to figure out the drill.

I hate this. She pulled up beside Vespucci as he palmed his doorlock. "Sir, if I could be allowed to make a suggestion?" She waited, her teeth grinding as Vespucci hesitated in his open doorway. She could see the mechanisms turning, his eyes flicking back and forth as he weighed his options. *You self-serving son of a bitch.* "I don't possess the authority to speak to them, sir. They're waiting to hear something from you."

"Ischi spoke with you yesterday." His voice held the barest tinge of verbal pout. "I saw him go into your office."

"Lieutenant Ischi brought me my mail, sir, as I'm sure he did yours."

"I didn't—" Vespucci stopped.

You didn't let him in the door because you're mad at him for liking me. "Sir, this is your department until Colonel Hals returns. I understand completely that I am in no position to presume any sort of authority. I am, of course, available to provide any advice you might wish—" the words ran together as he stiffened "—but I know where I stand." Her head pounded. "*Please*, sir."

That was the magic word. Vespucci shot her a superior smile. "A little different, dealing with a real department instead of that fly-by-night collection of losers you worked with, isn't it, Kilian?" He sauntered into his office and tossed his briefbag on his desk. "Give me a few minutes. Have everyone gather in the anteroom."

Jani flexed her left hand, the one hidden from Vespucci's sight. Formed a fist. Forced it open. "Yes, sir. Thank you, sir."

*   *   *

"—and the colonel requests I let you know that as soon as these rather intense meetings are over, she will be back in her office, just in time for our annual performance evaluations." Vespucci grinned at the chorus of mock moans and groans that greeted that portion of his announcement. His pleasure seemed genuine. He liked being the center of attention and the fountain of all Service wisdom, and his delight filled the room.

The group dissolved into happy gabble. Three of the techs jostled to sort the mail, while two others disassembled the brewer. *And peace reigned again in the valley.* All Jani had to do was roll over on her back, expose her throat, and point out the targets.

Ischi wandered up to her, his face lightened by a subdued grin. "Thank you, ma'am."

"Major Vespucci is second-in-command here, Lieutenant."

"Yes, ma'am." His eyes shone with wisdom beyond his tender years as he jerked a thumb toward the gurgling brewer. "Coffee?"

Jani bit her lip to keep from smiling. "Why, thank you, Lieutenant. Just let me get my cup."

Jani sipped from her Central United mug, and grumbled foul words in Acadian as she scanned the report she had transmitted to Hals's system the night before. Vespucci, now sufficiently persuaded as to his worth to do his job, had taken it upon himself to make changes that would have resulted in the document being bounced back from Legal within the time it took an outraged paralegal to smash his fist into his touchboard. She deleted one of his "corrections," ignoring her bleating comport until the fifth squawk.

Lucien's face in no way resembled the sunny visage she had come to know. More overcast, with a threat of storm. "Where were you this morning?"

"I peeled out early." She tapped her board again, deleting a phrase that would have resulted in twelve crates of cabinets being classified as small arms. "I was nervous."

"*You?*" He wadded a sheet of paper and bounced it off his display. "How did it go?"

"Hals had spoken to Vespucci yesterday morning. He sat on it the whole damned day."

"A pouter. I knew it." He smiled proudly, a professor watching his valedictorian strut across the stage. "But you charmed it out of him."

"I feel like I need a shower."

"Want some company?"

"Good-bye." Jani thumped the disconnect with a fast chop of her open hand, then returned to debugging her report.

Her comport squawked again. This time, she caught it on the first alarm. "Damn it, Lucien, leave—!" She choked back the balance as she found herself staring at Frances Hals's puzzled countenance.

"Good morning, Captain."

"Ma'am!"

"I'm still alive."

"We were beginning to have our doubts."

Hals offered a tired grin. "So was I." She massaged the back of her neck. "Things started out badly. But once Eiswein realized you were right and Foreign Transactions had legitimate cause to complain about how Diplo treated us in this matter, it was all over but the drafting of the formal report." She stared out of the display. "You look surprised, Captain."

The only thing worse than taking the shot is finding out you took it for nothing. "I only heard about a meeting with Eiswein and a revamp of FT, ma'am."

Hals ran a hand across her eyes. "*When?*"

"This morning, ma'am. I spoke with Major Vespucci and requested he address the department. People were starting to get edgy, if you know what I mean."

"I told him to use his discretion. Unfortunately, he takes that as permission to keep his mouth shut." Hals's look of tired disgust didn't bode well for Vespucci's future in FT. "Things are in the draft stage, so I can't be too specific about details. Suffice it to say, General Eiswein was extremely interested to hear all the things I had to say about how the idomeni regard documents examiners. I haven't spent the past day and a half getting my ass chewed on. I've spent it helping to assemble a proposal that should, if it gets past the Administrative flag, result in FT being reclassified as a Diplomatic adjunct."

Jani laughed. "Burkett will flip."

"Serves him right. The day the first of my people start Dip School is going to be one happy day for me." She stared off to the side, her expression pensive. "Do you understand any German, Kilian?"

"Very little, ma'am. Enough Hortensian to get by."

"Does *Scheißkopf* mean what I think it means?"

Shithead! Luckily, coffee beaded nicely on summerweight polywool. "Yes, ma'am, I believe it does," Jani said as she dabbed at her trousers with a dispo.

Hals nodded. "Eiswein muttered that a lot when I told her how Burkett tried to lock us down." She yawned again. She looked like she'd been wrung out and tossed in a corner to dry. "I'm exhausted. I need a shower and a hot meal and about ten hours' sleep."

"Would you like me to do a room sweep and bring you some gear?"

"No, thank you. My husband brought me a kit. He's a civilian, but he's learned to pack in a rush with the best of them."

Jani started. "I didn't know you were married, ma'am."

"Nineteen years." Hals's face closed. "The past few weeks have made for an interesting time."

"Children?"

"Three. All in prep school." The dulling in her eyes hinted at the pressure the situation had brought to bear on her life outside Sheridan. "We're on our way to getting this straightened out. Can't come soon enough. I hope to be back in the office in a few days."

"My Office Hours with Burkett is scheduled for tomorrow." Jani knew she couldn't discuss the matter with Hals *per se*, but a hint that she could anticipate a cancellation of the little get-together would have done wonders for her mood.

"Yes." Hals's dour countenance gave away nothing. "He may try to get his last licks in. I understand he's working up a head of steam over rumors he has heard that aren't really rumors a'tall." Her thin smile allowed a glimpse of an agreeably vile sense of humor, but the curtain soon fell. "We didn't do our careers any favors, but we did our jobs, and the entire department is going to benefit from it. It's a good feeling." She nodded. "Captain."

"Ma'am." Jani waited for the display to blank before turning back to her workstation. She dumped a few more of Vespucci's edits, then set the unit to standby. She had picked up her cup and was just about to leave in search of fresh coffee when her comport alarm bleeped again.

"Jani." Friesian's face held the contented fatigue of a workman who had taken a step back to admire his handiwork. "Could you be at my office within the hour? I have some news for you."

"If this goes as planned, with no paper snafus or further visits to the idomeni embassy, your hearing should take place late next week, and your discharge early the following." Friesian tapped a happy drumbeat on the tabletop. "A week and a half from now, you'll be a civilian again."

Who are you kidding, Jani thought. *I'm a civilian now.* They sat in the breakroom down the hall from Friesian's office. The room faced the lake. Brightly colored sails of assorted watercraft shimmered like pearly scales on the water's calm surface, while lakeskimmers whizzed in all directions like skipping stones.

"Try to restrain your excitement." Friesian pushed back in his chair. The flexframe hummed as his weight shifted.

"I'm sorry." Jani felt genuinely contrite. He had looked so proud as he described the terms of her discharge. "I just have a difficult time accepting that I'm being let off the hook."

"Off the hook for *what*?" Friesian took a swallow of his black coffee. "The missing-movement charge is a harsh one. You're losing half your pension, many of your benefits, and if not for the medical aspects, you'd be facing a dishonorable discharge. Hell, they're even letting you go out a captain— they had every right to bust you to lieutenant!" Dark circles rimmed his eyes, and his skin had greyed. He looked as drained as Hals.

It's the pressure of their jobs. Had to be. It couldn't have anything to do with the fact they worked with her. Could it? She looked at her hands. They had grown so cold that the nail beds looked blue. "It's not that I'm not grateful. But compared to some of the things I've gone through in the past few years, this didn't make the top one hundred. I expected . . . much worse."

"Well." Friesian got up and walked across the room to the vend coolers. "The only thing you have on your plate now besides the hearing is to provide some info to Colonel Chandra Veda. She's the SIB investigator assigned to your case." He patted his pockets in search of a vend token. "I pledged your cooperation in some other investigations she's closing out. She just wants some information about Rauta Shèràa Base. She also mentioned some questions about Emil Burgoyne."

"Borgie." Jani looked toward the window. The reflection of the bright sun on the lake made her films draw and her eyes water, forcing her to squint. "We called him Borgie."

"Borgie had problems with Neumann, from what I could glean from your ServRec. Some were rather serious."

"Neumann pushed him. He enjoyed tormenting him."

"He pushed him into at least one assault on a superior officer."

"Trumped-up charge." Well, not really. Jani had helped Borgie wash Neumann's blood out of his short-sleeve herself.

"Borgie admitted to having an affair with his corporal. Nothing trumped-up there."

"Yolan Cray." Jani could see them now, the short, dark-haired Borgie and the willowy blond Yolan. "At Rauta Shèràa Base, a good-looking body belonged to whichever member of base command laid claim to it. Yolan was attractive. She went to Borgie for protection, and things took off from there."

Friesian's lip curled. "He worked the situation to his advantage, you mean?"

Jani recalled the light in Yolan's eyes the day she showed Jani a ring Borgie had given her. It hadn't been expensive— Borgie had his pay docked so many times, he barely cleared enough to cover his incidentals. A plain silver band—you'd think he'd given her the Commonwealth Mint. "They loved one another. Maybe to you, it was a threat to order and discipline. You have a different measuring stick against which to judge it. To me, it came as a relief. At least it was clean."

Friesian plugged his token into a cooler slot and removed a sandwich. "You can say things like that to me. It won't go beyond these walls. But keep your opinions to yourself when you talk to Veda—she tends to be a little straight-laced."

"I'm glad she can afford to be." Jani wedged her hands beneath her thighs to warm them. "I assume you're going to sit next to me when I talk to her, too."

Friesian tore the wrapping off his sandwich and tossed it into the trashzap. "You're damned right," he said, as the polycoat paper flashed, then flamed to powder.

CHAPTER 20

Jani checked in at FT after her meeting with Friesian, and found the desk pool scrubbed and straightened to its former glory. She finished editing her report back to its earlier pristine state, and forwarded it to Hals's system on a delay that would guarantee it wouldn't be opened until the colonel herself was at her desk to read it. She checked out for the day to sounds of Vespucci singing along with an opera recording someone had inserted into systems. He proved a remarkably sound tenor. Jani considered sticking her head in his office and recommending he transfer to the Entertainment Corps, but after some thought, she decided against it. Unaccustomed restraint on her part. She felt extremely pleased with herself, as though she'd passed a grueling test.

She returned to her rooms to find her comport message light fibrillating. A clerk from the Misty Center confirmed that they'd transmitted her communication to her parents, and that her salary account had been billed accordingly. Since she had yet to receive any salary, she owed them money. They had therefore applied to garnish her account, but she was not to worry since this was standard practice and would not reflect negatively on her credit rating.

"I didn't know I had a credit rating." Jani erased that message and went on to the next one.

"Hello, Captain!" Sam Duong appeared much happier than he had earlier, which probably meant his supervisor was somewhere else. "Can we meet tomorrow? I have news that may interest you." He fiddled with an object below display level. "I have entered the time into my handheld. I hope twelve up is fine. We can meet in front of the SIB. Please reply if not possible; otherwise, I will assume you will be there."

"Damn." Jani held her finger on the response pad, and debated sacrificing Lucien's soccer game. She would have liked to barge in on Duong and see what he information he had. And to see how he was doing. Whether he enjoyed his shrimp tea. If he remembered anything now, rather than just knew.

"Lucien would kill me." He had, after all, sacrificed his relationship with Sports and Activities in order to bring her Niall Pierce. Pierce, who kept turning up. Who followed her. Who stared into his beer like a man with a rip in his soul. Yes, she needed to meet Pierce.

She hit the pad for the last message.

"Hello, Jani." Pimentel glowered at her. "You missed your appointment today—"

Damn again.

"—so I've rescheduled you for tomorrow at sixteen up. Please be sure to stop by, or else I will track you down using every tool at my disposal." The display blanked, leaving Jani to stare at the slow fade to standby blue until a glance at her clock told her she needed to get moving.

She showered, then donned her base casuals for the first time. The trainers were dull white, with removable sock liners. The T-shirt fitted more snugly than she'd have liked, and the shorts, while attractive and comfortable, were above all, *short*. She couldn't recall the last time she'd shown her legs in public. Baggy clothing and no makeup had been her uniform of the day for almost two decades. Unattached women attracted unwanted attention in the places in which she'd been forced to earn her keep. She'd learned to avoid trouble.

But that isn't an issue anymore. That sort of trouble had become something to welcome, to embrace with open arms. *Somebody nice and safe, I think, like a test pilot.* Much more dependable than any I-Com lieutenant of her acquaintance.

Just before she left, she buzzed the Misty Center and asked if any messages had arrived for her. It was ridiculous to expect a reply so soon. If nothing else, the laws of physics dictated against it. But it didn't hurt to make sure she had given them the right code. Just as it didn't hurt to turn her comport on its base so that she could see whether the message light blinked as soon as she opened the door.

Jani found a seat on the end of the half-filled bank of bleachers, away from the bulk of the crowd. Both teams still warmed up. She could see Lucien's towhead flash in the sun as he trotted downfield and lifted a soft pass to one of his teammates. He spotted her as soon as he turned upfield, and froze just long enough to catch a return off the side of his head. Amid rude laughter, he ran to the sideline.

"Where were you?" His face was flushed, his blue-and-gold striped jersey already sweat-soaked. "I waited by the field house for over an hour."

"I had things to do."

"Like what?" Before she could answer, he jerked his head toward the opposite sideline. "He's over there."

Jani looked across the field. Pierce stood near the cooler bank. He wore base casuals—his arms and legs were as tanned and hardened as his face. Sunshades shielded his eyes—Jani couldn't tell whether he watched them or not.

Lucien glared at her. "He was standing there when I arrived. He took off his shades to watch me stretch. He hasn't budged. I don't know whether to water him or ask him out."

Jani wrinkled her nose. "He's not your type."

"Ha-ha. Laugh, I thought I'd die." He wiped his face with the hem of his jersey, flashing an attractive expanse of flat, tanned stomach in the process. "I should have fitted you with audio pickup. He's the wound-up type that blurts incriminating details, I know it."

"I'll be fine."

"You will? *Good.* I'll tell Nema you said that. Maybe it'll buy me a ten-minute head start."

Jani watched Lucien fidget with his sleeves. It would have been a stretch to call him jumpy. Concerned, more like. Definitely concerned. "What are you so worried about?"

Lucien bent close to her ear. "Because before I thought he was just a hard-ass, but now I know he's strange, and you can't predict what strange will do." One of his teammates called to him. "Don't let your guard down." He loped back to the middle of the field to join the referee and the Specials' captain.

The Specials, clad in plain green, won the token flip and elected to receive. Both teams huddled, broke, then spread out in formation. The starting whistle blew. The crowd whooped as the ball sailed.

Jani followed the arc of the ball's flight. As she did, she caught a flicker of motion out of the corner of her eye.

"Excuse me." Pierce brushed by her, stepping over her bench seat to the one behind. His voice fit him—rough, middle-pitch, nasal. Victorian accent. He wasn't much taller than she was. Solid muscle, though—the bench creaked when he sat.

Jani waited.

"He's not your type."

Jani turned and looked up at him. Against the ruddy, worn skin of his face, his scar glinted like something polished and new. "Are you talking to me?"

"Pretty boy." Pierce's sunshades obscured his eyes—even up close, Jani couldn't tell whether he looked at the field or at her. "He knows it, too."

"So do you, apparently."

"What makes you say that, Jani?"

"He told me you've been watching him."

"Bugs him, does it?" Pierce grinned. Nobody would ever call him pretty. "Good to know."

"You did it on purpose?"

"Pretty Boy's been asking questions about me. I traced back his comport calls."

"You have a search lock on your name?" One that could override any protections Lucien with all his I-Com knowledge had most assuredly put in place. "Isn't that excessive?"

"I have a right to know if people are talking about me."

"Sounds like you're concerned with what they're saying."

Jani searched Pierce's face for a twitch of muscle, any movement that would betray fear or nerves. "Now why would that be?"

Pierce hesitated. "Because they'd miss the point." His grating voice dropped to a whisper. "They wouldn't understand." He removed his shields to rub his eyes, then quickly shoved them back on. "Take your Service record," he said, speaking normally. "Anyone reading it would assume you to be a willful, arrogant, insubordinate screwup. Would they be right?"

Jani glanced toward the field in time to see Lucien look in her direction. He almost missed a pass in the process—one of his teammates yelled at him to wake up. "To an extent." She tried to think of something to say that would drag the conversation back on course without spooking Pierce. "Sounds like you've been asking questions, too."

Pierce crawled down from his seat to the open space next to her. "Actually, I have a few that only you can answer." His voice turned lighter, sharper. "You've been in and out of the PT ward as much as I have lately." His bare knee brushed hers as he leaned toward her, the reddish hair glinting like finest wire. "What's the verdict?"

Jani edged down the board away from him, rubbing the place where their skin had touched. "You read my ServRec. You tell me."

"Well, there are your physical difficulties, caused by your hybridization. The rumored bioemotional problems—same cause." Pierce's Victorian twang had softened. Now he sounded thoughtful. Scholarly. "Do you remember the transport explosion?"

"According to my ServRec, I wasn't on the transport."

"I've heard that rumor—I don't believe it. I don't think Shroud could have gotten his hands on you any other way." Pierce tilted his head. Jani still couldn't tell what he looked at. " 'Hurled headlong flaming from th' ethereal sky, with hideous ruin and combustion.' "

What? Jani felt a gnaw of curiosity. Coupled with her wariness, it made for an interesting combination, like admiring the snake while waiting for it to strike. "I don't think you got *that* from my ServRec."

Pierce cracked a smile. His scar contorted his curved upper lip, exposing the jagged point of his eyetooth. "Milton. *Paradise Lost.* Book One—the expulsion of Lucifer from Heaven." One shoulder jerked. "I wasn't drawing any comparison. The imagery just seemed particularly apt." His head dropped. No problem determining where he looked now. "Your arms and legs don't look different. They're the same color. Same shape."

I should have worn the damned pants. And a long-sleeved shirt. "The leg had to be switched out earlier this year," Jani snapped as she crossed her arms in front of her chest. "The arm's new, too."

Pierce detected her annoyance, and pulled away from her. "I didn't mean to be forward. Just making an observation." He nodded toward the field just as the crowd noise ramped. "Pretty Boy just made goal."

Jani watched Lucien run across the field, arm pumping. She took her cue from his display—times like this didn't call for subtlety. "You're framing an innocent man for documents theft. Why?"

Pierce drew close again. "If you ever got to know me, you'd see we have a lot in common." He held one hand in front of him. " 'Full of doubt I stand, whether I should repent me now of sin by me done and occasioned, or rejoice much more that much more good thereof will spring.' " The open hand closed to a fist and lowered to his knee. "Book Twelve. The archangel Michael shows Adam the future of the human race just before he's cast out of the Garden, the eventual triumph of good over evil. Adam is comforted. He realizes his suffering has a purpose." His voice grew harsher, scolding. "You should read more, Kilian. It soothes the soul."

He just admitted he set up Sam Duong. It wasn't the sort of admission that was worth a damn legally—for one thing, she didn't think Pierce was emotionally stable enough to testify. But it was enough for her. "Do you really believe that it's worth destroying a man's reputation to save yours and Mako's?"

"What's one man's reputation? We have a way of life to protect."

"You broke the law at J-Loop RC when you forced out the Family hacks. Fine—nothing wrong with that. But now you're attacking an innocent. You call that honorable?"

"For the good that thereof will spring." Pierce thumped his fist against his knee. "Yes, I do." He flinched, muttered a curse, and reached into the pocket of his shorts, pulling out a handcom. "I have to go." He muttered a few words into the device, then stuffed it back in his pocket. "I can send you a reading list, if you'd like. To your office or your TOQ suite, whichever you prefer." He stood and nodded to her. "Let me know." He looked as though he practiced for the parade ground as he strode away, back straight and arms swinging, around the end zone and down the steep incline that sloped from the Yards toward the base proper.

The game continued past sunset, the usual combination of blown calls, sloppy play, and outright confusion. The Wonderboys, unfortunately, weren't. Final score: five to four in favor of the Specials.

Jani joined the crowd of players and spectators that milled around the coolers. She found Lucien standing by the ice dispenser, scooping melt out of the drain with a dispo and pouring it over his head. "You had a good game. Scored twice."

"Three times. Glad to see you paid attention." He slipped into soft-spoken French. "I saw him take off. What happened?"

"Nothing. He got a call."

"Did he say anything interesting?"

"He thinks we have a lot in common." Jani filled a dispo with ice chips and popped one into her mouth. "He thinks I should read more."

"Strange—I knew it. Anything about Duong?"

"He admitted he framed him." He seemed to have admitted other things, too—Jani just couldn't figure out what they were.

Lucien pulled his sodden jersey over his head and snapped it like a wet towel. "I knew I should have fitted you with a pickup." He walked toward the field house. "Shower," he called out in English as he vanished through the door. "Out in ten."

Jani passed the time tossing ice chips into the trashzap and watching them crack and steam. " 'Hurled headlong flaming.' " Though in this case, sputtering described it better.

She pondered Pierce's odd explanation. "He's been following me because he wanted to talk to me. He wanted to make me understand." Understand what? That Sam Duong's reputation was a fair price to pay to cover up his and Mako's character assassinations? "That's what you think, Niall."

"You're talking to yourself again."

Jani turned to find Lucien grinning at her. He'd changed into clean casuals—his hair was towel-damp, his cheeks shiny from lazoring. He looked so fresh and normal—a balm to the senses after the bizarre Pierce. She found herself grinning back. "And you're eavesdropping again."

"It's the only way I can find out what you're thinking." His gaze drifted down, settling on her legs. "Maybe during our next match, you could stroll around the end zone and distract the opposing goalie. I'll run it by the guys, take a vote."

"Stop it."

"But it's for the team." He yawned loudly. "So, back to the Club for dinner? It's a cookout tonight."

On cue, the odor of grilling meat drifted across the Yard, borne by the breeze. Jani's roiling stomach tightened in rebellion. "I'm not hungry."

"You have to eat."

"I need to do some things first." See if her parents called. Check on Sam Duong. Figure out what Niall wanted her to understand. "Let's go back to my room."

Lucien pursed his lips and shouldered his duffel. "Whatever you say."

The TOQ lobby was empty. The sounds of the 'Vee filtered in from the game room. Jani took the stairs slowly, keyed into her suite, checked the comport message light. Nothing. She patted the top of the display and wondered if Mako had ordered her room bugged. "I wonder if Pierce is covering up more than chicanery at J-Loop Regional?"

"I guess I can't leave your side now that he knows you suspect him." Lucien slipped his duffel off his shoulder and let it drop to the floor. Jani tried to back away as he closed in, but the divider that separated the bathroom from the sitting area stopped her. He leaned into her and let his lips brush hers. So light. The barest touch. His breath smelled of mint, like her favorite lunchtime leaves.

Jani tried to turn her head away. "There's a time and a place."

"Right here." Another kiss. "Right now."

"You call this protection?"

"Of course." He placed his hands on the wall on either side of her head. "After Nema gets his—" He kissed her cheeks, her eyes, along the lines of her jaw, her neck. "—and Justice gets theirs—" He lingered over her pulse points, raking them lightly with his teeth. "—this is what's left for you."

Jani leaned harder against the wall as her knees threatened to buckle. *I can't do this now.* Her heart pounded. Her clothes grew tight. *Maybe I can.* She wrapped her arms around him, pulled him close, felt his hard muscles beneath her hands. He buried his head in her neck and murmured things in French that made her gasp.

As they pulled at one another's clothes, Jani heard a cough. She looked over Lucien's shoulder.

Rikart Neumann sat in an armchair at the far end of the room, near the window. He wore desertweights—the tan shirt and trousers faded as she watched. "Tsk, tsk." He shook his finger at her—Jani could see the curtain through the translucent skin and bone. "You always were one for the boys, weren't you, Kilian?" he said as he vanished.

Jani pulled her hands from Lucien's back, bunched them into fists, brought them down past his arms and up through, breaking his hold and pushing him backward.

"What the hell!" He stumbled and sprawled across a low table. "What's the matter with you!"

"Get out."

"What!" His unfocused gaze sharpened. "Why?"

"Because I said so."

Lucien stared at her. His breathing slowed. "You know, I see the way you look at me." He'd reverted to English. Crisp. Sharp. Cold. "The feeling's mutual." He pushed himself into a sitting position. "Look, you're sideline—I'm mainline. We don't work together. No lines crossed. Is that what you're worried about?"

Jani shivered and hugged herself as a fat chuckle sounded from the far corner of the room. "No."

"Then *what*?" He boosted to his feet. "Pierce thinks you and he have things in common. Well, you and I have things in common, too. We know how to work people. We keep it simple and travel light, take what we want and leave the rest. We're a matched set—why waste it?"

Just as Jani opened her mouth to speak, Neumann reappeared at the bedroom entry. He held a finger to his lips. Then he formed an O with his index finger and thumb and poked his other index finger through the circle. In. Out. In. Out. "You do it because you like to," she said hurriedly. "I do it because I have to."

"Oh, really?" Lucien picked up his duffel. "I don't understand you completely, and, frankly, I think you're wrongheaded about a lot of things. But I never figured you for a tease, and I sure as hell never figured you for a hypocrite!" He hit the doorpad and left without looking back.

A greasy snicker sounded. "Looks like your little rent boy took off, Kilian." Neumann's form had disappeared, but his voice remained. "I don't think you can support him on a captain's pay. He's Cabinet class all the way. You don't earn enough to cover his mint-flavored oral rinse."

Jani pressed her hands to her ears and stumbled to her bed.

"Think you're off the hook because Mako says he'll cut you loose?" Neumann's voice sounded from one dark corner, then another. "Well, think again."

"You're *dead*!" Jani fell back against her pillows, pulled her damp shirt from her sweaty skin, and breathed deeply and slowly.

When the fluttering in her chest subsided, she eased to her side and struggled to her feet. Bedrooms felt too much like hospital rooms—she stumbled into the sitting area and lay on the sofa. It was too short to sleep on—one bolster caught her in the back of her neck, the other, just below the backs of her knees—so she curled her legs and hunched her shoulders and resigned herself to discomfort.

The inactive comport display reflected the dim light that seeped around the window seals. Jani watched it until Neumann's mumbles lowered to nothing and the sweating stopped and she was able to fall into something resembling sleep.

CHAPTER 21

Sam disembarked the tramline that shuttled from the civilian apartment blocks to the base. Even at that early-morning hour, the heat enveloped; by the time he descended the stairs from the elevated passenger drop-off to ground level, he could feel sweat trickle beneath his shirt.

He stopped to study the building signs, and earned a muttered "watch where you're going" from the civvie who banged into his shoulder. *I hate this place in the morning!* Uniforms and civvies bustled in his path. Delivery skimvans laden with supplies blocked entries and walkways. Muffled rumbles emanated from the weapons ranges, echoing off buildings like thunder.

Sam cringed as a sharp report sounded—he stepped off the walkway and ducked beneath the sheltering shade of a black maple until his pounding heart slowed. Of all the things he hated, the booming roll and reverb that issued from the ranges topped the list.

But it was louder this morning—like bombs. *They've broken out the Y-40s today.* The latest-model long-range shooters made a great deal more noise than had their predecessors, the V- and T-series, but design improvements had supposedly made them safer and easier to control.

"Yes, this one will only blow your target to bits if you want it to." He tucked his briefbag under his arm and dashed out into the open. The faster he found a quiet indoor haven, the better he would feel.

He hustled into the safety of the South Central Facilities lobby and removed his handheld from the outer pocket of his bag. *Where am I going?* Who could find their way when surrounded by all these bloody identical buildings!

He flipped through his list of "Reminders." *Odergaard is my Tech One . . . my name is Sam Duong . . . I live in Flat 4A-Forrestal Block.* He paged to the next screen. *South Library!* That's where he wanted to go. A good place to do Gate research, or rent a few hours on a workstation, or catch a nap before the start of a second-shift day.

"Are you all right, sir?"

Sam looked across the lobby at the desk corporal, who eyed him with concern. He forced a smile. "Just taking a break from the heat." He waited a few more minutes, then rose and walked back outside. *I am going to the South Library.* He followed the signs and markers until he reached the five-story white scancrete box.

He crossed the lobby, then wandered aimlessly through the stacks. Departed through one of the side doors. Hurried down the connecting walkway to one of the many satellite office buildings that dotted the base, which was where he meant to go all along. Darted down the hallway and disappeared into the first vacant office he found. It made sense for an archivist to go to a library. Therefore, a library was the last place he wished to be. He suffered from a brain tumor, not stupidity.

Sam didn't know for sure whether someone followed him. The movements he'd glimpsed in entryways and beneath trees the previous night as he walked across the Yard to the tramline platform could have been tricks of moonlight and shadow. The display flutter when he tried to use the comport in his flat could have been random interference from base systems. The trip of his heart each time he locked eyes with a stranger or heard an unfamiliar sound could be due to his medical condition, not the ancient portions of his brain telling him to beware.

No one knows what I found. He and Tory had journeyed

to Chicago, to the Active Vessel Archives building. He'd been helping her search for an old equipment record when he'd uncovered the Station Ville Louis-Phillipe cargo transfer. Technically, it did belong in the unsecured bin in which he'd found it, since it contained no obvious Service markers. Only the date, time, and dock entries linked it to the CSS *Kensington*, and that would only set off alarms if you knew what date, time, and dock entries to look for. Which Sam did. Some details managed to stick in his mind, despite Dr. Pimentel's fears and his own disintegrating self-confidence.

He reached into his briefbag's inner compartment and once again reassured himself of the transfer's presence. Encased within its flexible plastic slipcase, the document crackled, the aged parchment dried, almost brittle to the touch. Cheap colony paper, a simple record of what was loaded onto a certain ship at a certain time. Not meant to be saved.

Food. Nothing unusual there—it made sense that the *Kensington* would load more supplies to feed its extra passengers. But synthetics and high-density nutritionals would be the consumables of choice. *Not real meat.* And certainly not real meat packed in agers. Sam had archived active vessel records for many years, and the only ships he recalled taking on agers were command vessels with high-level guests to impress, not combat vessels in emergency status. The containers took up too much room; they required specially trained technicians to maintain calibration or the contents would spoil. If Mako had wanted to feed his evacuees high-quality protein so badly, that's what the kettles were for.

Sam nestled into a chair, maneuvering it so it faced the door. Captain Kilian would approve of his actions, of that he felt sure. She seemed a cautious soul. He hugged that thought close as he did his briefbag, and waited for the hours to pass before their meeting.

He arrived at the SIB a few minutes before twelve up and sat on one of the tree-shaded benches in the building's front yard. He wiped his sweaty face with a pre-dampened dispo, and checked the transfer record again. Then he looked up—

his heart lifted as he watched Kilian cross the lawn from the direction of the South Central Base complex.

She wore summerweight trousers, but with the dressier white shirt Sam had seen Yance wear when he had to give a presentation. Unlike most Service clothing, it flattered a woman's figure. The wrap styling accentuated Kilian's waist and bust while the crossover collar framed her dark face.

She terrified him physically—so tall and straight, a woman of line, not of curve. Still, he found himself appreciating her with a bolder eye than he normally would have dared; he felt a surge of pride as he watched other men's gazes follow her. *My Captain of Dark Ice.* He stood as she approached the bench.

"Mr. Duong. I hope you're well." She smiled. "We don't have a lot of time. I'm scheduled for an important meeting at thirteen up. I didn't arrange it, so I couldn't move it. Sorry."

"You have so many meetings." Sam remained standing, finally gesturing for her to sit down first. "This one must be very important. You look very nice."

"Thank you." Kilian dropped her briefbag to the ground. She lowered to the edge of the bench, then moved down with a start as though something surprised her. "It's Office Hours. With a mainline general. I might live." She tensed, hunching her shoulders like Sam did when people pressed around him in the lift.

He leaned toward her. "Are you feeling all right, Captain? You don't look well."

"I'm fine." She had lost her smile. "Would you mind if we went somewhere else?"

"Where?"

"Not indoors." A loud blast sounded from the ranges, and she flinched. "The covered walkways, maybe? I know you don't like the beach."

"I will walk on the beach." Sam injected his voice with a confidence he didn't feel and hoisted his briefbag to his shoulder. "If you're with me." He looked down at her—was it his imagination, or did she shiver? "It's the noise from the weapons ranges, isn't it?"

She stiffened, then nodded. "That's not helping."

"We could go in—"

"*Not inside*." She offered a sheepish curve of lip that was more grimace than grin. "I'm feeling a little crowded today."

They walked silently across the East Yard, then down the flights of steps that descended to the beach. Sam held his breath as he stepped onto the sand and sank in up to his shoe tops. He stopped. Took another step. Stopped again.

Kilian reached out to him. "Give me your hand, Sam."

Sam held out his hand, sighing as Kilian closed her fingers around his. They felt cool. Dry. She had a strong grip for a woman. He felt her strength course up his arm, through his body.

He looked up the shore and saw the red, blue, and green splashes of sun umbrellas, running children, a group in base casuals struggling to right a volleyball net. *There's nothing to be afraid of here.* Not on this sand. Not now.

Kilian led him to a round wireframe table that was sheltered from the relentless sun by a red-and-white-striped awning. "You said you had some news that would interest me?" She released him, dragged a chair into the center of a wide strip of ruby light, and sat heavily.

Sam looked at the place where she'd touched him—he imagined the imprint of her fingers, like a signet. He slid into the chair opposite her and reached into his bag. "I found this in the city." He tucked the transfer into the fold of that morning's issue of *Blue and Grey*, and pushed it across the table toward her. "Early morning is the best time to search through Active Vessel Archives. The security is not all it should be."

Kilian opened the newssheet—her eyes widened as she studied the document nestled within. "Cargo transfer."

Sam nodded. "Check the date/time stamp."

Kilian did. "Well, well." Her voice emerged stronger, surer. She didn't look cold anymore. "You wanted to see how my idomeni-made scanpack worked—that's the story if anyone asks, OK? I scanned the newssheet." She waited for Sam to nod before she reached to her belt and removed the device from its pouch. "Where did you find this?"

"In an unsecured bin, while I searched for something else."

Sam glanced up and down the beach, on the lookout for spectators. "There's nothing on the document that identifies it as Service paper. That's why they let it go."

"All they had to do was check the date." Kilian activated her scanpack; the palm-sized unit's display shimmered bright green. "That tells me that whoever took the other records had little or no experience with documents. Covering the main doc trail is a snap, it's the peripherals that'll trip you up every time." She brushed the 'pack's bottom surface over the document in a regular left-to-right, top-to-bottom pattern. When her scanpack display flashed green, she deactivated it and returned it to its pouch. "It's the real thing," she said as she fingered a browned corner. "Not high-quality paper. I'm amazed it held up for eighteen years."

Sam nodded. "I don't think that bin was opened much. We got lucky."

Kilian studied the transfer. "Agers. Two of them." She looked across the table. "Feeding those evacuees well, weren't they?" The act of examining the paper had energized her—her dark eyes glittered.

Sam swallowed. When Yance looked at him the way Kilian did now, it never boded well for some poor would-be paper fiddler. "The evacuees were Family. I suppose they were entitled." He scraped the soles of his shoes against the scancrete. "I think I wasted your time—that document means nothing."

Kilian stared out toward the lake, where a couple of wave-gliders banked and weaved across the still surface. One glider cut a turn too sharply—his iridescent board shot out from under him and tumbled through the air. "Mako faced a court of inquiry when he returned to Earth." She waited for the board to strike the lake surface before turning away. "He mishandled remains. Ebben's, Unser's, and Fitzhugh's."

"Caldor's." Sam squirmed under Kilian's startled stare. "Her death cert had gone missing, too."

"So it did." Kilian crossed her legs and locked her hands around her knee. The red light that filtered through the awning rouged her complexion, making her look sunburnt. "How many died during the evac, total?"

"Sixteen."

"That's a lot of bodies to store in three cramped ships."

"The morgue coolers—"

"Three per sick bay. That's nine bodies—what did they do with the other seven?"

Sam rubbed his stomach. The conversation made it ache. "Body bags in the hold?"

"Want to know what I think?" Kilian smiled, a frosty twist of lip that reminded Sam uneasily of Pierce. "I think they ran out of body bags. And someone thought, oh aren't these convenient, and emptied out the meat and shoved the bodies in the agers. They probably thought they were reefer units." She chuckled. "I'd have hated to be the poor bastard who cracked those seals after two months." Her happy expression vanished when she looked at Sam. "Sorry. My sense of humor." She sat forward and spread her hands out on the tabletop, spacing them so that they both were bathed in red-tinged light.

Sam imagined the shadowing as the thinnest film of blood. "Captain, are you an augment?"

"Yes."

"Dr. Pimentel told me things, too. About agitation and feeling sick."

She smiled brilliantly. "You remembered that!"

"Yes." Sam tried again. "Should you be sitting in the red like this?"

The smile turned strange. "I find it energizing." She grew serious. "Has a mainline colonel with a nasty facial scar been turning up at the SIB over the past few weeks?"

"You mean Niall Pierce?"

"*You* know him, too?"

Sam shook his head. "I know of him, from the Rauta Shè-ràa Base files."

"He was part of the evac."

"Yes. And I saw him at the hospital once. He was there to pick up scan results. I haven't seen him at the SIB."

"I have." Kilian stood up and walked out into the blazing sun. In the distance, the booms of the Y-40s shook the air, but she didn't seem to hear them anymore. Her timorousness had disappeared—energy seemed to ripple from her now, like heat from a roadbed. "Do you think you're being watched?"

"Yes." Sam's hands shook—he braced them against the table.

"Do you own a weapon?"

"No. You think I'll need one?"

"If you don't know how to use it, it may do you more harm than good."

"I'm very good at running and hiding."

"Not bad skills to have." The grim smile again. Then Kilian glanced at her timepiece. "I have to get going." She walked back to the table and hoisted her bag, then gestured to Sam with that childlike backward wave. "Let's go."

"No." Sam shook his head. "I want to sit here a while." He looked out over the water, at the lakeskimmers and sailboards. "Maybe I'll even walk in the sand."

"You're sure?"

"Yes."

The dark in Kilian's eyes softened. The goddess touched. "You're a very brave man."

"As long as I know you're here." Sam smiled up at her. "I couldn't do it alone. I could never do it alone."

Kilian started to speak, blinked, turned away. She strode across the sand, her step hurried. As though there were someplace she needed to go. Or someplace she needed to leave behind.

CHAPTER 22

Evan slept fitfully and awoke feeling restless. As pink-orange wisps of cloud drifted through the sunrise sky, he tended his roses, following the checklist Joaquin had given him to the letter. Hours passed as he applied nutrients and fungicides, cut back straggly branches, slaughtered the weeds that had dared poke through the raked and treated soil.

For the first time, he found himself enjoying the work. Sweat and repetition helped him think.

"So, Quino would rather think me brain-impaired than believe Mako killed the charges against Jani to save Pierce." Evan yanked at a stubborn pig's ear, breaking the plant at ground level. "He controls my access to secured information, which means I can't investigate further without his buy-in." He knelt and dug into the ground with his hands. After a few strong tugs, he wrenched the root free, spraying clods of dirt in all directions. "Shroud was right. Quino wants to cut me loose—he's tossing up that Haárin option as a smoke screen." Well, he had learned a lot about the esteemed Mr. Loiaza in the thirty years of their acquaintance. "You snake me, I may just make some notes about you, too." He wiped smeared earth from his face and hands and continued weeding.

"So who got to him, Anais or Roshi?" Evan paused in front of a creeping Charlie that had taken over a shady corner near the Wolfshead Westminster. "I'd bet Anais. Quino doesn't give a damn about the Service, but he sure as hell cares about Cabinet Court retainer fees."

He tore out the creeping Charlie with a hand rake, then collected the round-leafed tendrils and stuffed them into a decomp bag. In a few days, he'd remove the rotted plant matter and fold it back into the soil to nourish the roses, the vanquished enemy reworked for his purpose. Government in a nutshell, part two.

He collected his implements and concoctions, trudged to the small shed adjoining the house, and returned them to the appropriate hooks, racks, and shelves. Pulled the flask from his trouser pocket and took a draw.

The *breep* of the front-entry buzzer greeted Evan as he entered the house. Halvor had already departed to run errands, and Markhart worked upstairs before lunch, which left him with the unusual task of answering his own door.

He didn't check the security display to see who waited outside. If the door system announced a visitor, then his jailers must have already cleared them. So he released the panel, swept it aside, and found himself nose to nose with an agitated Hugh Tellinn.

"Mr. van Reuter." Tellinn looked over his shoulder, then back at him, his movements as stiff and awkward as they had been in Shroud's parlor.

Who does he want to pound into the carpet now? "Dr. Tellinn." Evan looked past the man to see if either of his neighbors had wandered to their front yards to check out the action in person. Both areas looked clear, which meant they had stayed inside and used scanners instead. "Come in."

The physician stepped inside. "Thank you for seeing me," he said softly. "I understand this isn't the best time for you."

"Not your problem, Doctor. Don't give it a second thought." Evan regarded Tellinn with a critical eye. *So, Val, you forsake young and dumb for old and smart and look what happens.* He gets jittery and seeks out the enemy. "Is this a medical visit?" he asked for form's sake.

"Only officially. So I could get permission to come here." Tellinn took a tentative step toward the sitting room. "I—I need—I need your help."

"I'm not in the position to help myself, much less you."

"Just hear me out. I think after you do, you'll change your mind." Tellinn walked around Evan into the sitting room, then glanced back at him in nervous expectation. "I'm here about Jani Kilian."

Oh no. Evan fell in behind him and sat in his usual lounge chair. "Val didn't send you here in an effort to bypass John, did he?"

Tellinn perched on the edge of the sofa. "No. If Val knew I'd come here, he'd kill me." He started to rock, a slight forward-and-back motion, like a continuous nod of the head. "I need you to contact Jani the next time you go to Sheridan. I need you to give her something."

Evan studied Tellinn's face for some sign he joked, but saw only dour sincerity laced with panic. "I won't be returning to Sheridan for some time." *If ever.* "The most serious charges against Jani are to be dropped, and she's to be given a medical discharge. Since that's the case, the SIB no longer needs what information I have to offer."

"But surely you can think up some excuse, tell your attorney that you've remembered something important." Tellinn stilled his rocking long enough to reach into his inner shirt pocket and pull out what looked like a cigar case. When he snapped it open, however, steam puffed—he removed a frosted cylinder the size of Evan's index finger. "She needs to have the contents of this syringe injected as soon as possible." He slowly inverted the cylinder, displaying the straw yellow liquid contained within.

Evan eyed the cylinder with dismay. For years, his own physicians had threatened him with similar devices. "That's a gene-therapy cocktail."

"Yes." Mild surprise dulled Tellinn's edginess. "If you know what it is, you must realize the condition she's in."

"I remember what you said in John's parlor. John didn't think you knew what you were talking about."

"Dr. Shroud had allowed his ego to come before the needs of his patient." Tellinn rendered his own diagnosis of the situation quickly and coolly. "I had to bribe one of his hybridization specialists to help me manufacture this. It's primarily designed to repair the defect in Jani's heme pathway, but it also contains components to fix the worst of her metabolic abnormalities as well." He resumed his rocking. "They're packing her with engineered carbohydrates because that's the diet prescribed for patients with AIP, but she's synthesizing idomeni digestive enzymes that are cleaving the molecules in different places, which is leading to the buildup of toxic metabolites in her tissues—"

Evan jumped in before the torrent of words turned to flood. "Dr. Tellinn! I can't help you!"

"But . . ." Tellinn stilled, and blinked in bewilderment. "Val said you agreed to help us. You felt guilty because of the way you treated Jani years ago and you wanted to make it up to her."

Vladislav's got nothing on you for dramatic nonsense. Evan squeezed the arm of his chair. His hand closed over a Crème Caramel petal left over from yesterday's encounter with Joaquin, and he rolled it between his fingers. "Dr.—"

"Call me Hugh," Tellinn interrupted hopefully.

Evan glanced at the wisp of flower in his hand. "It sounds as though you don't know the entire story where Jani and I are concerned."

"I confess, I don't keep up with events as well as I should." Tellinn's face lightened with an apologetic smile. "But Val said you almost married—"

"John Shroud has circumstantial evidence linking me to Jani's transport explosion. I had nothing to do with it, of course"—Evan's fingers worked harder, grinding the petal to fragments—"but it looks very bad, and I'm in no position to fight it. In other words, he held a shooter to my head. That's the only reason I agreed to perjure myself. I don't care what happens to Jani." He brushed the bits of rose to the floor. "But now that she's to be discharged, it's all academic."

Tellinn's eagerness evaporated. "No, Mr. van Reuter, not *all* of it." He glared at the cocktail cylinder, then shoved it back into its case. "You won't help?"

"I can't."

"Her organs will fail, one by one. Her brain will be irreversibly damaged. She will die."

"Even if I could talk myself onto the base and somehow arrange to meet Jani, I could never convince her to take anything from me." Evan felt his pocket for the flask, then pulled his hand away. *Not in front of the children.* "I assume you've tried to contact her Service doctors yourself."

"Just last night. Begged my way as far as a Roger Pimentel. Received a very cold, 'thank you, Doctor, but we have things under control' in response." Tellinn's face had paled to a Shroud-like pallor. He sat forward, elbows on knees, hands clasped across his forehead.

Evan looked over the top of Tellinn's head to the window and the outdoors beyond. He wished he'd remained outside, never heard the buzzer. "John loves her. If he has to resort to brute force or invoke compassionate intervention to get into Sheridan, he will."

"I don't think you understand the extreme animosity that exists between Service Medical and Neoclona."

"I know all about that. If John hadn't accused the Service Surgeon-General of promoting butchery last year when she refused to allow Neoclona to assist in the training of Service physicians, he wouldn't find him on the outside looking in now."

"There's more involved than that." Tellinn's face had the nauseated cast of a man who had bitten into an apple and found half a worm. "I think the Service higher-ups who remember the idomeni civil war hold John responsible for the destruction of Rauta Shèràa Base. They feel that if he hadn't angered the idomeni by getting involved in illegal research, there would have been much less outrage directed at the remaining humans as the war wound down."

"Knevçet Shèràa led to what happened at Rauta Shèràa Base, and John Shroud had nothing to do with that." Evan massaged the rough upholstery until his fingers stung. "How many times do I have to tell you, Doctor? I can't help you."

"She's been through so much."

"I hate to sound cold, but she brought a lot of it upon herself."

Tellinn stared at him, tired eyes searching in vain for something. Then he stood slowly and walked, back bowed,

step heavy. He paused in the room entry and turned back to
Evan. "Val tells me stories about Rauta Shèràa Base. He
leaves a lot out—I can tell from the way he jokes to fill the
holes." He hesitated, dark eyes reflecting the horror described. "He talks about the last night. The Night of the
Blade. The dead quiet when the bombing finally stopped, and
the Laum streamed out of their homes and lined up to be
slaughtered." He looked at Evan. "Humans don't line up to
be killed."

"Not unless they're forced, no."

"So the humans who died there probably weren't killed
by Haárin, because the Haárin weren't carrying the sorts of
weapons that could compel them to stop. Val thinks they
were executed by criminals for failing to come through on
contracts, or just to keep them from talking."

"That's certainly possible."

"Jani wasn't a criminal. She got into trouble for fighting
the criminals." Tellinn's hands twitched. He kicked at the
carpet—the tread of his shoe caught so that he almost lost
his balance. Gone clumsy again. "So how can you say Rauta
Shèràa Base was her fault? Seems to me quite a few *humans*
went over the edge there. Panicked. Rode the madness of the
moment. They're the ones to blame, not her."

Evan reached for his flask again. Stopped himself again.
"Jani won't die. Remember that she has Nema on her side,
and Prime Minister Cao knows she dare not anger him." He
stood, hoping that Tellinn would take the hint. "Something
will shake loose."

"I hope you're right." Tellinn accepted the invitation to
get lost. "Thank you for nothing, Mr. van Reuter." He headed
for the door—it swept aside, and he almost collided with a
grocery-carton-laden Halvor.

"I'll be outside," Evan informed the confused aide. He had
the flask out of his pocket before he stepped out of the house.

It would have been nice to officially blame the Haárin or
some criminal syndicate for the deaths of Ebben, Unser, and
Fitzhugh. That would have provided answers enough to cut
off the questions and the rumors that sprang from the events
of that night. And the magic Joaquin could have worked with

a few holos of the blade-cut dead or signs of ritual execution would have dispelled once and for all the cloud of suspicion hanging over Evan. *Nothing works like firm, hard paper.* From there, it would have been an easy leap to suppose Jani's transport crash the product of Haárin vengeance or criminal bungling. *And I'd have been out of this house by autumn.* He ducked into the shed, leaned against the sheet-metal wall, and emptied the flask down his throat. *If not for Roshi's screwup.*

He kicked at the decomp bag, distended by weed bulk and digestion gasses, and gagged as a warm belch of half-rotted vegetation stench puffed through gaps in the opening. He grasped the handle of the bag and dragged it across the floor to rest near the solvent storage ventilator. The digestion mechanisms built into the sack worked quickly—in a few days, there would be no sign of what the muck had been or where it had come from—

Something flitted in Evan's head, like a whisper. He picked through his myriad thoughts trying to recover it, but it wriggled away like a fish.

The madness of the moment. . . .

He stood in the doorway of the shed, Tellinn's words echoing in his head, and stared at the decomp bag until Markhart called him in to lunch.

CHAPTER 23

Jani set aside the issue of *Blue and Grey* that she'd been paging through, and stifled a yawn as post–augie languor settled over her. Sitting in a stream of red light wasn't the medically approved way to deal with Neumann's hallucination, but she'd grown desperate since she'd awakened that morning to hear his off-key bass emerge from her bathroom. *I always dreamed of this, Kilian,* he said when he stuck his shower-damp head out the door. *All you'd have to do is strip and join me to make this moment complete.*

A few minutes later had found her trudging barefoot across the South Yard, wearing the same base casuals she'd slept in, duffel on her shoulder. It had still been dark, thankfully. No A&S-holes out and about to find her in sweat-stained dishabille.

Working on sleep-deprived autopilot, she had showered in the women's locker room of the South Central Gymnasium. Dressed. Applied makeup with a trembling hand. And walked out into the blaze of day to find Neumann leaning in the gymnasium doorway, waiting for her. He'd stood close enough for her to smell his breath drops, the cinnamon candies he had sucked incessantly.

I watched you through the gap in the shower curtain, and you didn't see me.

"Nervous, Jani?" Friesian shuffled through a file and made

a notation into his handheld. He had gone the "B" shirt route, as well. And had his hair trimmed.

"No more than usual, considering the circumstances."

"They will probably holocam this, even though it's a non-judicial. Just forget it's there and act natural."

Act natural, he says. She'd have a hard enough time staying awake. She had tried to give Neumann the boot by breakfasting decently, then making sure her morning in Foreign Transactions remained uneventful by locking herself in her office and letting her comport screen her calls. He hadn't shown up—she thought she'd beaten him.

Then he had reappeared during her meeting with Sam Duong, dogging her shoulder and offering advice on how to get Burkett off her back. Foul comments all, and some physically impossible besides.

So she drove augie to the edge, felt the white light in her head and the hurricane gales at her feet, and pitched Neumann over the side, at least for a while. *Roger would kill me if he knew.* But augie's neurochemical magic had worked wonders—she felt better than she had for a week. *Just a little wobbly . . .*

A gentle throat-clearing sounded from the opposite side of the anteroom. General Burkett's adjutant spoke a few words into her comport, then glanced at Jani and Friesian. "You may go in, Major. Captain."

Jani stood slowly, gripping the arms of her chair for support. She sniffed, smelled only filtered office air, and offered silent thanks. She followed Friesian to the door, let him palm it open, and preceded him inside. As expected, she saw Burkett sitting at his glossy bloodwood desk, glare at the ready.

She didn't, however, expect to see Frances Hals sitting across from him, nor another older, blond-haired woman who, judging from the stars on her collar and the scanpack on her hip, could only be Major General Hannah Eiswein, commander of the First Documents and Documentation Division.

I'm gonna die. "Captain Kilian reporting as ordered, sir."

"Come in, Captain." Burkett's gaze shifted to Friesian, and his frown deepened. "Major?"

"Major Piers Friesian, General. Defense Command." His voice sounded tentative as he looked at Hals and Eiswein. "I'm Captain Kilian's legal counsel."

"There's no need for that, Major." Eiswein smiled. She appeared companionable, with the sort of relaxed, unlined face that *implied* an even temper. "This isn't a disciplinary action."

Friesian shot Jani a befuddled look. His thick, black eyebrows knit. "Ma'am, my client was given to understand—"

"Circumstances have changed, Major." Eiswein smiled again, more coolly. "Captain Kilian's role here will be more in a consulting capacity. If you feel at all uncomfortable about this, of course you may stay. But you'll be wasting your time."

Friesian settled back on his heels, chin raised, eyes narrowing. Jani could read the questions in his expression. The concern. The stars.

"If it's all the same to you, ma'am, I'd prefer to sit in on this." He gave Jani a "be careful" nod as he walked to a small conference table that basked in the light of the office's window-wall. "I do possess top-level security clearance, if consultations reach that point."

"They shouldn't," Eiswein said softly as she withdrew a recording board from the briefbag by her chair. Pink-skinned and cushy, she looked the polar opposite of the tanned, narrow-faced Burkett. "Captain Kilian. The famous Eyes and Ears." She gestured toward the empty chair between her and Hals. "I've been looking forward to meeting you."

Hals offered the barest smile as Jani approached; the expression altered to one of concern as she took her seat. "Are you feeling all right, Captain?"

"Yes, ma'am." Jani caught herself on the chair arms just in time to keep from collapsing into it. "Trouble sleeping." She noted that Hals wore the less formal light grey "A" short-sleeve, as did Burkett and Eiswein.

We're overdressed, Piers. Jani looked around Burkett's office, a showcase of wine-red cabinetry and satin-finish steel, on the alert for hidden lieutenants with holocams. She faced front to find Burkett glowering at her.

"Looking for something, Captain?"

"Just admiring your office, sir." It took true force of will for her to smile at him. He made no effort to hide his feelings—the animosity rolled across his desk and buffeted her like a wave.

"Well, General, why don't we get started." Eiswein's voice, flavored by her German provincial accent, sounded at the same time soft and clipped. The rules of the game being what they were, if her sideline double stars had been able to stand up to Burkett's mainline single and quash any disciplinary actions against Jani and Hals, that meant someone in Supreme Command had thrown their vote her way.

Jani could imagine the scene. Perhaps it had even been Mako himself who had said, *you gave the wrong orders, Cal, and I'm ordering you to back off.*

Eiswein proved gracious in victory, at least for the time being. She ignored Burkett's choppy mood, and had only smiles for her two rebellious dexxie underlings. "Colonel, please bring Captain Kilian up to speed."

"Yes, ma'am." Hals activated her board; an open file bloomed on the display. "Captain Kilian is, of course, an old hand in dealing with the idomeni. She already understands our major issues."

"Such as figuring out the difference between what's important to us and what's important to them, ma'am?" Jani looked around innocently. Burkett met her eyes, his face like stone.

"But surprises still occur," Hals added hastily. "Scanpack health, for example, has suddenly become a pressing concern." Her voice lowered in genuine distress. "Lieutenant Domenici's 'pack suffered a stroke soon after we returned from the embassy. It can't recognize certain symbols anymore, and can't decode the right sides of chips. Scantech blamed the elevated temperature in the embassy. They said nutrient degraded, formed a clot, and blew out her fourth octant region."

Jani thought back to the embassy visit. Everyone had complained of the heat except her. "If 'packs are experiencing heat distress, the embassy interior must have been at least forty-five degrees. You need to switch out spent nutrient more often. Make sure you're using a warm-weather brand, and that fluid levels are topped off. Has that been the only stroke?"

Hals nodded. "Yes, although we have had some scares during previous visits. Transient ischemic attacks—the 'packs malfunction for a few hours, then snap back. Tech Service is starting to write papers about our problems, and that is a worry."

"Lieutenant Domenici will, in fact, need to have her 'pack replaced," Eiswein interjected. "I approved the requisition an hour ago. The damage proved so extensive that it's cheaper to grow her a new one than try to fix the old." She patted her own 'pack pouch absently. "They'll farm her cells tomorrow. It will be six weeks before she'll have something she can begin to teach." Her eyes bored into Jani's. They shone palest blue, like Burkett's steel. "So not only are we dealing with the replacement of an extremely expensive piece of equipment, but I'm also out one experienced dexxie in an already-stretched department for the time it takes her to retrain her 'pack. How long does that take on average, Colonel?"

Hals called up another screen on her board. "Four months, ma'am. On average."

"And that's assuming she returns to FT, of which there's no guarantee." The color rose in Eiswein's face as she hit her stride. "Dexxies get edgy when their equipment's threatened, and the knowledge that merely doing their *routine*, *uncomplicated* jobs could result in irreversible damage to the devices on which their livelihoods depend is enough to make them pretty damned edgy!" Her anger held a particularly distressing aspect, like being chewed out by your favorite aunt.

Burkett remained silent throughout, although he did twitch about in his leather-upholstered chair as though he needed to adjust his underwear. Especially after Eiswein spat out the words *routine* and *uncomplicated*. Direct quotes, no doubt. Jani almost felt sorry for him. If Eiswein hammered him like this in front of subordinates, what had she said to him one-on-one?

Scheißkopf? She struggled to keep a straight face. "So, along with the measurable loss in equipment and efficiency, FT may also find itself dealing with a serious morale problem."

Hals sighed. "There are so many minefields where the idomeni are concerned, things we think nothing of. We know we can't wear red. That we can't carry in food, not even so much as a pack of gum. My concern is that one or more of our rebellious souls might resort to sabotage. Considering how important the idomeni think we are, the magnitude of the perceived insult would be great indeed."

Burkett finally opened his mouth. "And you've made no effort to supply me with the names of those souls, Colonel, despite my repeated requests."

"Give those souls the tools to maintain their equipment and you'll stop the revolution in its tracks." Jani pulled her scanpack out of its pouch and studied the underside. "My 'pack was manufactured on Shèrá as part of a joint humanish-idomeni project. Lots of effort went into synthesizing the heat-dissipation system. It's functioned flawlessly for over twenty years. I don't even consider it exceptional anymore." She looked at Eiswein. "Did anyone talk to Three through Six about this? They have the same type unit I do—they could have advised you on what to expect."

"Three through six?" Burkett muttered crankily. "What does that mean?"

"The Captain is referring to her fellow Academy graduates." Eiswein made a notation into her board. "The funny thing is, Captain, that whenever we dexxies talk about the fabled Academy days, we talk about you, and we talk about the late Hansen Wyle. The others don't make the cut." She regarded Jani intently. "Shortsighted of us, was it not?"

"Ma'am," Jani replied. Eiswein's examination possessed a distinctly maternal quality, if one's mother had the talent for seeing through to the back of one's head. "If you're going to keep working with the idomeni, you need to act. Right now, FT is taking all the hits. You need to start dishing out."

"That's Diplo's job," Burkett growled.

"From what I gather," Eiswein countered, "any negotiation with the idomeni must take place on many different levels. They believe existence is a series of incremental steps, like multiple stairways approaching from all different directions, and every undertaking is approached the same way. Any resolution of this Lake Michigan Strip matter will be reached in the records room as well as the negotiating room."

"My thoughts on that, I believe, have been added to the record, General."

"Yes, General, but be that as it may, we have our mandate from Supreme Command—"

Jani glanced sideways at Hals at the same time Hals glanced sideways at her. Then Hals activated her stylus and executed a quick sketch. With a few rapid strokes, she outlined a pudgy matador, cape in one hand, scanpack in the other, advancing upon a snorting bull that had been branded on his backside with a single large star—

Jani faced front and focused on a point on the wall above Burkett's head.

"—and participate in this process, we will." Eiswein smoothed an errant lock of hair behind her ear and eased back in her chair.

Burkett drummed his fingers on his desktop. Once. Twice. Thrice. "Could we just ask the idomeni to turn the heat down?"

"You could, sir," Jani answered carefully. "But it would be better if you made a bigger splash. They know you're miserable—all they have to do is look at you. They're enjoying watching you sweat, both literally and figuratively."

She paused before continuing. "A visual display of your adjustment to their conditions would act as an issued challenge, and win you a little of your own back. It needs to be something obvious, something the idomeni can appreciate. They find us so difficult to read that an explicit action by us would both please them and take them by surprise." A spot of personal whimsy popped into her head, and she tossed it out to the house. "Wear base casuals the next time you're called in."

Hals sighed. "God, that would be *so* comfortable!" She starting making notes. "Do you think we could bring little cooler units, too? The ones you can set up on your desk—"

"*Colonel!*" Burkett's bronzed skin flared maroon. "That's outrageous!" He thumped his fist on his desk. "I'll be damned if I ever represent my Service in a T-shirt and trainers."

"Don't forget the shorts, sir." Jani heard a tiny, strangled sound emerge from Hals's throat. Burkett twisted around in his chair to face her, but before he could erupt, Eiswein cut him off.

"Calm down, General." She beamed like Mère Christmas. "I like it."

Burkett's jaw dropped. "General—!"

"Well, why not! I'm always hearing about the idomeni's playful side, their need to make and accept challenge, the constant one-upmanship they seem to thrive on. And here we are, with a golden opportunity to stick it in their ear, and you want us to back off in the name of *propriety*?" Eiswein gave the word a gamy twist, making it sound like something nice people didn't talk about.

Burkett looked stricken. "Aren't there any alternatives?" The hard look he directed at Jani held a hint of pleading. "What did you wear, Captain, when you were stationed at Rauta Shèràa Base?"

"We were issued desertweights, sir."

Burkett nodded in relief. "We can ship some of those in from Bonneville or Aqaba. We'll have them in a couple of hours."

Hals shook her head. "Base casuals are an official part of the Sheridan-issue uniform set, sir. If you name it Uniform of the Day for our trip to the embassy, no matter how strange it may seem to some, we are technically in A&S compliance. But desertweights are *not* an official part of the Sheridan-issue uniform set; therefore, we would need sign-off from A&S before we could even place the order."

"We're in a crisis situation, Colonel."

"Yes, sir. The problem is, sir, that if you go to A&S with this type of request . . ." Hals faltered. "It's the Joint Perception Committee, sir. The Cabinet-Service group that monitors how the civilian public perceives the Service. They'll get wind of it, and once they do they're going to stick their— get involved."

One little vein stood out in Burkett's temple. "Which Cabinet Ministers sit on that committee?"

"Exterior Minister Ulanova, for one—"

"Scratch that," Eiswein entoned glumly. "Ulanova would kick our sand castle over just to watch us cry." She pondered. "We place the nice, aboveboard order for the desertweights, via A&S, and amass our weapons for the fight. For this next visit, which is scheduled for early tomorrow morning, we go casual."

"You need my buy-in for any off-the-beaten-path scheme." Burkett's voice had thinned. The stressed metal had been drawn very fine, and seemed about to snap. "I want it on the record that I disagree strongly with our constantly and consistently putting idomeni sensibilities before those of our own people." He didn't look at Jani as he spoke; he didn't have to. "Why are we always giving in to them?"

"They gave in to us just by the act of coming here," Jani said to the side of his face. "Just by the act of living here. We've discussed this before, sir. Your refusing to see the point doesn't make it any less valid or any less important."

"In other words, what's a little dignity if it saves us the Lake Michigan Strip?" Eiswein deactivated her board and stuffed it back in her briefbag. "Your buy-in, as you call it, would certainly make the row easier to hoe, but if it doesn't prove forthcoming, I suppose we'll have to carry on without it."

Before Burkett could counter, a voice piped from the far corner of the room.

"Ma'am? Sir?" Friesian spoke quickly, as though he'd been trying to fit a word in edgewise for some time. "If Captain Kilian is to leave the base so soon, we need to clear her through the JA immediately." He looked at Hals. "Colonel, with whom did you talk to arrange clearance for the captain's previous trip off base? I did not receive a restricted-movement repeal related to that trip, and with her status, it's vital I have those on file."

Burkett stared at Jani. "You're restricted to base?"

"Yes, sir." She cast a wary eye at the four confused faces watching her. "I assumed everyone knew."

"I did, but . . ." Hals fell silent.

Burkett seemed to be having trouble wrapping his mind around Jani's status, too. "You were under *official* restriction when you traveled off base to the embassy?"

"Yes, sir," Jani answered, more harshly than was prudent. "Is there a problem?"

"I don't understand this at all." Pimentel stood in front of the imaging display and flipped through the multiple deep-tissue scans of Jani's right arm. "Where did the calcification come from?"

One of the many new medical faces that had surrounded Jani for the past two hours spoke up. "My best guess is that when they implanted the chip at Constanza, they used standard nerve solder, which is, of course, human-compatible." She nodded toward Jani. "Captain Kilian rejected the solder as foreign material and sealed it off from the rest of her tissue. In sealing off the solder, she sealed off the rest of the chip as well, causing the security function to fail."

"Not all the way." Jani massaged the crook of her right arm, from where William Tell Pimentel had withdrawn about half her blood. "My arm hurt like hell as soon as I passed through the Gate. By the time we returned from the idomeni embassy, it had gone numb."

The internist waved a hand. "Captain, trust me, 'hurt like hell' doesn't begin to describe the pain restrictees feel when they try to leave their allowed area. Prisoners pass out. We've even had a few try to cut the chips out themselves— luckily, we got to them first." She wandered up to the imaging display. "Has anyone notified the Judge Advocate?"

Jani had been thinking longingly of sleep, but mention of the JA jarred her alert. "Why do you need to call them?"

"Your chip's security function needs to be reset. Only someone from the JA can do that." Pimental studied the image again, and shook his head. "Judging from the looks of this thing, they'll need to insert a new chip. We're going to have to keep you here until we can perform the surgery." He walked to the door, the rest of the medicos falling in behind him. "Major Friesian is holed up in the sunroom. I'll speak with him. Under the circumstances, I think he should notify the JA."

The removal of Jani's calcified ID chip and the implantation of her new one were performed in a cramped operating theater, under the official eye of a blasé sergeant major who observed the magnified interior of Jani's lower arm without a blink of discomfort.

They anchored the chip with surgical glue rather than nerve solder. They couldn't risk using anesthetic, the neurosurgeon told Jani, because of her history of idiosyncratic reactions to common medications. Instead, after they clamped her arm into the surgical sleeve, they applied pin blocks that supposedly disrupted nerve transmissions just as well. They didn't. Not without the magnetic-pulse adjuncts, which they couldn't use because a magburst could blitz the new chip. Pimentel stood behind her and massaged the knots out of her shoulders, and they gave her a dental appliance to bite down on so she wouldn't damage her teeth when she clenched her jaw.

After the neurosurgeon finished, she recommended cold packs for the pain. Jani's street Acadian reply drew blank stares from both her and Pimentel. The sergeant major, however, betrayed her origins by chewing her lower lip and staring at the display until her eyes watered.

As soon as Jani had been settled with a cold pack and instructions for caring for the incision, everyone left. Except Pimentel.

"I'm sorry about that, Jani." He dragged a stool near her surgical chair and sat. "I've scheduled you for an appointment with someone from Gene Therapeutics tomorrow."

Jani repositioned the cold pack. "I thought you wanted to wait."

"I don't think we can." Pimentel stared at his hands. For

the first time, his voice sounded tentative. "I ran a routine liver-enzyme scan while we were waiting for your imaging analysis. I'm seeing values I've never seen before, and I'm not seeing things I should see." He looked at Jani, eyes pitted by circles, skin grey. The self-confident physician of only a few days ago seemed never to have existed. "Internal Medicine has a team of med techs working to develop assays that can identify and quantify your enzymatic activity. Hepatology has advised we farm your liver immediately so we can start growing a replacement, and so we can assemble an adjunct in case you go into failure."

"I feel *fine*." Jani forced her voice to be strong. "Not great, but not that sick. My department is required at the idomeni embassy tomorrow morning. I *have* to go."

"Not if I feel you're in danger," Pimentel replied, in a voice that sounded surer than it had all afternoon.

Jani spent over three hours in Gene Therapeutics being sampled, scoped, and scanned. More pin blocks, this time augmented by the magnetic pulse. Together, they deadened the pain, though not the eerie sensation of *things* being removed from her abdomen.

The med techs' cobbled assays told the hepatologist some of what he needed to know about the state of her internal organs. That allayed Pimentel's fears sufficiently that he agreed not to admit her. He did, however, make her spend a few postop hours in the sunroom. Just to be on the safe side, he said, which didn't make Jani feel safe at all. She cheered up a little, though, when Ischi stopped by on his way home to the BOQ to drop off her paper mail.

"You didn't have to do this, Lieutenant," Jani said as she laid out the few thin envelopes before her on the table. One contained an offer to join the South Central Players, while another held an invitation to the All-Base Volleyball Tournament.

"Oh, yes I did, ma'am." Ischi leaned down and with one finger, tapped a crimson-edged white envelope out of the stack like a trickster picking his card. "Read the front."

"One North Lakeside." Jani felt her tender stomach clench as she peeled the envelope seal and removed the stiff, gold-edged card. "Admiral-General and Mrs. Hiroshi Mako cordially invite you and a guest to attend an Open House . . ." Her voice faded.

"How about that!" Ischi bubbled. "Some people wait for *years* to get their invitation. But you've only had your number a couple of days."

Oh, I think someone's had my number for longer than that. "Yeah," Jani replied. "How about it."

CHAPTER 24

The next morning dawned, as had all the previous ones, clear and hot. Jani stood by the people-mover, dispo of fruit drink in hand, and watched the rest of Foreign Transactions gather. She'd had an early night—Pimentel's dour pronouncements concerning the state of her health, combined with the lack of news from the Misty Center, had made her too grumpy to socialize. She'd remained in her rooms. Read newssheets. Debated calling Lucien and decided against. Discussed Niall Pierce's odd behavior with Val the Bear.

She had also waited for Neumann to reappear. He hadn't. At least something had gone right.

The sound of laughter brought her back to the present; she watched the rising sun illuminate her coworkers' sleepy eyes and sheepish grins. Dressed in T-shirts, shorts, and trainers, scanpacks hanging from belts and shoulder slings, they looked like Sheridan's first team in the all-dexxie Olympics.

"What do you think, Captain?" Colonel Hals gestured toward the milling group. Ischi, athletic-looking enough to appear at home in the abbreviated uniform of the day, busied himself checking off names on a recording board. Meanwhile, the less toned Vespucci, red-faced and fidgety, assisted a couple of underlings with last-minute 'pack assessments.

Jani eyed assorted flaccid limbs. "I think there's going to be a stampede on the gym when we get back." She looked

256

at Hals, who regarded her impatiently. "When word of this leaks out, the self-appointed arbiters will have plenty to say."

"That's a given." Hals sipped her steaming coffee. "What about the Vynshàrau?"

Jani bit into a slice of carefully scanned breakfast cake. The smell of the coffee hadn't agreed with her stomach, but otherwise, she felt good. Not one bit sleepy. Hyper, actually. Floaty, as though she'd drunk a glass of wine. "Officially, I think they'll be relieved. I can't predict individual reactions."

"But you went to school with them?"

"Yes, but we didn't mix."

"Except for Hantìa?"

"Only because she approached us."

"Wasn't that unusual? I would have thought they'd have waited for you to come to them. I thought that except for Tsecha, all the idomeni felt themselves superior to you." Hals coughed out Nema's official name. A good job, as though she'd practiced.

Jani shrugged. "The Vynshà hadn't yet ascended to rau, so they still had room to maneuver. It was up to the Laumrau to hold the snobbery standard." She flashed a smile she didn't feel. "Hantìa was disputatious, even by Vynshà standards. She liked sticking her fingers between the bars."

"Did any of you ever bite?" Hals grew restive as the silence lengthened. "I'd like an answer, Captain."

Oh hell. It never failed. Why did the events from your past that you hoped remained buried forever always disinter themselves at the worst possible time? "I . . . hit her, once."

"You *hit* her!" Hals lowered her voice as people turned to look. "Define *hit*."

Jani mimed a right uppercut. "It was our first term at Academy—"

"I don't need a history lesson."

"Yes, ma'am, you do. She found out that Hansen Wyle and I had been sneaking food into our study carrels. We stayed in the equivalent of a dormitory, but we couldn't eat or even store any food there. If we wanted to eat, we had to travel to the human enclave, two kilometers outside Rauta Shèràa's perimeter. It took an hour or more to skim there on an average traffic day. Three or more hours to make the round-trip. We already traveled there twice a day for regular meals. We had so much work to do, we couldn't spare the extra time." Jani felt a sick chill. "And we just got tired of being hungry." Even decades later, the episode bought back feelings of guilt. Fear. Anger. "We tried our best to follow their dictates, and only bring in the kinds of foods that were sold on the futures markets on a given day."

"She threatened to fink?"

"She would have gotten us expelled. Not even Nema could have saved us from that one." Jani clenched her hand. "She came to my room and told me what she was going to do. She has a very aggravating laugh, even for an idomeni." She heard it in her head now, that monotonic staccato. "I was scared. Upset. I thought I'd blown it for everybody. Before I knew it, I had knocked her to the floor."

"What did she do?" Hals's voice was flat.

"Blinked. Stared right at me, which surprised me. Picked herself up off the ground and left."

"That was it?"

"Yes, ma'am." Jani worked her fingers. She could still remember her aching knuckles, Hansen trying to console her as he packed her hand in ice.

Hals shook her head. "And you think that in spite of that run-in, she accepts you now?"

"She knows I killed twenty-six Laumrau at Knevçet Shè-ràa. They all do. They accept it. Like I've said before, they'd be insulted if you tried to hide me or pretend I didn't exist. It would be an affront to their intelligence." Jani sighed at Hals's confused look. "It's difficult to explain. Honoring the unpleasant isn't a sensibility most humans are familiar with."

Before Hals could respond, a stiff-looking young woman approached them. She wore dress blue-greys cut with a main-line stripe, and eyed the bare limbs around her with distaste bordering on horror. "Lieutenant Guid, ma'am." She saluted Hals. "Judge Advocate's office." She offered Jani only a vague nod, in acknowledgment of the fact that she represented the prosecution while Jani embodied the prosecuted.

Hals gestured for them both to follow her to the other side

of the people-mover, away from prying eyes. "Lieutenant Guid is here to see about your chip, Captain."

"I was starting to wonder about that." Jani held out her still-sore right arm to the pinched young woman, who removed a tiny blip scanner from her trouser pocket.

"This release is on a timer." She ran the scanner along the inside of Jani's arm. As soon as it beeped, she tapped it against the bandaged area, leaving a red dot behind. Then she removed a stylus from her shirt pocket, activated it, and placed the glowing orange tip against the dot.

Jani felt a warm tingle at the site, followed by a painful jolt as feedback from the chip radiated through incised tissue and nerve. Her arm jerked.

Guid struggled to hold the stylus in place. "You must return to Sheridan within four hours, Captain." The stylus emitted a sharp squeak, and she released her grip as though Jani burned.

"I asked for six, Lieutenant." Hals had paled when Jani's arm started twitching. She stood a long pace back and declined to draw closer. "I distinctly remember petitioning Incarceration for six."

"Four hours, ma'am. That's standard."

"This is a decidedly nonstandard situation."

"Then you need to take it up with Incarceration, ma'am." Guid repocketed her devices. "Someone will be available at oh-nine."

"You—" Hals struck her bare thigh with the flat of her hand—the impact sounded like a slap. "Thank you, Lieutenant. That will be all." She grudgingly acknowledged the young woman's salute. "Damn it," she said as the representative of justice disappeared over the rise, "that's cutting it close."

Jani flexed her arm. Liberated felt no different than trapped. *Not yet, anyway.* "If what I felt before was any indication, when it kicks in, it kicks in full-force. It won't increase gradually."

"Should we have a medic standing by?"

"Do you believe we're going to be there more than four hours?"

Hals paced in a tight circle. The casuals accentuated her plump roundness—she looked like she should have been carrying a trowel and a flat of seedlings rather than a scan-pack and the weight of an entire department. "Burkett's been good about making sure our time isn't wasted. According to what I've been told, we're just supposed to validate the prov-enance of some survey grids and maps being used in the talks."

Jani ran the toe of her shoe along a hairline fissure in the walkway. "Hold off for now. If it looks like our visit will run over, we can call. It shouldn't take them long to get there. All they have to do is blow the chip out with a magburst." She peeked around the mover just in time to see the amused sergeant who would serve as their driver amble down the walkway.

Two orderly lines formed in front of the vehicle's fore and aft doors. Hals hung back, gesturing for Jani to remain with her. Ischi bustled past them, recording board tucked under his arm, eyes shining at the prospect of diplomatic derring-do. "We're going to Camp Ido!" he sang as he leapt aboard the mover. "We're going to Camp Ido!"

Vespucci approached them, white knees flashing in the sun. "Everything's airtight, ma'am." He remained with Hals, waiting pointedly until Jani broke away and headed for the mover.

Jerk. Jani took a seat near the rear, one row up from where Hals and Vespucci would sit. As they pulled out of the charge lot, she glanced out her window. Lucien sat alone on a bench beneath a stand of trees, a place hidden from view from the charge lot, but visible now. He looked up just as the mover passed by, a morose expression on his fallen-angel face. He wore summerweights. And a packed holster. Jani watched him track the vehicle until they floated around the corner of an Admin building and out of sight.

Everyone seemed relaxed as the trip began. Ischi even tried to organize a sing-along, but as soon as the mover passed beneath the Shenandoah Gate, the first verse of "All Around the Campfire" dwindled to a few halfhearted warbles. Then one of the civilian techs said, "Shut up," very softly. Ischi shot her a hard look, but kept his protests to himself. Jani looked over her shoulder at Hals, who stared back, face set.

The nervous backward glances started as soon as the mover ramped onto the Boul. Jani felt them like gnat bites, and did her best to ignore them. But the growing tension managed to wend around her calm—she started when Vespucci touched her shoulder.

"I hope you know what you're doing, Kilian." He tugged at the neck of his T-shirt as though it choked him.

"This was *Eiswein's* call, Major." Hals's voice was tight. "Kilian may have suggested, but it was Eiswein's call all the way."

Vespucci's mouth opened, but one glance at Hals and it snapped shut.

Jani turned around to face the front. Everyone else did, too.

The mover traversed the same route as had Burkett's skimmer. Through the Bluffs, then onto the Boul artery that ran within view of the lakeshore. Soon, the Chicago skyline filled the windscreen; some of the older, reflective-glass towers flashed the light of the rising sun.

Temporarily blinded, Jani didn't spot the demiskimmers at first. But as the mover veered toward the lake and her viewing angle changed, she saw them glide over the water toward the city, metal skins gleaming. They banked in groups of three, first rising, then swoop-landing out of sight amid the buildings lining the shore.

"I'll bet my 'pack they're coming from HollandPort," Vespucci said. "That's the shuttleport on the eastern shore that's set aside for idomeni use."

Idomeni, coming to their embassy. Jani counted the demiskimmers, and lost count after thirty. *Lots and lots of idomeni.* Important idomeni, to command demis. Along with the rest of FT, Jani watched the graceful craft bank and glide.

Whatever it was, it looked big, and she hoped like hell that it had nothing to do with her.

* * *

The fingerprinted courtyard felt almost cool, sheltered as it was from the morning sun. Quiet, too, like the vestibule of a church.

"By the way," Hals said to Jani as she stepped down from the mover, "keep your fists to yourself in there."

Jani nodded. "Yes, ma'am."

They fell into their rank-line and walked up the short flight of steps and through the door. Six Vynshàrau diplomatic suborns bookended the entry this time instead of the single female who had stood for them before. Three males on one side, three females on the other.

Oh . . . shit. Jani looked past them down the hall, where even more suborns lined the way. Five on each side, lined up by sex. A total of eight paired escorts, one for each major god. Her mind stumbled over itself as she tried to determine the reason for the formality. So intent was she, she didn't feel Vespucci nudge her until he prodded her aching arm.

"Do you have any idea what's going on?"

Jani nodded, her stomach roiling. "Someone plans to offer challenge."

"*À lérine?*" He surprised her by pronouncing the term properly. Ah lay-reen, with a trilled r.

"Yes, sir."

"Who?"

"I don't know, sir." Someone who had arrived in one of the demis, perhaps. *But whom would they fight?*

They passed through the silent gauntlet to find Burkett waiting for them by the documents-room entry. Even dressed in casuals, no one could mistake him for anything other than highly polished brass. "Morden nìRau Cèel is here."

The Oligarch? A vague image of lanky height and dark hair formed in Jani's mind. She had never seen him in person, even though he had studied at the Academy at the same time she had. He didn't like humanish then. He still didn't.

"Just flew in from the Death Valley Enclave." Burkett's eyes were on Jani. "The PM is here with half the Cabinet. They're playing catch-up because no one can figure out what Cèel's doing here. He and Tsecha holed up in the main altar room as soon as he walked through the lakeside door—no one's heard a word from them since." He turned to her, his dislike swamped out by his need to know. "It's a challenge, isn't it, Kilian? A big one."

"Yes, sir," Jani replied tiredly. It figured that the knives and fighting part of the idomeni philosophy would be the part Burkett would get right.

"Think Cèel challenged Tsecha?"

"I hope not, sir."

"That would explain the number of demis, though—a formal bout between the Vynshàrau's secular and religious dominants would definitely draw a crowd." Burkett stood tall, hands clasped behind his back. "Not to mention precipitate an intrasect rift that would cripple the Vynshàrau's power and influence over their affiliated sects." His nostrils flared, giving his narrow face a snorting-stallion cast. Confusion to the Vynshàrau held definite appeal for him.

"You may think you want that, sir, but you don't." Jani caught a glimpse of Hals, who stood behind Burkett, mouthing an emphatic "shut up." "Nema has fervor on his side, but Cèel has forty years. Their mutual enmity's ground in the bone. À lérine may technically be ritual fighting, but knives have been known to slip. The Vynshàrau are the most pro-humanish born-sect, thanks to Nema's influence. You don't want anything happening to him."

Burkett looked down his nose at her. "Don't presume to know my mind, Kilian."

"I was in Rauta Shèràa the night it fell to the Vynshàrau. I repeat, you do not want anything to happen to Nema!"

"*I hear my name!*"

They turned as one toward the voice.

The overrobe churned less vigorously, befitting the formality of the occasion. "I find my nìa arguing with you again, General." Nema's face split in a ghoulish grin. "Such habitual disputation—you should declare yourselves. We have blades you may borrow for the task."

Burkett's face reddened. "We don't handle disagreements that way in the Service, nìRau."

"Ah." Nema cocked his head to the left as he cupped his right hand and raised it chest-high, his tone and posture indicating question of yet another aspect of humanish behavior. His eyes met Jani's, and he bared his teeth. "Nìa," he said, touching a fingertip to her chin. Then he looked at each of them in turn, examining them from head to toe one after the other. He reached into his overrobe as he did so, and removed a battered black ovaloid that twinned Jani's scanpack. His handheld, however, functioned as a Vynshàrau-humanish dictionary. It held French, English, and Mandarin, formal and foul, idiomatic and slang. The occasional amusing muck-up occurred, but Nema's research and extensive cross-referencing would have impressed any linguist.

He tapped at the worn unit's touchpad. "We have been *cooking you in your skins.*" He shut down the handheld and bared his teeth again. "And you have accepted challenge. A glorious thing. My compliments, General, for finally waking up." He thrust his hand toward Burkett and nodded vigorously as the man gingerly shook it. "Now, let us work, for we have much to do." He swept down the hall, the members of Foreign Transactions playing butter to his Sìah blade. "Come! Come! Much to do!" he cried as he vanished around the corner.

Burkett watched him, mouth agape. "He's a goddamned Pied Piper."

"And he's the only idomeni who can pipe a tune you can dance to," Jani said. "Remember that the next time you wish a knife in his ribs." She waited for Burkett's face to flare anew before she turned her back on him and walked slowly into the documents examiners' meeting room.

Jani braced her hands on the U-shaped table for balance and leaned back in her three-legged easel seat.

So where are Hantìa and company? Foreign Transactions had been validating documents for almost forty minutes, and the Vynshàrau had yet to make an appearance. *Only a couple of hours left.* Jani felt the muscles in her right forearm twitch. They knew what would happen if the princess didn't leave the party on time.

She looked at the others. Vespucci turned away as soon as she glanced uptable at him. She had caught him eyeing her several times, beetle brow knit in consternation. And dripping sweat.

She breathed through her mouth as Ischi leaned close to spread a set of nautical survey maps before her. His deodorant still worked. Barely. *Wish I could remember what we used in Rauta Shèràa.* A colonial brand, formulated for above-average temps. Limited distribution. Odds were it wasn't even manufactured anymore.

Wonder who could find out?

Well, there are my parents.

She imagined the dead comport light, and busied herself scanning the maps.

"How are you holding up, Captain?" Hals, seated next to her, asked for the umpteenth time. "There's ice water and electrolyte replenishers in a supply vehicle just outside the embassy perimeter." The easel seats, like all Vynshàrau daytime furniture, weren't designed for comfort. They also weren't designed for the average human—the one-four Hals was having a hell of a time keeping stable in a seat designed for a one-nine Vynshàrau. "We can break at any time—our mover can get us there in five."

"I'm fine, ma'am." Jani met Hals's examination head-on. "Really."

"You're not even sweating." Hals wiped the tip of her nose with the edge of her T-shirt sleeve just before she dripped on her aerial survey grid. "I don't know if that's good or bad."

"Could be heat stroke," Ischi chimed helpfully.

"I'm not moving around as much as you are," Jani said. "And I picked the seat by the vent."

"Moving hot air is still hot air." Ischi tugged his blotched T-shirt away from his skin. "I think we should invite the Vynshàrau to the base and stick them in the arctic test facility. Crank it *all* the way down."

"Thank you, Lieutenant," Hals said.

"Chip 'em out with chisels."

"That will be all, Lieutenant." Hals waited until Ischi found another ear downtable to complain into. "Was it like this in Rauta Shèràa?"

"Worse." Jani felt her forehead. Slightly damp. A little warmer than normal. "The only air-conditioning was in the human enclave. Once you entered the city, you were at the mercy of nature and idomeni utilities." *I know the symptoms of heat stroke.* She'd seen it enough in Rauta Shèràa. *I'm still lucid.* She felt fine.

The general buzz of conversation died as work claimed everyone's attention. So intent were they, no one looked up when the door opened.

"Ladies and gentlemen."

Heads shot up. Hals had a better view of the door than Jani. Her breath caught. "It's Burkett. He looks sick. Or mad as hell. I can never tell the difference."

Jani twisted in her easel seat too quickly and grabbed the edge of the table to keep from tipping over. "Anyone else?"

"The PM and some Ministers—Ulanova, damn it—Tsecha and all the Vynshàrau dexxies and a whole bunch I don't recognize and—oh damn! Cèel's there, too!"

Jani balanced on the seat rungs to peek over Hals's head, and caught a glimpse of the Oligarch. He was half Nema's age, lighter-skinned and darker-haired. They were arguing— you didn't need to be a trained Vynshà-watcher to interpret the choppy hand movements and twisted facial expressions. Hantìa stood with them. Her hairloops had been gathered and clasped. Instead of the tan-and-grey clothing of a documents suborn, she wore white lightweave trousers and a sleeveless overshirt. "The better to show the blood." Jani pressed a hand to her churning stomach.

"What?" Hals glanced back at her, frowning.

"Remember when I promised not to use my fists, ma'am?"

"Yes?"

"I'm going to have to take it back."

"Kilian, what are you talking about?"

"You know that challenge that's going to be made?"

"The guessing games stop *now*, Captain."

"Yes, ma'am, I believe they will." Jani watched Burkett break away from the group and walk along the table toward her, followed by Nema.

Hals leaned close. "What are you talking about!"

Jani slid off her seat. "Twenty-five years later, it's finally Hantìa's turn."

Before Hals could ask any more questions, Burkett stopped in front of Jani. "Captain."

Jani nodded. "Sir."

"I imagine you don't need to be told what's going on."

"No, sir. Hantìa's requested permission of nìRau Tsecha to make challenge. He gave her leave. Then he made the request to you, as my most high dominant. I'm assuming you're reluctant."

"Yes." With Burkett, uncertainty came clothed as stiffness and an inability to look one in the eye. "I understand refusal is an insult." He stared at a point somewhere over Jani's shoulder.

"Without cause, yes. Simply not wanting to fight isn't enough. Health reasons can serve, but I'm here working, so it's difficult to argue that I'm unfit." Jani flexed her hands. It was safe to say she was already warmed up. "It's ceremonial fighting. Doesn't last long. Injury occurs to the arms, mostly. The shoulders. Superficial wounds. They leave ugly scars, because of the types of knives used, but they're not in themselves dangerous."

"Nonetheless, I've messaged Doctor Colonel Pimentel. Nothing proceeds unless he's standing by. I asked him to bring a trauma surgeon, as well. Something someone said about knives having been known to slip." Burkett lowered his voice. "I am deferring to your judgment, Captain. I've never acted as someone's second before."

"Sir, Captain Kilian has been at Sheridan less than two weeks." Hals's voice was strained. "She's spent more than half that time in hospital, and remains under close medical supervision. She is in no condition to fight anyone. I don't care how ceremonial it is."

Jani looked uproom at the assembled Vynshàrau. She recognized several of them from her Academy days. *Hey, a class reunion.* "It's not a fight to the death. I don't need to be in top form. It's simply a declaration. Hantìa and I are acknowledging to the world that we hate each other's guts." She stared at the female, who turned to look in her direction.

Jani nodded; Hantìa bared her teeth. "That shouldn't take long."

Nema, who had remained uncharacteristically silent to that point, stepped forward. "I have accepted challenge sixty-seven times, and offered challenge twenty-two times." He extended his arms and pushed up the sleeves of his overrobe to his elbows. The silvered remains of old scars, accented by the occasional red slash of a fresher wound, crosshatched the bronze skin of his forearms and wrists. "It is an honor to be challenged by one such as Onì nìaRauta Hantìa. She shares skein with Cèel, through their body mothers." He tilted his arms back and forth. The scars, jagged and raised, seemed to shimmer in the roomlight. "Such an esteemed enemy is greatly to be wished."

Hals and Burkett both stared at the wounds. "Hantìa and Cèel are *cousins*?" Burkett asked. He sounded choked.

Jani looked at Nema, who patted his pockets for his handheld. "In a way. Vynshàrau family organizations are difficult to explain." She shut down her scanpack and stuffed it into its pouch. "Right now, I need to get ready, and since the opening ceremonies can get a little protracted, I can't afford to waste any time."

Burkett glared at Hals. "I thought you took care of that, Colonel."

Hals glowered back. "They gave me *four* hours, sir."

"I specifically asked for six."

"Well, askin' ain't gettin' around here, is it!" Hals closed her eyes. "Sir, I apologize—"

Burkett ignored her. "Captain—"

Jani held up her hands. "I realize you're both upset because you're confused and hot and completely out of your element, but I know what I'm doing, so there's no need to worry." She handed her packpouch to Hals for safekeeping and ducked under the table. "Let's try to maintain a united front, all right, Spacers?" she called out as she emerged on the other side. Nema bared his teeth and beckoned to her, and she followed him out of the room.

CHAPTER 25

"To which god do you pray, nìa?" Nema pointed to the cluster of statues and symbols arranged atop the altar. The beads, medals, and smaller figurines had been obtained from the pockets of members of Diplo and Foreign Transactions, while the larger pieces had been hastily acquired from nearby shops by an Ischi-headed strike force. "You have more than we. Such confusion." He backed away, so that Jani could step up and choose. They were the only two in the embassy's secondary altar room. Normally, both foes would have offered prefight sacrifice in the same place, but since such a profound difference in religion existed, the home team had been granted use of the primary room, a windowed veranda that contained shrines to all the Vynshàrau's eight dominant gods.

I, meanwhile, get the closet. But it was a nice closet, quiet and cooler than the rest of the embassy. Nema had chosen to accompany her, a fact that had visibly irked Hantìa and resulted in even more heated discussion between Nema and Cèel. *He's declared himself my supporter.* In the face of his ruler. In spite of Knevçet Shèràa. *I have to fight well.* Her stomach ached from tension.

She picked up a small stone elephant. "Ganesha, the god of wisdom. I prayed to him when I was little."

"Ah." Nema took the tiny figure from her and examined it thoughtfully. "Why did you stop?"

269

"I don't know." She picked up the teakwood seat on which the elephant had rested and studied its minute carvings. "Maybe I didn't think it helped." She set the seat back down on the altar. "Sometimes, he's called Vinayak, when he's worshipped as the god of knowledge, and other times, he's called Vighneshwer, when he's honored as the remover of obstacles."

"Ah." Nema handed the figurine back to her. "Do you worship any gods that are less complicated?"

Jani smiled. "My mother is Brh Hindi. My father grew up Freehold Catholic, and converted to the Hortensian Presbyter just before I left for the Academy." A memory of the baptism ceremony flashed in her mind's eye, and she almost burst out laughing. *They held it outside. It was cold and the pool leaked and the minister wrenched his back dipping Mrs. Louli.* "I guess the answer is no."

"Then I believe the remover of obstacles would be a good god for now." Nema looked around the room. "What does he demand as sacrifice?"

Jani set the elephant back on its seat. Then she stripped some petals from the blanket of bright orange cymbela that had been draped across the altar, and sprinkled them before it. "Help me, Lord," she said, just as she had when she was eight and asked for the wisdom necessary to pass maths.

She knew her father would be disappointed if he somehow discovered she hadn't given his God a chance, so she picked a plain gold cross from the collection and whispered a quick Act of Contrition. The one formal prayer she remembered. She knew many informal ones, spoken from the heart, usually a variation of "please, God, get me through this." Any God. Whichever one cared enough to listen. And up to now, she'd managed to survive it all and didn't despise herself any more than she ever had, so someone must have thought her worth the bother.

"We must go, nìa," Nema said. He watched Jani as she set the cross back down on the altar. "You feel strong?"

"Yes, nìRau."

"Hantìa will try to draw much blood. That is her way."

"I understand."

"If she fights too vigorously, you must knock her down, as you did before."

Jani stared at Nema. His expression was bland, for him. Grim Death in Repose. "You knew about that?"

"Yes, nìa." He rearranged the draping of his red-rimmed cuffs. "I know all."

"You could have told me."

"No, nìa." He walked ahead of her, which since he was her dominant was a serious breach of protocol. "You prefer your secrets, even if they are secret only to you."

"You've come to know humanish so well?"

"Humanish have no place in this." His auric eyes seemed to glow. "I know Rauta Haárin. I know you."

The room was oval, windowless, with smooth, dun-colored walls and floor. A high ceiling, the light provided by simple sunglobes suspended from helical chains.

The audience had already assembled. Humans filled the banked seating on one side, idomeni, the other, each following the idomeni convention of lower ranks to the rear. That allowed Prime Minister Li Cao a seat of honor on the floor, very close to the action. Closer than she would have liked, judging from the way she jerked back as Jani walked near the edge of the fighting circle.

Anais Ulanova sat at Cao's side, the slight elevation of her seat denoting her lesser status. "An interesting way to start the day, is it not, Captain?" No false bravado was detectable in her voice or manner. In fact, she seemed rather bored. Somewhere in her ancestry lurked women who yawned during executions.

"Yes, ma'am." Jani shot an encouraging look toward the back rows. Hals stared back, grim and tight-lipped. Ischi sat behind her, edgily tapping his feet. Vespucci chewed a thumbnail. Burkett sat arms folded, eyes on the floor.

The Vynshàrau side looked even cheerier. As ranking secular dominant, Cèel sat in a very low seat, mere centimeters from the floor. The best seat in the house, idomenically speaking, belonged to Nema as ranking religious dominant and, as such, Cèel's propitiator. Like Cao he rated the floor itself. Jani watched him lower slowly, his back straight, his face unreadable. *He won't root for me.* Not openly, anyway.

As the challenged, the choice of blades fell to Jani. She considered the assortment laid out before her. Long and short, curved and straight, all bearing the stark elegance and implied efficiency that marked classic Sìah workmanship.

Her earlier self-assurance ebbed as she hefted a couple of the longer blades. The incision in her arm pulled every time she squeezed. *When was the last time I fought with a knife?* Not stabbed someone, but *fought.* Like any other martial art, it required training. It also took skill to fight without seriously hurting your opponent. Hantìa had trained for ceremonial bouts like these since she was old enough to walk— her experience showed in her heavily scarred arms. *I only know how to cut and run.*

Jani settled for a short, straight sword that resembled a really nasty carving knife. Hantìa bared her teeth when she saw her choice of weapon. She picked up the matching blade and made several skillful cuts through the air.

Show-off. Jani tilted her blade back and forth. The anodized wireweave, fine as spider silk, shone beneath the lamps like multicolored threads. The razorlike wires would shred as they cut. The wounds she'd receive would sear as though rubbed with salt, while the edges would heal raised and ragged.

Pain. The prospect worried her. As much as she disliked Hantìa, she didn't want to fight this fight. Not because she didn't know what she was doing, and not because she feared the pain. But the aches and twinges she'd tolerated for years were different from the agony experienced when someone cut you with a knife. And kept coming. And kept coming.

Augie likes that kind of pain. She could sense him in the back of her mind, telling her exactly where she needed to strike. He didn't fight for the beauty of the process. He didn't fight to make declaration, or honor any god. He fought to hurt. He fought to kill.

The status of humanish-idomeni relations again depended on what she feared, and how she felt, and where she aimed.

Please God, don't let me kill her. Any God. Whichever one cared enough to listen.

As if on cue, hushed conversations silenced. All eyes shifted to the two females standing in the middle of the room.

"We will begin now," Hantìa said in informal High Vynshàrau, her voice level and without gesture. She circled Jani, arms opened wide, slightly bent at the waist. *Hain.* The Stance of Welcome. A great position if you wanted to be gutted.

Get it over with. That was augie talking. Jani blocked him out. *"Yes,"* she answered, forcing herself into the same stance as Hantìa. *"We will begin now."* The soles of her trainers squeaked against the bare floor as she maneuvered. That and the pound of the blood in her ears were the only sounds she heard.

She played it safe at first, blocking Hantìa's tentative initial thrusts, restraining the urge to come in behind the blocks and do damage of her own. She knew Hantìa, a skilled fighter, would try to draw her in. *She wants a quick shot.* A chance to cut near an elbow or a wrist, to nick a tendon and impede Jani's ability to wield her weapon.

Hantìa struck repeatedly. Jani parried attack after attack, each more confident than the last. Her incised arm ached. The impacts Hantìa threw behind the blows forced her back, left her off-balance. Open.

I am not weak. Yes, she was. *I'm—not tired.* Yes, she was. Sweat flowed. Her knees trembled.

Her hands dropped.

Hantìa struck. Blade in. Blade out.

The gash tore Jani's left arm from elbow to wrist. The wireweave worked its magic, making vessel-grown nerves sing as though real. One note. High and long. Rose-pink carrier welled and dripped, squelching beneath her shoes as she dodged Hantìa's follow-up.

"Bring your hands up! Cover—!" Ischi's shout, silenced mid-warning.

No coaching allowed. Jani raised her hands just in time to avert another blow. Carrier flowed down her arm and coated her hand. It didn't clot as quickly as blood. It would remain liquid for the balance of the fight. She'd drop her knife if she tried to switch hands.

Her heart pounded. Skipped a beat. A side stitch stabbed like an internal knife. Hantìa's face wavered. The room darkened.

Jani's heart skipped again, then slowed. Like new life, the pain ebbed. She knew why.

Hantìa again closed in, arms spread wide, torso exposed. *You owe me!* augie shouted. *Hit her now!*

Jani ignored the fatal opening. She blocked another thrust with her injured left arm. Found her chance. Slipped her blade through.

Hantìa jumped back, blood streaming from the hack across her right bicep. Her dominant arm. Jani saw her wince as she tried to grip her blade. Heard the mutters from the Vynshàrau side of the room, the muffled "yes" from hers. She could hear the rasp of Hantìa's pained-tinged breathing. See every bead of sweat on her face. Smell the syrup sweetness of the carrier mingled with the metal tang of blood.

Time slowed. Motion. Jani saw Hantìa's answering blow coming as if she'd announced it. She swept aside the blade edge with her right arm, driving the Vynshàrau back toward the wall, taking the cut as she knocked the knife from her hand. *Follow it in.* She did. *Grab her around the neck.* She did, the slickness of her left hand forcing her to grip Hantìa's throat so tightly she could feel the pulse.

Either side of the neck. Just under the jaw. Do it. Do it!

Jani pressed Hantìa against the wall. Pushed tip of blade against hollow of throat. Saw, for one fleeting moment, the alarm in the Vynshàrau's cracked marble eyes.

Then she stepped back. *"Declaration is made."* She switched the blade to her left hand. No matter if it slipped now. Edge to right forearm, taking care to avoid the bandage. Back. Forth.

Somebody screamed. It wasn't her.

"Finished!" Nema bounded to his feet. "A marvelous fight, and truly. Full of hate—a glorious thing!" He swept toward them, eyes alight. "My Eyes and Ears' first declaration.

When she turns my age, her arms will look as mine, I predict!"

"I'd be dead by then." Jani opened her left hand and let the blade fall. Metal clacked softly against coated flooring.

"No, no, no. You will be most gloriously alive." Nema picked up the blade, turned to his side of the room, and lifted it above his head. His eyes focused in Cèel's direction, he lowered it slowly and wiped the edges on his sleeves, leaving behind ragged smears to complement the neat red trim.

Hantìa approached her. "You are cut more than me." She sounded disappointed. "I should demand rematch." She grasped Jani's left wrist and turned it, examining the wounded animandroid flesh. "Does that hurt?"

"Yes."

"Good." Hantìa nodded, her tone as clinical as John's at his most detached. "Mine, also." She studied the cuts on Jani's other arm, touching the self-inflicted one that signaled the end of the bout. "The wound you gave yourself is worse than the one I gave you."

"No surprise there."

Jani turned, catching herself just before it devolved to a wobble. "Good morning, Doctor."

Pimentel scowled. "Good morning, Captain. It's been hours." He wore medwhites instead of summerweights. A woman stood behind him. She wore medwhites, too, and a stunned expression. She also toted a sling bag. Without being asked, she reached into the bag, pulled out a stylus, and handed it to Pimentel.

"Let's see how far gone you are." He frowned as he stepped around the carrier drying on the floor. Then he activated the stylus and flicked the light in Jani's eyes.

Red light. Pulsing. This time, she wobbled.

"We have to get you out of here now." Pimentel pocketed the stylus and gripped Jani by the elbow.

"No!" Nema's hand locked around Pimentel's wrist. "She cannot go. There are ceremonies. There are—"

"NìRau ti nìRau." Jani slipped her fingers around Pimentel's wrist and pried Nema's fingers away. "I'm wearing a security chip on a time release. I have to go back."

"But your first *à lérine!*"

"NìRau." Pimentel massaged his abused wrist. "She should never have left the base in the first place." His voice shook. "She is sick, weak, in the first stages of augie over-drive, and if I don't get her back to Sheridan within thirty minutes, there isn't a pin block in existence that will stop her from going into shock."

"*À lérine* must be properly closed." Cèel swept through the Vynshàrau gathering. On closer examination, his face looked familiar. If Val Parini could be jaundiced and stretched, he could pass for the Oligarch's twin. "You forced this, Tsecha. Now we are to be cheated of what small order we could have salvaged." His English held only the barest born-sect throatiness. His clipped disapproval was more eas-ily detected.

Nema rounded his shoulders. "My nìa won."

"No finesse. No beauty. She beat back nìaRauta Hantìa like Haárin. Like humanish. The fight ended before it began." Cèel's chin jutted. Since he had typical Vynshàrau bones, he had a lot to jut. "I could declare it no fight at all."

In other words, your girl lost, so you're kicking the gameboard over. Jani fingered the bout-ending wound on her right arm. "If that was no fight, why am I bleeding?" She held up her arm in front of Cèel's face. He didn't look at her, of course, but he knew she was there. "*I found opening. I disarmed. I won.*" She slipped easily into the stylized pos-ture of High Vynshàrau, despite the growing agitation caused by augie's dressing up and finding nowhere to go. "*I should challenge you for questioning me.*" She raised her left hand, palm facing down, and turned her head to the right in injured pride. "*I do challenge you for questioning me.*"

Vynshàrau and humanish fell silent.

Cèel looked at her in his periphery. His eyes were unusual for a Vynshàrau, neither brown nor gold but a pale sea green that contrasted sharply with the tarnished gilt of his skin. "You have no right or cause to challenge me," he said in English. "You do not understand hierarchy."

"But lousy sportsmanship, nìRau, I understand perfectly." She turned her back on Cèel's puzzled glower. "Ask my teacher to explain it to you. He has the handheld." She headed for the exit. Pimentel hurried after her, followed by his colleague.

Nema cut past, around, and through to catch Jani up. Desjarlais at his best never moved better. "Your first declaration." He sounded giddy.

"Hantìa had been training as a Temple archivist." Jani touched the wall every so often just to make sure it was there. "Instead, she's here as an examiner. You forced her to change her life's work. Then you brought her here, because you knew she would challenge me. You knew if she did, it would force Cèel to acknowledge me because they share skein. Gotten devious in our old age, haven't we, nìRau?"

"You are angry, nìa?" Nema's voice wavered in disbelief.

"You set me up."

"You must assert yourself as my heir, nìa. You must fight for your acceptance."

"I am not your heir! I will never be your heir!" She darted out the doors and toward the first vehicle she saw, a Service grey triple-length with a caduceus and two silver stars etched on the rear door. She turned to Pimentel. "Carvalla's staff car?"

"It's fast." Pimentel closed in behind her. "Hals told me what happened. Somebody at the JA is going to get their ass handed to them on a plate." He yanked up the door and pushed Jani inside. The other doctor followed close at his heels; Burkett, to her surprise, brought up the rear. He yanked the gullwing closed. The vehicle shuddered.

"Let's go!" Burkett thumped the privacy shield with his fist. The skimmer lumbered out of the courtyard, then picked up speed as it hit the skimway.

CHAPTER 26

"How are you feeling?" Pimentel again flicked the stylus in Jani's eyes. Muttering darkly at whatever he saw, he dug into the sling bag and pulled out a larger scanner with an attached sphygmomanometer cuff.

"Flicking red lights in a challenge room—you're lucky Cèel didn't ask you to choose your weapon." Jani rested her head against the seat back. The smooth leather felt odd. Damp.

"So is he." Pimentel wrapped the cuff around Jani's right arm, but as soon as he hit the contraction pad, the pressure caused blood to well in the gashes. "I need to close those wounds."

Jani sniffed. The upholstery smelled, too, like wet rodents. "You can't close them. They have to heal naturally."

Pimentel punched at the scanner pad. The device squeaked in protest. "It looks like someone went after your arms with a piece of sheet metal." He took the blood pressure reading, then stripped off the cuff. "Even with your augie, they're going to scar."

"They're supposed to." The smell intensified. Her stomach churned. "The uglier the better. It means your hatred has been well and truly declared."

A ripple of dismay crossed Burkett's face as he watched Pimentel scrabble with his equipment. "What did Tsecha mean when he called you his 'heir'?"

Jani found Burkett's queasiness amusing, which told her how badly off she was. "You're aware of my medical history?"

A sharp nod, followed by hesitation. "You're turning into one of them."

"No, not completely. I'm hybridizing. The ambassador thinks after I hybridize completely into a half-human, half-idomeni, I can begin training as his religious replacement."

"Chief propitiator of the Vynshàrau!"

"Yes, sir."

"You won't have to worry about that once Gene Therapeutics gets started on you," Pimentel muttered as he and the trauma surgeon took turns attaching pin blocks leads.

"My God." Burkett rested his head against the seat back. "I hope I did the right thing letting you fight Hantìa."

"You would have insulted the Oligarch if you hadn't." Jani paused. The damp rat smell had ramped to an appalling stench, and she tried to breathe through her mouth and talk at the same time. "Then who knows, he might have challenged you." She smiled. Cruelty could be fun, with the right target. "I'd brush up on my bladework if I were, sir. You may need it."

Burkett looked at her. Outside, the workday was just beginning for most inhabitants of Chicago, but his long face already showed the effects of a head-on collision between a rough morning and an afternoon that promised more of the same. "You held your augie in check during that fight. I could tell."

Jani's smile faded. "Yes, sir."

"That takes . . . an extreme amount of willpower."

"I've learned how to control him. All it takes is practice." A wave of shivering overtook her. She could hear her teeth chatter.

Burkett swallowed hard, then twisted in his seat and thumped his fist once more against the privacy shield. "Damn it, hurry up!"

"Yes, sir!" The young man's voice sounded tight. "We're almost topped out, though." The skimmer's insect hum increased in pitch. They had left the last of the city buildings behind. Forests and parks now whipped past in a series of green blurs.

"The Bluffs." Jani grinned. "I know people who live here, but I don't think they'd admit to the acquaintance." She sniffed. Amid the wet rat, she detected the unforgettable rank of corpse. "Roger?"

Pimentel looked up from the recorder display. "Yes?"

"Does this cabin smell funny to you?"

"Do you recall that smell, Jani?"

Jani nodded carefully. "A cellar. On Guernsey. Spring floods—we found all these dead rats in the cellar. Drowned. And a body—"

The trauma surgeon thrust the recorder at Pimentel and dived into the bag. "She's accessing sense memory. We need to take her down now. If she flies off, we may not be able to control her."

"No!" Pimentel grabbed her wrist. "We only have a few minutes to set up the pin blocks. We take care of the pain first, then we worry about her augie!"

A sharp tingle, like an electric shock, radiated through Jani's right arm. "How much time do we have left?"

Pimentel checked his timepiece. "We're still supposed to have fifteen minutes!" He turned and pounded on the panel. "Speed up!"

"I'm going as fast as I can, sir!" The driver's knuckles showed white as he clamped down on the wheel. "I'm losing her on the curves as it is!"

"You should have called for air transport, Colonel," Burkett snapped.

"I tried, sir." Pimentel's hands flew as he clamped the pin block array around Jani's forearm. "I couldn't get approval for an in-city trip."

"Then you should have lied!"

"I'll file that recommendation away for future use, sir, thank you!"

Jani stiffened as the second wave broke like a studded club across shattered bone. She reached out her carrier-encrusted left hand. Pimentel grabbed it and squeezed. "I didn't think it would give any warning." She winked at him. "Write it up. Maybe you can get a journal communication out of it."

Pimentel thumped the block touchpad with his free hand. "I've just activated the blocks, Jani. Hang on for a few more seconds."

"That's easy for you to s—!" Her back arched as the third wave hit. No mercy this time. No quarter. And, after a split second of white-hot pain that exploded from within like a swallowed shatterbox, no consciousness.

She inhaled.

No rats, this time.

Metal.

Antiseptic.

Hospital.

Jani eased open her eyes just as Morley's familiar face poked into view.

"Don't move too much. Your arm is going to be pretty sore for a couple of days."

Jani looked around as well as she could. It wasn't worth the effort. This room mirrored her last room, which in turn mirrored the one before that. "Are you still on afternoons?"

Morley checked the readouts on the monitors surrounding Jani's bed. "In answer to your unspoken question, you've only been out four hours. It's about what we expected. There are only two sedatives we could risk using on you, and neither is worth much. They pumped you full as soon as they skimmed you into Triage, but your augie fought off most of it."

"Oh." Jani stifled a yawn, then ran a tongue over her dry teeth. Her head throbbed. She swallowed again, and detected the tell-tale odor of berries. "They took me down, didn't they?"

"They had no choice." Morley held a straw to Jani's lips and supported her head as she drew down a wonderful swallow of cold water. "You came to a few minutes after the chip stopped emitting, and you came up swinging. You wouldn't let anybody touch your arm." She pulled the straw away.

Jani gazed longingly after the water. "What else happened?"

Morley grinned. "First Pimentel stormed over to the JA's and went critical all over Incarceration. Turns out their four-hour grace period really equaled three hours and forty-five minutes. The traditional warning shot, they said. Endangering the life of my patient, Pimentel said. I think it was the attempted murder threat that really made their day. Some of them are augmented, but they're going to be reluctant to come here for their precautionaries for quite a while." She dragged a chair between the monitors and sat down.

"Watching what you went through with that chip shook the hell out of Burkett—he was green-faced when he shot out of your skimmer. Tore off to the JA Executive Offices right behind Pimentel, sweaty casuals and all, and threatened everyone within shouting distance with a charge of treason, saying that what happened to you endangered sensitive negotiations, thus imperiling Commonwealth security. *Then*, last but far from least, the idomeni ambassador called the A-G. Something about the Oligarch's extreme displeasure and the disruption of sacred rituals. He also mentioned Lord Ganesha?"

"He's a Hindu god."

Morley chuckled dryly. "Talk about threats to body and soul. Everyone at North Lakeside must be afraid to walk outside for fear of lightning strikes." She thumped the arms of the chair and rose slowly. "Well, I'm going to let you get some rest. Pimentel will be around soon, if he hasn't staged an assault on Base Command." She straightened Jani's sheet. "Hit the rail pad if you need anything."

Jani licked more cotton coating from her teeth. "I'm really thirsty now."

"Thank the sedative for that," Morley said. "We need to hold off. Your fluid levels are satisfactory, but post-takedown vomiting is still a threat, and the usual antinausea meds we give might do you more harm than good."

Jani stuck out her tongue at the closing door. "I have such glamorous illnesses." She stared at the ceiling, hunting for any interesting blemishes that would set it apart from the other hospital ceilings she had known.

"Hello, Kilian."

Jani raised her head too quickly. The room spun.

Neumann sat in Morley's recently vacated chair. He wore desertweights. A rancid smile. "Didn't think you'd see me anymore, did you?"

Jani stared at the years-dead man. "Guess the takedown didn't."

"Yeah. Can't trust technology. Pin blocks. Shooters. Pulse bombs." He straightened so he could look over at Jani's bandaged arm. "So, your marble-eyed buddy set you up. With friends like him, who needs a death sentence?"

"I was never in any danger."

Neumann snorted. "Shows what you know. Hell, you said it yourself. Knives have slipped during those little bouts before, and Cèel's a hard-liner who'd like nothing better than to offer a prayer of thanks over your corpse."

"But instead, Nema forced him to accept me." Jani tried to sit up, and made the mistake of using her right arm for support. Stars exploded. She slumped back against her pillow, breathing in quick gasps to keep those precious sips of water where they belonged. "He's ten steps ahead of all of you. Always was. Always will be."

"You better hope so. Your continued existence depends on it." Neumann stood and walked to the window side of the room. The wash of daylight highlighted odd shadows in his pale tan uniform, darkenings across his torso, his right trouser leg and sleeve. "Yeah, he's got them all running scared."

"Cao can't afford to lose whatever idomeni support she has." Jani sat up, this time more carefully. "Colony-Haárin trade increases every month. Financial stakes are huge. The colonies will vote her out of office the second her policies affect their pocketbooks."

"Since when did you become a political analyst?" Neumann sneered. "Well, you were always good at flummoxing those too ignorant to know better." The taunting expression turned self-satisfied. "But you never fooled Acton van Reuter. And you sure as hell never fooled me."

"I *killed* you."

Neumann shrugged. "My shooter caught in my holster." The front of his shirt had darkened further. Looked shiny.

Wet. Red. "You'd have never outdrawn me in a fair fight." He turned from the window to face her. The blood from the shooter entry wound in his abdomen had soaked from the V of his collar to below his beltline. "But you don't know a goddamned thing about fair fights, do you, Kilian? All you know is fucking your way to the top and interfering with your betters."

Jani watched the bloodstains bloom. The killshot. The exit wound that blew out his right leg. The wound in his right arm, that seeped instead of bled. That was where the shelving had fallen on his corpse during the first round of Laumrau shelling, severing the dead arm. *He's a hallucination.* Yet he seemed more real than any person Jani had seen that day. *Big as life and so damned ugly.* "One of the last times I spoke with Evan, he sounded as though he missed you. Why?"

Neumann leaned against the window. The blood from his damaged arm streamed down the glass. "Evan was a good kid. Normal blowouts growing up. The drinking—that started way too early, but Acton wouldn't listen to me." He smeared a line of blood with his finger. "Evan understands tradition. He respects it."

"What he respects are the privileges of being the V in NUVA-SCAN."

"Ours by right of conquest, Kilian, paid for with those names on the Gate. Top dog gets the best cut of meat—first law of life in the Commonwealth."

Jani watched Neumann draw on the glass in his blood. One line. Another. Then crosshatches, like a small grid. *He's here for a reason.* Her ghosts always appeared for a reason. It was her job to figure out what the reason was. "Speaking of dogs, ever run into Ebben, Unser, or Fitzhugh?"

Neumann drew an *X* in one box. "Once in a while."

"Did they ever tell you who killed them?"

"Oh, now she wants information." He filled another box with an *O*. "Even though she knows I can't tell her anything she doesn't already know or have the ability to figure out." When the blood on the window became too thinly spread to work with, he refilled by dipping a finger in his oozing arm.

"No, Kilian, you have to work for your supper like everyone else. No more easy rides. No more getting by on your Two of Six mystique."

"That mystique was the reason you forced my transfer to the Twelfth Rovers." She watched him puzzle over the half-filled grid. "You need a naught in the upper-right corner."

"Oh, thank you." He drew it in, then cut a diagonal slash through his line of *O*'s. "Being dead plays hell with the ol' cognition." He took a white-linen handkerchief from the pocket of his short-sleeve and wiped the window clean. "You think Pierce had something to do with their deaths." He tucked the bloody cloth away, then crossed his arms and leaned against the pane. His right arm shifted as he applied pressure—the elbow slipped down.

Jani tried to sit forward. Every time she moved, her right arm throbbed. "I know he did. It's just a question of what."

"He already told you. At the soccer match."

"He said we had a lot in common."

"Nah. He did you two better." Before Neumann could explain what he meant, the door swept aside. Lucien stood in the open entry and peered cautiously into the room. "Who are you talking to?"

Jani eased back against her pillow. "Just myself."

"Just myself," Neumann mimicked. "What a choice you have. Keep your mouth shut and piss him off, or tell him the truth and have him think you're crazy." He minced to Lucien's side and blew him a kiss. Then he pulled at his own belt. "Tell you what, Kilian. I bet he shows you his any second now. Then I'll show you mine, and you can tell us which is bigger."

Jani shot back in disgust, "I didn't know you had one, you son of a bitch."

Lucien stiffened. "What did you say?"

"Nothing."

"I'm only here because Nema ordered me to come. If you want me to leave, just say so."

"No." Jani waved toward the bedside chair. "I'm just tired. My arm hurts." She watched Neumann wander to the far corner of the room and turn his back. He stood hunched, right shoulder jerking up and down. Jani shifted so the seated Lucien blocked the view.

"You're not supposed to have visitors, but Nema wants an eyewitness account of your condition." Lucien's heavy-lidded stare moved over her as Neumann's grunting sounded from the corner. "So, how do you feel?"

"I just had my arm yanked out of its socket from the inside. How do you think I feel?"

"Nema said you fought most as idomeni. He crowed to me for over fifteen minutes. If he's doing the same thing at the embassy, Cèel's ready to kill him."

Neumann spun around. "Hey, Kilian, look what I can do!" He tugged at his right arm, gasping in fake surprise as it came away in his hand. "Wave bye-bye to Aunt Jani." He held it by the wrist the way a father would his son's arm, and worked it up and down. The limp hand flopped like a dying fish.

"Are you all right?" Lucien glanced at the monitors. "I don't want to be the one to tell Nema you look really sick."

"I'm fine."

"I heard you're going to a party tomorrow night."

"From whom?"

"Ischi. I stopped by FT to hear what happened. He wouldn't shut up about you, either." Lucien's peeved look altered to angel innocence. "You know, that invitation says you can bring a guest."

"Boy, that's a friend." Neumann had given up waving bye-bye, and now played one-sided patty-cake. "You're lying there half-dead, and all he can think about is trolling for new victims at Mako's shindig."

Jani watched Neumann toy with his limb. "Stop by during morning vis and I'll let you know."

Lucien eyed her sourly. "Is that a hint?" Something banged against the door, and he hunkered down as if to dive under her bed. "I better get going. After what I heard about Pimentel, I don't want him to be the one to find me." After an obvious pause, he leaned down and gave her a brotherly kiss on the cheek before slipping out of the room.

"Isn't that sweet?" Neumann tossed his arm onto the top

of a metal-frame table, and struggled to adjust his leg. Judging from the balletlike turn-out of his foot, it must have slipped from its tenuous mooring. "Well, Kilian, it's been lousy as ever. I'll leave you alone. Let you *digest* it all." He limped to the door, empty right sleeve soaked and dripping. Then he slapped his forehead, returned to the chair, and picked up the limb. "Forget my head next." He waved good-bye with the detached arm. " 'Course, I'd have to give you a chance to blow it off first." He exited through the door, literally, the blood from his blown leg squelching in his shoe.

Pimentel visited toward nightfall. He wore summer-weights. Dress "B" shirt. Creases sharp enough to shave with. Eminently suitable for reaming North Lakeside ass.

We'll see, he said, when Jani asked him about Mako's party. He transferred data from the monitors to the recording board containing Jani's chart and gingerly examined her right arm. He seemed distracted. He asked her questions about Cal Montoya's diagnosis, and about John, and left without saying good night.

Morley brought her a snack. Not fruit sludge, but nutritional broth. Chicken-flavored. Spicy. With crackers, even. Jani savored it like a meal from Gaetan's.

Wonder if Neumann will come back. The prospect angered rather than scared her. *He's part of me.* Like Cray, and Borgie. She'd seen them the last time she visited Chicago. *They helped me solve a murder, too.*

Her door had opened wide before she realized it had opened at all.

"Captain?" Sam Duong slipped in, then skirted to one side so no one in the hall could spot him before the door closed. "Shh. I don't want Pimentel to see me."

Jani looked him over. He wore civvie summerweights. No sign of an outpatient bracelet. "Are you all right?"

"Yes." He eyed her in bafflement. "I'm on dinner break. I just stopped by to visit. See if you needed anything."

"A working brain."

"What?"

"Sit down, Sam." Jani watched him as he walked to Lucien's recently vacated seat. He looked a little wobbly himself—he gripped the chair arms the way she did, as though he'd fall off if he didn't hang on tight. "I've been thinking about Pierce."

Sam shot her the same aggravated look Friesian and Pimentel had been bestowing on her since her arrival. "You shouldn't be thinking about him. You should rest. Get better." He looked at her arms. "You fought. Now you should recover."

"Pierce and I have a lot in common. He told me so himself."

Sam chuffed. "You have nothing in common with him! You're lovely and he's—" His face darkened with embarrassment. "He's not."

"You shepherded the paper, Sam. Do you remember why I'm here?"

"Stupid reasons. No proof."

"I was wanted in connection with the death of my commanding officer." Jani knew Sam admired her, and it pained her to destroy it. But better he should know her for what she was. Better she should tell him things he couldn't remember. "I killed him."

"No—!"

And Pierce—She gasped as Neumann's words hit her like a punch. "And Pierce did me two better." She slumped forward and pounded the mattress with her fists. "Two better. Two better. Two better!"

"Captain?" Sam leaned forward, bracing his hands on the edge of the bed for support. "You look like you did under the awning. I don't think you should look like that now."

Jani thumped the bed, her right arm singing in time. "Pierce killed them, Sam."

"Keep your voice down!"

"For the good that thereof would spring. Then he stole the documents connected with my case because they could lead back to him. And he stole other documents and put them back and set you up to take the blame."

Sam stared. Then he clapped his hand over his mouth to muffle his cry. "I did not put them there!"

"No." Jani massaged her aching arms. "Pierce was sent to

do a very important job. Doing that job would have been the first step in saving the Service, the Service he'd come to love, thanks to Mako. The Service he'd come to see as his life." She held out her hand, as Pierce had. "It was night. The air reeked of panic and the stench of burning bodies. The Haárin had constructed the Ring of Souls around Rauta Shèràa—he was one of the happy few who witnessed the Laum line up to be slaughtered and tossed on the burning piles."

Sam closed his eyes.

"The base was a shambles, I'll bet. Partly from the Haárin bombing, partly from the efforts of Ebben, Unser, Fitzhugh and the rest trying to cover their tracks. But that was all right. Pierce was a weapons runner in the life he's left behind. He was used to thinking on his feet. Improvising." Her voice dropped. "Up to a point. I'll bet he was just supposed to arrest them. But they ran. Toward the city. The shuttleport. He'd never find them then." She looked at the stricken Sam, who still held his hand over his mouth. "What do you do? They're human and you're human and it's all going to hell and they're running. What do you do?"

Sam spoke through his fingers. "I yell for them to stop. The MPs always yell—"

"They *don't* stop, Sam! They keep running. A few more seconds, and they'll be gone. What do you do?"

Sam had raised his hand to object, but the protest caught in his throat. Instead, he raised his arm higher, straightened it, squeezed off. "I . . . shoot them."

"You shoot them." Kilian nodded. "And you know that no one can die by shooter on the Night of the Blade. So you shove the bodies in agers to rot them and hide the cause of death. Call it an awful mistake if anyone complains. Then you spend the next two decades building a career and trying to forget that one night when it all went to hell, when you became the thing you'd been sent to destroy."

"But Caldor—?"

"Not involved. She was only put into one of the agers to make it look like an accident." Jani thought back to Pierce on the day of the match, wound to snapping with anxiety, bursting with all the things he wanted to tell her because they had so much in common. "Could you stop by the hospital library and get me a copy of *Paradise Lost*?"

Sam eyed her strangely. "I suppose so." He took his handheld from his shirt pocket and entered a notation. "I'll go right now."

"Wait. Is there someplace you can spend the night?"

"Well." Sam frowned. "Tory invited me to her eighteenth birthday party. She feels *sorry* for me." He moaned in pain. "The music alone will kill me."

"You should go. You should pretend to get very drunk. Make someone put you up for the night. It should all be over after tomorrow."

"What's tomorrow?"

Jani forced a smile. "You're not the only social butterfly around here. I've been invited to a party, too."

CHAPTER 27

It took Evan several days to work out what must have happened. He ransacked the Family records that he'd been allowed to keep, searching for any references to Rauta Shèràa Base from the early days of the civil war through the evacuation and the long journey home.

Bless you, Mother. Since Carolina van Reuter was an Abascal by birth, she had persuaded her brother—the then–Exterior Minister—to copy her on the Mistys he received from both Rauta Shèràa and Ville Louis-Phillipe, the colonial port nearest Shèrá. The fraternal generosity should have ceased for security reasons as soon as conditions in Rauta Shèràa became dangerous, but owing to the pressure applied by the frantic Carolina, they never had.

Evan had found the messages, encased in parchment slip-cases and bound with dark blue cord, in a set of silver brocade boxes stashed in the closet-sized spare bedroom. Well, that explained why Joaquin hadn't claimed them. He must have taken one look at the containers, assumed Carolina's personal missives, and allowed his sense of gallantry to overwhelm his lawyerly reason.

Good old Quino. Evan arranged the most important messages in a neat row atop his desk and reread them. In a court of law, they'd be considered insufficient evidence. Too many gaps that needed to be filled in by Evan's memory and his gut instinct.

"That's where the court of public opinion comes in." Or rather, the court of public opinion that mattered.

The first marker on the trail was a communication from J-Loop Regional Command to the Consul-General, who had relocated his offices to Rauta Shèràa Base after the Haárin started shelling the city. A timetable, informing him that three cruisers, the CSS *Hilfington*, the CSS *Warburg*, and their flagship, the CSS *Kensington*, were being sent from Station Ville Louis-Phillipe to evacuate the human enclave.

The ships would take on additional supplies in preparation for the evacuees. They would also take on additional weapons. T-40 shooters, both short and long-range. Screech bombs. Smoke screens. No blades of any sort, however. Regional Command didn't want the Haárin to think humans wanted to challenge them with their ritual weapons of choice.

Evan underlined the sentence about the blades, and continued reading.

Since the ships would be fully outfitted prior to their arrival, no stops would be made on the way back to Earth. Most of the evacuees were Family members and affiliates, highly placed officials with heads crammed with sensitive information. They needed to be returned to the mother world as soon as possible for debriefing.

Evan underlined that sentence twice. "So why the detour back to Station Ville Louis-Phillipe, Roshi?" That could be discerned from the next two documents.

The defense Mako assembled to justify the return trip had been carefully assembled, with enough basis in fact to withstand examination. His argument, combined with his proof of Family criminal wrongdoing and his threat to make it all public, had allowed him to keep his career.

Facilities and Environmental were taxed to the limit, Mako had written. *Space was at a premium.* Therefore, there was no room to house "exceptional cases," those who could batter already-tenuous morale and endanger other passengers and crew. One evacuee who suffered from claustrophobia was put ashore at the Station, as was an odd case who had taken to lurking in the women's showers.

It surprised Evan to see that he had been one of the examples cited in Mako's defense of his sidetrip.

> *Mister van Reuter refuses to eat. He sleeps fitfully, and has been found wandering in restricted areas of the ship. If his condition does not improve soon, it's the recommendation of my medical officer that we put him ashore at Station Ville Louis-Phillipe, since it is her belief that he poses a danger both to himself and the other passengers and crew of the Hilfington.*

The name of the *Kensington* medical officer turned out to be Sophia Carvalla. *So she was in on it, too.* Evan didn't meet her during the journey, although he did recall meeting her at a party several years back. Seemed a sound woman. Just the sort her frazzled colleague from the *Hilfington* would consult with concerning his highborn problem patient.

And Mother got to read this fresh from the receiver. No wonder she had fallen apart at the sight of him. "I wasn't that much of a problem." True, he refused to eat. And he had trouble sleeping. But his appetite had never been the sturdiest, he had always suffered from insomnia, and the lack of liquor had made both situations worse.

Yes, I infiltrated a restricted area. Suicide had crossed his mind, and he wanted to see what the weapons lockers had to help him along. But that only happened once. At the start of the trip. When the memories were still fresh.

He opened the bottom drawer of his desk and unearthed a bottle.

"So they put two people offship, and topped off supplies." Took on prepack rations. Medical goods. And two meat-filled objects referred to only as *TD4J1* and *TD4J2*. Evan's intuitive leap with the decomp bags had led him to ask Halvor to make a special trip to question their grocer. Yes, the model numbers were old, but she recognized them. Agers. Meat-curing chambers.

Or meat-rotting chambers, if a person wasn't careful about the settings.

Which led to the fourth document, a handwritten communiqué from the unlucky clerk who had been the first to crack the *Kensington* hold seals at Luna Station.

> *. . . hosed them out. Shoved them into hold, Gleick said. Too many evacuees, not enough room. No time to care for the dead—they had the living to worry about.*

Mako, of course, took full responsibility for the error. "But it was no accident—he rotted those bodies for a reason." This was where the leap in logic came. Gut instinct.

Evan stood, stretched, walked around his tiny office. Adjusted the window controls and let the first light of day into the room. It had been years since he'd pulled an all-nighter. Good to know he still had it in him when he needed it.

"The way Ebben, Unser, and Fitzhugh died points to Pierce. Pierce killed them. Maybe he planned it himself. Maybe his criminal cronies sent him. Whatever happened, he shot them. Then he realized that if it was discovered they died by shooting, he couldn't blame the Haárin. So he ran squealing back to Daddy Mako."

And Daddy Mako fixed. By disobeying orders and detouring to Station Ville Louis-Phillipe to take on the agers, then shoving the incriminating shooter-burnt corpses in the meat boxes and cranking the settings to maximum. "The putting-ashore of the two nutcases was a decoy." As was the addition of the SFC to the mess. "Make it look like an accident by throwing in a nobody."

It must have been a difficult decision for Mako to desecrate an innocent like that. Or was it? Survival instincts had kicked into overdrive by that point. A man could find himself capable of anything when faced with the loss of everything he valued.

"Yes." Evan leaned against the window and took another swallow from the bottle. "I can't have been the only one to figure this out." He knew he possessed a sound native wit, and he could reason in the policy stratosphere when he needed to. *But it's all here.* All someone needed to do was comb and piece, and Families paid people lots of money to do just that. *He wrote a paper on Macbeth, for crying out loud. A story of a murderer driven mad by guilt. Jesus, Roshi, how could you let him walk around loose?*

"So here I have it." His great defense—one-third bluff, one-third bullshit, and one-third hard fact. "Government in a nutshell, part three." He hoisted the bottle in the air and toasted himself for a job well-done.

Before he could seal the self-congratulation with more bourbon, his door buzzer sounded.

"You're up early, sir." Halvor blinked blearily at him, then at the documents covering the desktop. "Is something wrong?"

"No. Not at all." Evan felt so pleased with himself, he even smiled at the young idiot. "What's up?"

Halvor yawned. "It's Mr. Loiaza, sir. He's here. He says he needs to speak with you."

"That was last night. As of this morning, she's still in hospital." Joaquin dabbed at the corner of his mouth with his napkin. "The idomeni are in quite the happy uproar. Tsecha actually told the Exterior Affairs correspondent for the *Tribune-Times* that the embassy had finally been properly blooded. I suppose that means that was the first bout that had been fought there. One doesn't know whether to be relieved or appalled." He wadded the linen square into a ball and tossed it onto his plate. "What utter savagery."

Evan picked at his omelet and snatched glances at Joaquin's face. The lawyer's expression remained placid. He seemed to have enjoyed the hastily assembled fare Markhart had prepared. They had elected to eat outside, and the man had joked amiably about the fact that the two-seat table filled the miniscule patio.

Evan took a sip of coffee. Too damned bland—he hadn't thought to lace it until they'd sat down to eat. He set down his cup. Tapped the rim of his plate with his fork. Waited. "What does it mean, Quino?" As if he didn't know.

"It means Kilian had been officially acknowledged by the Oligarch. It means she's proven her usefulness to the Commonwealth in a way we wouldn't have thought possible months ago." Joaquin stared out toward the cramped rear yard, the truncated banks of roses. "It means we need to talk, Evan."

"Yes, I—" Evan looked into Joaquin's turtle-eye stare, and his tale died in his throat. Better to hold his fire until he could see down the enemy's gullet. "You first."

"Thank you." Joaquin shot the cuffs of his charcoal day-suit. Even in the morning heat, he kept his neckpiece snug and his collar fastened. "You were never a man for weasel words. Well, outside my chosen profession, neither am I. I've been forced to admit a couple of things to myself these past few days. One is that taking you on as a client was the greatest miscalculation of my career."

Evan tried to probe Joaquin's expression. No use looking for signs of joking—at their level, one didn't kid a fellow about tossing him over the side. He forced a laugh through clenched teeth. "If you cut me loose now, I'll have a hell of a time bringing a new attorney up to speed for my trial."

Joaquin smiled coolly. "There will be no trial, Evan. Anyone as politically shrewd as you must have figured that out by now. The Service's refusal to charge Kilian with Neumann's murder negated your usefulness to them. It also gutted her usefulness to you. You needed her, Evan. You needed a foe with as many strikes against her as you could uncover in order to draw attention away from your own missteps."

He's saying you *now. Not* us. *Not* we. "The charges against me are independent of the ones against Jani. There's no reason for them not to proceed."

"If they did, you'd have a greater problem." Joaquin *tsked* in disgust. "I should have seen it coming. Mako had his own agenda all along. He stuck Kilian in the Psychotherapeutics ward as soon as she arrived at Sheridan—she's been in and out like a fiddler's elbow ever since. It's on paper that she's not entirely well between the ears. Attacking a sane alleged murderer is one thing. Engaging in the character assassination of a woman diagnosed as mentally incapable of defending herself would not have been the way to rebuild a political career. Thus does the Service guard its own." He took a linen square from his jacket pocket, dipped a corner in his glass of ice water, and patted it over his forehead. "Let's walk. It's stifling to sit in this heat."

"It's stifling to sit, period." Evan rose shakily, leaning on the table for support. "They can't just shunt me aside."

Joaquin locked his hands behind his back. He walked easily. No shakes. No nerves. Just another morning spent setting someone adrift on the stormy Family seas. "The evidence against you seems to have disappeared. No surprise there—Lady Commonwealth has a long reach. It doesn't do to reopen old wounds with the idomeni, who in their distinctly odd way have accepted the fact that Kilian is alive and in the public eye. It doesn't do to appear fragmented before the colonies."

Evan shook his head. He still found it hard to comprehend. His screwed-up Jani, the fulcrum on which two civilizations balanced. "She means that much to them?"

"On the day she's discharged from the Service, Felix has pledged to withdraw its lien against Fort Constanza. In addition, the Channel Worlds will sign a pact promising full cooperation with Exterior's efforts to rein in the runaway smuggling operations based in their sector." Joaquin leaned over to sniff a fully opened Nathan Red. "And let us not forget nìRau Tsecha, who just last night put forth an offer of GateWay rights to the Samvasta Outlet, the granting of which will shave one week off Outer Circle long-hauls." He plucked a partially opened bud and inserted it in his collar notch. "I don't relish telling you this, but we're both realists. It's moved beyond you, Evan. You're yesterday's news."

Evan kicked at a clot of soil. It exploded into powder against a stand of rocks. "What do you get out of this? A Cabinet Court retainer fee? NUVA-SCAN contracts?"

"I had those before. When I took you on, I lost them, one by one. Now, I'm getting them back."

"So you're working for them now. You didn't come here as my attorney. The Families sent you here to make me an offer."

"Offer? No. They sent me here to tell you the way it's going to be." Joaquin kept his turtle gaze fixed on the roses. "Arrest will be rescinded. Gradually. You'll have this house, and a stipend with which to run it. Your personal assets will be held in trust for a period of five years, during which time your conduct will be monitored. Behave, and when the term ends, you get the money. Step out of line even once, every bit reverts to the Treasury."

"The personal assets are nothing compared to the NUVA holdings!"

"Which reverted to the company on the day of your arrest." Joaquin shot a quick look at Evan's shoes, as if assuring himself of the distance between them. "After a year or so, a board meeting or two is a possibility, but only as a courtesy. You will have no voting rights."

"You can't confiscate my family's property!"

"Consider it reparations." Joaquin hesitated. "Some of us were very fond of Lyssa."

That was easy when you didn't have to live with her. "You said no proof existed."

"There's trial-quality proof, and there's the opinion of people who watched you grow up." Joaquin plucked a dead leaf from the stem of a Tsing Tao Pink. "If several members of the Cabinet had their way, you'd spend the balance of your life on a Lunar construction site welding transport frames. As it is, you'll have your native sky above your head and native soil beneath your feet. And you'll be cared for." His mouth twisted. "All the *medical* treatment your heart desires."

Evan followed Joaquin's gaze, still fixed on the flowers. Why did people love roses? All he saw were twists and thorns; their pungent perfumes, released by the first wash of sun, sickened him. "I'm too young to be shut away like this—I'll go mad."

"You don't have a choice."

"I'll demand a trial. I'll name names." Evan nodded firmly. "The van Reuters weren't the only ones who made money off Knevçet Shèràa technology, and they weren't the only ones with something to hide. I could tell you—"

"Who will listen to the ravings of a mentally impaired maintenance alcoholic? I received a copy of John Shroud's medical findings last night. Suffice it to say that if a person asked you if it were night or day, they'd be well advised to look outside first." Joaquin turned to him, stiff and formal, thirty years' acquaintance gone by the boards. "The sad end to a promising career, perhaps, but you did it to yourself. I'm only glad your parents aren't alive to witness the fall." He nodded. "If it's any consolation, you went farther than most of us thought possible. Good-bye, Evan."

Evan watched Joaquin walk up the shallow incline, the leather soles of his shoes sliding on the grass. He grappled with the urge to grab a spade from the shed, to run the man down and split his skull.

He slipped and hit his head. Honest, Officer. It was Chicago, after all. The Bluffs. The ComPol dealt with accidents like that all the time.

Instead, he shoved his hands in his pockets. When Joaquin disappeared through the doors, he made his own slow way up the slope. His feet dragged. His perception played tricks. The house seemed to draw farther away the closer he came—he knew if he turned around, he'd see himself standing at the bottom of the yard, staring back.

He closed his eyes. When he opened them, he saw Elba in all its poky homeliness sitting where it always had. He reentered the cool quiet of his tomb, closed himself in his office, and entered a code into his comport. It wasn't a personal code—he had to threaten several peons before he was sent through.

The pasty face formed on the display. "Evan." Shroud scowled. "What do you want?"

"Your head on a plate, you son of a bitch!" Evan sank into his chair. "You gutted me."

"Well, in the end, it did seem the best way to ensure Jani's safety." Shroud's voice rose and fell, a singsong of mock condolence. "What are you upset about? You won't face trial. You won't die."

"I'll go public—"

The voice flattened. "The comlog ensures that you will do no such thing." Shroud sat back. He wore medwhites. Greyed circles beneath his blue-filmed eyes combined with his chalky aspect to make him look like a nervous patient's worst nightmare. "Don't contact me again, or I may recommend hospitalization. Trust me, that's the last thing you want."

Evan opened a drawer, drew out a bottle, then put it back. "Tellinn was here."

"That doesn't surprise me."

"He says Jani's dying."

Shroud gave the smallest start. For an instant, he looked ready to crumble. But just for an instant. "Good-bye."

Evan stared at the blank display. He didn't move until a shadow cut across his view. He glanced up to find Markhart standing deskside, regarding him thoughtfully.

"Mr. Loiaza seemed confident this morning, sir. I hope that means things are going well?"

"Things are great."

"How many for lunch?"

"One." He tasted the sound of the way it was. "Markhart, you said your sister worked at Fort Sheridan, didn't you?"

Markhart nodded. "Half shift in one of the snack bars. But only two days a week."

"Is today one of those days?"

"No, sir. Tomorrow is, though."

Tomorrow. Evan swallowed down a growl of frustration. *Take advantage of it.* That would give him plenty of time. To word things properly. To decorate the few facts he had with just enough bluff and bullshit. "Ask her if she'd do me a favor."

Markhart stared at him. "Sir—"

"Nothing illegal." Evan grinned reassuringly. "I'd just like her to deliver a note. To a friend."

CHAPTER 28

Pimentel balked when Jani mentioned attending the A-G's garden party. She wore him down over breakfast and had him convinced by lunch. But late that afternoon, when Lucien arrived with her gear, he wavered once more.

"I don't like this one bit." He watched Lucien lay out Jani's dress blue-greys on her bed. "You're in no condition to be discharged, much less attend a party."

"It's not like I'm going to dance the night away." Jani nestled in her visitor's chair and tucked her bare feet beneath her. "It's just a sedate little gathering. I'll make small talk, avoid the buffet, drink water, and lean on the lieutenant for support when necessary."

The supportive lieutenant continued his silent organizing, setting out her mirror-polished black tietops and running a cloth over her dress lid's black brim. Then he reached into his duffel and pulled out hairwash, makeup, and underwear.

When he removed the bouquet of miniature roses, however, Pimentel's eyes goggled. "What the hell?"

Lucien turned to him and smiled. It was an odd expression, one Jani hadn't seen before. It wasn't a broad smile, or a boyish grin, but a half-mast bend of lip accompanied by hard-eyed evaluation. It said that he liked doing things like this, and would do them for the colonel if the colonel wished. It added that he would do a lot of other things for the colonel, too, if the colonel were at all interested.

Pimentel shifted uneasily. "I have to go." He nodded brusquely to Jani and darted out the door.

Lucien looked at Jani, shrugged, and arranged the flowers in a handy water glass. He had already donned his blue-greys; his glossy hair had the look of a fresh trimming.

Jani watched him bend and turn—it was a pleasure, as always. "He's a happily married man."

"Most of them are." He glanced at her slyly. "Jealous?"

"Only if I thought you gave a damn."

"You mean there's hope?" He dawdled over the bottles, rearranging them according to size. "Guess I'm going to have to learn to give a damn."

"You'd need a different implant in your head."

"Oh well, so much for that." He rummaged through the bag, then turned it upside down and shook it. "That's it. I don't believe I forgot anything."

Jani counted the containers vying for space atop the small dresser. "No, I don't think you did, either." She untangled her legs and stretched her stiff muscles. She still couldn't support any significant weight with her right arm; getting up meant sliding to the edge of the chair and boosting upright with only her left arm for stability. Since the animandroid flesh was still sore, her legs felt rubbery, and her back ached, it resulted in a significant portside lean.

Lucien took a step toward her. "Do you need help?"

"I'm fine."

"You're bent into a letter C."

"I'm fine."

"Let me be supportive."

"Maybe later." She straightened, flexed her right arm, mouthed an "ouch," and walked to the bathroom.

Lucien drew alongside and paced her, step for shaky step. "I can wash your back."

"Go harass a nurse." Jani leaned against the bathroom entry. "Track down Morley—she's ripe for conquest."

"No, she's not." Lucien kicked at the floor. "I know her."

"Is that a fact?"

"She's a lot like you."

"I knew there was something about her I liked."

*   *   *

"You're up to something." Lucien helped Jani ease into the passenger side of a wheeled scoot. "You are being too damned . . . *military*."

Jani unbuttoned her jacket and flared the bottom outward to avoid rumpling it. "I thought that's what you wanted."

"If it crossed my mind for one second that you were doing it for me, I'd check myself in for a takedown." He squeezed behind the steerbar. "You saluted Pimentel, fer chrissakes."

"He's a superior officer."

"He almost readmitted you on the spot." He pressed the vehicle charge-through. The motor hummed to life, and they trundled up the track designated for wheelworks. Progress proved slow; brisk walkers on the adjacent path passed them easily, and one wag shouted that the playground was in the other direction. "You aren't going to tell me a thing, are you?"

The landscaping kicked up a few grades as they crossed the Memorial Quad that separated South Base from North. Colonial shrubs outnumbered native; the flowers possessed the glassine petals and jewel colors that were the current fads among plant designers. "What do you want to know?"

"I want to know if I'm going to be court-martialed!" Lucien tapped an agitated song on the steerbar. "I know it's a minor consideration for you, but we don't all have your complete disregard for the things normal people care about!"

"You're normal compared to me, huh?"

"What the hell is that supposed to mean?"

"Nothing." She waited until his fidgeting eased. "I know why they're discharging me."

"Nema and the colonies will raise holy hell if they don't, that's why." Lucien glanced at her. "You don't think so?" He looked away, his hands tightening on the bar. "Anybody ever tell you that you think too much?"

"Only anybodys trying to hide things from me." As if to illustrate her point, the Base Command complex came into view. "It's bigger than I thought," she said, as they passed building after building. "How many people work there?"

"At any given time, about half." Lucien didn't even bother to grace his own joke with a smile. "*Well?*"

She told him. When she mentioned Sam Duong's framing, he threatened to toss her out of the scoot. By the time she explained about the agers, Pierce's ghosting, and the timing of Mako's invitation, his protests dwindled to the occasional sharp question.

The working portion of Sheridan gave way to the leisure regions. After passing the Officers' Marina, they puttered through a sprawling park. Another turn of corner and the A-G's whitestone residence loomed into view, a boxy, four-story edifice that resembled a well-landscaped office building more than a home. Uniforms and dressy civvies streamed in from all directions, guided by the faint glow of half-lit patio lights.

"The tent's on the north side," Lucien said halfheartedly, as he wheeled the scoot into a remote charge lot. Then he muttered something dark and Gallic, and smacked the steer-bar with his open palm. "What do you need me to do?"

"Just stay within shouting distance." Jani patted her trouser pocket, checking for the slip of paper she'd tucked there. Sam had made good on his errand—she had spent most of the previous night reading snatches of *Paradise Lost* beneath the covers. Memorizing. Making notes.

She slumped into her hard seat, tried to figure a way she could get through this without depending on Lucien for help, and realized she couldn't. She still didn't know where he and duty parted company, didn't know the point at which his fear of Nema outweighed his loyalty to the Service or whoever else had laid claim to his attentions.

Lucien sighed loudly. "Shall we go?"

"I guess." Jani tried to slide out of the scoot by herself, but her right knee gave out, forcing her to wait for assistance. She leaned against Lucien so heavily he murmured in pleased surprise, and they joined the rest of the crowds streaming toward the Residence like ants toward the world's largest honey trap.

*   *   *

The years spent as Anais Ulanova's protégé had trained Lucien to deal with situations most people found daunting. He negotiated the social reefs and shoals of the tent like the seasoned sailor he was, dropping bon mots and names, eliciting greetings, laughter, and the occasional lustful stare.

Jani just nodded, mumbled "good evening," and watched the master. "You're good," she said, when they finally took a break and laid claim to a table near one of the numerous buffets.

"Ani gave a lot of parties." Lucien had collected ice water for her and a piled plate of hors d'oeuvres for himself. "It was either learn to play the room or check coats and work in the kitchen."

"She made you work?"

"One less temporary staffer she had to hire. One way or the other, she always got her money's worth."

Jani surveyed the scene around her. The tent was immense, and already filled from end to end. The buffet tables and bars that lined the walls were crowded, and the soundshielding fought a losing battle with the noise level. "Didn't you care for her at all?" She knew as soon as she'd asked that it was a stupid question. Partly inborn and partly inserted, Lucien's ability to care stopped at the end of his nose.

He shook his head, dark eyes blank. "She gave me what I wanted. Nice room. Nice skimmer. Clothes. Money." He had chosen the most select offerings from the buffet, exotic seafood, cheeses, mushrooms, and breads. "When I graduated prep school, she wangled me an appointment to East Point. I ranked fourth in a class of fifteen hundred and seven. That qualifies as good return on investment, by any measure."

"Why the Service?"

"I . . . like rules." He had the sense to smile. "Most times. I like knowing what I'll be doing the next day."

"Then why me?"

"You're for the rest of the time." The smile turned saucy. "When I'm in the mood to be totally confused." He glanced out at the milling crowd. "Speaking of which, do you expect something to happen, or are we supposed to force their hand?"

"I think it's happening now," Jani said, as an unfortunately familiar face came into view.

The dress blue-greys looked hand-tailored rather than line-cut, and the number of ribbons and badges arraying his chest was formidable. Despite that, Niall Pierce should have given up long ago. His damaged face and sinister air would forever mar any attempt at North Lakeside polish. Jani took a swallow of water and held it in her suddenly dry mouth. *Wonder why he never got his face fixed?* Maybe the ragged scar served as his equivalent of the healing gashes on her arms. *Wonder if whoever gave it to him is still alive?*

"Good evening, Captain Kilian." He waved for her to remain seated, his quick smile appearing snarl-like in the tent's subdued lighting. "Heard about your match. Congratulations are in order, I understand."

Jani swallowed the water with an audible gulp. "Thank you, sir."

Pierce looked at Lucien, who had stood up like a good looie, and his manner frosted. "Lieutenant. Tough loss the other day."

"Yes, sir."

"Your sweeper stinks."

Despite his social training, Lucien's grin visibly tightened. "We're working on replacing him, sir."

"The sooner, the better." Pierce then caught Jani by surprise by offering her his arm. "I wondered if you'd accompany me on a tour of the house, Captain."

"Sir." As Jani rose, she shot a sharp look at Lucien, whose return glare could only be interpreted to read "he outranks me." She held Pierce's arm as lightly as she could, and allowed him to lead her from the tent.

"You should watch him." Pierce's 'across the Yard' voice lifted easily above the party din. "I've been asking a few questions of my own. He meets with Justice Ministry officials every day."

"I know." Jani brushed off his look of surprise. "If he's

so dangerous, why do you go out of your way to twist his tail?"

Pierce shrugged. "I've no use for his sort. Self-serving. No loyalty to anyone or anything save themselves."

"When did you acquire your experience with his sort—during your weapons-running days?"

"My crimes are no secret."

Aren't they? Jani tried to pull away from him, but he tightened his hold on her arm. Not hard enough to hurt her, but hard enough.

"I waited to hear from you concerning the reading list," Pierce said. "I've prepared one especially."

"I've been very busy."

"You're never too busy to learn."

"I'm sure you're right." Jani glanced back over her shoulder and down the fabric tunnel that connected the tent to the house. *So much for shouting distance,* she thought as she watched Lucien's silvery thatch disappear amid the crowd.

The tour began and ended in the same place, a sitting room on the second floor. It no doubt resembled every other sitting room where such discussions had ever occurred. The chairs were large and well padded, the windows darkened against any threat of accidental observation. A sideboard held a narrow selection of hard liquor. The basics—whiskey, gin, vodka. A bucket of ice.

She recognized Admiral-General Mako. General Carvalla. The three-star had to be Gleick, the base commander. There was also a two-star she didn't recognize, but no one seemed inclined to make introductions.

"So." She stepped inside. "Let's get the story straight now, in case it ever comes up. Where were we during the time this meeting never took place?"

Carvalla fidgeted. Gleick scowled. The two-star swirled his whiskey.

Mako smiled. "You were touring the house with Colonel Pierce. You stuck your heads in this room, and spoke with General Carvalla, who had a yen to sample my excellent vodka in private. A display of Channel World curios in my library held your interest for quite some time. Then you and the colonel returned to the party."

"Shouldn't I be able to describe these fascinating curios?"

"Colonel Pierce will take you to see them after our meeting."

"And what about you and General Gleick and General . . . ?" She thought her prompting obvious, but no introduction to the silent stranger followed.

"We will see to ourselves, Captain." Mako's smile dimmed. "Thank you for your concern." He gestured toward a vacant chair near the center of their grouping. "How are you feeling?"

As Jani sat, she sensed Pierce move behind her chair. "I'm fine, sir."

Mako turned to Carvalla. "Is that true, Sophia?"

"Her test results are as screwy as ever." Carvalla sipped from a small, frosty cylinder with a silver handle. "Roger's worried that the readings we're getting aren't telling us what we need to know. He's desperate enough to contact Shroud."

Jani recalled Pimentel's edginess. "He's changed my diet. He's manufacturing a new liver for me. Is there something else going on I should know about?"

"Not one for the military courtesies, are you, *Captain*?" That was Gleick. Grey-haired. Bullet-headed. Face like a fist.

"No, I'm not." She withheld the "sir" deliberately, and watched him squirm. "But I didn't think you'd mind, seeing as we all have so much in common." She did a slow three-count. "Officer-killers, all."

CHAPTER 29

Everyone stared at her. Jani sensed Pierce, still behind her, like you'd sense eyes in the forest.

Finally, Mako broke the tension with a small snort of humorless laughter. "Not much for preliminaries either, are you, Jani?" He wiped a hand over his face, regarded his empty tumbler. "That's fine. Neither am I." The angle of his chairside lamp highlighted his fatigue-grooved jowls. "I gather you arrived at this conclusion during your explorations with the odd Mr. Duong?"

"He's not odd—you just made sure everyone thought so!" Jani sat back as tiny flecks of darkness bloomed and faded before her eyes. "My attorney had difficulty locating Rauta Shèràa Base documents I told him should have existed. Documents I'm charged with having neglected."

"Indeed," Gleick growled.

Jani looked at the man. He sat rigidly straight—she would have bet her 'pack the clear liquid in his glass was water. Physically, he looked nothing like Durian Ridgeway, but she could see the similarities just the same. The cutting voice. The air of judgmental superiority. *Behind every great man stands a creep with a shovel.* "You know, General, I bet you made one hell of a poop boy."

"*How dare you, you*—" Gleick had half risen out of his chair, but settled back in shocked surprise when Mako held out his hand.

"Sit down, Gunter." The look he gave Jani was stern, but not unkind. "I've known Spacers like you before. When their expertise is needed, none are better. As you proved yesterday, at the idomeni embassy." He nodded slowly. "But your times are few and far between, and those betweens are the career-killers, aren't they, Jani?"

Throwing a fistful of stars at me didn't work, so now you're trying understanding. "I had the sort of career that killed itself. I conducted audits on Rauta Shèràa Base—that was no way to win friends." *Stay on course—don't let him distract you.* "One thing I learned is that the reason documents disappear is because they lead to bigger and better things."

"Paper disappears because nobody cares about it," Gleick grumbled. "It disappears because it doesn't matter."

Jani ignored him. "The *Kensington* shipping records, for example, that described the loading of two agers."

Mako waved a dismissive hand. "I admitted in closed-door sessions long ago that in our haste to free up space for evacuees and supplies, we accidentally packed bodies in unsuitable containers."

Jani nodded. "Yes, and it's a shame that that story doesn't hold up, because it's nice and simple. Short of space, let's get these bodies out of the way—whoops, we loaded them in the wrong sort of box, but we were in a hurry, you see. SFC Caldor was a sound move. Good randomization. If a little nothing colonial got stuck in an ager, well, it couldn't have been planned. Had to be an accident."

A cloud passed over Mako's face. "I did not consider Caldor a 'little nothing colonial,' Jani."

"Then I stand corrected." Jani touched her face—the skin felt hot and dry. Her heart pounded.

"Are you all right?" Carvalla set her drink on her chairside table, and sat forward. "Get her some water, please, Niall."

Mako looked at Jani, then at Carvalla. "Sophia?"

"I don't like how she looks at all."

"*I'm all right.*" Jani sat back, inhaled deeply, tried to relax. But when she attempted to cross her legs, the right one wouldn't work. She couldn't even lift it off the ground. "The question is, why go through the trouble to rot the bodies? What was it about them that you couldn't afford to let others see?"

She looked up just as Pierce leaned over to place the water glass on her table. His eyes proved his only handsome feature, rich gold-brown, like honey.

"They deserved it." His voice held an eager rasp, as though he felt he had to convince her.

Jani nodded encouragement. "They ran, and you had to stop them because they were headed into Rauta Shèràa, and once they disappeared into the city, you'd have lost them for good."

"They deserved it. Do you know some of the things they did?"

"I lived some of the things they did." Her dull tone made Pierce cringe. "You were just supposed to arrest them, weren't you? Those were your orders. But they ran. And you're another of Mako's Spacers—it was between-time for you. He gave you your big chance, and you let him down." They'd begun to breathe as one. Short. Sharp. Inhale. Exhale. " 'Which way I fly is Hell; myself am Hell.' "

"Book Four, Satan's entry into Paradise. Out of context. You need to study before you can toss lines at me. I lived it!"

"What did you do, Niall, blow them apart with a long-range?"

"*They deserved it!*" His beautiful eyes described the ugly details. He held out the glass to Jani with a tentative hand. As if whether or not she took it from him would forever define something between them.

Jani took it. "I can't argue with that." She sipped the metallic-tasting water and set it down. "I can't argue with that at all. But the problem isn't whether I agree or disagree, the problem is that I *know*." She looked at Mako, Carvalla, and Gleick in turn. "So, that's my side. I'm assuming you asked me here to give me yours."

Gleick's lip curled. "We don't owe *you* any explanations."

Mako closed his eyes. "*Gunter.*"

"Damn it, Roshi, stop coddling her! She didn't do it for the good of the Service, like—"

"Like we did?" The eyes that opened held the dimming light of a suddenly older man. "No, Spacer Kilian didn't kill for the good of the Service. She killed because people were dying horribly, and she wanted to make it stop." Mako tipped his glass back and forth. It had been empty since Jani entered the room. Looked, in fact, as though it had never been filled. "Isn't that true?"

Jani listened to the sound of ragged breathing behind her. Pierce, reliving Hell. "Does it matter?"

Mako held out a hand, palm facing up. "Perhaps not." But something in the way he looked at her indicated that it did. When he donned his uniform and appraised himself in his mirror, he no longer felt the way he wanted to. And he blamed her for it.

Jani read his single thought easily, followed its flarelike track. "You'd have me executed, if you could. But I've become a symbol. The Channel Worlds would make trouble, and that could increase the dissension between the colonials and Earthbounders in the ranks. And you know a fragmented Service would lose against the idomeni. Nema's hinted at that, hasn't he? War. I think you blinked where that was concerned. He couldn't have convinced Cèel to go to war over me. But you had seen the Haárin fight in Rauta Shèràa. You didn't want to chance battling them with divided troops."

"You credit yourself with formidable influence, Kilian." Gleick still couldn't let go the old standard. "You're nothing."

Jani breathed, but couldn't sense her chest rise or fall. Her legs felt numb. She wondered if Pierce had poisoned the water. "If I'm nothing, then have Pierce escort me to the brig. Process me. Treat me the way I should have been since you nailed me on Felix. Prosecute me—for Neumann's death." She stopped to catch her breath. "Stop throwing roadblocks in the way of Colonel Veda's investigation. Then watch her reach the same conclusion I did, because any investigation of Knevçet Shèràa will lead her right back to

Rauta Shèràa Base on the Night of the Blade."

Gleick's mouth moved, but no sound emerged. Carvalla tossed back the balance of her vodka. The silent two-star, whom Jani had forgotten about, watched her unmoving, like a snake on a rock.

Mako finally spoke. "What do you want?"

"What do I *want*?" Jani tried to shrug. "Nothing." Her limbs felt leaded. "To be left alone."

"A job befitting your training?"

"Anyone with a scanpack can earn a living."

"But people will still think you a killer. They'll think you got away with it."

"I don't care what people think of me."

"Don't you?" Mako cocked an eyebrow. "This isn't some Outer Circle backwater, Jani, this is Chicago. The Commonwealth capital. Home base for all us Earthbounders of whom you think so little. You're the Eyes and Ears, a famous woman. Nema has formally declared you. Your days of hiding are over. What some people in this city think of you will shape your life." He touched fingers to forehead in a mock salute. "The Prime Minister and the Exterior Minister, for example. Let me commend you. You've managed to acquire some very powerful enemies in a very short time."

"I'll leave Earth."

"Your medical condition prevents that. The only facilities that can treat you properly are located here. From what Sophia tells me, if you left Earth now, you could be dead in a month."

"That's ridiculous." Jani paused to breathe. "I feel fine."

"Why are you so determined to make it hard for yourself?" Mako gestured to the silent two-star, who set down his glass and reached into his inner tunic pocket. "Li Cao is agreeable to releasing you, but to appease some of her more vocal critics, she needs a victim. It's a matter of record that the late Sergeant Emil Burgoyne threatened the late Colonel Rikart Neumann on several occasions. The Judge Advocate is prepared to make a ruling that all evidence points to him as Neumann's killer."

Jani looked at the eerily silent man, who had taken a piece

of paper from his pocket and now noiselessly unfolded it. "You're the Judge Advocate General?" He nodded. "You want me to hand my sergeant over to save myself?"

"*Your* sergeant?" Mako smiled coolly. "He's dead, Jani. I hardly think he'll mind."

"He didn't do it!"

The JA held up his piece of paper. "Even the most cursory glance at the late Sergeant Burgoyne's record would give one pause, Captain." He again reached inside his tunic and removed a stylus. "All we need to close the case is a signed statement from you that you witnessed such threats, but failed to report for fear Sergeant Burgoyne would turn on you as well."

Jani looked from Mako to the JA. "Are you familiar with the concept of untoward influence?"

The snake didn't blink. "We have a Service to protect."

"I trusted Borgie at my back."

Gleick snorted. "You consider that a recommendation?"

"I wouldn't trust *you* out of my sight!" She felt her eyes grow heavy. "He was worth twelve of any one of you." Her shoulders slumped. "He was worth twelve of every one of you."

Pierce touched her shoulder. "Kilian, take the deal."

Jani shook him off. " 'Ease would recant vows made in pain,' Niall. Book Four, again. That's another way of saying I don't want to wind up like you." She sat forward. The room darkened. "I stood here. Neumann stood"—she stretched her aching arm, and sighted down—"four paces in front of me."

"Five." Neumann sat on the arm of Carvalla's chair, detached leg swinging sideways from his hip, back and forth like a pendulum. "And I was a little off to the right, but keep going, keep going. I'll dance at your execution yet."

"Not with one leg, you won't."

"Captain?" Carvalla glanced at the chair arm in alarm. "Are you all right?"

"*Five* paces." Jani pointed her finger at Neumann. "He told me about the patients." She squeezed the imaginary charge-through. "He made me an offer, too." Neumann blew her a kiss.

Mako and Carvalla looked at one another. Mako's eyes widened, and Carvalla sat back.

"I understand guilt," Mako said.

"No, if you did, you'd have locked down Niall long ago. He kept turning up, and I had to ask myself why?" Jani kept her finger pointed at Neumann—it felt as weighty as a long-range. "I shot Neumann. I didn't know whether he had drawn his weapon, and I didn't care. I'd have killed him if he'd been unarmed. If he'd been sitting at his desk. If he'd been asleep."

"Brava." Neumann stood, bowed to her and clapped his hands. "Do you want me to kick my leg across the room for emphasis?"

"I killed him. Then Yolan died. Then the patients. Because of me. Then I killed the Laum. Then Borgie and the rest of the Twelfth died. Because of me." She stopped to breathe. "I almost died, but John stuck his nose in. I wish he hadn't."

Pierce whispered, "Jani—"

"I admit to murder, yet you'll hand me the lie to save myself. Why?"

Mako had the gall to look humble. "Because you are a good Spacer who deserves a second chance."

"And you're the honorable man who'll give it to me." She watched him watch her. "I'm not honorable. I've known that for years. It's difficult, at first, admitting that you're no better than what you are, that you'll do whatever it takes to survive. Deal with whatever devil rears his head. But it gets easier as time goes on. Doesn't it, Roshi?"

"I'm offering you a new life."

"And all I have to do is abet the libel of a dead man." Jani held up her left hand so she could shake her finger. Since the arm felt numb to the shoulder, she had to watch to make sure she did it. "No, I'm wrong. You can't libel the dead. Supposedly." She let the arm drop. "I killed Neumann."

"The evidence doesn't exist."

"I admit it freely."

"The court will not accept your word as anything but the guilt-ridden ramblings of a traumatized woman," Mako said. "The world outside court is, of course, a different story."

"You have paper proof concerning Borgie?"

"Of sufficient scope that guilt can be assumed, yes."

"Where is it?"

The snake glanced up from his paper. "Hidden, Captain."

Jani nodded. Across the room, Neumann clucked his tongue, then stuck it out at her. She stood up slowly. "Good evening."

Carvalla tried to rise as well, but Mako held up his hand, and she sat back. "Good evening, Jani. You know where we are if you should change your mind."

Pierce caught up to her just outside the door. "They're giving you a chance." He grabbed her sore arm and spun her around. "Take it and run!" Jani stifled a scream, and he released her like hot metal and backed away.

She waited for the haze in front of her eyes to clear. "I said I couldn't argue with you about killing them. I meant that. But there are limits—you know that better than I do." She pulled the slip of paper from her pocket. "I had to write this down. No time to memorize everything. We're still in Book Four. It seemed to describe you so well." She blinked at the paper until the words came into focus.

" 'Horror and doubt distract his troubled thoughts, and from the bottom stir the Hell within him.' " She heard Pierce speak the words as she read them, and slowed her voice to pace his. He knew it better than she did, after all. " 'For within him Hell he brings, and round about him, nor from Hell one step, no more than from himself, can fly by change of place.' " She paused to breathe, and heard Pierce pause beside her. " 'Now conscience wakes despair that slumbered; wakes the bitter memory of what he was, what is, and what must be worse; of worse deeds worse suffering must ensue.' " She folded the paper and slipped it back into her pocket. "I think that means it's only going to get worse from here. I think it means Sam Duong and Borgie are only the beginning." She looked past Pierce's sliced face, and spoke to the unscarred man. "Smearing Borgie bothers you the most, doesn't it? It should. Shame on you, Sergeant. He was one of yours." She turned her back on him and walked slowly down the hallway.

"So, what do we do now?" Neumann crab-walked beside her, cartwheeling his arms, pushing the right one back up his sleeve every time it slipped.

"SIB."

"Oh, Christ, I hate that place." As they walked through the foyer, he looked toward the door leading to the party tent. "Where'd your rent boy run off to?"

"I don't know."

"Guess it's just you and me, Kilian. At each other's throats, just like old times."

"Just like old times."

CHAPTER 30

The other techs had gone on break. Sam sat at his desk and picked through his perfunctory task. *Alphabetize these lists, Sam,* Odergaard had told him, while strangers guarded his dead.

"Mr. Duong?"

Sam looked up. Kilian leaned against the wall of one of the other cubicles. Hanford's, the gum-chewer. He wanted to warn her that if she wasn't careful, she would stick to the partition, but something about the expression on her face told him she wouldn't appreciate the joke.

"Captain." He stood slowly, one eye on the entry, on the lookout for breaktime returnees. "How was your party?"

"Can you get into secured records?" Kilian's light brown face was purpled, as though she'd been running. Yet she didn't sweat—her skin looked papery, as though it would tear if Sam touched it. She stepped forward, dragging her right leg. She had undone the collar of her dress tunic—a crescent of white shirt showed in the V. "I need—Sergeant Burgoyne's record." She stopped to breathe. Her eyes glimmered with fever. "Can you get it?"

"I—don't have the codes."

"Can you find them?"

"I need to break into Odergaard's desk."

"What kind of lock is it?"

"A single-finger."

318

"Those are easy."

They both smiled, in spite of the odd tension, and her strange behavior.

"They're going to smear him." Kilian's smile faded. "Borgie. They're going to say"—again, she stopped to take a breath—"he killed Neumann. But he didn't—I did."

"Because of us?"

"Yes." Kilian stared at him, her eyes filling. It was a terrifying sight, that abject vulnerability in one so contained, like watching the ground fissure at your feet. "You're Simyam Baru, aren't you?"

"Yes." Sam sagged against the desk. He felt so weak, but just on one side. He touched the right side of his face, tracing the jagged outline where the skin had peeled. Up to his temple, then alongside his ear, the line of his jaw, to his chin. "I wondered when you'd recognize me."

"You don't look the same."

"Neither do you, Captain." He felt a rush of compassion for her, this woman who lived only to dash herself against rocks. "But people are more than their faces, are they not?"

Kilian slumped against the partition, then edged along it and around the corner, finally scrabbling for purchase on the brink of a vacant desk. "How did you get away?" She squinted at him and blinked repeatedly, as though she had trouble focusing.

Her vision is going. He felt for his comport pad. "I should call the hospital—"

"Answer the question."

He pulled his hand back. "Orton had been our driver during our previous expeditions. She had never handled a people-mover of that size before, but—"

"Orton couldn't see. They'd severed her optic nerves so they could input directly into her visual cortex."

"The best pilots handle a craft by feel."

"Not to that extent."

"I was her eyes. I told her where to steer."

"Right over a blind jump and into the path of a Laumrau scout." Service disgust for all reasoning civilians dulled

Kilian's overbright eyes. "I saw the flash from the roof of the hospital."

"I was never a soldier, Captain." Civilian disgust for all things Service darkened Sam's voice. "I did not understand the concept of ambush until too late." He touched his face again. "Orton died. Fessig. I was the only one to survive the crash."

"Any injuries?"

"My left arm." He flexed it. "Broken."

"How did you get—to Rauta Shèràa?"

"I walked for hours. The sun at my back. Toward the city. Just when I thought I could walk no farther, I was rescued by a group of xenoanthropologists. They had been conducting research in the central plains, and had received the evac order from their inpost in the city." Sam watched as Kilian's shoulders rounded, slumped. *She's too weak to sit up.* "How did you get here from the party?"

"I swiped a scoot and don't change the subject!" Again the pause to breathe. "Who were the xenos affiliated with? A university? A collective?"

"I was in no condition to inquire."

"Can you recall any of their names?"

"No." He had tried to remember. He recalled snatches of faces—dark eyes, kind smiles—but he could never remember more. "They bandaged my face and arm as best they could and took me to the shuttleport in Rauta Shèràa. From there, I begged passage from a merchant transport bound for Phillipa."

"How did you pay? Did your rescuers pass the hat?"

"No." Details had always been fuzzy there, too, but considering the circumstances . . . "I begged. They let me on."

"No one would have given a billet to a broke and injured incoherent."

"Compassionate people exist, Captain, even in shuttleports."

"Name one." Kilian squinched her eyes shut. Opened them. Shook her head. Then she paused, tensed, as though she heard a far-off sound and was trying to place it.

"Do you hear something?" Sam watched the doorway, on the lookout for returnees.

"No one important." She muttered under her breath, as though she argued with someone close by. When she finally looked at him, rage glittered in her fevered eyes.

"Everyone says—you're sick." Her voice shook. "You have a tumor in your thalamic region that induces—a type of amnesia. You can't recall your own past, so you substitute other people's. For some reason, you've fixated on Knevçet Shèràa—and Simyam Baru. It makes sense. You're both Bandan. Similar, physically. But he's dead, and you are, and have always been, Sam Duong." She wiped her hand across her cheek, and looked down at the floor. "Too much coincidence, otherwise. Why, after all these years—would you wind up here?"

Why, indeed? That area of Sam's life had always been fuzziest of all. *Why am I here?* "So I could thank you." Yes, the relief that flooded him as he spoke told him those were the right words. "For trying . . . for trying to save us. I knew, if I waited here along enough"—his voice quickened as his assurance grew—"if I waited here long enough, you'd show up. Eventually."

Kilian stared. "Thank me—?" Her voice cracked, and she pressed a hand over her eyes.

Sam fixed his attention on the door to allow her some privacy. And to watch for his officemates, who would be filing in any moment now.

Kilian wiped her eyes with her tunic sleeve, and looked across the gulf of years at him. "Could we try to get hold of Borgie's—"

The alarm klaxon blatted. It pounded eardrums with physical force, pressing around them with walls of sound.

"It's a fire drill." Sam swept the work orders into a drawer, and locked it. "Only a fire drill, Captain." He looked over at her. "Follow me—"

Kilian sat rigid on the edge of the desk. Her eyes had gone black glass, her skin, dun clay.

"Captain." He stepped up to her, nudged her arm, then grabbed her shoulder and shook. "It's just a drill!"

"You have to get out." Her breath smelled like sweet vinegar. "They're coming—"

"*Duong!* Move your ass!" Odergaard stuck his ever-red face in the door. "It took us three minutes to clear the floor last time. You know we need to break two!" His voice rang down the hallway. "*Move! Move! Move!*"

Kilian had hidden behind the partition during Odergaard's short tirade. Now, she jerked. Gasped. "*Run.*"

"Captain—"

"*Run.*" She looked him in the face, but whatever her eyes saw, he knew it had nothing to do with him, or anything else in the here and now. "Get out while you still have a chance. Neumann's made a deal with the Laumrau. They're going to perform tests on you. You'll die. You have to go *now!*"

"But they check for stragglers after everyone is outside—"

"Let them." She grabbed him by the elbow, dragged him out of the office, and pushed him down the hall toward the exit. Then she took off in the opposite direction and disappeared around the corner, her stride an odd skip-walk because of her stiff right leg.

He stood in one spot, the siren blare squeezing him until he thought he'd scream. *Run! Neumann's coming!* He pelted down the halls, his weak leg causing him to stumble, up the stairs, through the building entry, out the door, and collided with—

He looked up into the face that stared down at him, saw white and death and eyes like ice. This time, he did scream.

"Oh bravo, John." Another man slipped an arm between Sam and certain doom and pushed them apart. His hair was light brown, his skin pale, but he looked like night next to the grey-suited thing beside him. "My name is Val Parini. This is John Shroud." His voice held that clipped, professional calm that reminded Sam of flavored ice—sweet, cold, nothing. "We're looking for Jani Kilian—do you know who she is?"

"That lieutenant said she fled here from the party." Shroud stalked to the SIB entry, his white skin glowing beneath the chemical discharge of the security lighting. "We need to get her out now. If what Pimentel says is true—"

"What do you mean, *if!*" Pimentel of the surgery threats broke away from a nearby huddle and strode toward Shroud, his finger raised like a shooter, medwhites fluttering in the night breeze. "Are you doubting my veracity *again*, Doctor?"

Parini stepped between Shroud and Pimentel. "If you two don't shut the fuck up—!"

A Spacer in black night fatigues ran past them. "The doors are all locked," she said to a similarly garbed figure who'd been talking to Pimentel. Behind her came outlines. Many outlines.

As Pimentel's black garb drew closer, shadows resolved into a pushed-up hoodmask. Hair like corn-silk. "Did you try the emergency exits?" the young man asked as he pocketed a handcom.

"They're locked from the inside."

"Shit." The handcom beeped, and he slapped it silent. "Is anyone left in there with her?"

"Not according to the Fire Drill Teams. Everyone present and accounted for." The young woman hesitated. "Sir, I think she's gotten into central systems. That means she's controlling all access and environmental."

"Override from South Central Facilities."

"I tried them. They can't. She's blocked them."

"How!"

"She said one-finger locks were easy." Sam floundered when he realized everyone had stilled to listen to him. "That—that's what she said."

"Does she know that much about structures?" one of the fatigues piped.

"She was a registrar and a smuggler," another said. "She knows where to look and where to hide."

Glum silence fell. They turned as one to look at the building, as if to assure themselves it was still there.

"Her ID chip's rigged with a security lock," someone mumbled. "Just blast her one and get it over with."

"*Who said that!*" Shroud's voice boomed over their heads. "Captain Kilian is gravely ill. She requires immediate hospitalization. She is unarmed and a danger to no one but herself. If you spot her, mark her position and notify a med immediately." He turned to the corn-silk blond, and his voice dropped. "She is unarmed, isn't she?"

"Yes," Cornsilk said. Both men sagged in relief.

Shroud's ice stare sought out Sam. "Is she hallucinating?" Sam nodded.

"Do you know who she sees?"

"I think that's rather obvious, John," Parini said. "Considering the circumstances."

"You need to get in there." A thin, dark-haired man broke away from another huddle that had gathered by an ambulance. "Carvalla said she was showing signs of respiratory distress."

"Her breathing isn't right," Sam said. Again, he hesitated as everyone quieted to listen to him. "She's dragging her right leg."

"Did she seek you out?" Shroud asked, broad brow furrowing.

"That's Mr. Sam Duong," Pimentel said. "I told you about him."

"Oh." Shroud's gimlet eyes narrowed.

"Can we get back to the matter at hand?" Parini snapped. "We know her neuropathy's progressing. Is paralysis ever complete?"

"Rarely," the dark-haired man said. "It's not unheard of, however—"

"Answer the goddamn question, Hugh!"

"Could she stop breathing! Yes!"

Shroud paced the sidewalk. "We need to get in there."

"We're rousting someone from the JA with a spotter so we can pinpoint her location using her chip." Cornsilk's handcom squealed once more. This time he answered. Barked one-word questions. Signed off. "The cracker team is on their way with ramming equipment. They'll be here in two minutes."

"We may not have two minutes," dark-haired Hugh muttered. A ragged look passed between him and Parini.

"What the hell?" A single voice lilted in wonder. "What is she doing?"

Everyone turned, and watched as section by section, floor by floor, the lights went out all over the SIB.

CHAPTER 31

Jani flashed the stylus, flicking closed the last UV switch, shutting down the hospital's interior lights as she had the entrance-exit controls and the ventilation. It would be difficult to see her way out of the central-utilities chase with only the sulfur glow of emergency illumins to light the narrow walkway, but it was safer that way. The Laumrau monitored the building systems using remotescan, and aimed shatterboxes at any area that showed signs of electrical life.

"I should have thought of this before the first wave." The barrage that followed her killing of Neumann and the subsequent fleeing of the Laumrau staff to the safety of the hill camps. The barrage in which Yolan died.

"If fucking were thinking, you'd be a genius, Kilian." Neumann's voice sounded from a pitch-dark corner of the chase. "Otherwise, you're boxed rocks." He had followed her into the guts of the building as he had through the halls and offices, offering sarcasm and useless advice as she broke into desks and cabinets in her hunt for weapons and handy objects like the stylus.

"You only started calling me stupid after I turned you down." Jani closed the switch box and turned to walk to the door. Tried to walk to the door. Her right leg hung her up again. "I think your bias is showing." She leaned against the wall and tried to shake the feeling back into the numb limb.

"Still time to make up for any regrettable lapses in judgment." Neumann stepped between her and the door and waggled his bushy eyebrows. She would have maneuvered out of his reach if she could have seen him approach, but he seemed to follow quantum rules when it came to movement. First he'd be one place, then another, with no transition she could see.

"I'd rather be found dead in this basement," she said as she brushed past him, close enough to smell his cinnamon breath. His thick, grasping fingers closed around her arm, and she struck out. His cry of pain and rage as her fist connected with the point of his chin was worth the agonizing shock that rang from her knuckles to her shoulder.

"You're gonna get your wish, Kilian!" he called after her as she exited the chase. His voice sounded muffled, as though his mouth bled.

The thought made her smile.

"*Borgie!*" She sagged against a wall and struggled for breath, then grabbed for a door handle for support as her legs crumpled beneath her.

"He ran." Neumann leaned against the wall opposite and folded his arms. "Left you high and dry." The right arm slipped, and he shoved it back into place with a muttered curse.

"He'd never do that."

"Could, would, and did, Kilian." Neumann fussed with his bloody sleeve. "You always put your faith in the wrong people."

In the distance, a dull thud echoed. Jani pushed away from the wall, and looked down the hall in the direction of the sound. "What was that?"

"How the hell should I know?" Neumann ratcheted his leg, which had twisted out of position. "Maybe it's company."

"Second wave?" Jani limped down the hall. The thud sounded again, this time with a higher pitch.

"Shatterboxes don't thump, you dumb bitch, they sing." Neumann shambled toward her. "Sounds like a door ram to me."

"I set all the main doors to close before I deactivated the access controller."

"So whoever's out there is going to have to ram through a whole lot of doors before they get to us. Great. That should make them good and pissed by the time they get down here." He squinted. "What's that stuff yorking out from the stairwell?"

Jani looked to the end of the hall, where a thick stream of gaseous muck billowed under the sealed door. Gaseous, fuchsia-colored muck. "They're lobbing pink." Jani's throat closed at the memory of the thick, cotton-candy smell. "Pink's *heavy*—it drifts down."

"And we're in the basement." Neumann laughed. "Good job, Kilian. You've set yourself up to suffocate to death."

"Pink's *heavy*—the cloud will settle around my knees."

"And what knees those are." Neumann's leer stripped her trousers away like paper. "Well, the real one, anyway. The fake one, however, could be in for a bit of malfunction. In fact, those animandroid limbs of yours might be just what those little beasties need to whet their appetites for the comports and workstations."

Jani tapped the fire-alarm touchbox inset in the wall by her head. "It washes out if you catch it fast. You can hose bright red air clean in seconds." She removed the purloined UV stylus from her pocket, activated it, and pressed it to each corner of the alarm pad in turn. As she touched the last corner, the plastic shield disconnected and fell to the floor, revealing a host of fire safety contacts, all clearly marked. Elevators. Alarms. Extinguishers.

Jani touched the stylus to the Extinguishers slot. With a series of hisses, reservoirs in the walls and ceiling opened. Liter after liter of fire-retardant foam spewed from inset sprayers, coating all surfaces in heavy white cream.

"*You idiot!*" Neumann covered his face with his hands and dashed into the nearest clear space.

Jani followed. Stopped in the entry. Looked around. *What's a vending alcove doing in an idomeni hospital?* That disquiet made way for greater concerns when she saw that no foam streamed from any orifices in the alcove walls or ceiling. Any pink that wended down the hall would find refuge here, seeping into the air-handling system through the floor-level vents.

"I don't believe you did that!" Neumann spat foam, coughed foam, blew it from his nose and scooped it from his eyes and ears.

"Anything that can push the pink out of the air and down will work long enough for me to think of what to do next." Jani slapped foam from her arms and face as she opened the coolers, the cabinets, and dispensers, looking for anything she could use as a hammer. As Neumann muttered and sputtered, she yanked opened the last door.

What the—! She reached out, picked up what her eyes saw and what her mind called impossible. The long handle, that seemed molded to fit her hands. The sensuous curve of blade. What a Sìah fighting ax was doing in a vending alcove janitor's closet, she had no idea, but she wasn't going to argue with providence. She swung it at the plastic cooler and dispenser connections—water geysered to the ceiling and rained to floor.

"They're coming, Kilian." Neumann sloshed to the door and stuck his head as far as he dared into the jetting whiteness beyond. "Those bashes are sounding closer and closer."

Jani swung the ax through the private rainstorm, and heard another sound, a sound she knew Neumann couldn't hear. A sound of her very own.

Do that again, augie whispered as metal cut the air. *I like it.*

"Hey, Kilian, stop making like the Ride of the Valkyries. We need to find the way to the subbasements. I thing they're in the stairwell."

"I'm not going anywhere." Jani stilled the blade, held it up to her face, and caught sight of her bright eyes in the mirror metal.

You owe me, you know. Augie whispered sternly in her ear.

Jani nodded in agreement. She was never meant to escape. Never meant to be free. She was meant for steel and rainbow edges glistening in the light. "Didn't you say something recently, sir, about me waiting for the chance to blow your head off?"

"What?" Neumann turned to her, his eyes widening in gratifying horror as he watched her cut patterns in the air. "That was a joke, Kilian."

"Strange. I didn't think it funny."

"We have to get out of here!"

"Why do you care?" Jani contemplated the blade's wispy Sìah tracework. "You're dead."

"I'm not armed, Kilian." Neumann pulled his right arm out of its sleeve and waved it at her. "I mean, I'm really not."

"Haven't you figured out that among all my other sterling qualities, I'm also a dirty fighter when need be?" Jani slashed the ax through the rain—the very molecules screamed in agony.

"Kilian!" Neumann backed too quickly, and slipped on the carpet of water. "We can work this out!" He fell backward with a loud splash, then scuttled cripple-crablike behind the shelter of a table.

"No. No." Jani's voice reverbed inside her head. "I've had just about all I'm going to take from you."

Neumann shot upright from behind the table like a pop-up toy. "I'm ordering you to desist!" He tried to skirt to one side as Jani closed in from the other. His detached leg shot out from beneath, sending him sprawling across the tabletop. For a perfect moment, he lay on his stomach, arm spread out to the side, neck exposed.

Jani sidestepped into position. Swung the ax up. "*Declaration is made*," she said as she brought it down.

Neumann's head bounced off the table and across the alcove floor like a deflated soccer ball across a soggy field, leaving a red stream in its wake, finally rolling to rest against the bottom hatch of the beverage cooler. Jani limped over to it, nudging it with her foot until she could look into the staring eyes.

"You're gone. You're dead. You lose. I got them all out." She hesitated. "Except for Yolan." But then, she hadn't seen Yolan's body, so maybe she got out, too. She grinned in long-delayed satisfaction. "They're out of your reach forever. Yours and Acton's and Evan's." She let the ax slip from her grasp and fall to the floor. From down the hall, voices, confused and angered, deadened by foam, resonated flatly. They didn't sound like Laumrau, from what she could discern amid the slosh and shower of falling water. *Sounds like English.* How silly. She turned slowly and walked to a chair to sit, and wait.

"The patients are gone. Borgie and crew are gone. You stay behind. Think that's an even trade, Kilian?"

Jani wheeled. Her tietops shot out from beneath her, sending her careening into the wall. She cracked the back of her head against uncoated brick. Lights spangled before her eyes as she sagged to the floor.

Neumann's head rolled away from the wall. It spun to a stop in the middle of the floor and righted itself with a couple of wobbly loops.

He blinked the water out of his eyes. "You can't murder the already-murdered, Kilian." A gurgle bubbled up from the throat he no longer had. "I'm going to stay with you forever and ever and ever. Till the day you die. Which from the looks of you just might be today."

Jani slumped farther down the wall as augie leached away. Her legs had numbed. The room had greyed. Breathing seemed too much trouble.

"See you in hell, Kilian." Neumann winked at her, and smiled.

She fell to one side. Gradually became aware. Of the water. Soaking her hair. Running down the walls. Like tears. Puddling around her. Immersing her. Drowning her. Like in her dream. Drowning.

Sinking. Deeper.

Deeper.

Deep—

CHAPTER 32

Sam huddled in the passenger seat of an abandoned scoot and watched the turmoil unfold around him.

The fireskims arrived first, great scarlet brutes that spat out HazMat teams and equipment with startling efficiency. The teams entered the SIB through the ram-blown doors, fighting against the relentless stream of bodies in foam-covered night fatigues who struggled to get *out* through the same narrow openings. Startling descriptives in several languages cut through the still night, following the inevitable soggy collisions.

Sam hid in his seat as the members of a spent HazMat team clustered beneath a nearby tree.

"Foam." An older woman's voice, exhausted and disbelieving. "All four fuckin' upper floors. And the basement. And the subs."

"First floor's the worst," said a younger man. "Those jassacks with the ram punched through a support wall into the relay station behind and ruptured an air-filter array. Microbial sieve everywhere!" He cracked the tip of a nicstick and passed it to the woman. "The conference-center auditorium looks like the world's largest strawberry sundae."

"There were no fires," another team member said with a yawn. "Who the hell set off the foam?"

"Some nutty captain. Her augie went south—guy from Security said she broke into desks and cabinets, found a UV stylus someone had rigged to building frequency."

"No one outside Facilities is allowed to have a stylus!" The older woman groaned. "You can reset a whole building with one of those things."

"Apparently, some people keep them around as personal environmental adjusters." The younger man activated a nic-stick for himself and turned to look at the SIB, now ablaze with lights and teeming with activity. "When was the last execution we had around here?"

"Thirty, thirty-five years ago."

"Well, there's going to be one toot sweet when they find whoever the hell that stylus belonged to." He pulled off his hood and pushed a hand through his matted hair. "Never saw a mess like this in all my life."

Sam watched the group smoke in tired silence, then turned his attention back to the still figure standing alone atop a low rise. John Shroud hadn't moved from his station since the ambulance arrived, a heartbeat behind the fireskims. He'd made no attempt to approach the lone skimgurney that had been pulled from the building, its burden obscured by attached monitors and emergency techs. The sole movement he made had been a clenching of one fist when a monitor alarm blared, causing the level of commotion around the ambulance to escalate accordingly.

Val Parini, his shirt pulled from his trousers and his jacket long since discarded, broke away from the anthill activity and trudged up the small elevation.

"How can you just stand up here like a goddamned tree?" He planted himself in Shroud's path and folded his arms.

"Because I can't do any good down there." Shroud's voice was level, matter-of-fact. "My years as a trauma man are long behind me. All I'd do is get in their way."

Parini hung his head, then dropped his arms and plodded a circle around the other man, finally coming to rest at his side. "A foam-encased mound by the name of Pascal informed me that if Jani dies, Nema is going to pick us off one by one like free range targets."

"Let me worry about Nema," Shroud replied quietly.

Parini shrugged. Coughed. Sniffed. "John, what the hell did we do?"

"The best we could at the time."

"Did we?" His breathing grew more and more shaky. Then he leaned against Shroud and pressed his face against his chest.

Shroud placed an arm around his shoulders. He remained quiet, his face like carved stone, and let Parini cry. Then he jostled him gently, the way a father would his son. "Val? Val, pull yourself together."

"Yes, John." Parini pushed back. Ran a hand over his face. Coughed again.

"Val?"

"Yes, John."

"I've spoken with Pimentel. If it looks as though—" Shroud stopped. Closed his eyes. Exhaled with a loud huff. "We stay with her until the end, and *we* pronounce her. We owe her that much."

"Yes, John." Parini's eyes squinched like a squawling babe's. Then he lifted his chin and swallowed hard, his face as masklike as his friend's.

All during that time, dark-haired Hugh stood at the base of the rise, watching. Parini beckoned to him as soon as he realized he was there, and the younger man strode briskly up to them.

"She's seizing. Your specialist thinks they should perform a DeVries shunt. Her Hybrid Indicator Indices are skied— he's worried about excitotoxic brain damage." He tugged at his sweat-soaked shirt. "They need to get her to Cryo."

"Those shunts have an astoundingly low success rate—he is aware of that?" Shroud's voice sounded dull, as if he knew the answer. "Is that the only problem?"

Hugh hesitated, then shook his head. "Hepatic failure's imminent. I'm worried whether the adjunct has the capacity to clean her up. Pimentel says they haven't been able to harvest a viable transplant. Cal Montoya's searching all Earth facility banks for possibilities, but—" He had already backed halfway down the hill. "I think we better go."

"Hugh!" Parini trotted after the man, who didn't slow or even give any sign that he heard him.

Shroud remained in place. He watched the crowd disperse and distribute themselves amongst other vehicles as the crew loaded Kilian's stretcher and closed up the ambulance. His eyes followed it as it fast-floated away, sirens blaring, lights flashing.

Sam struggled out of the tiny scoot and ran to his side. "What does that mean! What you said?"

Shroud glanced down at him, a cocked eyebrow the only sign of surprise on his long, monkish face. "Mr. Duong, isn't it?"

"What's the matter with Captain Kilian!"

"It's difficult to explain to a layman."

Sam dug deep, and came up with his "oral defense committee" voice. "Do. Your. Best."

Shroud stared. "My specialist wants to insert devices into Jani's neck and brain that will bypass her circulatory system and perfuse the brain with a solution that can both nourish it and prevent and repair damage from the seizures she's having." He broke eye contact, and focused on the grass at his feet. "But that's not her only problem. Some foods she's eaten and drugs she's taken in the past few weeks have poisoned her, and her liver is failing as a result. The toxic metabolites that have damaged that organ could affect others, as well. We don't know whether an artificial liver can do the job, and we can't locate a tissue replacement."

"She will die?"

Shroud stiffened. Then he picked his nails. The steady *click click* cut the still night like cricket chirps.

"Why did you do it?"

"Is that any of your business?" Shroud glanced at Sam, and offered a sad smile. The expression erased years, but as with Kilian's tears, the hint of exposed psyche rattled. "If you must know, I truly believed I was helping her. I was . . . very fond of her, and I wanted her to live forever." He turned away. Took one unsteady step, then another. Finally, he thumped his thigh with a cage-wire fist and quickened his stride, reaching the last remaining skimmer just as it was about to depart.

Sam remained atop the little hill and watched the vehicle float away. "No one lives forever, Dr. Shroud." He walked down the hill toward the SIB. The lawn in front of the building looked like a depot, the fireskims having been joined by a small fleet of empty tankers that had been bought over to "hold the foam." Activity, while still bustling, had slowed from "what the hell!" to "steady as she goes" as the discovery phase of the cleanup operation gave way to the actual cleaning-up.

The HazMat crews had disabled the building alarms to allow for the rapid deployment of hoses, suction pumps, and portable ventilators. Sam walked up to the staging area with the sure step of someone who had every reason to be there. He slipped a ventilator helmet over his head, freed a pair of boots and a coverall from the pile of discarded safety equipment, and dressed. He had to fold over the coverall sleeves twice, and the amount of material he had to stuff inside the boots impeded his ability to walk. But even the best-fitting safety gear made people look like they'd dropped a load in their pants, so Sam decided he looked just fine.

Most of the cleanup centered around the first-floor conference facility. Someone had already tacked up a banner over the doorway leading into the space. Operation Soda Fountain had been crossed out in favor of Operation Scoop, which had in turn been countered by the less poetic, but more apt, Operation Suck. Rows of vacuum pumps already filled the huge rooms with their characteristic spluttery sounds. Sam walked past chest-high dollops of bright pink foam, and felt for one crazy moment like an explorer in a children's adventure story.

The stairwell leading into the basement proved gratifyingly empty. He limped down, unable to avoid the sticky, whipped-cream mounds that swallowed his boots to the knee. The hallway itself had avoided a major influx of microbial sieve, although he could easily trace the pink-outlined trails of those who had preceded him.

The tech bullpen . . . well, shambles seemed appropriate.

Sam pushed a mountain of white foam from atop his desk—
it *flooped* to the floor and continued to advance across the
lyno like pyroclastic flow. He removed one coated glove,
touched open his drawer, and removed the box of shrimp tea
Kilian had given him.

He unfastened the front of the coverall, stuffed the canister
inside, closed himself back up. If he stumbled into anyone
now, he'd say that he'd come down to recover his mess card,
and gladly accept the three-day suspension he'd draw for
crossing the hazard line.

Sam slooshed into the hall. The foam damped out sound—
the vacuum noises that had filled his ears in the stairwell
proved barely detectable here. *So quiet.* Like a hospital. He
looked in the direction Kilian had disappeared, then slipped
through the hip-high layer of fluff.

On his way down the hall, an opened fire-alarm station
caught his attention. Someone had painted a large yellow X
over the gaping hole, through which assorted connections
could be easily seen. He smiled, thinking of Kilian popping
the cover and inserting the stylus. He relished the thought of
her creating mayhem. He prayed she would remain alive to
make more.

The vending alcove, the source of so much lousy tea,
looked appropriately tatty. The floor was covered with a
runny, white-streaked liquid, a blend of foam and . . . what?
Sam saw the broken water connections, the spray still covering the furniture and counters, and shook his head.

"What was she trying to do?" What had happened at
Knevçet Shèràa that she thought smashing water valves an
appropriate response? Did she try to drown Neumann? The
Laumrau? Did she even know what she did?

He kicked something as he crossed the floor, and bent to
retrieve it. *A turnstick.* The long one Janitorial used when
ceiling lights needed switching out. One of the polywood
ends was cracked and dented. *She used this to smash the
valves.* His mind plundered the thought. *What was she trying
to do?* He had a right to know. They were in this together,
after all.

Together.

Sam's eyes stung. He coughed, as Parini had coughed, to loosen his clenching throat. He leaned on the turnstick like a cane as he walked to the janitor's closet to return it to its rack.

Together.

All these years, he had known, in his bones, that despite all evidence to the contrary, Jani Kilian lived. As proofs of her death cropped up all over the Commonwealth like mushrooms, he treated them as conjecture only. Anecdotal evidence, not even worthy to be dubbed hypothesis. He knew her to be out there, somewhere. He knew that someone else had survived the hell he had lived through. He knew he wasn't alone.

He opened the closet door and inserted the turnstick back into its niche. He touched the places where Kilian's hands might have gripped, and a cry caught in his throat as the first hot tears spilled. He stepped into the closet, inverted the bucket used to catch leaks from the coffee brewer, sat down, and wept.

He wept for Eva, and for Orton, and the others. But mostly, as much as it shamed him, he wept for himself. This was what it meant, to choose Simyam over Sam. *If she dies, I'll be the only one.* The only one left to remember. The only one left to bear the weight.

She felt like this for years. The thought caught him like a sharp blow. His breath stopped, starting only when he consciously forced himself to pull in the air. *She felt like this . . . so alone.* The sole survivor.

He stripped the helmet from his head, let it fall to the floor.

"I don't want to be the only one! I don't want to be the only one!"

Then he thought of the dying other, and finally wept for Jani Kilian. Wept as Parini and Shroud refused to. Wept as people in HazMat suits splashed into the alcove and stared at him. Wept until Odergaard, much less red of face than he had ever seen him, escorted the two white-garbed men into the storage room and led him away.

CHAPTER 33

Quiet, cool, whiteness. It stretched around Jani for as far as she could see. She slept in it—it nestled her like velvet, soft as the wings of angels. She couldn't walk in it—when she tried, she sank in to her hips and fell over. But that was all right. She didn't want to walk anyway.

Neumann only bothered her once. He sprayed pink foam in all directions as he slopped toward her, his head nestled beneath his good arm. His mouth still worked, unfortunately. She told him to go to hell and he stalked off, muttering about colonial lack of respect for their betters.

At times, she'd see one in an assortment of faces. Male. Female. Dark. Light. Flashes only, barest traces of variety in an endless sea of white.

Sound. Her consciousness revolved around sound. It ebbed and flowed like the tide, fingering the white space with swirls of imagined color.

"—and after Gruppo Helvetica wins the Cup and I take your money, I'm going to—"

"—and the Lake Michigan Strip talks are still ongoing, but it looks better from our end. The Vynshàrau have backed off, just like you said. They've even turned the temperature down! And I spoke with Tsecha last week. Hantìa was with him, and he said, " 'Colonel Frances, you must tell—' "

"—foam everywhere, and guess who has to work cleanup

detail for three fuckin' weeks because everybody said I should have been watching you—"

"—so Piers and I are having a little informal contest, to see which one of us has a heart attack first—"

"—I never stopped loving you. Please come back—"

"—I'm not mad at you anymore for ditching me in Felix Majora, but you owe me dinner for putting me through hell—"

Blues. She heard happiness in most of the voices, and happiness touched her as blue. Even the complainer, who muttered about lost gloves and crap in his hair. Granted, at times his voice radiated into violet, with the occasional flash of scarlet. Self-pity, she sensed. Worry, about himself.

But blues, mostly. All the emotion that touched her came to her in blue.

Except love. Love was white, like the velvet that enveloped her. She recognized the color of the voice.

A brick crushed her forehead. Every time she tried to open her eyes, it pressed down more and kept them closed. She raised her arm and tried to push it away, but something wrapped around her wrist and stopped her.

"L'go." She tried to pull away, and the grip tightened.

"Get Shroud."

"Roger will have a fit if we don't call him."

"Then get 'em all!"

Running. Swoosh of a door.

"Le' go!"

"Please don't struggle, Jani, you'll pull out your IVs."

"Lemme go!"

The brick smashed down.

"M'head."

"That's swelling from the shunt, Jani. Your head will ache every time you move it for a few more days."

Jani concentrated all her strength and will on forcing apart four parchment-thin flaps of skin. Slits of light. Stabs of pain. She closed them, then tried again.

Shapes. Surrounding her. Watching her.

A flash of white. Bending close.

"Hello." John's thin face filled her view. A smile. Light green eyes, the milk skin beneath cobwebby with fine lines.

"I remember you." Jani's words came slow, slurred. Poured, rather than spoken.

"And well you should." A last, wider smile. Then nothing.

"Me next." Val's head replaced John's. New haircut since Felix. Shorter, more Service-like.

"Cousin Finbar—is it really you?"

His smile broke like sunrise. It was one of their Rauta Shèràa jokes. He'd probably hurry to the nurses' station after he left her to jot happy notes about her long-term memory.

"Me last." Scraggly blond hair and bloodshot eyes.

"Hi, Rog. Consorting with the enemy?"

Pimentel grinned sadly. "I had no choice. Patient before pride." Val made soothing noises, but he ignored them.

"Hmm." Jani smiled. "Had your heart attack yet?"

His eyes widened. Twin rounds of pink bloomed in his sunken cheeks. "Not yet. Any minute now, though." He exhaled with a *whoosh.* "You remember that?"

"I remember lots of things." She turned her head as much as she dared and looked at John, but he pretended to fuss with the IV leads and refused to meet her eye.

A DeVries shunt, a procedure developed by and named after her least favorite *living* person in the Commonwealth, had been performed. The exit and entry scars, located at her hairline on either side of the base of her skull, pulled and tingled every time she moved her neck. She had a new liver. It was undersized since they'd been forced to insert it when it was still in its early growth stages, but it would reach full form and function within months. To fill the gap, they'd implanted a partial adjunct to help it along.

Beyond that, no one would tell her what had happened or what had been wrong with her. Her nurses fobbed her questions off on her doctors, who in turn fobbed her questions off on each other. Pimentel chewed his lip to blood. Val oozed charm and changed the subject. John, she saw not at all. That worried her more than anything else.

They wouldn't give her a mirror. She discovered the first time she touched her scalp that they'd shaved her head in order to jack in the shunt main and attach the moniter buttons. She estimated length as best she could with her thumb, and guessed that her new growth consisted of a centimeter of wave. Unaided hair growth averaged fifteen centimeters a year. Hers had been on the slow side since her rebuild. *I've been out over a month?* She checked the color in the curved reflection of her IV stand. Still black. No bald patches requiring implants.

They'd left her *à lérine* wounds alone. The gashes had healed to ragged red lines on her right arm, thinner, paler threads on her left.

They had removed her eyefilms. Threat of infection, Morley said. Green-on-green orbs goggled at her, warped to skewed ovals by the tubing surface. She turned away from them repeatedly, only to have morbid fascination draw her back. Judging from the blasé reaction of the nurses, however, her eyes' appearance bothered her more than it did any of them. A day and a half passed before someone honored her request for filmformer—the male nurse who finally brought it expressed disappointment that she'd decided to cover them. Several of the guys had commented that they liked the way they made her look.

Big pussycat, indeed!

By day two, the headaches eased enough that she could sit up. On day three, they removed the IVs and fed her soup. She shocked everyone on day six by walking the halls. Especially Pimentel.

"Your progress is mind-boggling. I'd ascribe it to the recuperative abilities of youth," he said as he squired her back to her room. "But you're older than I am."

"Watch it, Roger." Jani kicked off her slippers and perched on the edge of her bed. "So what do you think it is?"

He looked at her with the same hangdog expression he'd worn since she awoke, and left before she could demand he answer the damned question.

*   *   *

"Why did I release the retardant foam?"

"*That's* the million-Com question, isn't it?" Lucien propped his feet up on her bed and tipped back in his chair. "And not just the stuff in the ready tanks, but the stuff in the reserves and in the lines. You activated the synthesizers, too. Overrode the metering sensors. Yup, you shoved a UV finger down its throat and the whole damned system just went *blech*."

Jani grinned. "I'm sorry about the cleanup detail."

Lucien had the decency to look uncomfortable. "Pimentel organized the tag-team talkers. He said you might recall what we said while you were in coma, so we had to be careful."

"Thanks for not taking the advice to heart."

"*You* hand-polish brass fixtures for three weeks and try to restrain your enthusiasm!" He eyed her with an expression of patience sorely tried. "Oh well. Nema says hello."

"Next time you see him, tell him hello back."

"He's inevitable, you know. Inexorable. All those *in* words." Lucien hunched deeper into the chair. "Besides, if you came around, you could keep him off my back. 'Lucien, you must tell my nìa—! Lucien, you must—you must—!' "

Jani studied him for some sign he might be joking, and couldn't find one. "If it's so bad, request a transfer."

"No." Lucien studied his nails. "It's still interesting."

"Haven't figured out how to work him yet, have you?"

"I'm going to ignore that. What he really wants is to see you. He has to hold off, though. Ceèl is still ticked about being forced to acknowledge you. Nema said he has to throw him a bone or two before he can mention the possibility."

"Did he really say 'throw him a bone'?"

"Yeah. That handheld of his has been getting a workout."

Before Jani could learn more, the door opened and Val sauntered in. He was sharply attired as always—dark green trousers and a patterned shirt in greens and browns. Late summer afoot. "Hello, I was on my way to a meeting and—" His eyes drank in Lucien, and his face lit. "I'm sorry, Jani, I didn't realize you had visitors. Lieutenant Pascal, isn't it? We spoke once during the night in question, but we've never been formally introduced—I'm Val Parini."

Lucien cast him a bored glance, then ignored him. "I have to get back to work." He rose and bent close to Jani. "I'll stop by this evening."

Jani tilted her head to receive his now-customary peck on the cheek. She wasn't paying attention, so she couldn't slip from his grasp when he wrapped his arms around her and pressed his lips to hers. He kissed her so hard she either had to open her mouth or risk a serious bruising. He tightened his grip when she tried to pull away, and nipped her lower lip when she pinched his thigh.

"*Speaking of ten-minute head starts,*" Jani said in brisk Acadian when they finally broke apart. Lucien answered with a smirk, then brushed past Val as though he wasn't there.

Val waited for the door to close before speaking. "I don't think osculation *français* is on your list of prescribed meds."

Jani struggled to find a less distracting sitting position—stimulation of one highly sensitive region tended to travel. "You're just jealous."

"Nonsense. Merely concerned for your welfare." His expression grew thoughtful as he strolled around the end of the bed and flopped into Lucien's chair. "I've read his psych evals. Nasty augment he has. You deserve better."

"I've seen him without his shirt—he's just what the doctor ordered."

"Not this doctor." Val adopted a look of serious concentration. "Selfish. Narcissistic. Incapable of sympathy, much less empathy."

"No sloppy emotions to complicate matters—just the way I like it."

"You're not—" Val faltered. "You're not his only *interest.* Or his only loyalty, if I can even use that word in connection with him. He can't be trusted."

"You have been digging, haven't you?" Jani met his gaze—he dropped his first. "I have him figured out."

"Think of the opportunities you're letting slip away."

"Keep John out of this."

"Did I mention a name? I was speaking of life in general—did I once mention my best friend, my business partner, one of the wealthiest men in the Commonwealth?"

"It didn't work the first time. What makes you think now would be any different?"

"The best amongst us acquire certain traits as they age. Maturity. Patience. The ability to give and take."

"We're talking about the same John Shroud, aren't we?" Jani racked her brain for a suitable change of subject, and pounced on the first thing she thought of. "How's Hugh? Morley said he was here the night I was admitted, but I haven't seen him."

Val's rakish air vanished. He looked away, hands clenching. "He wants to visit you, but only if he knows he won't run into me. I'm meeting with Cal Montoya in the city tomorrow, so he'll stop by then."

"Emergency ditching in the lovelorn sea?" That had been another one of their Rauta Shèràa jokes. Jani suddenly felt the need to make him smile.

He did. A little. "White chocolate cheesecake—what did I tell you?" He picked at his trouser leg. "And he got upset. About you. Reading the files was one thing, he said, but seeing in the flesh what John and Eamon and I had done . . ." His hand stilled. "He's submitted his resignation. He's leaving Neoclona."

"I'm sorry."

"Yeah." He looked at her, eyes darkened with concern. Fear. "I asked you on Felix, and you didn't answer. I'm asking you again." He tapped his fingers against his thigh, faster and faster, as though building up momentum. Or courage. "Do you hate us?"

"You saved my life," Jani said, jumping at the pat answer. But Val's desolate look informed her that she wouldn't slip out from under that easily. *How do I feel about you?* Master go-between. John's apologist extraordinaire. She shrugged, catching herself as the scars from the shunt pulled. "Val, if we'd met under normal circumstances, I think we'd have been great friends."

"Jani?" Val's eyes dulled in question. "We're friends *now*."

"In a way." Jani studied her hands. Had the real skin grown darker than the animandroid? More bronze? If she compared herself to Nema, would she see a difference? "But you're a scientist, and by all accounts a good one, if a little shifty on the follow-through. I think you're anxious to see how the experiment turns out."

"Don't be so sure," Val said, too softly. "You haven't been on the other side of that door for the past five weeks."

"No, I've been on the business side." Jani's voice thinned as her throat tightened. "Every time I ask somebody a question, they dodge or clam up. What did you do to me?"

"You're not in any condition yet—"

"*Val.*"

"John ordered us not to tell you until he deemed you ready, and he hasn't deemed you yet!"

"Hasn't he? Well, the next time you see him, tell him to get off his ass and deem away!" Jani kicked off her covers. "I'm going for a walk."

Val scrambled to his feet and hurried around the bed to her side. "Are you sure you're up to it?"

Jani eased her legs over the bedside and probed with her toes for her slippers. "Yes. I may even venture outside this time—it's a beautiful day."

She found herself the focus of all eyes as she shuffled down the hall on Val's arm. White coats smiled. Waved. Offered the occasional "Howya doin', Captain?"

"It's hotter than hell out there," Val said as he escorted her to the front entrance. "One circuit around the flower beds and I'm bringing you back in."

"I thought you had a meeting."

"Shit." He glared at his timepiece. "Stay put. I'm going to find someone to go with you."

As soon as Val disappeared from view, Jani took off in the opposite direction, weakened muscles distorting her walk into a limping skip. She had gotten the lay of the land during her previous visits—she knew exactly where she needed to go. She cut through an empty conference room. Up another hall and down a utilities chase.

The Basic Research Group dominated the east wing of the ground floor. Jani pressed the buzzer of the door leading into the largest, best-equipped lab. It swept open.

John sat at a large desk in the middle of the room, hunched over a recording board. Atop the surrounding benches, analyzers clicked and data-transfer stations chirped. In the background, a hint of music from a hidden system. Elgin. Or was it Mozart?

"Put the sequencer on the bench nearest the window," he rumbled. "Leave the samples on the cart."

"Where do you want me to put the violin?" Jani asked as she dragged a visitor's chair over to the desk.

John's head shot up. As soon as he saw her, his face colored candy pink. The cruel blush clashed with his jacket, a crossover cowlneck in palest pearl grey.

"Val told me you still play." Jani sat and swung her feet up onto the desk. The left leg worked fine, but the right still needed hoisting.

"Play?" John blinked in confusion. He'd filmed his eyes to match the jacket—the argent irises glittered like fish scales. He'd have cut a sinister figure if not for his face's boiled-lobster glow. He sat back and tossed his stylus on the desk. "Oh. Yes. Once in a while. I'm out of practice, though." He raised his left hand and ran his fingers along an imaginary violin neck. "I'm losing my calluses."

"Shouldn't let that happen—it'll take months to grow them back." Jani glanced around the lab for something else to comment upon. The featureless white walls? The blaze of summer, visible through narrow windows? Finally, she caught sight of a familiar device atop one of the benches, and shook her head. "Coffee brewer in the lab? For shame. Where's a safety officer when you need one?"

John's expression lightened. "I was about to make fresh." He rose and crossed the floor with the loose-limbed, liquid walk that age hadn't changed. "Do you want some?"

"Sure." Jani settled back and watched him brew the coffee. The surroundings were more posh and the circumstances less perilous than they'd been eighteen years ago, but in a way, it was as though nothing had changed. As though they sat in the same basement office and listened to the same recordings. As if nothing existed outside the walls that enclosed them.

She studied him, something she hadn't yet been able to

do. He stood one-nine, but as always, his thin build and penchant for monochrome clothing made him look even taller. His hair shone in the diffuse room light, so white and crisply trimmed it looked like a plastic cap. Jani could still recall its feel between her fingers, like shredded silk.

She pushed the memories aside and concentrated on the man who stood before her now. Time's passage had done him a favor. *Homely* had become *striking*. Strangeness had become style. *Congratulations, Johnny—you won. Just like you told me you would.*

The brewer gurgled and hissed. Dark aromas filled the room, heavy enough to cut with a Sìah blade. John poured and stirred, then ambled back to the desk and handed Jani her cup. Unadorned ivory ceramic—weighty and solid. "Black?"

"You remembered." Jani held it to her nose and inhaled the almost solid essence. "I drink this, I won't sleep for a week."

John frowned. "Val claims it etches tooth enamel." One nearly invisible eyebrow arched. "He told me *he* made you coffee on Felix, and you liked it."

"I *drank* it—it was either that or die." Jani sipped, then tried to think of the words to compare Val's bellywash with the nectar she tasted. "Trust me, you have nothing to worry about."

John smiled. "That's what I thought." The expression flavored his voice warm brown, like the coffee. He stared into his cup, then sighed. "I'd like to think this is a social call, but I'm guessing you came here for a reason." He returned to his side of the desk.

Jani nodded. "I waited for you to visit. When you didn't, I decided it was time for the mountain to come to Muhammad."

"You needed your rest." John gripped his recording board by the corner and pushed it back and forth. "Your recovery has progressed splendidly." He looked at her, and his metal eyes softened. "You look . . . wonderful."

Jani tugged first at the lapel of her mud blue robe, then at her pillow-mashed curls. She felt the heat flood her face—

at least her skin contained enough melanin to obscure matters. "Pimentel thinks I'm healing like a kid. He's never seen anything like it." She labored to maintain a casual tone. "What happened?"

John set down his cup and tented his hands. "Your condition, when we pulled you out of the SIB, was extremely grave. Your liver was failing, and your metabolism was deranged. You began seizing—those seizures were of sufficient scope and severity we feared permanent brain damage. The DeVries shunt—"

"—cut my brain off from the rest of my body until the hepatic adjunct cleared toxic metabolites out of my system so I'd stop seizing. That much I extracted from a nurse named Stan, who is quite taken with my pussycat eyes." Jani flexed her right hand and compared it again to her left. The light was brighter here—did they still look different? "What else?"

John ran a hand along his jacket crossover. "If you're upset, we can discuss this later—"

"*No.*" Jani lowered her feet to the floor—the right one hit with a *thump*. "We discuss it now."

"You have a new liver."

"*I know that.*" She leaned forward and set her cup on the desk hard enough that coffee splashed over the side. "Pimentel was treating me for acute intermittent porphyria, a disease he thought you gave me when you rebuilt me. Is that true?"

"Don't say 'rebuilt.' You make yourself sound like a machine." John drummed his fingers on the desktop. "Yes, you suffered from a porphyria-like disorder that affects a scant percentage of the idomeni population."

"An *idomeni* genetic disorder?"

"Yes." The drumming altered to a slower turn of finger, as though he pressed a string. "The idomeni tissue we used when we grew the new organ was taken from an unbred born-sect. The born-sects don't bother to repair manageable genetic miscues until the member is ready to breed. Sometimes, not even then. I didn't learn that until after you . . . left." He glared at her. "Ridiculous, but there it is." Whether he referred to the idomeni practice or her running away, he didn't make clear.

Jani's skin prickled in alarm. "Which sect?"

Another curl of finger. "The disease is most common in Vynshàrau. It affects point two percent of their population."

"Did you use . . . Nema's tissue?"

"*No!*" John's face flushed anew. "Use your head, Jan! I despise him—do you think I'd give you his tissue?"

"Right." So she wasn't related to Nema in any bizarre ways. Make that any *more* bizarre ways. "You repaired this disorder?"

"Of course. Then . . . things snowballed."

"Snowballed?"

John nodded. "You suffered from one or two arcane connective-tissue disorders, and a defect in glycosamino-glycan metabolism. And a glycogen-degradation defect that I believe accounted for more of your symptoms than the porphyria."

Jani pressed her hands together. Were the fingers of her right longer than her left? "Human defects or idomeni defects, John?"

John's hand stilled. "Defects."

"Human or idomeni?"

"Jani—"

"Answer me! On a percent scale, how human was I when I came in here and how much has that number decreased in the last five weeks?"

John leaned forward. "Jani, your transplant incision is almost completely healed, and you were operated on only two weeks ago. Every patient we've seen who was ever treated using a DeVries shunt remained bedridden for at least six months and required extensive rehab. Rehab that, I may add, was seldom entirely successful. Only twelve percent of those patients recovered sufficiently to live unaided." He nodded firmly, as though that proved his point beyond doubt. "You're walking around on your own and engaging in complex social interactions after five weeks. And your distinctive personality"—he eyed her in injury—"doesn't seem changed in the least." He touched the fingertips of his left hand to the desktop, raising and lowering each in turn, like slow scales. "The advantages of hybridization are becoming more and more obvious, and we've learned better how to take what we need and leave the rest behind. You won't change physically—well, not much more, anyway—and the health benefits—"

"You pushed me farther down the road. Hybridized me at a much faster rate than would have occurred naturally."

"We had no choice! The disorders you could have developed if we hadn't—"

Jani held up her right hand. Maybe the skin hadn't yellowed—maybe it was the light. "If I went to Cal Montoya or one of your other facility chiefs and asked them to make me one hundred percent human again, would they be able to?"

John shook his head. "You've altered too much. They wouldn't know where to start. You could develop more life-threatening disorders, the treatment of which could lead to more problems."

"So you did this for my own good."

He looked at her. His long, sad face was the first thing Jani had seen when she opened her eyes after the explosion. For a time, it had been the last thing she had seen when she closed them at night. "That has always been our foremost consideration."

Jani crossed her wrists and compared the skin color. Maybe the animandroid skin didn't tan like the real thing. Maybe the muddy hue of her pajamas made her look more sallow than normal. Maybe. "Val worries that I hate you both, but I don't blame you for what you did in Rauta Shèràa. You were young and thought you knew everything, and you were honestly trying to help me."

"Of course—you know we were—"

"But that was then and this is now. Could you have modified your all-or-nothing approach? Made do with the shunt and the adjunct until I was conscious and could make an informed decision?" She looked at the man who had saved her life in the way he thought best because he loved her. The man she'd fled when she realized what his love meant. "An-gel—"

John's breathing quickened. "Jani—"

"—could you have *asked*?"

He buried his head in his hands. "It was the only way to ensure your complete recovery!" He looked at her over the tops of his fingers. "You can trust me," he said, his voice gone velvet. Soft, enveloping, suffocating velvet. "I know more now than I did then."

"You may know more about the science, John." Jani reached for her cup—more coffee sloshed over the rim as she pushed it farther away. "But you don't know a damned thing more about me." Her knee gave out when she stood, and she almost lost her balance. John reached out to help her, but when he looked her in the face, he sagged back in his chair and let her go without a word.

CHAPTER 34

The next morning, Jani entered the sunroom to find Hugh Tellinn sitting on a lounge, leafing through a holozine. Almost three months had passed since she'd first met him at Neoclona-Felix. In the interim, his hair had been inexpertly trimmed into a flip-ended mop, and his state of sartorial disarray had further deteriorated. He turned pages with a rapid, slap-hand motion, as though sitting in the sunroom set his teeth on edge.

Then he looked up. "Jani!" It was the first time she had ever seen him smile. The expression split his face from ear to ear. Instead of a thirty-five-year-old man with a bad haircut and grab-bag taste in clothes, he looked like a boy who had opened his birthday box and found the puppy. She could imagine Val performing handsprings for a chance to savor that open-faced happiness.

"Hugh." She walked slowly to a straight-backed chair opposite his lounge. She could sense his examining gaze, knew he watched her posture and coordination, whether she walked easily or had to concentrate on how to place her feet. "Do I pass, Dr. Tellinn?" she asked as she sat.

"You look good." He tossed the 'zine aside and sat forward, his hands clasped. "I'm glad." The brilliant smile wavered. "I assume Val told you what happened."

"The barest bones." Jani sat back, grateful for the support the stiff framing offered her muscles, which still tired quickly. "The less he discusses a breakup, the more it bothers him. He spent all of fifteen seconds summing you up."

Hugh blinked. "Really?" He tugged at a stretched-out cuff of his dull brown pullover. "I was very fond of him, too. But sometimes that isn't enough."

"He said you resigned from Neo."

"Yes."

"That was a drastic step."

"It was the only way. I knew it from the start. Every time I tried to talk about you, Val would nod and pat me on the back. Told me he understood my concern. Five minutes later, John's rattling off a list of all the things they'd try the second they got their hands on you." Hugh rubbed his cheek. His face looked drawn. Thinner. "I lived with them for over three months. Longest ten years of my life."

"Three months seems the turning point. That's how long I lasted, too." Jani felt a warm rise of concern for her fellow veteran. "What are you going to do?"

Hugh's shoulder twitched. "I have family in Helsinki. I thought I'd visit them for a time. After that?" He rocked his head back and forth. "Bullet train through the China provinces. Ski in the Andes. I've never been to Earth and I have enough savings to see me for a year or two. Who knows what I'll do?"

Jani covered her mouth with her hand to hide her grin. Was there anything funnier than listening to a workaholic discuss vacation plans? "You'll hook up with a hospital within a month," she said through her fingers. "You won't be happy until you're up to your elbows in glands."

That smile again. "You're probably right. What about you?"

"I'm stuck here until I'm stabilized to the world's satisfaction." She crossed her legs. Right over left, no hoisting required. "My lawyer told me yesterday that my adjudicating committee met two weeks ago and tried me *in absentia*. Sentence, ninety days, commuted to time served. Alice loses some privileges, but she keeps her head. I'll be discharged from the Service two minutes after I'm discharged from here." *Don't be surprised if they process you in the lobby,*

Friesian had added dryly. "I'll need to find a place to live.
A job."

Hugh cocked an eyebrow. "Val had mentioned hiring you
into the Neoclona Documents Group."

"*Not bloody likely.*" Jani looked at Hugh to find him regarding her with sad amusement. "I didn't mean that the way
it sounded."

"I understand. Believe me." He pressed his knuckles to his
lips. "Well, I just wanted to stop by and say so long." He
stood awkwardly, his too-large trousers rumpled and bagged
at the knees.

Jani started to speak. Hesitated. Tried once more. "Could
you do me a favor? I want you to read a MedRec." She
handed him a slip of paper on which she'd written a name.
"Then I want you to come back here, so we can talk about
it."

One hour passed. *This is taking longer than I thought.* She
knew that Hugh suffered a disadvantage not being a neurologist, but she felt sure he'd grasp the essentials. He'd read
her Rauta Shèràa file. He'd make the connection.

Several patients had wandered into the sunroom for their
postbreakfast/prelunch newssheet reading by the time Hugh
returned. He paused in the entry, searching faces. When he
finally saw her, the life drained from his eyes. He shoved his
hands in his pockets and slouched across the room.

"I spoke with Roger." He reached out to her. "We're going
to meet with him." He maintained his gentle grip on her hand
as they departed the sunroom and negotiated the halls.

Pimentel sat at his desk waiting for them. Jani memorized
the details of his office, the bookshelves, the watercolor, the
view, in the sincere hope she'd never see them again.

"Jani." He glanced at Hugh. A look of back-and-forth argument passed between them. *You start. No, you start.*

Jani sat down in her usual chair and rubbed her damp
palms over her pajama-clad thighs. "Well?"

Hugh walked behind Pimentel's desk and perched on the
windowsill. His choice of seating gave the scene an "us versus them" flavor. "Roger told me that Sam Duong had named

you his next of kin." He turned to look out the window. "He was admitted the same night you were. Discharged two weeks ago." He toyed with the light-transmission touchpad, the taps sounding harder as he continued talking. "During his stay, he revoked your NOK designation. Legally, therefore, you have no right to know anything about his condition."

Pimentel occupied his own nervous hands by paging through a file. "However, he did mention to me things that he wished he'd told you. I'm taking that as permission to discuss him with you. Besides, the faster we clear this up once and for all, the better for both of you." He pushed a hank of hair out of his eyes. "He spoke about you quite a bit. He even volunteered to help talk you through your coma, but I refused to allow it. He was too weak to be subjected to that sort of stress. We operated on him the night he was admitted."

Jani tried to read Pimentel's closed expression, his careful wording. "You removed the implant?"

Hugh sighed. "No." He finally turned from the window. "Sam Duong suffered from a benign neoplasm affecting the paramedian posterior region of his thalamus—"

Jani tapped her temple. "A mass in the middle of his head. Thank you. Roger told me all about it."

"Jani and I have discussed the particulars of Sam's condition. She believes some of the experiments the Laum conducted involved augmentation of the thalamus." Pimentel removed sheets of coated parchment from the file and laid them on the desk in front of him. "I have to admit, some of the things you said jolted me. So I contacted Bandan Combined University and requested they send me whatever ID they had for Simyam Baru." He slid three pages of parchment across the desk toward Jani. "I also requested that they search their records for a Sam Duong. Three men with that name turned up. Two still work there. The third left about five years ago, to take a job as a civilian archivist with the Commonwealth Service at Fort Sheridan."

Hugh turned back to the window.

"I took a sample from Sam. It matches that of the Sam Duong who came here from Banda. It doesn't match Simyam

Baru's." Pimentel sat back slowly, gaze locked on her face. "Simyam Baru and Sam Duong are not the same man."

Jani looked from one scan to the other, her heart tripping, her hands damp. "Yes, but scans can change. The Laum may have conducted unrecorded experiments with tissue hybridization for all I know. I mean, look at me. My current scan doesn't match my Service scan." She kept reading. Line after line of comparator code. All different.

All different.

"Service ID scans are trace scans, Jani. Suitable for quick and dirty ID, in most instances. However, your ServRec also contained a full genomic scan, which was used to confirm your ID on Felix when the trace IDs didn't match up." Pimentel's voice remained low and steady. Calm. "The Bandans are similarly thorough. The scans they sent are full genomics. No chance of error or mix-up. No chance of confusion."

Hugh left his window seat. "Through a skillful melding of coincidence and storytelling, Sam Duong built himself a past to replace the one he'd forgotten." He rounded the front of Pimentel's desk and sat on the edge, close to Jani.

Pimentel picked up the story line. "He worked at the university at the same time Simyam Baru did. He may have even met him, but he can't remember and we'll probably never know." He cleared his throat. "Nothing would give me greater pleasure than to tell you, yes, it's possible someone else survived Knevçet Shèràa. But I will not lie to you. As a physician, I cannot, and as a friend, I will not." He reached across the desk and touched her hand. "I'm sorry."

Jani put a hand to her throat. The ache in her chest made it hard to breathe. "There's no chance?"

"Simyam Baru and Sam Duong are two separate people, Jani. No, there's no chance whatsoever." Pimentel paused. "Sam wanted me to tell you he's sorry. He said the thought of being the only one left with those memories terrified him into seeking help. He didn't want to be alone." He forced a smile. "He called you his 'Dark Ice Captain.' He said you were stronger than he was, and that he hoped you'd understand."

Hugh moved in behind her and placed his hands on her

shoulders. "I wish the answer could be different. I wish something could be returned to you, for all you've lost." His touch melted the tightness. Jani leaned forward and rested her head on the desk; Hugh didn't let her go until she stopped crying.

Pimentel walked her back to her room. He sat in the visitor's chair instead of on his usual perch at her footboard, as if he thought she might not want him too close.

"Jani." He eyed her uncomfortably. "Are you all right?"

"Yeah." Jani circled to the far side of her room, and leaned against the window.

"You're sure?"

"I'd bet my license."

Jani traced a finger over the glass in the same place Neumann had sketched tic-tac-toe with his blood. "Did he tell you anything about that night? I don't remember what happened from the time I arrived at the A-G's party."

Pimentel shook his head. "He knew you hallucinated. He hinted you spoke with Neumann, but when pressed, he became highly agitated." He smoothed a hand over the freshly made bed. "At that point, it was enough for me that he didn't want to be Simyam Baru anymore. That he realized there was a Sam Duong out there that he needed to recover. Rebuild." He thumped the bedspread, which was so tightly tucked it *whumped* like a trampoline. "Speaking of rebuilding . . ."

"Are you going to say something about the SIB?"

"No." He chuckled. "I wondered if you were up to . . . taking a call?"

Jani saw the controlled eagerness in his face, and felt her heart skip. "From whom?"

"Someone real, who's been worried sick about you for the past five weeks." He hesitated. "And, I'm guessing, for a hell of a lot longer than that."

"You'll be all right by yourself?" Pimentel pushed Jani's chair close to the display. "After what you just went through—"

"I'm fine." She pushed the chair back to a more comfortable viewing distance.

"I'll be down the hall." He glanced back at her over his shoulder. "If you need anything."

"Thank you, Roger." Jani fingered the Misty replay activator pad, and hoped he couldn't see how her hand shook. "I mean that."

"Sure." Pimentel eyed her somberly, then slipped out.

She tapped the activator once. Twice. Third time proved the charm. The display blued. Lightened. The face formed.

"Janila?" Her mother squinted, as though she could just see Jani at the other end of a very long tunnel. At the age of sixty-seven common, Jamira Shah Kilian looked so much as she had nineteen years ago, it took Jani's breath away. Only the faintest wisps of grey lightened her black hair, gathered in a knot at the nape of her neck. Her brow and cheekbones were broad, her nose an arched curve almost Family in its sharpness. Her skin, a shade darker than Jani's, bore a few fine lines at the corners of her brown eyes, which still shone large and bright. As always, she wore a brightly colored short-sleeved tee—Jani knew her loose, belted trousers would contain a multitude of colors to complement the current turquoise hue. She had drawn two horizontal downcurves of henna in the middle of her forehead, which meant she had visited the Brh shrine that day. She kept a smaller shrine at home, and only visited the neighborhood sanctum when she wished to pray for something special.

Jani looked away from the display toward the wall opposite until her eyes stopped swimming.

"It's very vexing not being able to see you to speak to you," her mother continued. "I was quite shocked when I saw your new face. So much like my grandmother Jamuna, my father's mother whom you did not know. I had grown so used to you looking like your father, to see my family in you now—" She held a hand to her mouth as the seconds passed. Ten. Twenty.

The hand dropped. "I have received so many messages these past weeks. Some of them have been quite . . . startling. So many doctors, reassuring me you are all right. That told me how sick you were. You can imagine my thoughts."

Jani rubbed her forehead and imagined her hands around Val's throat. It would have been his idea, of course, to re-assure her parents that she was just fine, then to nudge John into doing the same. And Roger. And God knows who else.

Her mother reached out and touched the display, her eyes soft with apology. "Your father is not here. He is helping Oncle Shamus install systems at Faeroe Outpost. He has been there two months common already, and the delays still mul-tiply like *lapin*. He is furious, but if they do not install the relays now, they will miss the peak of the tourist season and have to wait until next quarter to renew the permits and you know how anxious Shamus becomes. Already, he jumps at loud noises. Of course, most of those loud noises are your father. But it is for the best. He would only want to go to Earth immediately to see you, and Dr. Pimentel warned us you need time to recover. Without undue strain, he said. He seems very worried about that. I quite like him. He seems . . . normal." Her unexpressed opinion of John and Val rang loud and clear.

"Your Colonel Hals also messaged. I quite liked her. Solid woman. Lots of common sense. If she is your friend, you are lucky. I feel I have less to worry."

She inhaled shakily. "It was very silly—" Her hand went to her mouth again. "Silly of you to think we would not want to see you. You're our daughter, our only child—" She once more touched the display. "I can't talk to a blinking screen. I want to talk to you in the same room. I want to hold my Jani-girl—" With that, all semblance of reserve shattered. She sagged forward, her face buried in her hands, shoulders shaking. "I don't want to cry in this booth by myself. I want to cry with you. Tears should be shared." She sat up and wiped her eyes with a tattered dispo.

"I will send another message in a few days, when I can talk without crying. Dr. Shroud told me I should send as many as I wish, that Neoclona will pay. That is very gen-erous of him, but I do not like to take advantage." Her eyes narrowed, lit with a sharp light Declan Kilian always referred to as "roasted almond." "But maybe I will. I most look for-

ward to meeting him, Janila, when we come to Earth."
Again, the melting. "*Beaux rêves, ma petite fille. Au revoir.*"
The display blanked.

Jani wiped her face. Then she touched the reply pad. She
talked for almost an hour, telling her mother about life on
the base. Acadia Central United's continuing quest for the
Cup. The weather. Her upcoming life in Chicago, that she
had not even planned. Three months' nonexistent income
shot out into space when she pressed the touchpad, but if
Neoclona could pay for her mother's messages, they could
pay for hers, too. John owed her that and more.

Discharge came one week later. John and Val, who had made
themselves scarce since Jani's blowup with John, were nowhere to be seen. Morley helped her pack, while Roger lectured her on diet and the need to take it easy. In order to
stave off the heart attack he'd threatened her with for weeks,
she relented and accepted his offer to carry her full-kit duffel.
When he staggered under its weight, she took it back and
told him to stop being silly.

Friesian waited for her in the lobby. To Jani's surprise,
Hals stood next to him. They both wore dress blue-greys;
Friesian held a bouquet of mixed colonial blooms that looked
suspiciously like those growing around the buildings in
North Lakeside.

"Remember what I said about a table in the lobby?" He
handed her the flowers, then pulled a sheaf of papers from
the documents case that rested on the floor at his feet. "I was
being optimistic." He handed her the papers along with a
stylus, then turned around. "Sign the bottom of pages one,
four, and twelve, then touch the fingertips of your right hand
to the sensor square at the bottom of page twenty."

Jani handed the flowers to Hals and dropped her bag to
the floor. Using Friesian's back as the table, she wrote the
coda to her Service career. "Any surprises?" She tapped him
on the shoulder to indicate she had finished and handed the
documents back to him.

"Nope. It's just like I told you." He slid the papers into a
Service courier envelope, returned them to the case, then

handed the case to a mainline lieutenant who had appeared out of nowhere. "Your first pension payment will be deposited into a general account at the Service Bank by month's end," he said as the lieutenant departed. "Go to any branch in the city to arrange transfer to your own account."

"Take your shooter badge," Hals added with a grin. "They'll give you two tickets to a Cubs game."

As Jani shouldered her duffel, she caught sight of another full kit resting beside the lobby sofa. "Whose is that?"

Friesian held a hand to his heart. "I'm shipping out. In two hours, I catch the shuttle to Luna, then the *Reina Amalia* back to Constanza. There's already a new brief waiting for me on board."

"Here's your hat, what's your hurry," Hals said softly. "The lawyer shortage at colonial bases is a well-known fact."

The three of them stared over one another's heads and struggled to keep the smiles off their faces.

Friesian broke away to the sofa and gathered his gear. Then they walked out into the burning afternoon. A steel blue four-seater hovered in the Ten Minute oval in front of the hospital. Friesian raised a hand; the officer behind the wheel waved in response.

"My ride is here already. Imagine that." He offered Hals a sharp salute. "Colonel. It was a pleasure meeting you."

"Likewise, Major." Hals saluted in return. "Safe trip."

Friesian turned to Jani, and held out his hand. "It's been . . ."

"Yeah." Jani laughed. "Sorry for all the excitement."

"Maybe in a few years, when the dust has settled, we can hook up. Have a good, long talk."

"Sure." Jani agreed easily to a meeting she knew would never take place. Time would interfere. Distance. Or most likely, sweet reason. Friesian would realize that he didn't want to know what he didn't know.

She waved to him one last time as his vehicle skimmed out of the oval. "I wonder what's waiting for him on Luna?"

"A nice attempted murder, he said." Hals frowned. "He may have been joking." She adjusted her brimmed lid and led Jani to a rent-a-scoot stand.

Jani glanced back toward the hospital. Through the tinted scanglass, she could see Niall Pierce standing in the lobby window, dressed in pajamas, his bathrobe wrapped tightly around him. She hesitated, then raised her hand in farewell. He kept his hands buried in his robe pockets; she could feel his eyes follow her as she boarded the scoot, and it pulled away.

"I'm sorry none of us made it in to see you the past few weeks," Hals said as she steered along the path.

Jani broke the code of that remark. "How is Burkett?"

Hals grinned. She seemed more relaxed now. Her shoulders had unclenched, and her hand rested easily on the steerbar. "He's been surprisingly helpful. He arranged for everybody in FT to attend the weekly Diplo update meetings. And we'll all attend Diplomacy School, which means we all wind up with Foreign Service entries in our records. Nice little notation, come promotion time." She glanced at Jani. "He sends his regards, by the way. Trusts you'll make yourself available for consultation once you're settled."

"Tell him to get out his expense book. Advice from the Eyes and Ears will not come cheap."

"I think he knows that." For the first time, the contentment left Hals's face. "I could have used you here. Our interactions with the idomeni are going to get more and more complicated, and no one else here has your experience."

Jani glanced in the side mirror and watched the South Central Base recede from view. "You can handle the idomeni. As for me, well, I seem to encourage your unconventional side."

Hals nodded grudging agreement. "There is that." She steered into the drop-off oval adjacent to the station. "What time is your train?"

"Seventeen up." Jani checked her timepiece. "Just enough time for me to buy a newssheet and something to eat."

Hals helped Jani with her gear, then ambled around the oval. "Speaking of which, if you could suggest any newssheets or periodicals we should subscribe to, I'd appreciate it." She glanced down the stairs that led from the train platform down to the charge lot, and stopped. "Oh. My. God."

Jani hurried to the railing to find Lucien looking up at them from the middle of the half-empty lot. His hair glimmered in contrast to his black T-shirt. His beige trousers were tasteful, but *fitted*. Black sunshades covered his eyes. The skimmer he leaned against looked like an oil droplet in a stiff headwind, and cost more than the entire population of Base Command made in a month.

Hals exhaled with a whistle. "Don't tell me—that's your nurse." She shook her head in wide-eyed wonder. "Next time I have a day off, maybe we can meet for lunch. You can tell me Tsecha stories." She sneaked another glance at Lucien. "And anything else you think needs an airing."

"Sure." Jani smiled. "Thanks for calling my folks, Frances."

"No problem, Jani." Hals gripped her shoulders in a quick hug. "Be seeing you."

Flowers in hand, feeling like an underdressed bride in her base casual tee and trousers, Jani descended toward the vision that awaited her.

"Hello." Lucien met her at the foot of the stairs. "I had the afternoon off. Thought you might need a ride into the city."

"That was nice of you."

"I have my moments." He tossed her duffel into the boot as though it weighed grams and not kilos, then helped her into the skimmer as though nursing actually was on the agenda.

Jani snuggled against plush black leather and ran her hand over the polished ebony dash. "Mind if I ask?"

Lucien maneuvered out of the lot and ramped immediately onto a Boul artery. "One of the Caos, in a small way. Husband's spending the summer touring the colonial holdings. She's spending the day sucking up to the in-laws."

"Does she know you're spending the day with her skimmer?"

"That's not nice."

"Sorry."

The Plan involved finding Jani a reasonably priced hotel,

followed by a recon mission to get the lay of the land and possibly dinner. However, she had certain criteria that needed to be met regarding the hotel. By the time they found an establishment with easy access to train stations and major thoroughfares, a secure entry, and a room from which she could view the comings and goings on the street outside *and* rapidly access stairwells, emergency exits, and alleys, the clock had struck midnight and then some and her self-appointed guardian angel was muttering mutiny.

"Guess the lay of the land will have to wait until tomorrow." Jani stood by one of the room's narrow windows and checked her timepiece. "Make that later today."

"That was ridiculous." Lucien lowered to the small couch, testing the cushions with skeptical probes of his fingers. "Everyone who was looking for you found you and threw you back—you're off the hook."

"Humor me."

"I've been doing that since the day we met. I'm getting tired of it."

Whoops. Jani perched on one of the built-in window seats. Outside, the city lights shone. Ten floors below, skimmers coursed, bearing people who never had to worry whether their backs were covered. *I wonder what that's like?* Looks like she'd get the opportunity to find out. "Most folks have some kind of celebration on Discharge Day." She looked at Lucien, who looked perplexed.

"Who else do you know in Chicago?"

Jani pretended to ponder. "Only you."

His expression changed to one of profound concentration. "I'm signed out until oh-eight-thirty." He picked his words like delicacies from a tray. "If that will help you make up your mind."

Jani took in the cityscape one last time. Then she fiddled with the window adjustments until she found the privacy setting. The cast of the scanglass altered subtly, blocking the view from prying eyes.

"If you're toying with me again," Lucien said as she walked toward him, "I'm going to be really, really upset."

"You're so suspicious." Jani straddled him, eased down

onto his lap, and wrapped her arms around his neck. "Looks like I have a lot of fence-mending to do." She planted butterfly kisses on his forehead, his lips and cheeks, at the same time brushing her fingertips along the back of his neck until he shivered.

"I should say so." Lucien didn't waste much time on preliminaries—he had gotten the lay of her land long ago. He pulled her shirt up over her head. The bandbra followed. He eased her onto her back and finished undressing her; his clothes soon joined hers on the floor. He looked like a young god in the half-light, down from the mountain to help her celebrate her freedom. He didn't tell her he loved her—she wouldn't have believed him if he had. Love was something he did and was good at; right then it was what she needed. First, he said things to her that made her laugh. Then he did things to her that made her cry out.

Then it was his turn, and the first press of his naked body atop hers was a shock she didn't want to recover from for a very long time.

CHAPTER 35

Evan sat on the patio, his chair in the shadows, glass in left hand, right hand dangling over the side. The second bottle of the day, half-empty, rested on the table at his left elbow. He had decided to wait for as long as it took, but it had been a hell of a day. First, news of Jani's discharge had filtered in via Markhart. Then his attempts to reach several old friends had been bounced back, along with the notice that their services would not accept calls from his code.

One up. He'd give the son of a bitch until one up. Then he'd retire to the cool quiet of his office and compose a second letter to a wider audience.

He flexed his aching knee, then tensed as a rustle of leaves sounded from the rear of the yard. Something rattled closer, careless in its approach, like one of the neighbor dogs on a gallivant.

A few meters beyond the edge of the reflected streetlight, the sound stopped. Then, silently as the predator he was named for, Mako glided into view. He wore dark clothes—long-sleeved shirt and trousers. His hands hung at his sides, empty.

Evan tossed back the balance of his drink. "You took your goddamned time."

Mako grunted as he stepped onto the patio. His dark shoes made no noise on the flagstone. "I don't know if you heard, but we've been dealing with an incident. Neoclona has turned my medical services upside down and Cao and Tsecha are watching my every move." He sank into the only other chair, which Evan had taken care to position in the light. "Now, I'm here."

"How much interference are you throwing out?"

"Enough. I've been properly fitted against every sort of electronic surveillance." The soft patter of ergonomic clicks sounded as Mako shifted in his seat. "You'd be more comfortable, I'm sure, if you put that knife away."

Evan's right hand clenched. The knife, a serrated bread slicer taken from the kitchen, comforted him with its cool heft. "If you don't mind, I think I'll keep it."

"Put it away, van Reuter. If I'd wanted to kill you, I'd have done it a half hour ago, when you stepped into the bushes to piss."

"You were out there?"

"I've been here for over an hour, standing out by your lovely roses, watching you drink." Black eyes, scarcely visible through skinfolds and cheekbone, closed in pain as Mako worked his neck. "Killing you would provide me some repayment for the hell of these past weeks, but not enough." He opened his eyes, and gazed at Evan in quiet disgust. "What do you want?"

Evan flexed his right arm, gone numb from the position and the tension. "Just a foot in the door. Idomeni consultant. Seat on a Service-civilian commission. A chance to get in the 'sheets once in a while, keep me from gathering dust." The final words hung up in his throat. "I'll take anything."

"Bah-hah." Mako's rough laugh bubbled like a stuck drain. "You'll take anything *now*. I know you, van Reuter. Once you get that foot in the door, you'll force your way in and start stuffing your pockets."

"It's the Family way." Evan smiled. "I'm getting a renewed taste of the Family way. I catch the lucky break, comparatively speaking. I'm one of theirs, and they don't want to risk setting any unfortunate precedents with the tang of revolution in the air. That makes the verdict death by shunning." He refilled his glass. "But you're an outsider, Roshi. You're pro-colonial, in spite of your protests that you're apolitical, and what you pulled at Rauta Shèràa Base sure as hell proved that you're anti-Family. They'd chew you up and play flipstick with the bones."

Mako sat back, his spine straight and stiff as a flagpole. "If what you say about your predicament is true, who would believe you?"

Evan had prepared his bluff for that one. "The Unsers, for starters. Jerzy Unser's married to Shella Nawar, who just happens to be the Justice Minister's daughter. What's more, they all get along. I predict a domino effect."

Mako exhaled shakily. A long silence followed. Finally, a rumbling sigh. "These idomeni. They are a trial."

Evan's heart leapt. "Aren't they, though."

"I daresay we could use some advice, from time to time."

"Thank you, Roshi."

"Have you got another glass?"

Evan, as it happened, did. He filled it, then took care to maintain his distance as he handed it to Mako. Cornered animals could still strike, even when they seemed subdued. His fingers ached from gripping the knife handle.

But Mako remained seated. He even said, "thank you." Neither offered a formal toast, but they did sip at the same time. A deal sealer, of sorts, although Mako would never admit it and Evan would never think to push.

"You bollixed some of the details."

"But the essential argument is correct?"

Mako grunted an affirmative, his eyes fixed on nothing.

Somewhere down the street, voices carried in loud farewell, followed by the dull *thunks* of skimmer gullwings, an insect chorus of activation whines.

"Where'd you park?" Evan asked.

Mako swirled his drink. "Three blocks over. House party. Skims everywhere." He looked deflated. Exhausted. "I offered her a way out."

"She didn't take it, did she?"

"She had no choice."

"But she didn't say 'yes.' And she didn't say 'thank you.' And she made you feel like the scum of the earth for offering. Welcome to the club, Roshi." Evan stared at the stained flagstone at his feet. "Need a refill?"

But when he looked over at Mako, he saw only an empty chair, a half-filled glass balanced on the arm.

CHAPTER 36

Jani slipped out of bed, then showered and dressed. She took care not to trigger the lights—she needed to get where she was going by a certain time and she didn't want to risk waking Lucien. Odds were if he did wake, he'd simply want to make love to her again. But he was a curious soul, and would definitely question why she felt the need to stumble about in the dark at 0400 when she could be playing with him or for that matter, just *sleeping*.

She considered leaving him a farewell comport entry or a handwritten scribble on a piece of hotel stationery. Something to leave him mumbling imprecations as he drove back to Sheridan in his Family paramour's husband's skimmer. Instead, she blew a kiss to the tangle of arms, legs, and sheet sprawled across the bed and left.

The air was thick with pavement heat, the night sky faded to grey velvet by building lights. Chicago never truly slept, but it did take the occasional breather and early morning midweek appeared to be one of those downtimes. Few skimmers, delivery vans mostly. Fewer pedestrians. Jani bought coffee from an automated kiosk, then hurried down the main streets and byways she had mapped in her mind the night before. She didn't need to ask directions. She had done more during the previous night's hotel search than search for hotels.

Service Archives loomed like a holoVee castle on a corner

across from one of her rejected hotels. She walked in the front door and directly up to the desk lieutenant, and handed her one of the IDs she had cobbled together during her short stint in Foreign Transactions, when she still thought she needed to plan her escape.

She waited for *Kisa Van, Major* to ring up clean and green, then she wandered from stacks to stacks, and eventually found Sam Duong huddled on the floor, picking through slipcases.

"Good morning, Mr. Duong."

His breath caught, but when he looked up and saw her, he grinned in relief. "Captain." He shook his head. "No, not Captain. Not anymore." He brushed nonexistent dust from his hands and stood. "How did you know—?"

"You said morning was best to do Gate searches. Not the best security. I guessed."

"I'm surprised you remembered." Sam struggled to his feet, gripping the shelving for support.

"I understand you were in hospital the same time I was?"

"Yes. I wanted to visit, but Pimentel didn't think it a good idea."

"He's a worrier. How are you?"

"Fine. You?"

"Fine. You had surgery?"

"Yes. Pimentel says it went very easy. Drill, freeze, cut, cut." Sam flicked two fingers in imitation of a pair of snips. "I don't mean to sound rude, but how did you get in here?"

"You don't want to know."

"Hah!" Sam grinned. "Want do you want?"

She told him.

"I don't often make the entries themselves." Sam activated the workstation, nestled in a closetlike office down the hall from the stacks. "It's possible my passwords have expired." He uttered a few Bandan phrases, then sat forward so the display could get a good scan of his eyes. It took several minutes—the workstation was old and required coaxing— but eventually the correct screens burbled up from the system depths. "Go ahead."

Jani hesitated until he turned to her, brows arched in question. "Cray," she finally said. "Yolan. Corporal. C-number M-four-seven-dash-five-six-dash-two-eight-six-R."

Sam uttered codes, touched pads, waited. "Next."

"Burgoyne. Emil. Sergeant. C-number M-three-nine-dash-one-four-dash-seven-seven-I." Jani studied the scuffed brown lyno, the ancient paper notice tacked on the wall notifying users to clean up their trash. "Can you place the names where you want, or do they have to fall in alphabetically?"

"I can force-fit."

"Then put Borgie's name right at the top of the entry arch. I want Mako to drive beneath it every time he enters and leaves the base."

Sam uttered another password. "Next."

Fifteen names, by the time they finished. Fifteen C-numbers. Then Sam punched the touchpad one last time, and spoke the final password, and fifteen new names etched themselves in the Shenandoah Gate.

"I give it a week." He shut down the workstation and tipped back his chair. "Two, tops. I'm not the only checker they send out, and the names are monitored regularly."

"Can't let colony names get on that Gate."

"Almost as bad as inmates taking over the asylum."

They both smiled.

"I need to get going." Jani stood and held her hand out to Sam. "Take care of yourself."

"You, as well." He took it gently. "Jani."

Who do you think you are now? Jani couldn't make herself ask him that, either. Instead, she settled for wishing him good-bye, and hurried from the room before she thought of any more questions he could never answer.

The desk smiled. "Did you find what you were looking for, Major?"

"Yes, I did." Jani nodded briskly to the young woman and walked out of the archives building into the new light of day. The walkways had filled in the scant time since she'd entered. The skimways had clogged. She darted between the stalled movers and taxis and down a side street, flicked the

Kisa Van ID into a trashzap, then stopped at the first decent-looking café she found. Time for a leisurely breakfast, before the Documents Examiners Registry opened at 0700. The day was young, and Jani Kilian had a lot to do.

Four hundred years ago, an advanced society faced
a worldwide crisis and decided to pin their hopes for
survival on the colonization of five distant planets.

Now, centuries later, Colony Fleet
is finally nearing its destination.

From Susan R. Matthews, acclaimed author of
*An Exchange of Hostages, Prisoner of Conscience,
Hour of Judgment,* and *Avalanche Soldier*
comes a thrilling new science fiction tale
of adventure and discovery . . .
and what it takes to survive the unknown.

"A welcome addition to the canon of
classic science fiction novels. In COLONY FLEET the
meek have inherited the earth, and the bold face
untold dangers in carrying humanity to new worlds."
—Michael A. Stackpole

COLONY FLEET
Susan R. Matthews
0-380-80316-X/$6.50 US/$8.99 Can
In bookstores October 2000